# see
# jane
# date

## melissa senate

**RED
DRESS
I N K**™

First edition November 2001

First mass market edition 2003

SEE JANE DATE

A Red Dress Ink novel

ISBN 0-373-25027-4

© 2001 by Melissa Senate.

Dedicated in memory of Gregory Pope,
who (among his many contributions to this world and
my life) single-handedly redeemed the blind date.

And to...
My parents, Linda and Neil Flechner,
my brother, Joseph Senate,
and my sister, Marge Liguori,
with love.

# *One*

Depending on where you got your information (say, *Cosmopolitan* magazine, the hostesses of the *View* or my aunt Ina), there were well-documented ways to go from single to married in New York City without: A) kissing fifty frogs, B) unwittingly sleeping with a serial killer or C) settling.

Unless you were me. I'd be lucky if I got to kiss *five* frogs before I dropped dead from Another Saturday Night Alone Syndrome. *Why* was I still single at age twenty-eight?

My friend Amanda: *"You don't need a boyfriend to be happy, Jane."* Um, actually, you *do*. Did I mention she's living with someone?

My boss Gwen (unsolicited): *"You'll find love when you stop looking."* Really? I've never heard that one before!

My friend Eloise: *"You have high standards. Not that*

*there's anything wrong with that.''* No annotating required.

My engaged (younger) cousin Dana: *"You're negative, that's why!"* Just wait till you meet *her.*

*Cosmo: "You gotta put it out there, girlfriend!"* Like I *didn't* own a Miracle Bra in every color?

Me: *"Because you can do everything everyone suggests, and it still won't make the man you can imagine having kids with love you back. Or even ask for a second date."*

What was my aunt Ina's suggestion for finding true love? It had something to do with a certain "perfectly nice looking fellow" she'd met in the hallway of my grandmother's apartment building. He'd been taking his trash to the incinerator, and—oh, forget it. I might just as well let her tell you herself.

"It's one date!" Ina Dreer yelled into the telephone. I held the cordless away from my ear. "A couple of dances at a wedding, some small talk. And you get three hundred thousand dollars! You can't go on one lousy date for your grandmother? For *me?* For that kind of money? Why do I even bother? Tell me, Jane, why do I even bother?"

I mentally finished Aunt Ina's monologue for her: *Go ahead, Jane, be single. Never get married. End up all alone like your great-aunt Gertie, God rest her soul. So what if I promised your mother—God rest her soul—that I'd watch over you? So what if she worked her whole life to support you after your father died so young? What do you need with three hundred thousand dollars anyway?*

Actually, dear, sweet, guilt-tripping Aunt Ina had a point there. I *did* need the three hundred grand. My apartment was seven hundred and sixty-two buckeroos a month (rent-stabilized)—which was super-cheap by New York, New York, standards, but hardly one-quarter of my gross monthly salary. Which, according to *Mademoiselle* and *Glamour*—and probably *The Wall Street Journal*—was the guideline for what you should pay for housing.

Plus, I'd been sleeping on the same lumpy futon for six years, ever since I moved to Manhattan from Aunt Ina's spare bedroom after graduating from college. With three hundred thousand big ones in the bank, I could finally afford a real sofa bed. Ina had sprung for the futon as a college-graduation and first-apartment present. She'd also narrowed her ever-suspicious pale blue eyes at the ten-by-twenty-one-foot studio I was so excited about as though it came complete with muggers and rats, then ordered custom-made "burglar bars" for the fire-escape window and hired an exterminator for me.

What else would I do with that financial windfall? Immediately DKNY my wardrobe, which was currently limited to career separates on sale at Ann Taylor and Banana Republic. I aspired to DKNY, which was three promotions away.

"Jane Gregg, am I talking to myself here?" That was followed by Aunt Ina's trademark deep sigh.

The pack of Marlboro Lights on the table in front of the futon was taunting me. I was dying for a cigarette, but it would kill Ina if she heard me inhale, and I loved her too much to disappoint her. My aunt didn't know I'd started smoking again. I'd quit for one day six months ago and made the mistake of telling her about my big achievement. I'd never seen her so happy—well, except for when her daughter, Dana, got engaged two years ago. How could I tell her I'd only lasted seven hours as a former smoker?

"Aunt Ina, I would meet this guy, but I'm sort of dating someone right now." Lie. Big, fat lie. "It wouldn't be right to go out with another guy. No, you don't know him. No, I don't want to say too much, or I'll jinx it. Yes, he's nice. And would you stop worrying about Grammy's money? She's not going to disinherit me just because I won't go to Dana's wedding with the schlub who lives next door to her. He's not my type, anyway, okay?''

'' *'Sort of dating,'* she says,'' Aunt Ina mimicked. I could imagine her shaking her strawberry-blond head. She loved repeating what people said in the third person. '' *'Not my type.'* What do you know—you've never even met Ethan. He's not a schlub! He's a perfectly nice looking young man. *And* he has a big-deal job working with money. Not like the artsy-fartsy weirdos with gunk in their hair who you and your skinny friends run around with. He's from Texas. That means he knows from respecting a young lady. Oh, what am I wasting my breath for? Go ahead, Jane. Be single! Never get married....''

I tried to conjure up a vision of Ethan Miles, the three-hundred-thousand-dollar Incinerator Man. I doubted he looked anything like Matthew McConaughey or whatever other hot actors hailed from the Lone Star state. Granted, I wasn't about to win the Miss New York Pageant, but at least no one would describe me as ''perfectly nice looking.'' *Please.* We all knew what that meant. And Ethan Miles lived in *Queens,* for God's sake. Separated from my seventy-six-year-old arthritic Grammy by one white wall. What marriageable man, especially a transplanted Texan, lived in Queens, next to elderly people? If he was such a catch, why didn't he live in *Manhattan?*

It was true that Grammy had inherited three hundred thousand dollars from her spinster sister, Gertie. Ina was afraid that Grammy, long widowed, would disinherit both Dana and me because we didn't visit her enough. Gram thought weekly Sunday get-togethers involving pastrami sandwiches, German potato salad, butter cookies and liv-

ing room piano recitals were de rigueur. Disagreeing with
that concept was the only thing I had in common with
cousin Dana, Ina's only child. At family functions, Dana
liked to roll her eyes and announce that my sarcastic
tongue would keep me single *and* out of Grammy's will.
Which tended to send Ina into a tizzy about how I'd have
to live on my twenty-six-thousand-dollar salary for the
rest of my life.

What Aunt Ina didn't seem to understand was that I
had a master plan. And even if the plan failed miserably,
I was still due a four percent raise in three months. If you
added my five percent Christmas bonus, I'd be earning
just over twenty-eight thousand by the new year. That
wasn't bad, was it? According to my friend Amanda, you
were doing okay career-wise if your salary matched your
age in thousands. I was close. Although in February, I'd
be twenty-nine.

"Did you buy your bridesmaid shoes yet?" Aunt Ina
asked. "If you need money, don't be proud. They have
some nerve charging so much for shoes that aren't even
leather!"

Yeah, try one hundred and thirty-five smackers. "Pale
peach peau de soie pumps, two-and-a-half-inch princess
heels. I know. I'll get them. Don't worry."

"'*Don't worry*,' she says," Aunt Ina snapped. "You
have a final fitting for your dress next Saturday, Miss
Smart Aleck. What are you waiting for? The shoes to
mysteriously appear in your closet?"

Yes, actually. That was exactly what I was waiting for.
"I'm getting them this weekend, okay? My friend Eloise
is going shopping with me. She knows good shoes."

"The one who dates the foreigners?"

I tiptoed to the door and knocked hard. "Aunt Ina, I
have to go. Someone's at the door."

"Honey, listen to me," Aunt Ina whispered, as if anyone but my uncle Charlie was in her apartment with her. "Both you and Ethan Miles have been invited to Dana's wedding without guests. What's so terrible that you walk into the Plaza Hotel together, sit at the same table? It'll make your grandmother happy, and what's the crime that everyone will think you're a couple? You'll feel better, trust me."

Only married people and singles who lived with significant others could bring dates to Princess Dana's wedding. Losers like me—and Ethan Miles, apparently—had to come alone. The reasoning seemed to be that at $225 a head, Dana shouldn't have to pay for a casual fuck's prime rib.

"Should I give him your number?" Ina asked. "You shouldn't have to attend a wedding alone at your age. I understand it's a little humiliating."

No, actually statements like that one were *a little humiliating.* Besides, I was twenty-eight, not thirty-two, for God's sake!

"Aunt Ina, I told you. I'm *seeing* someone. It wouldn't be right to go to the wedding with this Ethan guy, okay? I really have to go. Love you! Bye!"

Even if I never had another date, I was not going out with Mr. Incinerator. *Ever.* And I most certainly was not taking him as my date to Dana's wedding, an ostentatious snooze-fest ruining a perfectly good Sunday two months from now on August 2. Like I needed Miss Superiority to know I was so desperate for a boyfriend that I was dating Grammy's next-door neighbor? No thank you. The guy took out his trash in front of people! Besides, it was bad enough that I had to go to the wedding at all.

No, actually it was worse: I was a bridesmaid. At least the dress wasn't as embarrassing as it could have been. I personally wouldn't have chosen peach—a color no one looked good in—as my wedding party's color scheme, but then again, it wasn't *my* wedding, as Aunt Ina reminded me every time I "made a smart remark" about Dana's abominable choices. Peach turned my dark brown eyes into two mud pies, and the dark brown of my hair into a mousy makeover "before." I should be grateful that at least the dress didn't have a big bow on the butt.

The Plaza Hotel. Who got married at the Plaza Hotel? *No one.* It was insane. A wedding at the Plaza Hotel must cost five hundred thousand dollars. No one got married there. Well, except for Ivanka Trump, maybe. And by the time she got married, even The Donald wouldn't be able to afford a wedding at the hotel he owned.

Twenty-four-year-old Dana Dreer, of the Forest Hills Dreers, was not supposed to get married at the Plaza.

Did I mention that her fiancé, a thirty-year-old from Far Rockaway named Larry Fishkill, started up an Internet company whose IPO made him an instant multimillionaire back when that was still possible?

Thank God I wasn't allowed to bring a date. Who would I bring? I didn't even have a gay male friend. Not having a date when I was invited to bring one—now *that* would be humiliating.

Ina finally said goodbye with her trademark long-suffering sigh and hung up. I put the cordless back on the recharger and returned to what I was doing before she called. Which was: choosing the perfect outfit for tomorrow's Super Day. It was now nine-thirty, which meant I had almost ten hours to decide on the perfect ensemble to accomplish the three most important things in my life, which were (in no particular order):

1) *Getting Promoted:* I had an appointment at nine sharp tomorrow morning with William Remke, president

and publisher of Posh Publishing. I'd been slogging away at Posh for six unappreciated years, three as an editorial assistant and three as an assistant editor. If I didn't get promoted to *associate* editor, I'd—well, who *knows* what I'd do? Maybe take an extra half hour at lunch or use letterhead as scrap paper—lots of it. I'd do something.

2) *Getting the Man:* For years I'd been fantasizing about Jeremy Black, my interim boss (my real boss was out on maternity leave). Jeremy was Posh's vice president and editorial director. Single (and straight), thirty-seven and a dead ringer for Pierce Brosnan. He was so movie-star good-looking that I had trouble uttering words and looking him in the eye at the same time. Which most likely accounted for the fact that he completely ignored me. Except when loading up my in-box with slush (sent by the hordes of would-be writers who didn't have agents) manuscripts.

3) *Getting the Enemy:* And *good.* She was a big part of the reason I'd had it with my lowly title. Natasha Nutley was a faux celebrity whose tell-all memoir I'd been assigned to as project editor. Did I mention that Gnatasha—oops, I meant *Natasha*—and I went to junior high and high school together? That I'd hated her tall, skinny, beautiful guts since I was twelve years old? No way would I let Gnatasha (the Gnat for short) think I was anything less than a senior editor making one hundred K a year who summered in the Hamptons and had a very good-looking, very successful, very adoring boyfriend who—

"Jane!"

Right on time. I ran down the foot-long, foot-wide hallway into the tiny kitchen, kneeled down on the black-and-white linoleum floor and opened the cabinet under the sink. "Hey!" I shouted over the little garbage can.

"Come on up. I need help! Don't forget the Super-Straight hair balm, okay?"

"Gimme ten minutes!" Eloise Manfred shouted back from the depths of the cabinet.

Eloise lived in the apartment below mine. The walls, floors and ceilings were so thin in our six-floor walk-up that we'd discovered we could chat the night away if she shouted toward her kitchen ceiling and I opened the under-the-sink cabinet. If either of us was ever being murdered in our kitchens, the other could call 911. I'd once told Aunt Ina that, thinking she'd stop worrying about my doorman-less building. She didn't.

Eloise and I worked together at Posh Publishing. During my first week at Posh, I'd mentioned I was apartment hunting, and Eloise told me about the vacancy right above her. She'd shown me a picture of her place and said the studio upstairs had the same layout. Rent-stabilized had been all I needed to hear. I'd rushed to the landlord's office with my entire life's savings in cash, which almost equaled one month's rent and one month's security (I had to borrow two hundred from Ina). With the exchange of cash, a clean credit check and the signing of a two-year lease, the little box was mine. My studio looked nothing like Eloise's decor-wise. She wasn't Posh's assistant art associate (a title almost worse than mine) for nothing. Eloise had done the most amazing things with flea market screens, sheer, silky curtains and blown-up black-and-white photos. I'd lived at 818 E. 81st Street for six years and still had the hot-pink plastic Parsons table I'd bought for my college dorm room.

If you were wondering how I could afford the apartment on my salary—which, trust me, was even more pathetic six years ago—it was all about budgets and credit cards. Aunt Ina taught me something about budgeting that

I actually listened to. It really worked. I got paid twice a month, so I put aside half my rent and utility bills with one paycheck, and half with the second paycheck. Then I paid myself fifty bucks in a savings account. The rest was walk-around money, food and subway fare. Everything else, like clothes, and shoes and stuff for the apartment went on credit cards. I had four: Visa, Ann Taylor, Macy's and Bloomingdale's. The only thing I ever bought in Bloomies was MAC makeup, but I liked having the card. Anyway, thanks to Ina's system, come bill-paying time I always had two halves of my expenses.

I heard Eloise lock up her apartment and jog the steep staircase to the sixth floor. Then I heard her stop, jog back down and unlock her door. She must have forgotten the hair balm.

Among the many things I loved about Eloise Manfred was that she was two years older than I was (the big three O), and didn't mind being single. In fact, she relished her freedom and the choices out there. She dated constantly. Younger men, older men, cute men, ugly men, musclemen, short men, bald men, hot men. All nationalities and colors and professions. Aunt Ina had met Eloise once. The three of us arranged to meet in my apartment for a trip to the designer outlets in Secaucus, New Jersey. This was during Eloise's Swarthy Man phase. She'd brought Abdul upstairs to introduce us, and Ina's arrival had coincided. Ina had taken one look at Abdul and instructed him to take Second Avenue to 42nd Street, then to go crosstown to the Lincoln Tunnel. Abdul, whose English wasn't too great, nodded politely and smiled, having no idea what she was talking about. Eloise and I hadn't either, for that matter. Until Ina had whispered to me, "Isn't he the car-service driver?" I'd held my breath. But Eloise had laughed and kissed Ina on the cheek. According to Eloise,

Aunt Ina was a classic. Another of the reasons I loved her so much.

Right now Eloise was dating a Russian immigrant hair-stylist named Serge. He looked like an Eastern European John Travolta, if you could picture that. They'd been see-ing each other for three months, and he adored her. Serge was an old-fashioned gentleman. He stood up when a woman entered a room, brought Eloise flowers before every date and complimented her pathetic attempts at cooking. A month ago, he'd raved about the new hairstyle that was all the rage in Moscow, and Eloise, being game for anything, had let him do his thing. When he trium-phantly spun her around to face the mirror, she had the Jennifer Aniston "do," circa *Friends* six years ago. She didn't have the heart to tell Serge that *Friends* was a few years ahead in America. Or that she'd already *had* this very hairstyle, like every other woman in the United States.

Eloise knocked her special triple knock, and I unlocked the dead bolt, the three lesser locks and slid off the safety latch. She was beaming, with her hazel eyes twinkling, which meant she was about to do me a very big favor. She liked making people happy.

"Don't say no," she ordered. She held out her hands and opened her fists; a one-carat diamond stud earring sat gleaming in each. Her mom had given her the heirloom earrings just weeks before she'd passed away from ovar-ian cancer. Those earrings were the most precious things that Eloise possessed. I knew what it felt like to cherish what your mother left you. I squeezed my eyes shut for a moment. Eloise laughed her don't-make-me-cry-too laugh.

I'd once asked her if she thought we'd be best friends if we didn't have the loss of our mothers (to cancer) in

common. Eloise had said definitely. I agreed. My mom
died when I was nineteen and a sophomore in college. I'd
already lost my father when I was nine. Eloise's mother
had passed away when she was eighteen. She never talked
about her dad, but she was very close to her mother's
mother.

"You're wearing them tomorrow, end of story," Eloise
announced, closing the door behind her. She pulled the
tube of Super-Straight out of the waistband of her jeans
and placed it on the Parsons table. "Natasha will definitely notice them. And they *say* Senior Editor."

I took the diamond studs and put them in my ears,
pushing back my hair to model them for Eloise. I mouthed
a *thank-you,* then admired the brilliant gems in the full-
length mirror attached to the back of my bathroom door.
"But El, do they say, My Very Successful Boyfriend
Gave Them To Me, So Take That, Natasha Nutley?"

Eloise laughed. "Say" was *the* word at Posh Publishing. That was how the big cheeses (meaning William Remke and Jeremy Black) decided if a book was worthy of
being published. It had to *say* something that would make
everyone buy it.

Last year, my boss, senior editor Gwendolyn Welle,
had stuck me with a former child actor's autobiography
that said: If You Read Me You'll Be Depressed For A
Week. *Sitcom Kid: No Laughing Matter* had landed on
the extended *New York Times* bestseller list at number
twenty-three, which for small Posh Publishing was as
good as number one. Remke had been thrilled. He threw
a big party in our loft office to celebrate. As the project
editor of the memoir, I got to take a two-hour lunch
(whoo-hoo). Gwen, who'd *acquired* the manuscript (but
did only one quarter of the work) got a huge raise. Jeremy, who'd done nothing but green-light the deal, got his

gorgeous mug and a special interview in *Publishers Weekly,* where he was heralded as the "brilliant mind behind the success of Posh's RealLife Books imprint." Posh's only imprint, mind you. And Remke got a gazillion stock options from our parent company.

A major television network was making a movie-of-the-week out of *Sitcom Kid: No Laughing Matter.* Eloise and I joked that the child actor playing the role of the sitcom kid would also end up homeless and addicted to drugs one day. Not that that was funny. Oh, wait. That reminded me. I *did* get something else for being project editor on the book: depressed for a week.

Eloise went into the kitchen and rooted around in the refrigerator. She came back into the main room with diet Snapple iced tea, then settled herself on the futon that dominated the small room. She leaned back against the pastel throw pillows, hugging one to her stomach.

"Okay. We've gotta focus. Which is more important?" Eloise asked, tucking her auburn Jennifer Aniston layers behind her ear. "Impressing the Gnat, scoring a drinks invitation from Jeremy or getting that promotion from Remke?"

That was easy. I grabbed the Snapple and took a sip, then handed it back to Eloise. The promotion would begin to negate the necessity of lying to semi-famous former classmates about my pathetic title at age twenty-eight. *And* it would impress Jeremy, who *could* possibly ask me out to celebrate my hard work and dedication to the Posh family.

"The promotion takes care of everything else," I explained, picking up the pack of Marlboro Lights. I almost knocked over the cheap plastic Parsons table; Eloise saved the bottle of Snapple just in time. I couldn't get a real coffee table until I had a real apartment, with a bedroom. I had to move the table every night in order to unfold the futon, which I folded back up every morning. Such was life in a studio apartment.

"Ugh! Only one left," I complained, lighting the cigarette. I took a good long, satisfying drag and blew out the smoke toward the ceiling.

Eloise plucked the cigarette from my fingers and took an equally long puff, then passed it back to me. "We have to quit." She said that once a week or so.

"Yeah, because walking down and up six flights to get a pack is the *real* drag." I inhaled, then exhaled. "Maybe we can get the bodega on the corner of First Avenue to deliver."

"One pack of cigarettes?" Eloise asked, searching the tips of her hair for split ends.

"The night clerk has a crush on you," I reminded her. "He's always staring at your chest when we go in there." Which, I should note, was much smaller than mine. She was a B, and I was the C. But she attracted more men. Maybe it was because she wore tight ribbed turtlenecks. I tended toward serious Ann Taylor jackets. As an artsy type, Eloise didn't have to dress too corporately.

She rolled her eyes and gestured for me to pass her the cigarette. She took a puff. "So your big meeting with Remke is first thing tomorrow, right? Nervous?"

I nodded, watching the stream of smoke rise up and disappear. Perhaps arranging a meeting to discuss my fate on a Friday wasn't such a hot idea, after all. If Remke laughed in my face (or the professional equivalent), it would ruin my weekend. I bit my lip and peered at myself in the mirror.

"You'll get the promotion," she assured me. "You've earned it. You just have to go in there and state your case. Don't let him intimidate you, Jane."

Ha. That was a joke. *Intimidating* was William Remke's middle name. He was very New York, very sophisticated. He looked like a less handsome version of Blake Carrington from that old television show *Dynasty*. Remke was meticulous—his hair, his suits, even his inbox. He liked his ''team'' to have a certain look, so he'd know we were his kind of people. Therefore, everyone at Posh had a very streamlined appearance and wore muted colors.

I'd modeled myself after Gwen, since it was her job I aspired to. She never wore jeans to work, so I never did. She worked till seven at night, so I worked till 7:01. She drank green tea and ordered exotic salads for lunch; I gave up Coke and brown-bagged ham-and-cheese sandwiches from home. She wore DKNY; I did my best to copy the look. I wasn't too great at style, but I had Eloise to help me. Eloise had the look naturally, but that was because she was from here—Manhattan, I mean. Private school on the Upper East Side and everything. She'd been obsessed with Anna Wintour as a teenager. Natasha Nutley and Fran Drescher from *The Nanny* had been my role models during high school. Natasha because she was everything I wished I could be. And Fran because she was from Queens.

I'd changed since graduating from Forest Hills High. That old saying about taking the girl out of wherever, but not the wherever out of the girl didn't hold true with me. You couldn't make it in the world of New York City publishing with the boroughs on and in you. So I'd worked hard. There wasn't a drop of Queens on me, accent included. No one would ever guess my bridge-and-tunnel origins. Sometimes I wondered if my own mother would recognize me. If she were still alive, that was. I think she'd be proud. Virginia Gregg always said I'd be a big-deal something someday. Aunt Ina always said I was trying too hard. But she didn't know how *hard* it all was.

"I can't take it," Eloise announced, blowing out a perfect smoke ring and smushing the butt in the ashtray. "I'm going down for a pack. I'll be right back."

I gratefully unlocked the door for her. I needed cigarettes to get through tonight. Tomorrow was major. I had the appointment with Remke, my first meeting with Natasha (over lunch), and because tomorrow was Friday, it was the last chance for Jeremy to suddenly realize I had breasts and a vagina and ask me out for Saturday night.

Like *that* would ever happen.

I eyed my reflection, wondering what else I could possibly do to make myself attractive to Jeremy Black. Gwen had once told me I looked like That Girl. All I remembered about the sitcom was that my mom used to watch it and crack up when I was little. I suppose there was a resemblance between me and a young Marlo Thomas, except I didn't have the flip to my hair. I did have similar sparkling dark brown eyes and shiny dark brown, shoulder-length hair and a pale complexion, but I was hardly That Girl. I was more Invisible Girl. At least as far as Jeremy Black was concerned.

Maybe I *was* trying too hard, like Aunt Ina thought. I wore prescription-free glasses a few times a week to make me look more editor-ish; they were knockoffs of a pair I saw on Julianne Moore in *In Style* magazine. Gwen wore glasses, too, but she may actually have needed them. My nails were always pale pink and short, per an article my mom had once read about Jacqueline Kennedy Onassis, who'd said that fingernails should be the color of a ballet slipper, and toes a classic red. My mom had idolized

Jackie O the way I'd idolized Fran Drescher. Thank God I hadn't taken my style cue from *The Nanny.*

I stared in the mirror, turning to the left, then to the right. I decided I was cute. Very cute, even. But I wasn't a hot babe. Not by any stretch. A few months ago I saw Jeremy leave a restaurant with his arm around a woman who looked like Heidi Klum. Nothing round on her except her perfect butt. Who was I kidding? Jeremy Black was *never* going to look twice at me—except to ask me either to make a copy of a manuscript or read his friend's sister's cousin's brother's girlfriend's manuscript and write a thoughtful revision letter.

I stuck out my tongue at myself like the twelve-year-old I felt like and dropped down on the futon with a big fat sigh. I suddenly wished I had that stereotypical single woman's cat to cuddle. There was absolutely nothing of comfort in my apartment. Except my photo of me with my parents, when I was eight. But you couldn't hug a photo.

"I'm back!" Eloise called through the door. I unbolted again, and she staggered in, out of breath. "Those stairs are going to kill us before these cigarettes do." She threw the fresh pack onto the Parsons table. "Okay—it's promote-me time! Let's do your makeup first, then your hair, then you'll get dressed. I'm thinking the black suit with the cropped jacket and—"

I threw my arms around her and squeezed. Eloise was all the comfort I needed sometimes.

We both lit cigarettes. "Oh, wait!" I said. "We need the ultimate inspiration."

In moments I had the Backstreet Boys' *Millennium* CD cranked up in my tiny apartment. Eloise laughed. Remke was trying to get the least-known, least-publicized Backstreet Boy (as if there *were* one) to write a tell-all memoir.

A told-to, tell-all, actually. Remke wasn't sure if cute nineteen-year-old singers could actually write or not.

Eloise and I sang along as she started working her makeup magic, showing me the steps in the mirror. The goal was sophisticated chic, yet natural. The light bronzing powder she'd whisked on my cheeks made me look slightly sun kissed—like an executive savvy enough to stay out of the sun during her weekend of frolicking with her successful boyfriend in the Hamptons.

My next-door neighbor pounded on the wall. Eloise and I rolled our eyes in unison, and I turned down the volume on my CD player.

An hour later, I stood in front of the mirror, grinning at Eloise. She beamed back at me through a puff of smoke and adjusted my black jacket and the little neck scarf. "You definitely *say* Promote Me."

Now all I had to do was recreate it tomorrow morning at seven-thirty.

*Squeak, squeak, squeak.*
"Oh. Oh, oh. Ohhhhhhhhhhhhh!"
I opened one exhausted eye and glanced at my alarm clock. The red glowing numbers were too bright. It was 6:38 a.m.

Opera Man's sex life was going to ruin my chance to get promoted. I desperately needed my remaining hour of sleep. I'd tossed and turned for hours last night, perfecting my opening speech to William Remke. It had been close to two o'clock when I finally conked out. I'd drifted off to sleep hearing the squeaking of Opera Man's bed and the strains of *Celeste Aida*. I should be grateful I'd slept through his girlfriend's orgasm, which this morning was so loud that I could hear her breathy little moans between *ohs*.

Opera Man lived directly across the hall, and we shared one long wall, which my futon was against. I had no idea what Opera Man's name was. Well, I knew his last name was Marinelli. But I only knew his first initial, "A," because "A. Marinelli" was on the sticky label on his mailbox and on his apartment door. I could hear almost everything that went on in his apartment. Including his sometimes annoying but mostly soothing obsession with opera. I got to hear all the major performances. He'd had some nerve pounding on my wall about a little teenybopper music when he blasted *Carmen* and had such noisy sex. Eloise and I figured he looked like Ricky Martin. Who else could make a woman scream like that? In the two years he'd lived across the hall from me, I'd never seen him. Except for Eloise and two other single women—one on the second floor and one on the fourth— I didn't know any of my neighbors and rarely ran into them.

"Oh, Oh, Ohhhhhh!" Too bad she didn't scream his name. I'd finally know what the "A" stood for.

Maybe Opera Man had done me a favor by waking me up so early. I could use the extra hour to get ready and eat something other than the usual cream-cheese-slathered bagel.

"Oh, oh. oh. Oh, yeah! Ohhhh!"

Sometimes I wondered if everyone in New York had a better sex life than I did. The last time I was naked with someone was when I dated Soldier of Fortune Guy, so dubbed by Eloise. He was a friend-co-worker of our friend Amanda's boyfriend Jeff. Soldier of Fortune Guy and I had gone out twice, and on our second and last date, I'd broken a big rule by sleeping with him before date four. In the morning, he'd served me instant coffee and an English muffin on a makeshift coffee table that turned out to be a stack of *Soldier of Fortune* magazines dating back to the Neanderthal era. I'd made the mistake of expressing my shock. We got into a huge argument, both snapped "Fine," and I slammed out of his apartment. He was the fourth guy Amanda's boyfriend had fixed me up with. That had been almost two years ago. Jeff had stopped offering up his friends after that episode.

I hadn't had sex in almost two years. And that last time hadn't been so hot, by the way.

"Oh. Oh. Oh!"

Opera Man himself never made noise. Only his partners.

My alarm buzzed, and I decided to let it buzz the *ohs* out of my earshot. Opera Man immediately pounded on the wall. I shut off the alarm.

Maybe the "A" stood for Asshole.

I lay back in bed and closed my eyes. I had more important things to do than wish I had a sex life. Like fantasize that Jeremy was Opera Man and I was his Oh Moaner.

## Two

"Jaaane."

I turned around and found myself standing way too close to Morgan Morgan, the assistant shared by Remke and Jeremy. Morgan Morgan was her real name, honest to goodness. She claimed that Morgan was her mother's maiden name and her father's last name, so her parents thought calling her Morgan Morgan was fated. I thought it was—

"William is ready to see you now, Jaaane." Morgan always drew my name out in a Long Island whine. She was twenty-two, fresh out of Barnard, pretty in a horsey way, and she had her eye on my job. She was not to be trusted.

I glanced at my watch. It was exactly 8:59 a.m. My meeting with Remke was set for nine. The man was never, ever late for anything. I glanced around the loftlike space of Posh Publishing to see if Eloise was around for a thumbs-up. She and her boss, Daisy, the art director, were huddled over slides on the light-box in front of the art department's wall of windows.

I shot Morgan an icy smile and walked past her and her puny cubicle, pausing for a second in front of Remke's door. *This is it. You're entering the corner office. About to demand your due! Deep breath, deep breath, deep breath. You can do it. Don't let him intimidate you!*

The door suddenly opened.

"Ah, there you are, Gregg," Remke clipped out as I stumbled inside. "Morgan!" he shouted past me, his head poked through the door. "Coffee! Let's go, let's go," he snapped at me. "I have a meeting in fifteen minutes."

*Fifteen minutes.* I had fifteen minutes to alter the course of my entire life. I closed the door behind me and took a few steps inside the gigantic office, which, no kidding, was bigger than my apartment. The sun streamed in from the floor-to-ceiling windows behind Remke's desk and glinted off his thick silver hair and his silver-framed eyeglasses. He picked up a stack of memos from his in-box and sat his six-feet, three-inch frame on the caramel-colored leather sofa adjacent to his desk.

Was I supposed to sit next to him? Or in one of the guest chairs in front of his desk, which didn't face him? I gnawed my lower lip, effectively eating off the lipstick I'd so painstakingly applied. Remke was thumbing through papers. My palms began to sweat. A bead of perspiration rolled down my cleavage. *Deep breath, deep breath.* I glanced out the window-wall. I could see the top of the Chrysler Building, the Empire State Building and—

"Let's go, let's go," he muttered, eyes on the memos. He said that a lot. *Let's go, let's go.* He said it at least a hundred times a day. It intimidated people so much that by the time they finally spoke, Remke was halfway down the hall.

I cleared my throat. "Um, yes, well, I wanted to talk to you about my future at Posh." I clasped my hands behind my back, not sure what to do with them. I wished I could belt out a confident statement the way Morgan Morgan could. I was six years older than she was, with six years of corporate experience, and I still said *um* and got sweaty palms. Morgan was very articulate. I doubted she even had sweat glands.

"Your future?" Remke repeated, thumbing away at the memos. "Why are you talking to me? Talk to Black. He's your direct supervisor now that Gwen's out on leave. In fact, you should wait till Gwen returns."

Remke referred to everyone by last name except for Gwendolyn Welle, which annoyed me to no end. I figured it was a chivalrous-respect thing. Remke liked Gwen, respected her. I could hardly stand Ms. Phony Baloney, and was delighted that she had taken an extended maternity leave. Four months instead of three, which meant three more months without her oppressive presence. But it most certainly did not mean I had to suffer through three more months without a promotion.

Most of Gwen's workload had fallen to me, except for two major authors she'd been courting (Jeremy had managed to sign both—women, of course—the moment he'd flown out to personally meet them, which had pissed off Gwen royally). I'd been working double time for six years, and triple time from the minute Gwen had waddled out the door with her baby-shower gifts. I *deserved* the promotion. I'd broached the topic with her before she left. She'd given me the just-keep-doing-what-you're-doing speech and brushed me off by telling me I had her blessing to talk to Jeremy and Remke while she was out on leave. One of the things I hated most about Gwen was that she was semi-decent to me. But that was only because she didn't see me as a threat. Talk about insulting. Why wasn't I threatening? I was young, smart and hungry. Wasn't I?

Remke was glaring at a memo. Lines were creasing his forehead.

I sat down in one of the guest chairs and twisted uncomfortably to face him. "Yes, well, um, I did speak with Gwen, and she suggested I talk to Jeremy or you, so, um, I discussed it with Jeremy, but he suggested I talk to you directly." Did I sound like an idiot? I was never sure if I made any sense when I talked to certain people, like Remke and Jeremy or anyone who intimidated me.

Given my inability to look at Jeremy and speak to him at the same time, you can imagine how my conversation with him had gone. He'd barely let me finish my sentence. Maybe because I'd been staring at his shoes.

"Morgan!" Remke shouted toward the door. "Where's the press release on the Natasha Nutley deal? Morgan!"

Doubly annoying was the inability to determine if Remke was calling Morgan by her first or last name. I liked to think he was using her last name.

A short knock was followed by the door opening. Morgan Morgan entered with a mug of coffee, which she handed to Remke. "It's right on your desk, Williaaam," she whinnied through her horsey mouth. She ever so efficiently trotted over to retrieve it for him.

Remke scanned the press release of Natasha Nutley's memoir, scowling. "Who wrote this?"

My cheeks burned. I felt Morgan's eyes on me, and I glanced at her. I could swear she smiled. She hid it, but I saw it. The bitch smiled!

I cleared my throat. "Um, I did?"

"Are you asking me or telling me?" Remke snapped, his ice-blue eyes narrowed at me over the rims of his glasses.

I'd spent four days (well, four sleepless nights at home, actually) writing and perfecting the 350 words on that piece of paper. Usually Gwen wrote publicity materials for the big projects, especially the initial press releases that announced a major sale. But thanks to her absence, I got to write up the impending publication of the Gnat's still-untitled memoir.

What could I have screwed up? Jeremy had approved the press release, which had been copyedited and proofread. All the pertinent information was there, and I quite cleverly, if I do say so myself, *told the story*. That was another Posh phrase, which meant emphasizing the key elements. Had I gotten the print run wrong? Called it a trade paperback instead of mass-market? Not focused enough on the scandalous nature of Natasha's doomed love affair with a famous actor? That was the heart—or lack thereof—of the Gnat's memoir.

Oh, God. Had I referred to Natasha as *the Gnat* in the press release?

"I mean, I *did*," I corrected. I could kiss the promotion goodbye. I was going to be an assistant editor for the rest of my life. Aunt Ina's fears had been realized. From now on, I'd have to spend Sundays with Grammy, eating pastrami and butter cookies and keeping my sarcastic mouth shut so she wouldn't disinherit me. I'd have to ask Ethan Miles to Dana's wedding. I'd be forced to watch Morgan Morgan's meteoric rise from editorial assistant to associate editor, skipping assistant editor because—

"This is damn good," Remke said, tapping the press release with his Posh Publishing pen.

Morgan frowned. I smiled.

"You help Nutley shape her memoir as well as you wrote this release and we'll see about that promotion to assistant editor, Gregg."

Morgan smiled.

My stomach twisted. "Um, William? I, um…I'm already an assistant editor. I'm, um, hoping to be promoted to *associate*—"

"Morgan, get Black in here," Remke interrupted. "Tell him we've got to talk about signing that Backstreet kid. Bring in our press kit, too. And more coffee." He leaned against the sofa and thumbed through more papers. "Gregg, like I said." He glanced up at me, then back down. "We'll see how you do with Nutley's manuscript. She brings a sophisticated level of celebrity cachet. And celebrities breed celebrities. We've got the budget to promote the hell out of the Nutley book, so there's no reason not to hit the *Times* extended list, Gregg. And if Jeremy can sign that Backstreet Boy, we're in the big leagues. And big leagues mean big budgets mean money for perks, like promotions. But don't you worry about that, Gregg. You just keep doing what you're doing."

Morgan smiled.

Why did big cheeses like to say that? I heard the just-keep-doing-what-you're-doing crap at every performance review. It only made you feel worse and more powerless than you already did. After all, *what you were doing* wasn't getting you *anywhere* but brushed off. Maybe Gwen and Jeremy and Remke would like to try living in New York on twenty-six thousand a year, reading manuscripts on the subway to and from work. Maybe Remke would like to choose between buying cigarettes or dinner on the night before payday because he was totally and completely broke.

Okay, okay—I was done whining. And if I quit smoking, I'd be able to afford the *super-sized* chicken fajita burrito from Blockheads, the cheap Mexican restaurant Eloise and I always went to, right? I knew that, okay? But how could I quit smoking when I couldn't even get through a conversation with Remke without uttering an *um?*

Remke tapped his pen on his Armani-covered thigh. "What are you both still doing here? Shoo. Go. We're done. Where's Black!"

Morgan lifted her nose as she walked past me out of Remke's office.

"Thanks, William," I said. "About the Nutley release. I was, um, really proud of that myself, and—"

"That's fine, Gregg. Thanks. Close the door on your way, out, will you?"

Well, at least I'd gotten a compliment. And a *maybe.* Well, more a *goal.* My glum spirits perked up a bit. I'd gotten *more* than a just-keep-doing-what-you're-doing, I realized. Remke had pretty much outlined a defined thing I had to do: get Natasha's book on *The New York Times* extended bestseller list. That was the only way I'd get promoted. Unless Jeremy really did manage to sign the Backstreet Boy and up the budget for everyone. But unless the Boy was gay, I doubted Jeremy could work his magic quickly, if at all.

"Gregg, where are you taking Natasha Nutley to lunch today?"

Hand on the doorknob, I turned around. "Um, the Blue Water Grill?"

He stopped thumbing. "Are you asking me or telling me?"

What was wrong with me? Why was I a blubbering mess with this man? Why was I so insecure all the time?

I could only be grateful Morgan Morgan wasn't around to shoot me evil smiles.

"The Blue Water Grill," I corrected with a firm nod.

"Fine. Keep it under a hundred. And keep her talking, too. This is the big time, Gregg. Natasha's a big fish for Posh. I've entrusted her to you instead of Black because you've got the school connection. Women yak, especially when they go back that far. Get her to confide in you. The goal is to help her reveal every sordid detail of the affair *and* to sign her to a sequel, focusing on her months in rehab. Rehab's sexy now. Do your best, Gregg."

Maybe he'd forgotten that he'd already given me that speech five times since assigning her memoir to me last week. "I will," I said, and slipped out of his office.

*Rehab is sexy now.* Remke was such a jerk. Sometimes I wanted to take my fist and punch him right in his facelifted face!

I had bigger problems at the moment, though. Like how I was supposed to take Natasha Nutley to lunch at the Blue Water Grill without going over a hundred bucks. I'd have to say no to an appetizer or a salad, order the pathetic filet of sole and a glass of tap water, and watch Natasha fork the best salmon in the universe into her perfectly outlined mouth. Correction: I'd have to watch her order it, then eat only three bites, so she could retain her supermodel figure.

I'd fill up on the Blue Water's incredible bread. The bread was free.

"Morgan!" Remke screeched from behind me. "Coffee! Where's Black?"

I headed for my tiny office, Remke's monologue swirling in my mind. A sequel. Celebrity cachet. *Please.* Natasha was a small-time actress writing a small-time memoir about her small-time affair with an actor whose identity she wasn't even allowed to reveal. Okay, so The Actor was rumored to be big time. So what? She'd milked his mystery identity and her supposed heartbreak for all it was worth. She'd sold her sob story to women's magazines, and she'd even managed to get booked on some B-list talk shows.

The whole thing was almost unbelievable. Because she'd stupidly signed some legal document The Actor had had drawn up, the Gnat was—by penalty of law—prevented from ever discussing or writing about the guy or her affair with him in any medium, including print, radio or television. She'd cunningly gotten around it by referring to him as The Actor and creating a buzz around who he was. *That* was the story, the scandal behind the scandal.

Who really cared?

Potentially five hundred thousand people, according to Remke. Which was why I had to devote the next two months to guiding Natasha in fleshing out her outline and writing the first three chapters.

Morgan was returning from the kitchen with another mug of coffee for Remke. Jeremy Black was right behind her. He nodded at me and walked toward Remke's office.

Suddenly everything moved in slow motion, and sound was barely audible.

The sun shining in from the windows across the left wall of the loft lit his thick dark brown, wavy hair and made his Caribbean-colored eyes even more…Caribbean-colored. Never in the history of the world had there been a better-looking man. He was honest-to-goodness *handsome,* movie-star handsome. James Bond handsome.

Thirty-seven years old, six-one, 175 pounds. Harvard—undergrad *and* M.B.A. He was smarter and more sarcastic than he was nice, but the VP and editorial director of a small, niche-publishing house was supposed to be a bit ruthless. He lived in a loft in Tribeca (mere blocks from where John F. Kennedy, Jr., and Carolyn Bessette had lived), worked out at the Reebok Sports Club next to people like Jerry Seinfeld and dated women who looked like models but were also vice presidents. The only thing I had in common with Jeremy Black was Posh Publishing. And that wasn't saying much.

I slipped into my tiny windowless office and groaned at the fresh stack of manuscripts Jeremy must have deposited in my in-box on his way to Remke's office. Great. Just in time for the weekend. Normally Jeremy would dump unsolicited manuscripts in Gwen's in-box, and she'd screen them for herself, then dump the losers in my in-box. So at least there was a chance for a "maybe" to be lurking in there. If I could spot a potential bestseller in the slush pile, I'd be promoted to associate editor in a heartbeat. And then my life wouldn't be contingent on Natasha Nutley's success.

Fat chance of that, though. RealLife Books wasn't just celebrity (and I use that term loosely) tell-alls. I'd had to suffer through poorly written, dull memoirs from nobodies about colon surgery (not sexy enough, per Remke), cocaine addiction (passé, per Jeremy), the I-hate-my-mother trend (whine, whine, whine, per me) and the I-grew-up-poor-and-ugly-until-I-became-a-supermodel phase (oh, please! per Eloise and her boss). Spare me. Spare us all.

The next *New York Times* extended list bestseller was doubtfully waiting for me to recognize its worth in the slush pile. I'd have to rely on making my name at Posh by getting the best work out of the Gnat, not that it would thrill me to see her succeed. The woman was milking her fifteen minutes off someone's else's ongoing fifteen minutes! Her celebrity was fake. So why shouldn't I milk my promotion to full editor off *her?*

Was that so wrong? After all, I'd been ordered to do just that by the president and publisher of my own company. And hadn't I learned that being Miss Nicey-Nice had gotten me to where I was today? A big fat nowhere.

The intercom on my telephone buzzed. "Jaaane," came Morgan's intolerable voice. "Your cousin Dana called while you were in Remke's office. She said you have the number."

"Thanks." I rolled my eyes and stabbed the intercom button off. Great. Now I'd have to call back Dana before I went to lunch with Natasha. Talking to my cousin generally made me feel nauseated. Then again, maybe calling her back now wasn't a bad idea. I couldn't afford to eat anything at lunch, anyway.

The intercom crackled again. "Jaaane—I forgot to tell you. She said to call her on her cell. She's at the Plaza till noon. Something about a pre-stroll down the aisle."

The unexpected sting of tears hit the backs of my eyes. *Stop it! Stop it! Stop it!* I ordered myself. *Do not lose it. You have a big meeting ahead of you.* So what if Dana's sipping tea at the Plaza and walking around with her stupid cell phone as she floats down the aisle in her own stupid mini-ballroom? You're having lunch with a semibig celebrity! A celebrity you even *know!* You're doing just as well as Dana. Better, actually. Dana didn't even work, unless you counted occasionally advising her neighbors about color schemes. Actually, that sounded pretty good.

I slumped over my desk, defeated.

My eyes landed on the tiny photo of my parents and me in a heart-shaped frame that Aunt Ina had given me. My dad, handsome and smiling, was lifting me up in his arms, and my mom was squeezing his biceps. According to Ina, who'd snapped the photo, I'd been three.

I wondered how my father would feel if knew that Dana was the one walking down the aisle of the Plaza Hotel in two months. Would he be disappointed? Shake his head and tell my mother I'd failed him?

Maybe I'd better explain. It had been Marvin Gregg who'd shown me the Plaza Hotel for the first time. *"See that fancy hotel, Princess?"* he'd said, pointing across the street as we strolled up Fifth Avenue. We were on our way to the Central Park Zoo for a Jane-and-Daddy-only-day. *"That's the Plaza. It costs a million dollars just to go inside. But that's where you're going to have your wedding. One day, I'm going to walk you down the aisle in the ballroom of the Plaza Hotel! Whaddaya think of that, Princess?"*

*"Daddy, I'm only nine!"* I'd complained, hands on hips. I remember staring up at the hotel and thinking it looked like a castle. That hadn't been the mere musings of a child. The Plaza Hotel *did* look like a castle.

*"Yeah, but you're gonna be all grown up one day, Princess,"* he'd said, squeezing my hand. *"And you deserve a million-dollar wedding. I tell you what. You find the guy, and I'll see what I can do. How's that sound, Princess?"*

*"Daddy, I wanna see the monkeys! Let's go, already!"* I recalled whining. And I remember him laughing. He'd twirled me down Fifth Avenue to the corner of 59th Street as though we were ballroom dancing.

Marvin Gregg died the next day of a freak stroke. He was thirty-six years old.

I'd never told anyone about that conversation. Not my mother, or Aunt Ina, or even any of my friends. It wasn't the kind of thing you told anyone. It was the kind of thing you just kept close to your heart. Sometimes it comforted you, and sometimes it made you cry.

"Jaaane!"

Now what? I stabbed the intercom button. "Yeah?"

"Remke said you should come up with title suggestions for the Nutley memoir and write back cover copy for the sales catalog before you leave for lunch. He wants both on his desk by noon." I heard the you'll-never-get-it-done-in-time triumph in Morgan's voice.

"No problem," I said cheerily, stabbing the intercom button and sticking out my tongue. Titles and back cover copy by noon. Great. I had only a hundred other things to do, not to mention going over my notes for the lunch meeting with the Gnat.

I checked my e-mail. Sixteen new messages. Nine were from Morgan: Remke's dictates for Posh employees. The use of blue pen was now against company policy, since it didn't mimeograph as well as black. Editors were never to use red pencil to edit, as copyeditors traditionally used red. Lunch was limited to one hour, except for author and literary agent lunches, which had to be approved in advance. The use of letterhead for scrap paper was absolutely forbidden. On and on and on. My favorite was: *The frivolous use of e-mail is strictly forbidden.*

I clicked open a message from Eloise. *Tell me how it went with Remke on our cig break! —E.*

What would I do without Eloise? I ignored all messages related to work and opened one from Amanda Frank, which had also been sent to Eloise. The three of us met without fail every Friday night for the Flirt Night Roundtable, which included gossip, venting about work, nine-dollar drinks, guy hunting and, of course, flirting. Amanda and her boyfriend had moved in together a year ago, so she was out of the running for the flirting part. But she never missed a Friday. Well, actually, we never did much *flirting* at all (we mostly eyed cute guys and occasionally tried to meet them). It had been Eloise who'd dubbed our early get-togethers "Flirt Night," and it had been me, the editor, who'd added the "Roundtable," since we discussed flirting more than we did it. The name had stuck. Each week for six years now, we'd traded turns at choosing the place to meet and arranging with everyone.

*Hey guys! How about TapasTapas, the new place on 16th off Union Square, for tonight's FNRT?* Time Out *mag says it's the latest Beautiful People hot spot and has great tapas. It's super-expensive, but oh well! Same time as usual. See ya'll later! —Amanda*

Amanda was a transplanted cowgirl from Louisiana. Honest—she was from a ranch and everything. She had long blond hair, something rare in New York City, and attracted a lot of guys our way every time we went out, which Eloise and I sincerely appreciated. I typed back a *Can't wait,* then clicked onto Word to start drafting titles and back cover copy for the Gnat's memoir.

*Title Suggestion:* **The Gnat Sucks.** *Back Cover Copy Headline:* The true story of Natasha Nutley, a bloodsucker squashed in her prime. Read it and weep tears of joy that you're not her!

I smiled. If only.

Natasha Nutley kissed the air close to my cheek. I couldn't even lampoon it as the Hollywood kiss; everyone I knew kissed like that. Well, except my own friends. Acquaintances and business associates air-kissed, sometimes going so far as to air-kiss both cheeks, as though they were European. If someone was willing to muss up her Bobbi Brown lipstick by actually kissing your flesh, she was your real friend.

Natasha settled her super-thin self into the chair across from me at a back table in the Blue Water Grill. I hadn't seen her in ten years, since graduation day at Forest Hills High School. She looked exactly the same…well, sort of. At least she didn't look twenty-eight. Maybe she'd already had work done on her eyes?

"Omigod!" she trilled one second later. "I see my agent. I have to go say hello! Excuse me, Janey?"

I nodded and forced a smile. Janey. Hardly an appropriate name for a big deal senior editor like me. (I wasn't going to tell the Gnat my *real* title.) I watched Natasha glide to a table full of tanned men. More air-cheek kissing.

I was grateful for the reprieve. When the hostess had led Natasha to my table, my heart started booming in my chest. Suddenly I wasn't even Jane Gregg, assistant editor at a respected publishing house in New York City. I was Jane Gregg, brainy loser at Forest Hills High.

Robby Evers's sixteen-year-old face and his tall, gawky body flashed before my eyes. My heart squeezed with sympathy for the lovesick teenager I'd been. The *heartsick* teenager, thanks to the Gnat. How I'd hated her.

I glanced over at where she stood laughing with the Tanned Men. How was it possible that she'd never looked more gorgeous? She was ten years older than when she'd had everyone at Forest Hills High wrapped around her pinky. But now, she had the beauty, body and mystery of a woman. And a truly beautiful woman, at that.

Actually, the Gnat looked a lot like Nicole Kidman. Down to the red Botticelli ringlets, the slightly upturned nose, the beauty and the height. All she was missing was Tom Cruise as an ex. Though if rumor had it right, The Actor Natasha had had the affair with was hot stuff himself.

Natasha Nutley had that celebrity *je ne sais quoi*. Whenever I saw famous people in New York, it was as though they traveled with their own soft lighting. They didn't look like ordinary people. And the Gnat was anything but ordinary. Ordinary people didn't get romantically involved with television actors who made *People* magazine's Sexiest Men Alive list. Ordinary people didn't become famous by not only sleeping with men who made the list, but actually having a *relationship* with them. According to Natasha's outline for the tell-all, she'd been his one and only for seven weeks.

On their first date, which had been in his bed (slut!), he'd made her (and every woman he got involved with, apparently) sign The Document. Which basically said that if Natasha discussed him or their relationship in any medium, or even with friends, The Actor could sue her for everything she had and everything she'd earn in the future. *Including* royalties of the tell-all. So why did she sign such a stupid, insulting document? Why did she even sleep with a man who'd handed her a legal document while taking off her bra? Every spotlight-seeking answer was explained in the outline she'd written for her memoir.

Ugh. It was all so personal! Usually I didn't feel squeamish about knowing the intimate details of a person's life—after all, nothing was too personal for the Flirt Night Roundtable, and I'd worked on a lot of tell-all memoirs. But Natasha Nutley? She was supposed to remain at arm's length. I wasn't supposed to know anything about her other than what I assumed and judged. And that was the way I wanted it. That her existence on this earth had been full of larger-than-life disappointments should have made me feel triumphant, but it didn't. It made me feel weird. And I wasn't sure why.

"Sorry about that!" Natasha sing-songed, sliding into

her seat with a toss of her red ringlets. The collection of silver bangles on her wrist jingled. "My agent's such a doll. He's delighted we're having lunch. He promises to come say hi before he leaves."

I smiled and sipped my tap water. "Great," I said, trying not to stare at her. How had ordinary Mr. and Mrs. Nutley, who lived right around the corner from the apartment building I'd grown up in, managed to create such a stunning human being? Judith Nutley was five foot three, tops, though she did have the curly pale red hair. Mr. Nutley, whose first name I forget, was tall and thin and had the Gnat's green eyes. But neither parent was a looker. Not like Marvin and Virginia Gregg.

"So, um, Natasha, why don't we get started on discussing my ideas for streamlining the first chapter, per your outline. As you know, Posh is thrilled that we'll be excerpting the first chapter in *Marie Claire,* and we'll need—"

"All business!" Natasha stated in a mock scold, her whiter-than-white teeth gleaming at me. "We haven't seen each other in what, ten years? I have to say, Janey Gregg, you look *adorable!*"

That was an insult. There was nothing more condescending than being called *adorable.* "Thanks, Gnat," I said, recalling how much she disliked her name being shortened. *If only she could hear that silent* G. "You look really great yourself."

"Don't I though?" She laughed, and her green eyes sparkled like the clichéd emeralds. It was so unfair. "I have the most amazing dermatologist. I'll give you his number, if you want. He'll zap those little lines right out from under your eyes."

What little lines?

"I still can't get over this!" Natasha exclaimed,

squeezing a lemon into her six-dollar mineral water. "I mean, Posh signs me, and who should be a big editor there but Janey Gregg from Forest Hills!"

"I'm from *here* now," I said. *Too defensive, Jane. Calm down.* "I live on the Upper East Side. My boyfriend bought in a brownstone on the Upper West, but I've always preferred the East Side." Why did I say all that? A boyfriend was one thing, but did I have to go into every phony detail? Apparently so.

"Ooh, a boyfriend—and he owns a brownstone! Well done, Jane!"

*Yes, well done,* I thought, cringing. *Don't ask me his name,* I sent to her telepathically. I didn't have the mental energy to make up a really good one. "Well, not the *entire* brownstone, of course," I amended, ripping off a piece of bread from the basket between us. "Just the apartment. It's a two-bedroom, so he has an office. I have an adorable studio I'm too fond of to give up, but it's a waste, really, since I spend most of my time at his place."

Once you got started, you couldn't stop. Really.

Natasha's ringlets bobbed as she nodded. "I know exactly what you mean. My boyfriend and I live on his houseboat docked in Santa Barbara. Who could live on land after that?"

Who indeed? Now did you understand why I had diarrhea of the mouth?

"So whatever happened to those quiet twins you used to pal around with?" Natasha asked. "Are you still close friends?"

I envisioned the Miner twins. Lisa and Lora. Tall, thin and as quiet as the Gnat surprisingly remembered. They had been my only friends back in high school. Lisa and Lora had listened to me whine and complain about the Gnat for years, nonstop when she'd stolen Robby Evers

from me. Now, every six months or so I'd e-mail either
Lisa or Lora, and she'd e-mail me back. They'd moved
to San Francisco for college and stayed there. They were
both married and had two children with a third on the
way. We'd stayed close for a few years, but distance and
different lives had had its usual friendship-killing effect.

"Not really," I said. "People grow apart—you know
how it is."

Natasha looked me in the eye for a moment. I wondered what she was thinking. How pathetic and mousy
and nerdy I'd been as a teenager? That I'd never had a
boyfriend? That I'd had only two friends—and I wasn't
even able to hold on to those friendships? Natasha had
had the entire school at her disposal for friends and boyfriends. She'd *defined* the popular crowd.

"I have a great circle of friends now," I added, reaching for my tap water. "Friends are everything. I don't
know what I'd do without Eloise and Amanda." Wow—
a true statement! Didn't I get a medal for that?

She nodded. "Pretty names. Hey, so did I mention I
keep an apartment on the Upper East Side too? It's just
a one bedroom co-op, and I'm rarely in town, but, like
you, I can't bear to give it up. It's my *sanctuary*.
Wouldn't it be darling if we were neighbors? I'm on 64th
between Park and Madison." She sipped her water. "But
you already know all this—you know my life story! Well,
not everything! Just the bare bones from my outline and
whatever you've read about me in the press."

Bare bones, indeed, but what more did I need to know
to judge her as an opportunistic, spotlight-hungry bitch?
I'd already been forced to grudgingly acknowledge that
the Gnat had written a decent outline of her ridiculous
life story. It had all the necessary elements for a page-
turning tell-all. Rags to riches and back to supposed rags

(I knew *Agnes B.* when I saw it) with the all-important moral about self-esteem. I'd say Natasha Nutley had a little too much self-esteem. So forget about considering for a second that there was anything more to her than met the envious eye.

Sixty-fourth Street. *No one* lived on 64th Street, and especially not between Park and Madison. That was like getting married at the Plaza. It just wasn't done, unless you were a gazillionaire.

So how had Dana Dreer and Natasha Nutley, two girls from Queens, managed to do the impossible? Maybe your name had to be alliterative.

"Omigod! *Natasha?* Natasha Nutley?"

Omigod was right. That voice belonged to my cousin Dana.

I turned to find none other than Dana Dreer gaping at the Gnat, her mouth hanging open in wide-eyed joy. Of all the restaurants to have lunch in, did Dana have to pick the Blue Water Grill?

Natasha stared at Dana, taking in her big blue eyes, her pixie blond haircut and her small frame in head-to-toe Prada (compliments of the Internet-millionaire groom-to-be). Suddenly Natasha broke out in a huge smile. "Dana? Little Dana Dreer?"

They both squealed. Dana ran over, the Gnat stood up and the two hugged. Natasha had been Dana's baby-sitter for a few years when Dana was around eight, nine and ten. You could imagine that this little piece of trivia was something Dana shared with everyone whenever she was in Forest Hills visiting her parents or Grammy.

"Jane *told* me she was editing your autobiography!" Dana exclaimed. "That's so exciting! Adding author to your already very impressive résumé!"

Natasha beamed. "Well, writing has always been my first love."

Oh, really? I thought her first love had been stealing other girl's almost-boyfriends right before major school dances. Without knowing or caring.

"Jane!" Dana mock-scolded, turning those still-wide blue eyes on me. "I called you this morning, and you didn't call me back. I wanted to tell you I found the perfect peach peau de soie shoes for you. There's a store on Lexington at 77th, right when you come out of the subway." She turned her attention to Natasha. "What a co-incidence running into you two here! I'm having lunch with my caterer—"

A waiter-model came by to ask if we were ready to order. I told him we needed a few moments. I noticed he eyed Natasha appreciatively.

"Wow! Little Dana Dreer!" Natasha said, shaking her head. "I can't believe it!"

"I'm not so little," Dana gushed. "I'm getting married in two months at the Plaza!" As if on cue, a slight pink flush appeared on Dana's cheeks.

Natasha sucked in the appropriate gasp. "The Plaza! Not too shabby. Did your folks win big at Lotto or what?"

"More like I'm marrying very well, if I do say so my-self!" Dana whispered with a chuckle as she held up her two-and-a-half-carat-encrusted left hand and wiggled her fingers. Could I throw up now? "Omigod, Natasha, you *have* to come! Please say you'll come! The wedding's on August second, a Sunday."

"Well, I'll have to check my book..." Natasha said with the flip of a ringlet. She plopped her Louis Vuitton satchel on the table and pulled out an appointment book, also covered in Louis Vuitton leather imprinted with hundreds of LV's. She flipped a few pages. "Let's see…August second, August second…I'm free!" she announced, slapping shut the book. "I'm in town for two months to work on the first few chapters with Janey's expert help, and then I'm flying back to Santa Barbara to write, write, write. So pen me in!"

I was shocked. Why would Natasha Nutley, faux celebrity, want to waste six hours of her fabulous life at Dana Dreer's wedding to Larry Fishkill? Even if it *was* at the Plaza?

"It's all right if I bring a date, isn't it?" Natasha asked Dana. "Sam's flying out from the Coast for the entire month of August, so…"

Dana beamed. "Of course!"

I stared at Dana. Her ex-baby-sitter, who she hadn't seen in ten years, could bring a date, but her own cousin *couldn't?* Dana probably figured that any date of Natasha's was either famous, recognizable or at least fabulous enough to add glamour to the guest list.

"So I'll get to meet Jane's boyfriend and your soon-to-be-husband!" Natasha said. "I just love romance!"

Now it was Dana's turn for shock and staring. "Jane's boyfriend?"

"He's *not* going with you to the wedding?" Natasha asked me.

"Well, I—"

"Jane!" Dana said, hands on hips. "Why didn't you *tell* me it got serious! Mom said you were seeing someone, but I didn't realize…of course bring him!"

I swallowed.

"So it's settled," Dana declared with a clap of her hands. "You're both bringing your men. I'll seat the four of you together at your own table. Good thing I'm having lunch with my caterer—I'll add three to the list right now!

Wow—I can't wait to tell everyone that Natasha Nutley is coming to my wedding! Mom and Grammy are going to flip!''

More air kisses. And then Dana finally flitted off.

Natasha leaned her elbows on the table and rested her face between her palms. "I'm dying to hear more about your boyfriend. Where'd you meet him? What's he do?"

My palms were sweating. I rubbed them against the napkin on my lap. "Natasha, *your* life is the one interesting enough for a memoir! Not mine. Wow," I added, glancing at my watch. "It's getting so late! I think we should order and get started on planning Chapter One. The outline noted that you want to start with the acting class you took as a kid, but I think you should open with meeting The Actor, then work your way back. You know, unfold your life story as it's relevant."

"You're the editor!" Natasha trilled with a smile, opening her menu. "But I want to hear about the boyfriend over dessert. He sounds yummy!"

Glad she thought so. Because I'd have to eat every made-up word.

## Three

Flirt Night Roundtable Discussion No. 8,566,932: the Supposed Boyfriend issue. Amanda, Eloise and I leaned forward at our little circular table across from the bar at TapasTapas as an Angelina Jolie look-alike set down our drinks.

Amanda waved away a stream of secondhand smoke with one hand and stirred her Tanqueray and tonic with the other. "Hey, maybe you could pass off Jeremy Black as your adoring boyfriend! The wedding's practically a work thing now that Natasha's going. I'll bet he'd go with you. Ask him, Jane!"

I couldn't even handle asking Jeremy if he'd had a good weekend at our Monday morning editorial meetings. I was suddenly going to invite him to a family wedding?

Deep sigh. "I can't."

"Bull's balls!" Amanda insisted. "You've been dying

to go out with him for years. It's the perfect opportunity. I'd ask him.''

Did I mention that Amanda Frank—who threw around phrases like ''bull's balls''—looked like a shorter (but even blonder) version of Faith Hill? She *could* ask out a man who someone might mistake for Pierce Brosnan. I, however, had just been described by the notorious Natasha Nutley as *adorable*. Which meant I was way, way out of the stratosphere of Jeremy Black's world.

Eloise took a sip of her merlot, then a drag of her Marlboro. ''She can't take Jeremy even if she got up the guts to ask him. The Gnat knows who he is.'' She turned to the left to exhale the smoke away from Amanda.

''But Jane brilliantly didn't mention The Boyfriend's *name*,'' Amanda pointed out. ''When she shows up with Jeremy Black, the Gnat will fall off her chair, and so will Dana! They'll both think you were too humble to mention that the mighty Jeremy was your man. Plus, you wouldn't even have to clue him in to what you were doing, Jane. He'd never have to know he was your fake boyfriend.''

''But I said my boyfriend lives on the *Upper West Side*,'' I reminded Amanda. ''And Natasha knows that Jeremy lives in Tribeca. I overheard part of his phone conversation with her last week when he was signing her to Posh. They were talking about where they're from and where they live now, blah, blah, blah. That's how the Forest Hills connection came up in the first place.''

Amanda stirred her gin and tonic. Eloise gnawed her lower lip. I chewed the tip of my stirrer.

''Well, you might *meet* someone in time for the wedding—you've got two whole months,'' Amanda said, tightening the low ponytail holding back her long blond hair. ''Maybe even tonight. We could go hang out at the

bar and start flirting. Or I could set you up with some
friends of Jeff's.''

Eloise and I raised eyebrows in unison. Been there,
done that. And did I really want to feel even worse than
I already did because of some horrific blind date? Even
Eloise had gone out with friends of Jeff Jorgensen. He
was cute and normal, if a little prone to an extended frat-
boy lifestyle, but the random guys who surrounded him
at work were not necessarily cute or normal, let alone the
all-important both.

''He's working at Ernst & Young now,'' Amanda
added. ''It's the hottest accounting firm in the world.
Which means a new pool of very successful possibilities.
You never know.'' She eyed my Cosmopolitan. ''I wish
I'd ordered that. After the crapola day I had, I could use
something pink and strong.''

I sipped the top of the cold drink and slid it over to
Amanda. She'd learned *crapola* from me and Eloise. We
both tried to use some of her ranch lingo, but you couldn't
say things like *bull's balls* unless you were the real thing.
Amanda was a paralegal at Lugworth & Strummold, one
of the biggest law firms in New York. She had no interest
in becoming a lawyer, but she loved her job. Sometimes
she talked about trying her hand at writing a John
Grisham–type novel and making use of her publishing
house connections.

Eloise and I had met Amanda a day or so after I'd
started at Posh, while smoking in front of our office building. (Amanda neither smoked nor worked in the building
anymore. L&S had moved to the Wall Street area four
years ago.) Anyway, two or three or ten times a day, the
three of us would stand puffing away on the corner of
Lexington Avenue and 57th Street. A few weeks of su-
perficial chats turned into lunch invitations, which led to

drinks invitations, which led to brunch invitations on the weekends, which led to the formation of the weekly Flirt Night Roundtable.

"Or, you could call up Max," Eloise suggested, peering at me for my reaction. "You *have* been wondering what became of him, so this would be a good way to find out."

I immediately shook my head. Why did just the mention of his name still hurt so much? I'd never call Max. I couldn't. Who knew if he was still with what's-her-name? Who knew if he was with someone else? And who wanted him to know that I was so desperate for a date that I had to ask my only ex-boyfriend to attend a function with me? A family function, no less.

Max and I had met in the men's department of Macy's. He'd been buying a shirt; I'd been looking for a birthday present for my uncle Charlie. And when I'd spotted Max, looking miserable and confused while sliding pants on a rack, I was smitten. Smitten enough to risk asking him if he thought an uncle would like the sweater I was holding. (Now there was a great way to meet marriageable men in New York. Only single guys bought their own clothes alone.)

Oh, wait a minute. Scratch that. I was forgetting that Max Reardon *hadn't* been a marriageable man. After a year of pretty serious togetherness, he'd fallen for someone at work, and that was that. Well, that had been that for *him*. I'd been left with a broken heart at age twenty-three. I immediately lost twelve pounds because I couldn't eat. Then I gained twelve pounds because I couldn't stop comforting myself with the Häagen-Dazs Eloise and Amanda brought me every day. I'd ended up exactly where I started: heartbroken and seven pounds overweight.

After two weeks of watching me cry and blow my nose and mope, Eloise had decided that she, Amanda and I should pretend we were tourists in New York every weekend. Each month we did a different borough. While Eloise and Amanda handed out tissues, I cried up the stairs to the Statue of Liberty's chin, gazed swollen-eyed through the viewfinder on top of the Empire State Building and sobbed over the railing of the Staten Island ferry. I cried while staring up at the World's Fair globe in Flushing Meadow Park. Cried through a Mets game at Shea Stadium. Cried during a Lilith Fair concert at Jones Beach. By month five, my tear ducts had dried up. I was over Max enough to notice how beautiful the flowers were at the Bronx Botanical Gardens and how incredibly cute some of the Yankees were. I'd tried to sell Gwen on the idea of *The Broken-Hearted Girl's Guide to New York City,* but she told me it was too gimmicky.

Max had been my first real boyfriend, and I hadn't had a real relationship since. Except for Soldier of Fortune Guy and two other short-lived romances, plus a couple of dates here and there with a maybe that always fizzed out, I'd been totally single.

Why? Amanda had Jeff. Eloise had her Russian. And I was surrounded by a Tapas bar full of women sitting across from men. What was my problem? Truck drivers and construction workers seemed to think I was cute enough to merit a catcall, so why couldn't I wrap a man around my little finger the way my friends could? The way Natasha Nutley could?

Amanda slid back my Cosmopolitan, and I slurped a sip.

"Nix calling up Max, Jane," Eloise said. "I totally forgot that your family knows Max. You can't pass him off as the new love of your life, and you can't pretend you're back together. Bad idea. I'm really sorry I even brought him up.''

I sent Eloise an it's-okay look. We all went back to chewing, gnawing and sipping.

Amanda pointed at me with her stirrer. ''Do the blind date thing, Jane. All you need is *one* guy to bring to a wedding. What have you got to lose?''

Eloise and I stared at her. There was no need to add a sarcastic response.

My silence, though, was enough of an answer for Amanda. She whipped out her cell phone. ''Jeff, guess who's willing to go out on blind dates again? Jane! Shut up—that was, like, *two* years ago! Got anyone for her?'' We all waited. ''No! He's bald! No, too short—Jane's five-six. Hmm. Oh, that guy? No way—he's cute, but an idiot! Jane's an editor—he's gotta be smart. Ooh—yes! Uh-huh, uh-huh, uh-huh…he sounds really good! Set it up.''

*Sounds* good? So Amanda had never clapped eyes on Mr. Uh-Huh?

Amanda clicked off her cell, her blue eyes twinkling. She leaned forward at the table and whipped her long ponytail behind her. ''Kevin Adams. Thirty-three. Senior Accountant. Lives in a brownstone off Central Park West. Jeff says all the admins in the office salivate over Kevin.''

I almost spit out my mouthful of Cosmopolitan. It was fate. Kevin Adams was exactly who I'd described to Natasha! Right down to the brownstone on the Upper West Side.

''He sounds good, Jane,'' Eloise said, nodding. ''Damned good.''

''Do it, Jane,'' Amanda seconded. ''Or it's telling Dana and the Gnat you lied. It's going out with Incinerator Man!''

They'd mistaken my look of shock for disdain. I burst
out into a grin and beamed at Amanda. "Tell Jeff to give
him my number. At home *and* work."

Eloise and I gave Amanda real kisses on the cheek and
disappeared down the steps into the Union Square subway
station. Both Grammy and Aunt Ina had made me promise never to take the subway. They refused to believe that
the New York City subway system wasn't the crime pit
it had been in the seventies when they'd been "career
women" with jobs in the garment district. Eloise and I
swiped our metro cards in the turnstile and headed for the
Uptown IRT line.

A woman pretending to be the Statue of Liberty stood
stock-still on a platform (she was painted silver), holding
a torch. An upside-down hat in front of her had a few
bills in it. Down a few feet, three teenagers played drums,
an open drum case in front of them without a coin. Eloise
and I stopped for a few minutes to listen to an overweight
gospel singer. We each threw the change from the bottom
of our purses into what looked like the case of an amp.

We slipped inside the 6 train just as the doors were
closing and grabbed two of the hard orange seats. A pack
of teenagers huddled together playing a hand-held video
game. An elderly man was clipping his fingernails. Two
or three sad sacks read newspapers or the ridiculous ad-
vertisements lining the top rim of the car. And six attractive women, all in their late-twenties and early thirties,
were dotted around, their Kate Spade handbags tight
against them as they read reports, books or stared blankly
out the dark windows.

Looking at them depressed me. I was one of them. Like
me, they'd spent a few hours after work with friends,
maybe even on a date, and now they were going home.
Alone. On a Friday at ten-thirty. To open their mail, check

out cable, root around in the refrigerator, flip through a *Vogue*, fantasize about promotions, boyfriends, marriage proposals and be depressed until sleep thankfully took over. One of the Me's caught me staring, so I shot my gaze upward to an advertisement for a local podiatrist.

"So tell me more about her," Eloise said as the train rumbled uptown.

"The Gnat?"

Eloise nodded. "Is she a total diva? All fabulous and tragically hip?"

I envisioned Natasha. "Yes and no. She is sort of 'super-fabulous' in the way you mean, but there's something I can't put my finger on about her. I don't have her figured out yet."

"You will, though. You're gonna know her inside and out after working with her on the memoir. Why is she going to Dana's wedding, anyway?"

I shrugged. Yeah, why?

Eloise was flung against me as the train short-stopped in the 42rd Street station. "Maybe she wants the free booze. Does she still have a drinking problem?"

"Not according to her book outline," I said. "And she didn't have any alcohol at lunch." Which, by the way, had come in just under eighty-five bucks. Maybe I could treat myself to a fifteen-dollar pan-seared salmon tomorrow night. That was practically a cure for Another Saturday Night Alone Syndrome. Even if you had to eat the salmon alone while renting a video. I glanced around the car at the Me women. Not one of them had that I-have-a-date-tomorrow-night contentedness in their "adorable" faces. "El?"

"Yeah?"

I kicked the toe of my sandal against the dirty floor. "You don't think what I did was pathetic? I mean, telling Natasha and Dana I had this great boyfriend?"

Eloise raised an eyebrow. "Pathetic? Try *necessary!* And you didn't tell Dana anything. Natasha did. You had no choice. Don't worry, Jane. I'll bet Kevin turns out to be everything you described and more. He'll ask you out for a second date, you'll start seeing each other, and suddenly you're bringing your boyfriend to Dana's wedding."

I laughed. Eloise was forgetting that stuff like that only happened to *her*. Serge had confessed his love on their fifth date. (She still hadn't said it back, by the way.) "I'm not gonna get my hopes up too high about Kevin. He's just a *possibility*."

Eloise raised her eyebrow.

"Okay, so my hopes are up," I admitted. "You'll dress me, right, Eloise?" She nodded. "Just think—this afternoon I had *no* boyfriend, then a *fake* one and now a blind date possibility who could become a *real* boyfriend. If he even calls."

*That* was pathetic, actually. Hoping that some guy you'd never even met would call you, then like you enough to want to go out with you again, all so you could dance with him in a hotel ballroom at a wedding that had been promised to *you* a long time ago.

But if you stopped hoping, stopped believing, stop playing the stupid game for even one second, you were doomed. You couldn't give up, ever. Because if you did, you'd be alone for the rest of your life, like my great-aunt Gertie. And all your hard work would be left in the form of an inheritance that would go to your undeserving relatives.

My eyes flickered over the date on my watch, and my heart stopped for a second. "Hey, El, do you know what today is? I almost forgot till just now. It's my parents' wedding anniversary."

Eloise gave my hand an empathetic squeeze. The train lurched into the 77th Street station so violently that we both had to grab on to the edge of our seats. We stood up and waited for the doors to open. "Let's stop for frozen yogurt," Eloise suggested. "Tasti D-Lite has fat-free hot fudge now."

We emerged out of the subway and ducked into the Tasti D-Lite on Lexington Avenue. I got chocolate marshmallow. Eloise got a twist of vanilla fudge and fake Snickers. We both got a dollop of fat-free hot fudge.

Content to lick our cones and people-watch, we strolled east to First Avenue, then north to 79th Street so that Eloise could buy the new *In Style* magazine at the kiosk on the corner. Catherine Zeta-Jones was on the cover.

Eloise smiled at the cute Indian guy behind the kiosk's counter. "Will you be a sweetie and drop the change and the magazine in my tote bag?" She held up her cone.

"Of course, anything for you," he told her, his dark eyes sparkling. He leaned over the counter and slid the thick magazine and some bills into her bag.

"You're a doll." She blew him a kiss as we headed away.

I usually loved watching Eloise in action. But right then, my heart felt like a big painful blob.

"Hey, Jane, let's make pit stop at St. Monica's Sunday morning to light candles for our moms and your dad," Eloise said as we walked past the huge church.

I nodded gratefully and licked a dripping stream of hot fudge off the sugar cone. We lit candles once a month, even though neither of us was Catholic. The whole idea had been Eloise's. She said you didn't have to *be* the thing to *do* the thing. You just had to want either.

Didn't I know it.

* * *

On Saturday morning, Eloise and I had gone shoe shopping at the store Dana had told me about. I walked out with a pair of $125 peach fabric shoes I'd never wear again and wouldn't be able to return. Eloise had then gone to meet Serge for lunch after his ESL class. He was studying to become an American citizen. Serge's friends at the hair salon had told him that American women worried that foreign men were only interested in green cards. So even though Eloise had told him she wanted to keep their relationship casual, he'd headed straight for the Immigration office and filed the necessary papers to get his green card the hard way.

And *I* was headed for my blind date with Kevin Adams! He'd surprised me with a ten-in-the-morning phone call, which, according to Eloise, was a good sign. It meant he was eager to meet someone, in the market for a relationship. Kevin had told me he was playing squash till eleven thirty, then had brunch plans, but he'd love to meet me for a cup of coffee—if I wanted to be spontaneous.

I did. And I happened to be free since my own fictitious brunch plans had suddenly fallen through. According to every person in the world, you never accepted a date for *that* day. You never accepted a date less than two days away, preferably three. Doing so was tantamount to telling the guy you had absolutely no life. Usually I listened to that crap. But I was on a major deadline. Dana's wedding was barely two months away. Anyway, we were just meeting for coffee.

At two on the dot, I neared DT UT (stood for Downtown Uptown), a trendy coffee lounge on Second Avenue at 84th Street. Kevin and I had arranged to meet on the side of the pastry counter, under the hanging roll of brown paper that listed the smoothies and shakes. I was to look for the guy in the navy blue sweater and jeans. Amanda via Jeff had provided the vital stats: tall, lanky, dark brown hair, brown or green or blue eyes—Jeff hadn't been sure.

I took a long drag of my cigarette as I approached the door to the lounge, then crushed it out. Had Jeff told Kevin I was a smoker? If he cared, he probably wouldn't have agreed to meet me. Maybe he smoked, too. I envisioned us puffing away in the ballroom of the Plaza, blowing smoke rings as we sipped champagne.

And then I remembered that guys who played squash didn't smoke. Should I step into the deli next door for breath mints? Hmm. It was already five minutes after two, and if I had to wait for the mint to dissolve in my mouth, I'd be late. It wasn't like I could meet my fake-to-be boyfriend while sucking on a mint. I cupped my hand, blew into it and sniffed. Seemed okay.

I pulled open the door and was immediately greeted by a Pat Benatar song that I hadn't heard since grammar school. Lisa and Lora Miner and I had listened to that album over and over and over. Pat Benatar knew from heartache, as Aunt Ina would say.

A short line was snaked around the pastry counter, but no tall, lanky guy alone, and no guy in jeans and a dark blue sweater. I glanced around at the overstuffed chairs to the side of the counter. A good-looking, dark-haired guy with what looked like hazel eyes sat reading *The New York Times*; he wore jeans and a white T-shirt. A giant-sized mug of coffee was in front of him, next to a scone of some sort. A gym bag was by his feet. An empty chair was next to him.

Well, that couldn't be him. Kevin Adams wouldn't be sitting down, or have ordered already. Plus, he said he'd be wearing a navy sweater. Two young women chatted away in the other two chairs, across from T-Shirt Man. Lining the lounge on the other side of the pastry bar were some hard-backed chairs. A few people were in those, but no one matched Kevin Adams's description.

I was dying for a cup of coffee. Should I order one and sip it while I waited? No. That would be weird. And probably rude. Plus, there was nowhere to rest the cup without getting in people's way as they moved along the counter to order and pay.

I glanced down at my watch. It was two-ten. So Kevin was ten minutes late. Big deal. Ten minutes late was actually on time in New York City. I should have been fifteen minutes late, so I'd be an extra-fashionable five minutes late.

I didn't know what to do with my hands; I was pocketless. Eloise had dressed me in a pale silver-gray camisole topped by a mesh black cardigan with only the top button buttoned, black stretch capris and low-heeled black leather mules. I'd told Kevin I'd be wearing black. No other women in head-to-toe black waited by the pastry counter, so there was no way he *couldn't* recognize me.

Two-fifteen. The door opened and a bunch of people entered. A couple with a baby in a stroller. Three teenage girls. A guy carrying a laptop. I started feeling self-conscious, so I pretended to study the blackboard menu hanging on the wall behind the counter.

I eyed T-Shirt Man in the overstuffed chair. He glanced up at me for a split second, then returned his attention to his newspaper. Geez. I didn't even merit a checkout. I hated that. A checkout or lack thereof was how you knew if you looked good in what you were wearing or if it was a bad hair day. Great. *Yesterday* had been a fine hair day.

Two-twenty. I pretended to study the menu again. My

palms were beginning to sweat, but I couldn't wipe them on my pants. I was starting to feel more and more self-conscious. Did people think I'd been stood up? *Had* I been stood up?

Two-twenty-three. Suddenly, T-Shirt Man was staring at me. He gestured at me to come over. I sent him a questioning look, and again he waved me over. So maybe it was a good hair day after all. Given that Kevin Adams was a very rude twenty minutes late, I saw no reason to pass up meeting a cute guy. With my luck, T-Shirt Man probably just wanted me to get him a napkin or a plastic spoon. I ventured over with a tentative smile.

"Hi," he said to me. "Are you Jane Gregg, by any chance?"

Huh? How did he know my name?

And then I saw the navy-blue sweater folded over the arm on the far side of his chair.

"I'm Kevin Adams." He extended his hand.

I felt my ears start to burn. "Why didn't you come over when I walked in? I've been standing right over there for the past twenty minutes. Didn't you think it was me?"

"Yeah, I knew right away, but my legs are *killing* me from playing squash." He smiled and revealed a gummy mouth. "My friend wiped the court with me. And I was so into this article about the Federal Reserve, I figured I'd finish it, then get up and let you know I was here. But every time I moved a muscle—" he exaggerated a grimace "—I was, like, whoa, dude, sit back down."

It was rare to want to pick up a pot of boiling water and pour it slowly over a person's head, but that was what I wanted to do to Kevin Adams at the moment. And because we were in a coffee lounge, there were two pots simmering on the burners, just waiting for me to lose it.

A total stranger had managed to humiliate me before our "date" had even begun. A gummy stranger, at that.

"So have a seat," Kevin said, gesturing to the chair next to him. There was a dusting of powdered sugar square in the center of the cushion.

*You don't have to marry him,* I reminded myself. *You just have to develop a casual relationship so that you can invite him to Dana's wedding.*

*If you don't tell him off and stomp out, you deserve him,* I warned myself. *He's clearly an A-level rude jerk.* But he fit the bill to a T. He lived in a *brownstone.*

Couldn't you cut me a break? I asked my brain. You were there. You went to high school with Gnatasha Nutley. She made your life miserable. She made you feel like the ugliest, dullest girl in town. She stole Robby Evers away from you before you even had a chance to feel his arms around you. You're just going to have to swallow your pride now in the name of saving it later.

"You have really beautiful eyes," Kevin Adams said.

Score one for Kevin Adams. He'd slightly redeemed himself. Maybe I'd judged him too hastily?

Yeah, and maybe one stupid compliment from a total jerk was all it took to make everything okay. I might have been desperate, but I wasn't stupid.

I dusted off the powdered sugar, sat down and smiled at my potential wedding date.

At three o'clock, Kevin Adams gingerly stood up. He made low, grunting sounds and contorted his features like the guys who lifted weights at the health club I'd stopped going to. I wasn't sure if he was really in pain or just a total wuss.

"So, I had a really nice time," he said, slipping the blue sweater over his head.

He had a nice body, I noticed, eyeing him as the sweater was over his face. Flat stomach, long legs. And he was really cute. Not Pierce Brosnan, but then who was, besides Jeremy?

So what if Kevin wasn't Mr. Manners? Not every guy had been raised well. Sometimes women had to train their men. The issue wasn't that he'd started the date without me and then invited me to join him when he was damned good and ready. Nor that he'd asked me to get him another soup cup of coffee while I got my own. The issue was that he was good-looking, male and lived on the Upper West Side in a brownstone. He was only gummy when he smiled.

I decided right then and there to accept a second date. If he asked. I'd gotten the impression that he liked me. Our date hadn't been very long, but we'd talked easily. Mostly about how great Amanda and Jeff were.

"So, um, Jane," he said, grabbing his knapsack. "I'll give you a call."

Oh. Everyone knew what that meant. An *I'll Call* meant: *I wasn't attracted to you, but you're a nice person, so, take care.* Why couldn't guys just say something like that outright? Why raise false hopes?

Kevin leaned forward awkwardly and air-kissed me.

I woke up on Sunday morning to pouring rain and a headache. Eloise had taken me out for Mexican last night; she'd insisted that a few stiff frozen margaritas would clear my mind of Kevin Adams. She'd been right. But now I had both a migraine *and* my memory restored.

At least I wouldn't have to go out in the downpour for *The New York Times*. I'd been smart enough to pick one up last night at the newsstand where Eloise had flirted with the Indian clerk.

I threw the comforter off me and shuffled into the kitchen to make a pot of coffee. *Oh man!* I mentally whined. *I should have bought milk last night.* I opened the fridge and shook the quart of skim. There was just a trickle left.

This clearly wasn't going to be a great day, but it had to be better than yesterday. Amanda had called last night to hear if she'd sparked a love match. I sugarcoated the report by telling her that Kevin and I didn't seem to have chemistry, but that if he called again, I'd be happy to go out again. *Which he wouldn't.* No way would I tell her the guy was a big fat jerk. Amanda had done me a favor by fixing me up. Plus, I couldn't afford to re-alienate my wedding date resource's boyfriend.

I flopped back into bed and lugged the heavy *Times* onto my stomach, dumping the sections I never read onto the floor (Automobiles, Sports, Money & Business, the front section). I grabbed Styles and turned to the wedding announcements. I always liked to look for people I knew. Maybe three times in my life I'd recognized a name. Two from college and one from Posh, an intern who'd left a long time ago. The main reason I read the wedding section was to check ages and jobs to see how I stacked up against them.

Lots of twenty-seven-year-olds were getting hitched. Elementary teachers at private schools were aplenty, as were Internet executives like Larry Fishkill. Ugh. In a couple of months I'd have the joy of seeing Dana and Larry's faces smiling at me from these pages.

I scanned the names—and stopped breathing.

Max Reardon's smiling face stared at me. His arm was around a pretty redhead with freckles. Reardon and Carmichael, the headline read.

*Max Reardon, 28, and Cheryl Carmichael, 26, both*

*Equity Analysts at the Bank of New York, were married yesterday at St. Stephen's Episcopal Church in the bride's hometown of...*

Tears plopped on the newsprint before I even realized I was crying.

I ran into the kitchen and opened the cabinet under the sink. But I broke into sobs before I could even utter Eloise's name.

The phone rang. My legs were useless. I couldn't even manage to stand.

The answering machine clicked on. "Omigod! Jane, it's Dana! I can't believe this! Larry and I are sitting here reading the paper and having breakfast, and guess who got married in *The Times?* Your ex, Max! Remember him? Omigod, can you believe it? The wife's so pretty! Doesn't she remind you of Natasha a little? Everyone's so excited that Natasha's coming to the wedding! Did you buy the shoes? Call me later. Bye!"

---

I tried and tried to turn off the alarm clock, but it kept buzzing. And then I realized it was the telephone. I sat up, forcing open my eyes. It was six-thirty in the morning.

My sheets smelled like stale smoke. I'd gone through two and a half packs of cigarettes yesterday. Amanda had valiantly stayed through the first chain-smoked pack and a half, but when her eyes had become as red rimmed and watery from the smoke as mine were from sobbing, I'd had to force her to leave. Eloise had emptied the ashtray for me every time it hit five butts and sprayed Lysol after each half pack.

The nicotine must have done serious damage to my brain cells. Because unless I was mistaken, I'd actually agreed to go on more blind dates with acquaintances of Amanda's boyfriend. Eloise had convinced me that giving

up and arriving solo at the wedding would only make the
Maxes and Kevins of the world *win*. But hadn't they?
Who had the energy to fight them anymore? I was going
to end up like Great-aunt Gertie. I might as well just
accept it.

And then Aunt Ina had called to ask if I was okay about
Max's wedding announcement. Her motherly concern had
been so comforting that I'd almost burst into tears on the
phone. Until I'd remembered that a woman with a supposedly wonderful new boyfriend wouldn't be so upset
about an old flame's wedding.

Amanda had said she'd take care of everything. She'd
whipped out the cell phone, and suddenly I had four new
blind dates all set up. Three for this week (Tuesday,
Thursday and Saturday) and one for next week (Tuesday).
If Blind Date #1 worked out, I could cancel #2, and so
on and so on.

"Yeah but, what if they're *all* busts?" I'd asked.
"Then what?"

Dead silence had followed. We'd agreed to worry about
that at Friday's Flirt Night Roundtable.

The phone shrilled again. I snatched the cordless.
"'Lo," I croaked into the receiver.

"Jane? Natasha. I'm so surprised to get you! I thought
I'd be leaving a message, since you said you usually stay
at your boyfriend's. Otherwise I wouldn't have called so
early."

Why was the Gnat calling me at *home*, anyway? She
was *work*. Not a personal friend.

"Jane? Did I wake you?"

"Um, no, I was actually doing my yoga tape." I
breathed deeply, held and exhaled. "My boyfriend's away
on business for a few days, so…"

"Oh, good then! I wanted to let you know I was planning to stop by the office this morning, if that's okay. Oh, I just realized I could have left you a message there, but you don't have a direct line, and I never remember your extension so... Anyway, I spent a good chunk of the weekend sketching out a first draft of Chapter One, based on what you said. You know, about starting at the present and letting the past unfold as required. Great idea, Janey. I think I've got some good stuff down on paper."

I leaned back against my smoky pillows. My hair reeked.

The Gnat was a little too awake for me. How could she be so coherent and on top of things at six-thirty in the morning?

"So I'd really like you take a look before I flesh it all out," Natasha added. "I mainly focused on why I signed the legal papers while you-know-who was practically inside me."

I cringed. That was just what I needed on a Monday morning following the Sunday morning I learned that my one and only serious boyfriend had gotten married: an earful on how Natasha had signed each letter of her name to the grinding motion of The Actor's expert sexual strokes.

I sat up and forced myself to focus. "Okay, so, um, it has to be later than ten, since that's when our editorial meeting usually ends."

"Ten's great," Natasha said. "See you later!"

I hung up and fell back against the pillows.

Was she *allowed* to call me at home? I'd have to set a few ground rules with the Gnat. She might have been a faux celebrity, but I didn't work twenty-four/seven. I was about to *date* twenty-four/seven, but that was another story. Who did she think she was, anyway, calling me at home?

This totally sucked. I couldn't wallow in my misery with my family, and now I couldn't even wallow at work. After all, I supposedly led a *fabulous* life, making a 100K a year with a boyfriend who owned a brownstone. That woman wouldn't care that her ex-boyfriend had gotten married. In the bride's hometown, no less.

But the real Jane Gregg did. Very, very much. So much so that she'd lit an extra candle in St. Monica's yesterday—to say goodbye to whatever lingering hope she'd unconsciously hung on to about Max realizing he'd made a mistake by dumping her.

Eloise had insisted it wasn't pathetic of me. It was closure, she'd said.

"Oh, oh, oh-oh" *Squeak. Squeak. Squeeeeeeak.* "Ohhhhhhhhhhh! Oh yeah!"

I banged against the wall and covered my face with my smoky pillow.

## Four

"The baby just pooped, everyone!" Gwen Welle announced from the speakerphone.

Even when she was on maternity leave, I couldn't escape her. She insisted on calling in for editorial meetings. Like anything important ever went on at these weekly wastes of time.

Could you tell I was in a bad mood?

The editorial staff of Posh Publishing had been in the conference room for half an hour, and all I'd learned was that a singer whose career had died in the eighties had signed on for a tell-all, as had a computer geek who insisted he'd been ruined by Bill Gates. Plus, our managing editor, Paulette Igerman, complained to Remke that Jeremy had changed the publication date of a book without alerting her. Paulette seemed to be the only woman alive immune to Jeremy's charisma. I didn't get it. Eloise was sure that Paulette was a lesbian.

"Morgan, order in a Continental breakfast for Jane's meeting with Nutley," Remke said, tapping his pen on the agenda. "Keep it under twenty."

I smiled. Morgan glanced at me with contempt. So, I'd done it. I'd crossed that golden line with Remke. I was now too important to order a fruit plate, a platter of Danishes and a gallon of orange juice from the gourmet deli down the street for my own meeting with an author. Morgan had to order it for me. That was something.

I felt Jeremy's gaze pass over me for a moment. What did he think of me? I honestly didn't know. I did know that he considered me hardworking. Gwen had offered that tidbit of praise from Jeremy in each of my performance reviews. And he seemed to think I had potential to be a good editor; he often entrusted me to do preliminary line-edits on his projects. But would he ever look at me? I mean, really look at me? Sometimes I had the feeling that Jeremy felt sorry for me. And other women like me. Which didn't include Morgan Morgan. Women who'd grown up on Thoroughbred farms weren't to be pitied when their twenty-thousand-a-year salaries were subsidized by their parents.

Jeremy knew I lived in a dumpy building and couldn't take taxis because I couldn't afford them. He'd seen me arrive at work every morning subway-sweaty in my Gap and Ann Taylor on-sale clothes. He knew I spent summers on a beach towel on the Great Lawn in Central Park, with a cooler of iced tea, manuscripts and tuna-fish sandwiches I made myself.

And I knew he spent his summers in East Hampton, dining on fifty-dollar lobster caught that day from an ocean he sailed on.

"Morgan!" Remke snapped, thumbing through papers

as usual. "Where's the P&L on the sex addict's autobiography?"

"It's the third from the last in your pile, Williaaam," Morgan said, a satisfied smile on her flat face.

Remke was trying to decide whether to do the sex addict's memoir in mass-market size or trade. Everyone at Posh had made a copy of the manuscript to read. It was really steamy stuff.

Remke pulled out the profit and loss statement and scowled at it. "Morgan, take this back to Ian, tell him to run it at three hundred pages, mass-market, at $6.99. The content justifies it. Plus, we'll give it a really hot title." Remke passed the P&L to Morgan. "Agreed, Black?"

Jeremy nodded. He was leaning back in his chair as though he were at the dentist. Remke sat at the head of the table, as always. Jeremy sat at Remke's left. The speakerphone was placed at Gwen's usual seat, to Remke's right. Paulette was next to Jeremy. I was in the chair *next to* Gwen's empty seat. Across the table, Morgan sat in a chair next to the empty seat beside Paulette.

We both knew our places. But *I* was moving up. Morgan would be busy for years trotting up and down the hall to the one- or two-person departments that made up Posh's publishing empire.

*"Hello,"* Gwen snapped over the crackle of the speaker-phone, reminding everyone she was on the line. "William, we're on your dime long distance, so let's wrap up, okay? So, Jane, how's the Nutley tell-all going, anyway?" She had on her phony concerned voice. "If there's anything you need help with, you know I'm just a phone call away, right?"

"Right," I chirped. *Yeah, right* was more like it. Even if I *had* a problem with the Gnat's manuscript, I wouldn't call Gwen. I'd have to listen to The Baby stories for twenty minutes first. What was it about new mothers? Why did they think anyone was interested in their Kegel exercises or the color of their infants' excrement? New mothers *never* shut up. Everything they said was so scary and sickening, it was a wonder any childless woman ever got pregnant on purpose.

Plus, Gwen was a major phony. She was okay as a boss, and she *was* really good at her job, but I couldn't stand her personally. She sort of looked like Christine Lahti, minus the killer body, and she was married to an even bigger phony, a hotshot on Wall Street. They lived in Chappaqua, three streets away from the Clintons. During her pregnancy, Gwen had had the mistaken impression that I was interested in her sonograms, and now, when she called to check in with me privately, her endless nanny sagas. She'd been through two nannies already, and the baby was only four weeks old. Eloise and I had whittled away the time on many a stalled subway ride home from work coming up with baby names for Gwen's kid. My personal favorite was *Not*. Not Welle. Eloise's was *Oh*. Gwen had chosen Olivia, so Eloise had sort of gotten her wish.

Jeremy leaned forward in his chair. He was having a private discussion with Remke. Morgan and I twiddled our thumbs. Gwen was silent. The baby had probably pooped again.

I stared at Jeremy's profile, since he was otherwise engaged. He had a strong, straight nose and a square chin chiseled out of—

"So, Gwen," Jeremy said, snapping me out of my appraisal of his beauty, "I'd like all unsolicited manuscripts to go to Morgan from now on." He glanced at the telephone. "With you out on leave, we're short staffed. Nutley's high priority, and I don't want Jane distracted by busywork Morgan can take on. For the next couple of months, Jane's going to be focusing on the Nutley book as Natasha writes the first three chapters and nails the outline. I'll handle the projects she's baby-sitting for you, Gwen, and I'll freelance out as necessary. We can get Morgan started on doing some preliminary line-edits, too.''

Morgan flashed a mouthful of teeth. For once, we were both pleased at the same time.

Remke eyed the telephone. "Gwen? Sound good to you?"

"Just fine," Gwen cheeped. "Although I'd like someone to look over Morgan's rejection and revision letters. I know Jane'll be busy, but perhaps she can take home Morgan's drafts and return them the next day with comments.''

*Excuse me?* It was bad enough that I had to work with the Gnat. *Now* I had to deal with a backstabber who was after my job?

Remke nodded. "Good idea, Gwen. Morgan, you're our screener now. Go to Jane with any questions or problems.''

Morgan shot me a dagger, then turned her suddenly thrilled expression to Remke. "Great, Williaaam! Thanks for the trust, everyone. I'm really thrilled to have this opportunity to flex my editorial muscles.''

What a suck-up. She was capitalizing on *my* success. Just like I was capitalizing on the Gnat's.

Jeremy nodded his cleft chin, then turned those magnetic Caribbean eyes on me. I immediately shot my gaze down to the table as though the scratches on the fake cherry wood were more interesting than his amazing bone structure. "I'll expect the first chapter of Nutley's memoir, excerpted, by next Friday.''

*Next Friday?*

"That's not a problem, is it, Jane?" Jeremy asked, tilting back in his chair again. "*Marie Claire* expects the excerpt in less than three weeks. Natasha gets two weeks to write the chapter, and you get a couple of days to excerpt it into twenty-five hundred irresistible words. I get one day to check it, and copyediting and proofreading get half a day. That gives us two days to spare for major problems."

Drop-dead gorgeous *and* a math whiz. "Next Friday's no problem," I said, daring to look at him for one and a half seconds. "I've had Natasha working all weekend."

"Good job," Remke cut in. "Keep it up. We're done here. Black, stay a moment. We need to talk about where we are on the Backstreet Boy."

*Next Friday.* How was I supposed to do *anything* this week but serial date? I'd have to work with the Gnat, train Morgan, go on four blind dates (with incredibly high expectations and rattled nerves) *and* mysteriously present a polished excerpt of Chapter One of *The Gnat Sucks* to Jeremy next Friday. My shoulders slumped.

I felt eyes on me. They belonged to Morgan.

No way was I letting *her* win too.


Morgan trotted after me to my office. I picked up the stack of slush manuscripts from my in-box and dumped them into her outstretched tanned arms. She was beaming. Perhaps the first genuine smile I'd ever seen on her horsey face.

I felt a drop of empathy for Morgan. She knew, like I knew, that all you needed was the chance. Once you got it, you either took it or someone else did. Morgan was taking it. In a way, I had to hand it to her, which, I literally *was*.

"So, um, Morgan, if you have any questions or want to know how I'd handle something, just come ask me, and I'll—"

"I learned how to read in first grade, Jaaane," Morgan said. "I think I'll manage just fine on my own."

Asshole.

My phone rang, and Morgan disappeared.

"Jane Gregg."

"Hi, Jane, it's Karen! Dana's maid of honor! How *are* you? I'm doing just great! I'm calling because I'm finalizing the plans for Dana's bridal shower, and I'd like to set up a meeting with the bridal party to go over the little details."

Like what? Who would clean up all the wrapping paper? Who would make Dana her stupid bow-encrusted shower hat? Who would take home all the disgusting, wilted deli meat and cookies? Dana's shower was a bunch of women sitting in a circle in Karen's gigantic Forest Hills apartment, watching Dana shriek "Omigod, I love it!" each time she opened another gift. The theme was French Kitchen, since France was where Dana and Larry were going on their honeymoon. How many dish towels with the Eiffel Tower on it did one couple need? And how often was I going to have be in the insufferable presence of Dana's friends before I spontaneously combusted?

Karen was a replica of Dana, only with light brown hair and bigger boobs. They'd been best friends since the third grade at P.S. 101. Karen was the kind of person who slowly looked you up and down. Twice.

"A meeting to discuss final details?" I said, checking my e-mail. "Don't you think that's overkill?" The shower itself was the Saturday after next. The bridal party had already gotten together a month ago to plan the shower.

Silence.

I felt a little guilty. "It's just that things are really crazy for me right now, so…" I clicked open an e-mail from Amanda. She wished me luck on Blind Date #2, which was scheduled for tomorrow night. Andrew Mackelroy. He was supposed to call me today to make a plan.

"We're all *busy,* Jane," Karen snapped. "And the shower's on the fourteenth—that's, like, in *two* weeks. The meeting will only be an hour or so. Look, if you don't want to be involved, just say so."

*I don't want to be involved.*

I rolled my eyes instead. "Of course I want to be involved, Karen. Just tell me when and where, okay? My other line's ringing."

"Saturday, at eleven-thirty at my place. First we'll meet, and the bridal party will head over to A Fancy Affair for our final dress fittings. Don't forget to bring your shoes."

How could I?

"Saturday at eleven-thirty," I repeated. "Can you give me your address again?"

She mentioned an address near Station Square.

"Okay, well, see you there."

I hung up and scowled at my wall calendar. I'd been hearing about Dana Dreer's wedding plans for the past two years. Why such a long engagement? Because of the waiting time to book a ballroom at the Plaza, of course. Getting married at the Plaza was more important to Dana and Larry than getting *married.* But now that the "big day" was two months away, I'd be hearing about it every second.

What did I have to look forward to for the next two months, besides working with Gnatasha Nutley and Morgan Morgan? Let me flip open my date book and share:

Note to self: cross off peach peau de soie shoes with two-and-a-half-inch princess heel. Got 'em.

*Saturday, June 6:* Wedding Shower Finalization meeting and Bridesmaid Dress Fitting #2, which meant spending another entire afternoon with Dana's insufferable bridal party. Did I mention that the dress cost me two hundred and twenty-five bucks?

*Saturday, June 13:* Wedding Shower. Which meant spending yet another entire afternoon with Dana's insufferable bridal party *and* Larry Fishkill's female relatives. It also meant buying an expensive present at Bloomingdale's or Williams-Sonoma, where she was registered.

*Friday, July 31:* The bachelorette party. At Hots, a male strip club. A repeat of the Wedding Shower Finalization group, but with dollar bills to stick in gyrating G-strings.

*August 2:* Wedding Day (crack of dawn): Zelda's Hair and Beauty Spa on Madison Avenue. Larry Fishkill's mother was springing for all the female relatives to have their hair and makeup done, plus manicures and pedicures.

*August 2:* (morning): Pre-ceremony pictures with the entire wedding party for Dana's personal collection. How long could a person keep a smile frozen on her face before her face cracked?

*August 2:* (early afternoon-2pm): Helping Dana into her $8,000 wedding gown and her Tiffany diamond studs, an engagement present from Aunt Ina and Uncle Charlie.

*August 2:* (2:30pm) The long, boring ceremony itself.

*August 2:* (4pm–midnight): The long, boring wedding reception. Dana had told her bandleader she wanted a heavy Celine Dion rotation. Her wedding song was "The Wind Beneath My Wings" by Bette Midler.

*August 2:* (10pm-ish) The tossing of the bouquet. The

horror movie all single women got to star in as they lined up like losers with hopeful smiles on their faces while stretching out their claws to catch the bouquet that promised they'd be next.

*August 2* (all day): Listening to Aunt Ina and Grammy look at me with pity and telling me not to worry, that my day would come.

*August 2* (all night): Sitting like a wallflower at the table with no one to dance with, just like at Forest Hills High.

The intercom buzzed. "Yeah?"

"Ms. Nutley is here to see you, Jaaane," Morgan said. "Coffee and Danish and a fruit plate are set up in the conference room. The deli only had the kind of orange juice with the pulp in it. I hope that's okaaay."

"It's fine. Thanks, Morgan. Can you tell Natasha I'll be out in a minute?" More like *five* minutes. I was a busy executive, not some lowly assistant editor who was so grateful for this plum project that she ran out enthusiastically to greet her star author.

The intercom buzzed again. "I'll be out in a moment," I repeated.

"Hey, it's me," Eloise said. "Pick up. I hate talking on speakerphone." I snatched the receiver. "Wanna come see the new Woody Allen movie with me and Serge tonight? We're going to the seven-twenty at the Beekman."

Serge was a huge Woody Allen fan. After he saw *Annie Hall* on video about ten times, he'd bought Eloise a tie and a vest. She'd had no problem alerting him to the fact that *Annie Hall* was almost thirty years old—and that the seventies fashion revival had thankfully come and gone.

"I wish I could, El, but I think I'd better work. I've got all those blind dates this week, so tonight's my only totally free night to slave over the Gnat's slutty life story.

Which she's delivering in person this morning—well, a draft of the first chapter, anyway. Jeremy wants the excerpt for *Marie Claire* by *next Friday*."

"Ugh. You *are* busy. So are you okay, I mean about yesterday?

"Yeah, I think so. I'm just gonna try and forget about it, if I can." Of course, Max's angular face flashed before my eyes. "Max's wedding announcement *and* that jerk, Kevin. Do you know that I actually called my machine a couple of times this morning just to see if he called? I didn't even like him! Hey, go take a peek at the reception desk. Natasha Nutley's waiting for me to come get her."

"Ooh—bye!" Eloise hung up. I could just picture her pretending she was dropping off a memo for Remke with Morgan so she could get a glance at the Gnat.

I figured my five minutes were now up. I stuck my head out of my office door and peered around the corner, which gave me a view of the reception desk—Morgan's open cubicle. The Gnat was deep in conversation with Morgan. I stared Natasha up and down, à la Karen, Dana's maid of honor. She was wearing a black camisole, black leather pants with a skinny cow-print belt and black high-heeled mules. I glanced down at my gray pantsuit, in which I'd felt perfectly professional three minutes ago. Suddenly I felt dowdy.

Deep breath, deep breath.

I grabbed my Gnat folder and headed down the hall with a smile plastered on my face. "Gnatasha!" I called out. "Right on time."

She flashed the whiter-than-whites at me. "I was just telling Morgan that I used to baby-sit your cousin. We were marveling at what a small world it is."

*Too* small.

"Has anyone ever told you that you look like Nicole Kidman?" Morgan gushed to Natasha.

"Um, so why don't we head into the conference room?" I interrupted, sweeping my arm ahead of the Gnat.

Remke appeared out of his office behind Morgan's cubicle. "Natasha! Lovely to see you." Remke and the Gnat air-kissed both cheeks and made small talk about "the Coast."

Jeremy came down the hall carrying a manuscript and cover mechanicals. "Natasha, you look wonderful, as always."

More air-kissing. More small talk.

I wondered what it would be like to air-kiss Jeremy Black. To be that close to his cheek. That close to his mouth, to those lips. I suddenly imagined his tongue probing deep inside my mouth, inside my—

"Jaaane, if you need the coffee urn refilled, you just let me know," Morgan said.

How sweet she was. "I sure will."

I led the Gnat inside the conference room. I sat at the head of the table, where Remke had been just a half hour earlier. I'd never sat in this chair before.

Natasha sat to my right. She placed her leather tote, this one imprinted with tiny *G*'s, onto Gwen's chair. She pulled out a red folder and opened it on the table.

I opened my own folder. My copy of her outline was peppered with notes in the margins. Why couldn't she read over my comments and do her work from home? Or better yet, from three thousand miles away, on the stupid houseboat where she now lived? Why did she have to constantly call and come over? Why couldn't she just fly back to "the Coast" and leave me alone?

"Coffee?" I asked, lifting the urn.

"Love some," Natasha said, steadying one of the mugs. "Wanna split a Danish?"

"Okay." I poured two cups of coffee. I was surprised she ate such things, let alone that she didn't launch into a diatribe about dieting. I thought actresses ate only spinach leaves and guzzled Ex-Lax.

"So, I'll leave you my first chapter to read later, but is it okay if I read you my opening sentence? I figure if it's too in-your-face, I'll know not to go that far with Chapter Two."

I poured milk into my coffee. She took hers black, I noticed. How minimalist. "Well, Remke and Jeremy always say to hook your reader with the first sentence, so the more in-your-face, the better. Go ahead."

The Gnat smiled, then lifted the page and cleared her throat. Her bangles jangled on her wrist. "I was fucking one of the most famous actors currently in show business when he handed me a legal document to sign."

I almost spat out my mouthful of coffee.

She frowned. "I told you it was straightforward."

She'd mistaken my surprise at her marketing savvy for shock. "No, it's great," I assured her as she took a tiny bite of her half of the Danish. "Perfect, actually. It's exactly what Remke hoped for."

"Really?" She was beaming. "I'm so happy! That means I'm on the right track."

Natasha Nutley was going to make my job even easier than I thought. I was as relieved as I was bothered.

"Jane Gregg."

"Oh, great—I got you and not voice mail," said a male voice.

"It's me," I confirmed, cradling the phone against my shoulder as I pulled a cigarette and a book of matches from my tote bag. I'd started having a major nicotine fit after thirty minutes in the Gnat's presence, so I'd excused myself to do something very important. Like get the hell away from her and sneak downstairs for a cigarette. This phone call was cutting into my puffing time.

Whoever it was—either one of the drones in the production department or the annoying Ian who crunched our profit-and-loss figures...or tomorrow night's blind date calling to confirm and set something up—had better make it snappy. I'd left the Gnat in the conference room to think over my editorial comments for the outline for Chapters Two and Three, which she'd focused too much on her childhood and not enough on life in L.A. and the struggle to break into show business. If Remke or Jeremy popped their heads in and found her alone, they'd wonder where I was. As nonsmokers, they wouldn't understand the need for nicotine. And as men, they wouldn't understand the need to escape Gnatasha.

"It's Andrew Mackelroy, Jeff's friend?" the voice said.

I sat up straighter in my chair and slipped the cigarettes and matches into my jacket pocket. "Hi." I immediately liked that he phrased sentences in the form of questions too.

"So, how does dinner sound for tomorrow night?" Andrew Mackelroy asked.

"Sounds good. I'm hungry already."

He offered a chuckle. "Great. You know, I sort of have this 'thing' I'm supposed to go to tomorrow night, and the best Italian food in New York will be served. Up for a surprise?"

I definitely liked Andrew. "Sure—I love Italian. Count me in."

How full of potential was this! He had a *thing* tomorrow night, and I had a *thing* in two months. That gave us two things in common already!

"Is it okay if we meet there?" he asked. "Yeah? You sure? Great. So the address is 563 Delancey Street, seven o'clock. I'm really looking forward to meeting you, Jane."

Delancey Street? Who had *anything* down there? And *was* there Italian food on the Lower East Side? Apparently so… I decided not to pre-judge.

"I'm really looking forward to meeting you," I said. "I'll be there, seven o'clock."

"Great. See you tomorrow."

I hung up and burst into a smile. I had a mystery date tomorrow night. At a thing!

I pulled out my datebook and flipped to Tuesday, June 2. I'd scribbled down the details Amanda had given me on Sunday afternoon. *Andrew Mackelroy, 30, Computer Engineer, Jeff's company. Five-eleven, dirty-blond hair, blue eyes. Good guy, family oriented, into sports.*

I was family oriented, too, sort of. And I did like to walk; that was a sport, sort of. I transferred the address he'd given me into my datebook and slipped it back into my tote bag.

I felt like doing a cartwheel down the hall, but opted instead to rush to Eloise's tiny office. She was peering at slides through a loop on her light-box.

"Guess who just called?" I whispered in her ear. "Tuesday's guy, Andrew! We're going out tomorrow night. Some surprise *thing* involving Italian on Delancey Street."

Eloise looked up. "Ooh—I'll bet it's a trendy gallery or club opening. The Lower East Side is beyond trendoid now."

I semi-frowned. "Should I wear something really hip? Like what?"

Eloise's intercom crackled. "El?"

It was Daisy, her boss. "Could you c'mere and bring the slides for the bulimia book?"

"Sure," Eloise said, pushing off the intercom.

Eloise was designing the cover of *Memoir of a Skinny-Minny Wanna-Be: My Bulimic Years.* The title was so long that hardly anything else could appear on the cover. Eloise had thought of placing a tiny digital scale between the title and subtitle, with flashing red numbers popping up and fading. *Skinny-Minny* was Gwen's book. I was "baby-sitting" it while Gwen was out, which meant I was being burdened with seeing it through all the phases of production *and* sending everything for approval by FedEx to Gwen's house. The cover mechanicals had come back with corrections and dried slime that looked like either baby food or baby barf. But thanks to Jeremy, I no longer had to deal with it.

"I'll plan a hipster outfit for you and bring it upstairs tonight," Eloise said, shutting off the light-box. "Oh, and I checked out the Gnat. She doesn't look *that* much like Nicole Kidman. And *hello?* Who wears leather pants past Memorial Day weekend, anyway?"

I kissed her, peered out of her office until I saw Morgan trot off somewhere, then sneaked out for the much-needed cigarette.

The tea kettle started shrieking in my kitchen just as I sat down to read the very juicy first paragraph of the Gnat's first chapter. I ran to the stove to turn off the burner.

Ten minutes later, everything I could ever want, for the next two hours, at least, was on a bamboo tray: a cup of apple-cinnamon tea, two chocolate-caramel rice cakes, a half-full pack of Marlboro Lights and an unopened pack, a lighter, an ashtray and two dark lead pencils. I carried my bounty into the main room of my studio and settled myself on the futon, the first chapter of the Gnat's memoir square on my lap. Cigarette lit and rice cake bitten into, I began reading.

*I was fucking one of the most famous actors currently in show business when he handed me a legal document to sign. Three pages preventing me from ever discussing him or our relationship in any medium to any media. He'd been trailing kisses up my thigh moments before he'd reached over me to the nightstand to pick up The Document. "It's just a precaution that my agent, manager, accountant and press people insist on," he'd told me between darts of his tongue against my clitoris.*

*One of* People *magazine's sexiest men alive was performing oral sex on me. Me, a small-time actress who'd never been cut a break. Me, Natasha Nutley from Queens, New York. The girl who'd never had a best friend. The girl whose parents thought she was a disappointment for as long as she could remember. The girl who'd managed to get two lousy lines on a prime-time hospital drama because she'd slept with the casting director's assistant's assistant.*

*Who was I not to sign anything anyone put in front of me? And who was I not to feel like the luckiest woman in the world because The Actor was making love to me? Making love. That was a laugh. Making a loser out of me was more like it.*

*Seven weeks. Seven of the most meaningful weeks of my life meant absolutely nothing to him. I'd re-*

*minded him of a girlfriend from drama school. He
later told me that was why he'd chosen me. And
while I thought he was falling in love with me, he
was simply getting blow jobs from a girl who'd
learned that was the way to a man's heart a long,
long time ago.*

Whip out the violins. And a barf bag, please. Did I
really have to read this pornography?

Remke and Jeremy would love it; it was *exactly* what
they wanted. Dirty words, sex and enough woe-is-me,
boo-hoo baloney to fill a big fat mass-market paperback
summer read. What a bunch of melodramatic hooey.

*Never had a best friend. Her parents thought she was
a disappointment.* Give me a break! Natasha Nutley had
had everything handed to her on a sterling silver platter
from the moment she'd flashed those green eyes and red
ringlets at her mother's obstetrician twenty-eight years
ago. Who did she think she was fooling? Maybe the
American people at large wouldn't know she was lying
through her capped teeth. But I did. *I'd* been there.

The first time I'd clapped eyes on Natasha Anne Nutley
was in the sixth grade at P.S. 101, when Mrs. Greenman
had introduced her as a new student to our class. The Gnat
and her family had moved into an apartment building
around the corner from my own. Aunt Ina, Uncle Charlie
and Dana lived in a building a few blocks away, where
Ina and Charlie still lived, a few more blocks over from
Grammy—and Ethan Miles, Incinerator Man. Natasha's
father had inherited his father's pharmacy and moved the
Nutley family to upscale Forest Hills from Flushing. To
this day I remembered Mrs. Greenman introducing Natasha with the pleased smile that had been previously re-
served for the class president.

Natasha had scored more invitations for roller-skating and McDonald's and slumber parties on her first day at P.S. 101 than I'd had in the history of my grammar school career. All the girls had wanted to be her best friend. And all the boys had salivated over her. Unable to take their eyes off her, they'd constantly failed tests or lost track of what the teacher was saying. Robby Evers included. I was always staring at him, so I was very well aware that he was always staring at Natasha and her budding breasts. She'd had her eye on Jimmy Alfonzo, the sixth-grade equivalent of James Dean or Dylan from *Beverly Hills 90210*. By science hour, day two, she and Jimmy were a couple. That was when I realized I could have a shot with Robby. Because the girl he wanted was already taken. There was nowhere for him to go but down.

I didn't have a lot of self-esteem in grammar school.

Robby Evers, who'd dreamed of being a hard-hitting journalist like his hero, Walter Cronkite, hadn't been interested in the skinny, quiet girl with the dark eyes and dark hair who hung around with the quieter and skinnier Miner twins. Not in sixth grade, or seventh, or eighth. Or even ninth, when my current C-cup-sized breasts had begun to make themselves known. In eleventh grade, Robby and I had been paired as partners in biology class. He'd been sickened by the idea of slicing open the dead frog, so we'd held the little knife together, my hand guiding his. With the first prick, he'd looked into my eyes, terror and discomfort forcing shut his own sweet brown eyes. I'd made him feel understood, and I'd made him feel *right*. And so Robby Evers began to notice me. Or my C-sized breasts, more likely. He still stared at Gnatasha, but she was involved in her on-again, off-again long-term relationship with Jimmy Alfonzo.

In biology and English, the two classes we shared,

Robby would show me newspaper clippings that he'd brought in to discuss in his social studies class and at meetings for the high school newspaper, which I'd joined to be near him. He'd go on and on about the injustice and the horror in the world around us and declare his intention to travel that world and document the atrocities so that everyone would be alerted and do something about it. I was in love. Robby Evers cared about everything. No other boy in Forest Hills High School gave a hoot about the ozone layer, let alone apartheid in South Africa. He was known for his intensity, and girls liked that, but the intensity combined with his awkwardness worked against him. He was going to be a foreign correspondent, and most girls at Forest Hills High had no idea what that was. I was going to be a poet. He liked that. Once, while I'd been passionately agreeing with him about the devastating photos of children starving in America, Robby had touched my hand. For three days I washed around the spot where his flesh had touched mine.

I'd been so sure he was going to ask me to the junior class semiformal, which was in two weeks. It would be my first dance. Every day after school I'd stop at Macy's and try on the pink gauzy dress I'd spotted while on a forced family shopping expedition to find Dana a dress for her own first dance at Russell Sage Junior High. (She was something of the Natasha Nutley of the seventh grade.) But a week before the dance, Robby still hadn't asked me. And suddenly, we were down to three days. In English class, I was gearing up to ask him, ever so casually, if he'd like to go with me. But then I'd heard the sound that accompanied Natasha Nutley everywhere she went: the jangle of bangle bracelets.

She was giggling and leaning over Robby's desk, her butt in the air. "So you'll pick me up at seven-thirty, right, Robby?'' He'd nodded, a speechless expression of bliss on his face. ''Don't forget the corsage, white with a pink ribbon to match my dress.''

*My* dress was going to be pink.

Robby watched her sashay her little hips back to her own desk, then pumped his fist in the air with a silently mouthed *Yes!* He'd passed me a note: ''Where do you buy a corsage, do you know?'' I'd written back that he should stop at Forest Hills Flowers on Queens Blvd, a few long blocks from the school. He'd smiled at me, and then hadn't taken his eyes off the back of Natasha Nutley's ringletted head for the fifty minutes of AP English.

I'd cried for three days. The day after the dance, I'd dared to ask Robby if he'd had a good time. He'd barely lifted his head from his desk. Said she'd canceled at the last minute, that she and Jimmy Alfonzo had gotten back together. He'd spent a whole hour at Forest Hills Flowers, he'd told me, only to end up throwing the corsage away.

The corsage that should have been mine. Robby Evers had been ruined by reality. Natasha Nutley had taken all his sixteen-year-old idealism and introduced the hard facts of real life. And Robby never touched my hand again.

Okay, okay, whip out the violins for me now, right?

As if on cue, the sweeping crescendo of an operatic overture burst through the wall. Opera Man must have gotten into a fight with his girlfriend. I didn't recognize the composer, but I knew drama when I heard it.

I lit a cigarette, took a long drag and leaned back against the futon as I exhaled slowly.

How was I supposed to carefully read and thoughtfully comment on Natasha's chapter while some Italian woman boomed next door? I pounded my fist on the wall. Opera Man pounded back, but he lowered the volume.

Five cigarettes later, I'd finished reading Chapter One.

Ten cigarettes later, I'd finished editing it. I'd penciled notes in the margins. *Expand here. Flesh this out. Show, don't tell.* I'd corrected her atrocious spelling. Natasha Nutley had apparently slept her way into high school AP English, too.

I reached for a cigarette—the pack was empty. Twelve butts littered the ashtray on the Parsons table. I hadn't even realized I'd smoked so many cigarettes. I stood up and stretched my legs, then crumpled the empty pack into the ashtray and carried the bamboo tray into the kitchen.

As the butts and ashes fell into the little garbage can under the sink, I could hear Serge shouting in his Russian accent. "I do not understand, El-weeze! In my country, when people love each other, they spend time together!"

"I need my space, Serge!" Eloise declared.

I thought only men said that.

A few minutes later, a door slammed, and heavy footsteps bounded downstairs. Then came the sound of Eloise unlocking her door and running up the steps. She knocked to the tune of the "Wedding March." "Open up, I have the best outfit for you for Trendoid Night!"

If I hadn't overheard that little tidbit of a fight, I never would have known that Serge had moments ago stormed out of Eloise's apartment. Eloise's expression gave nothing away.

"El? Are you okay?"

She opened my closet door and hung up the outfit, which involved lots of low-cut black matte jersey. "Yeah. Why? Oh, you heard that?" I nodded. "He's just so clingy, you know? I like to have nights to myself."

I tried to imagine wanting a night to myself when I had a boyfriend. I couldn't. I'd wanted to spend every waking and sleeping minute with Max; he was my only reference.

And if Jeremy Black were mine, would I tell him I needed space? I don't think so.

"Ooh, we're missing *Will and Grace*," she said, pointing the remote at my thirteen-inch television. "Let's watch it, then I'll dress you and we'll accessorize."

We dropped down on the futon and cracked up at something funny Grace's secretary said. At a commercial, I slipped the marked-up first chapter of the Gnat's memoir into a folder and dumped it into my tote bag. It was time to forget about Natasha and her semi-charmed life and concentrate on making my own exactly that.

## Five

Delancey Street smelled like a combination of rotisserie chicken, cigar smoke and garbage rotting in the rain. Where were all the quaint pickle barrels à la the movie *Crossing Delancey?* Where were all the kosher delis? Wasn't the Lower East Side supposed to look like it did at the turn of the last century?

"Ooh, mama!"

Three teenagers piled onto one child-sized bicycle sped past me, licking their lips at me and making kissing sounds. I decided to take that as a compliment. I'd worn a boring black pantsuit to work, then changed into my hot-to-trot date outfit, which I'd lugged to work in a garment bag. Eloise had done my makeup under the fluorescent lights in Posh's women's bathroom. Not that I was wearing much. According to Eloise, this season it was all about lips. Mine were currently lined and shined in Bobbi Brown's Raisin. Which was currently lining and shining the rim of my cigarette filter. I flicked the cigarette into a puddle of something lining the curb, then popped a Certs into my mouth.

Five thirty-three, 535, 537. I was getting close. Deep breath, deep breath. I still had a few blocks to go before I hit the address Andrew had given me.

The Lower East Side was the kind of neighborhood that was shared by the very old and the very new. Tiny, hunched-over elderly women in kerchiefs wheeled carts down the sidewalks; young trendies in bizarre clothes flocked into the bars, clubs and restaurants that had opened in droves. But as I walked farther down Delancey toward Chinatown, the trendy bars got fewer and fewer. The women pushing carts seemed to multiply.

Here I was—563 Delancey. It was a tenement, much like the one I lived in. A five-story brick walk-up. I leaned my head back and stared up at the ugly building. Five concrete steps led to a metal door. Perhaps the hipster club or hot art gallery was housed on the first floor. No sign, name or indication of an establishment was supposedly all the rage now for the hottest downtown nightspots. Places too cool to be revealed to the general uncool public. I headed up the steps in my three-inch strappy sandals, relieved that I'd let Eloise convince me to borrow her clingy, low-cut dress. I looked like hot stuff tonight. It wasn't every day I got whistles and licked lips from teenage boys.

A plaque of surnames, apartments numbers and buzzers was on the left of the door. *Mackelroy, 4R.* Did Andrew *live* here? Wouldn't he have mentioned the *thing* was in his own apartment? Maybe it was some sort of performance art? I pushed the round button next to Mackelroy.

"Who is it?" sing-songed a child's voice.

Who was that? "Um, it's Jane, I'm—"

The buzzer buzzed. I pushed open the door and was immediately overwhelmed by the smell of frying onions. A long, steep staircase loomed in front of me. I braced my palm on the banister and twisted my head to peer up in the dim light. I didn't see anything. But I could hear the basic apartment building sounds—muted televisions, telephones ringing, footsteps, voices.

My long dress twisted around my ankles as I negotiated the rickety steps. By the time I reached the fourth-floor landing, I was huffing and puffing, and a tiny drop of perspiration rolled down my cleavage. You'd think I'd be used to climbing four flights of stairs, considering that I had two more to go in my own building. Nope.

I fanned myself in front of 4F, took a deep breath, plastered on a friendly smile and walked across the narrow hallway to 4R. A little sticky label under the apartment number read MACKELROY. I pushed the bell.

"Who *is* it?" sing-songed the same childish voice.

"Get away from the door, Jenny!" snapped an older woman's voice. "Go put the soup bowls on the table like I asked you to."

I gnawed my lower lip. A few locks were turned and the door swung open. An attractive woman in her fifties or sixties pushed back strands of hair into her gray-blond bun, then wiped her hands on her apron. "Welcome," she said, extending her wiped hand to me. "You must be Jane."

Maybe not, I thought. Maybe I'm someone else, depending on who you are. I smiled—sort of.

"I'm Janice Mackelroy, Andy's mom. Come on in. Andy's going to be a little late. Tied up at the office again. The way they work you kids now, you'd think they were paying you a fortune."

Before I had a chance to process any of the above,

Janice Mackelroy took my hand and led me down a long, narrow hallway into the living room.

"Why don't you have a seat, and I'll bring you a nice glass of wine." She smiled, then disappeared.

I found myself walking farther into the room and sitting down on a sofa covered with plastic. It creaked. There was plastic on all the upholstered furniture. A rectangular glass coffee table was so close to the sofa that I couldn't lift my leg to cross it. A stack of coffee-table books on art and sailing and a purple glass bowl containing wrapped sour balls was set on the table. I thought about flipping through a book to have something to do, but I felt eyes on me. I followed the feeling to the stern face of an elderly man in a portrait above the television. I darted my gaze back to the top book. *Modern Sailors*.

"Are you Andy's new girlfriend?"

A nine- or ten-year-old girl with limp blond hair and a long, thin nose was staring at me. Her eyes were on my cleavage. She had the wariness of a girl who was picked on a lot. I sensed she was headed for a gawky phase that would be hell but that she'd end up exotic looking.

"Um, well, I don't know," I said, forcing a big smile. "I haven't even met him yet."

"So what are you doing here?" she asked.

Good question, kid.

"Uncle Andy had a girlfriend," the child said, "but they broke up. She dressed like you. Always wearing tight stuff and showing her boobies." Jenny pushed out her flat chest and did an exaggerated little dance.

Janice Mackelroy rushed into the living room, apology on her face. "Jenny, I thought you were Nana's helper. Come on back into kitchen. Don't bother your uncle's nice friend." Janice Mackelroy grabbed the little girl's hand and escorted her away. A few minutes later, the woman returned, a glass of wine in her hand. "Here you are, dear. I wish I could sit and talk, but I've got a kitchen full of pots simmering. I hope Jenny didn't bother you."

"Um, no, of course not. She's so cute," I said. "Reminds me of me at her age." That was an outright lie. When I was a kid, if I'd even dared to comment on a guest, I'd have been lectured for a half hour and denied television and Devil Dogs for a week. But Mrs. Mackelroy seemed to be working so hard on dinner that I couldn't bear to cause her any more trouble. "I'd be glad to help," I added. With what, I had no idea. Was Andrew Mackelroy's *thing* dinner at his parents'?

"No, I wouldn't hear of it," she told me. "You're our guest. Andy said you loved Italian food—I'm so glad. You're going to get quite a lot of it tonight."

I smiled—sort of. And Mrs. Mackelroy disappeared into the kitchen.

Several framed photos lined the top of the television. The plastic cover on the sofa crackled as I got up to peer at the family snapshots. The girl, Jenny, was in several, along with a slightly older boy, and a couple in their thirties or forties who I assumed were Jenny's parents. In the other photos were Janice Mackelroy, a man around her age and a younger man, blond, and woman, also blond. Was the younger man Andrew? The younger woman his sister? The mother of Jenny?

I felt Portrait Man's eyes on me and sat back down on the sofa. Another bead of perspiration rolled down my cleavage. If only I had my jacket with me. I was so inappropriately dressed for a family dinner. What would Andrew think? What would his family think? Who came to dinner at a guy's parents' house dressed for a nightclub? Well, that was Andrew's own fault, I reminded myself. He could have mentioned the *thing* was at his folks'.

"Why can't I go in the living room with Andrew's new girlfriend," I heard Jenny whine. "It's hot in here, Nana."

I plastered a smile on my face and ventured toward the sound of Jenny's voice. I stood in the doorway to a very warm kitchen. Mrs. Mackelroy stirred a gigantic pot on the stove top. Jenny sat at the square table, her head bent over a loose-leaf binder, her tongue sticking out in concentration.

"Um, Mrs. Mackelroy?" I said, "Are you sure I couldn't help? I feel guilty sitting in that lovely room doing nothing."

"Aren't you sweet," she said with a smile. "Well, if you're sure you wouldn't mind… Jenny, why don't you ask Andy's nice young lady friend if she'll be kind enough to look at your math homework?"

Um, that wasn't exactly what I meant. I didn't know what I'd meant. Setting out napkin rings, maybe? Wineglasses?

Jenny shot up off the chair, the loose-leaf binder in her hands. "Come on, I'll show you in the living room." She grabbed my hand and marched me back to the sofa, where she plopped down. I did the same. She opened the binder onto my lap. "Are you good at geometry or are you a total airhead?"

Before I could even register that, a key jangled in the door.

"Ma? I'm home. Ma?"

I shot up, which sent Jenny's loose-leaf binder to the floor. "Sorry," I said, bending down to pick it up.

"Airhead," Jenny announced. "Just like I thought."

I sneered at the ugly child as I handed her the binder.

"She here, Ma?"

I assumed he meant me. I also assumed that was the voice of Andew Mackelroy.

"In the living room. She's helping Jenny with her math."

"Ma!"

"She's pretty," I heard Mrs. Mackelroy whisper. "A little overdressed though."

"Shh, Ma, she'll hear you."

A tall, muscular guy with dirty-blond hair, blue eyes and a large nose appeared in the living room, carrying a briefcase. He looked Scandinavian. He was cute. Very cute. I even liked the suit, which had subtle pinstripes.

"Hi, I'm Andrew." He shook my hand and stared at my cleavage, then raised his eyes north. "I'm really sorry I'm late. Hey, hot stuff," he said to Jenny, ruffling her blond hair.

"Stop it! You know I hate when you do that," Jenny shouted, smoothing her hair back into place. She glared at Andrew. "Did you bring me something?"

He put down his briefcase and crossed his arms over his chest. "That's what you say to your uncle? You haven't seen me in, like, two days, and that's how you greet me?" A smile tugged at his lips. He snapped open his briefcase and pulled out a small paper bag. Jenny snatched it and stuck her nose inside. A huge smile split her sullen face. She pulled out a purple lollipop in the shape of a cat.

She ran off into the kitchen. "Nana, look what Uncle Andrew brought me!"

Andrew smiled at me. "Sorry I was late. It's nice to finally meet you in the flesh." The eyes traveled south again.

"No problem," I said, offering him a good-sport smile.

''And it's nice to meet you, too.'' I was waiting for the explanation.

Keys jangled in the door again.

''There they are!'' Mrs. Mackelroy exclaimed. ''How's my little birthday boy, huh? How's my big boy!''

''Nana! Stop treating me like a kid!'' demanded the cracking voice of a preteen. ''Ewww! What's Jenny doing here? It's supposed to be me and my friends only!''

''Stevie, apologize to your sister right now!'' A woman's voice.

''Go see your uncle Andrew,'' Mrs. Mackelroy said. ''He's in the living room.'' She lowered her voice. ''He brought a date.''

''Andy?'' The woman's voice. A female version of Andrew appeared in the living room, a friendly smile on her face. She and Andrew embraced, then she held out both hands to me and clasped my right hand. ''So who's this?'' she said, eyeing Andrew with a gleam in her eye.

''Jane, this is my sister, Danielle. Danielle, this is Jane. And this big kid here is my nephew!'' He swept up the kid over his shoulder. Delighted shrieks as the two played pretend wrestle. ''Happy birthday, Stevie!''

I stepped back and plastered my sort-of smile on my face, which I could tell from the reflection on the television screen expressed half horror, half you-never-know.

Danielle stuck out her hand. ''Nice ta meetcha.''

Knocks on the door. Bursts of childish voices.

''Wait till you see Stevie's birthday cake, kids!'' Mrs. Mackelroy exclaimed from the kitchen as a horde of boys rushed into the living room. Suddenly there was complete silence as the boys stopped dead in their tracks.

I very slowly sat down on the sofa, the sort-of smile draining from my face.

Seven or eight twelve-year-old boys stared at me. I

should amend that. Seven or eight twelve-year-olds stared at my breasts.

It seemed safe to surmise that the *thing* Andrew Mackelroy had been referring to was prepubescent Stevie's birthday party.

"Dinner's ready, everyone!" Mrs. Mackelroy called. "Come and get it!"

The boys tore into the dining room. If twelve-year-old boys had to choose between food and girls, they always chose food. I was never so grateful for that fact.

"It's all right, isn't it?" Andrew Mackelroy whispered. "I figured I'd get my nephew's birthday party out of the way, then we'd go to Little Italy for drinks."

"Sure, um, yeah," I said, good-sport smile on my face. "It'll be fun. I just love kids."

Ten minutes later, the first slimy, cold tortellini from the pasta salad was flung from a spoon into my cleavage. Much to the delighted laughter of seven or eight twelve-year-old boys.

"Yeah, so let's just go with the carafe," Andrew Mackelroy told the grim-faced waiter at Tutelli's Italian Ristorante. The ancient, gaunt man in a stiff shirt, vest and bow tie nodded and disappeared. Andrew had just finished explaining to me that a carafe and a bottle of wine both offered four glasses of wine, yet a carafe was ten bucks cheaper.

We were seated outside, on the sidewalk, at a table for two smushed between two square parties of four. Up and down the block and across the street were dozens of such restaurants, packed to overflowing inside and out, with lines snaking into the street. I noticed lots of couples at the tables, lots of families.

As Andrew glanced around the restaurant for good-looking women the way guys always did, I checked my lap and the front of my borrowed dress for stains. Luckily Mrs. Mackelroy had had a good supply of club soda, which I'd spent a good fifteen minutes dabbing onto my dress in the hot, steamy, smelly kitchen of the Mackelroy home. A faint orange-tinged smear remained on my lap. Eloise was going to kill me.

The waiter returned with the carafe of red wine and two old-fashioned wineglasses. He poured and left.

"So I guess you can tell I'm really family oriented," Andrew said. He raised his wineglass, gave it a little half lift at me and took a sip. I did the same. "We're pretty tight."

"That's nice," I said, for want of anything more original.

"How about you? You see your folks often?"

I never knew how to answer that question. If I said no, which was the truth, the guy immediately thought I was a parent-hating neurotic freak. If I added a quick "They're gone," the guy immediately asked, "Where?" If I said they'd passed away, it killed the evening. Guys never knew what to say after that or how to change the subject.

Generally I answered depending on whether or not I'd ever see the guy again. If I knew the date was a one-shot, I might say, "Yeah, a few times a month. They're just over the bridge in Queens." I loved saying that. For one evening, my parents would be alive again, just a subway ride away. They'd be dancing to Bruce Springsteen's "Glory Days" the way they did when I was young, singing the chorus at the top of their lungs.

My heart constricted in my chest and I sipped my wine.

"Oh, bad question, huh?" Andrew said. "I'm down with that. I know not everyone's close to their family. I was lucky, I guess. I'm, like, the only person I know who had a good childhood." He laughed, sipped his wine and glanced at the attractive blonde two tables over.

I envisioned sitting next to Andrew Mackelroy in a mini-ballroom of the Plaza Hotel. Andrew telling Natasha Nutley's houseboat-dwelling boyfriend that he was "down with" whatever Mr. Santa Barbara happened to be saying. Natasha, whispering a condescending "He's so endearing!" in my ear.

Suddenly a small noise erupted out of Andrew's mouth. A belch. "Sorry," he said. "All that soda at the birthday party, I guess." He let out an embarrassed laugh. "I have to say again, Jane, you really were a good sport back there. My ex-girlfriend was such a bitch. Every time we went over to my sister's and Stevie threw something at her or said something dirty, she'd start screaming her head off. He's just a kid, you know?"

I smiled. I wasn't nuts about Andrew Mackelroy, but he was a person like me, trying to find a little happiness in this world, this city. Who was I to judge him so fast? So the guy was family oriented. Since when was that a strike against him? Just because I'd lost my parents didn't mean that he couldn't have a good relationship with his own. Maybe we weren't each other's immediate types, but did that mean we couldn't go out again, see if there was some chemistry underneath all the snap judgments and expectations?

I was suddenly dying for a cigarette. And if Andrew Mackelroy and I were to get to know each other, if we were really going to give each other a chance, then it wouldn't be right if I tried to hide my smoking habit. As Andrew glanced around, I lit a Marlboro Light.

He immediately whipped his head to face me. "Oh, I didn't know you smoked."

My MO on a date had always been to wait. I'd wait till I was sure the guy was interested, and then, once I knew I had him on attraction, I'd light a cigarette and hope he'd find it alluring and mysterious and sexy, rather than vile and disgusting and health-endangering.

But wasn't that game playing? I was an adult. I smoked, and I was perfectly within my rights to do so at the moment. After all, hadn't Andrew felt perfectly comfortable belching in front of me and laughing it off?

He eyed the offending cigarette as though it were a bloody knife. "I wish I'd known you were a smoker. I'm, like, *really* allergic to cigarette smoke." He coughed for good measure.

I felt my cheeks turn red. "Oh, um, I'm sorry." I searched the table for an ashtray.

"I'll be right back," Andrew said. "Nature's calling."

Watching Andrew snake his way through tables and people and disappear inside Tutelli's, I took a long, fortifying drag of the cigarette. Why waste a perfectly good Marlboro while Andrew was in the bathroom?

"Excuse me, Miss? Miss? Hello? Miss?"

I turned around, expecting to find a woman about to complain to her waitress that her eggplant parmigiana was undercooked or overcooked. But instead, the entire family sitting directly behind me was staring at me. "Could you put that out?" the mother asked me. "Joey's got asthma."

I felt my face heat up again. There was no ashtray on the table. Now, not only had I probably caused Andrew Mackelroy to break out in hives, but I was preventing a child from breathing and about to add Litterbug to my list of habit-crimes. I dropped the cigarette under the table and crushed it out with my foot.

Joey glared at me, then broke out into a series of exaggerated coughs. His mother immediately fussed over him. The father was shaking his head back and forth, and suddenly I was the basis of a family argument. *"We're changing tables." "She put it out, calm down." "Well who knows if she's gonna light it again? I wanna change tables right now, inside, where there's a nonsmoking section. Get the waiter." "You're talking crazy, there aren't any tables. Look around, it's packed." "Okay, stop yelling at me." "I'm not yelling." "Miss, are you going to smoke more? Miss?"*

I turned around. "Uh, no. Sorry."

"Yeah, she's sorry," I heard the father mutter. "Joey, are you feeling okay?"

I was feeling like a leper—it went with the territory for a nicotine addict. Some smokers got indignant and refused to put out their cigarettes when faced with dirty looks and demands. They went on and on about how smoking was their right, and tough noogies if nonsmokers didn't like it. But I always felt guilty. In a crowded city like New York, someone was always waving away cigarette smoke on the streets. I hated to be the cause of someone's disgust.

Andrew Mackelroy returned, sat down and sipped his cheap wine. His attention was either thankfully or annoyingly diverted by the longest legs I've ever seen. My gaze started at the woman's strappy sandals and headed up the long, tanned legs to the slinky dress in swirling pale colors to the blond, straight hair, to the man she was walking with hand in hand.

Jeremy Black.

Jeremy turned around and laughed at something an older couple behind him had said. And once again, it was as though he were walking in slow motion; his entire entourage seemed to be, as well. I figured the older ones were either Jeremy's parents or the woman's. The four of them seemed too good for the gaudy, touristy streets of Little Italy. Their physical beauty, grace and perfection didn't belong here. I could just imagine Jeremy and his girlfriend humoring the parents and assuring each other that Little Italy would be *charming*. For the Jeremy Blacks of the world, Little Italy was a barely cute version of "slumming." I was grateful that at least Jeremy hadn't noticed me, looking, I was quite sure, the worse for my evening at Casa Mackelroy.

Depression, as hot and humid as the air, slapped me against the chest. I wanted that cigarette back. I wanted to be the woman Jeremy was walking with. I wanted those older people to be my parents, alive and well. I wanted to be the kind of woman who Jeremy would date, the kind of woman who schlubs like Andrew Mackelroy turned around to stare at, even when they were on dates with "adorable" women.

I had on strappy sandals and a sexy dress. But I looked nothing like Jeremy's date. And I never would.

"So Jeff mentioned you were an editor," Andrew said, once Jeremy's date's body was blocked from his range of vision.

"Assistant editor," I corrected, watching Jeremy and his group hail a taxi. They were probably headed for drinks in some club in Soho that didn't have a sign on the door. I drained my wine. Andrew immediately filled my glass.

"Actually, um, Andrew, I think I've had enough. Tell you the truth, I've got a raging headache."

"Oh. I could get you some aspirin or something."

"That's okay," I said. "I think I should get home."

"Should I put you in a taxi?"

"Um, no," I said quickly. "I'll just take the subway.
I'll be okay."

"Uh, okay, so I guess I'll just stay to finish the wine."

I stood up and slung my little beaded bag's long,
skinny strap over my shoulder. "So, bye."

Andrew Mackelroy stood up and awkwardly air-kissed
me. "I'll, uh, give you a call."

I smiled my sort-of smile and fled.

This was an *I'll call* I was grateful for.

I turned the corner and lit a cigarette. I smoked it fast
and didn't even appreciate it, then hailed a cab. I had no
idea where the nearest subway station was or which train
would connect me to the IRT. Which meant I was about
to be out seventeen dollars. Considerably more than Andrew Mackelroy had sprung on the entire night.

Opera Man was listening to his favorite Verdi master-
work, *Aida*.

Eloise's dress was scrunched in the bottom of my take-
to-the-dry-cleaner's bag, which was hanging off the doorknob.

And I was giving myself a homemade oatmeal facial,
which, according to the *Allure* magazine I bought at the
newsstand on the way home, was the newest cure for
stress.

"Tell your nice friend I said hello," the cute Indian
clerk behind the kiosk's counter had said.

The minute I'd gotten home I'd listened for sounds of
silence from the cabinet under the kitchen sink, which
would mean that Eloise was alone. But I'd heard the unmistakable sound of Eastern European male laughter. I'd
wanted to talk to someone. Someone, anyone. Eloise was
busy. Amanda was off-limits, since I couldn't complain
to her about Andrew. Aunt Ina was also off-limits, since

I wasn't supposed to be on a terrible blind date. The sound of Dana Dreer's voice would only make me feel worse.

Why didn't I have anyone to call?

The oatmeal mask hardening on my face, I pulled my address book out of my tote bag. The answer lay on each page I flipped through. I didn't know anyone I used to know. Why wasn't I friends with the people I was friends with before? Lisa and Lora, my only two friends from childhood, were across the country, leading their marriage-and-baby-filled lives. The few girls I'd hung around with in college had scattered too, and we'd lost touch the year after graduation. Eloise and Amanda were my only friends.

Why had I been so willing to let my friendship with the Miner twins dwindle away? I could call them right now, ask how they were, listen to cute stories about their children, cute complaints about their husbands, cute remarks about the San Francisco hills. I could breathe new life into a friendship that never should have petered out. I picked up the cordless, prepared to punch in Lora's number, but I noticed I had three messages blinking. I'd been so upset when I'd gotten home that I hadn't checked the machine. I pressed Play.

"I want to know who you think you are, young lady," came Aunt Ina's angry voice. "How dare you be rude to Karen on the telephone? She's your cousin's maid of honor, and she's been a godsend with the wedding plans. You'd better shape up that attitude, Jane, and—"

I pressed Skip. Hadn't I already been punished enough this evening? If dinner at the Mackelroys hadn't been enough, seeing Jeremy with his date certainly had been.

"Uh, hello, Jane? This is Ben Larson, Jeff's friend. I wanted to confirm our date for Thursday. I just found out that MOMA's open late this Thursday night for some anniversary celebration of something, so I thought we could meet at the information desk and check out the French Painters exhibit. How does that sound? If you'd rather do something else, I'm open to suggestions.''

Okay, Ben, here's a suggestion: Don't be a selfish cheapskate. Think you could handle that?

I was running out of Blind Date Excitement Energy. Two blind dates had sucked royally. Why would Ben Larson be any better? I couldn't even begin to imagine what fresh hell was in store for me at the Museum of Modern Art Thursday night. I grabbed my datebook and flipped to Thursday, June 4. *Ben Larson. Good-looking, super-smart. Brown curly hair, green eyes. Looks artsy. Works with Jeff.*

Next message. ''Hi Jane, it's me again, Ben Larson. I forgot to mention that I made reservations at a Japanese restaurant near the museum. Jeff mentioned you loved Japanese.''

Hmm. I most certainly did. Suddenly Ben Larson sounded better than he did a minute ago. Two bad apples didn't mean the whole bunch had worms. I had to remember that pearl of wisdom.

Ben Larson did not sound like a guy who'd belch or laugh when the first of three tortellini shells landed in his date's cleavage. He did not sound like a guy who'd analyze the financial difference between a carafe of wine and a bottle of wine. He did not sound like a guy who'd rather finish off that cheap wine than insist on seeing his date, suffering from a fake headache, safely to the subway.

I sat down on the futon and felt my face. The oatmeal was hardening nicely. Leaning my head back, I let the effects of the stress cure all and the strains of *O Patria*

*Mia* work their soothing magic. Ten minutes later, unable to move a muscle in my face, I headed into the bathroom to wipe off the mask. My face glowed shiny and new in the mirror.

That was what Ben Larson seemed like: shiny and new. A shiny and new possibility.

What was I moping around for? I had a great-sounding prospect for Thursday night. I had fresh-glowing skin. I was working on a high-profile manuscript for Posh. I had friends other than Amanda and Eloise.

I eyed my address book and the phone. A vision of the Miner twins, age seventeen, flashed into my mind. The three of us sitting in an arc in the Miner's living room, Lisa French-braiding my hair while I braided Lora's hair while Lora braided Lisa's hair. Natasha Nutley had come to school a few days prior with her hair in a French braid. The next day and for at least two weeks after, just about every girl with hair long enough had walked into Forest Hills High with a French braid.

I dropped back down on the futon, my shiny new skin a total waste. I had everything to mope about. I couldn't imagine calling Lisa or Lora and telling them the Fates of the universe were punishing me for some long-forgotten crime with the entrance of Natasha Nutley back into my life. I could hear myself complaining about her and could hear the silent condemnation in the Miners' voices. The *you're still carrying that around with you?* disdain. The *you're still single?* pity. The *what a loser you turned out to be* assessment. The *no wonder we didn't manage to keep in touch* judgment. And that would end my once-every-six months friendship with the Miner twins.

The phone rang. I figured it was Eloise, wanting a report on Andrew.

"Jane? Hi, it's Natasha!"

Did she know that it was 10:43 on a Tuesday night? Not 10:43 on a Tuesday *morning,* when normal business associates made phone calls regarding work. "Um, hi. What's up?"

"I'm sorry for calling so late, but I figured you'd be at the boyfriend's and I'd just be leaving a message."

She figured that a lot.

"I'm so excited, I couldn't contain myself. Guess what I just finished?"

"The entire manuscript?" Easy, Jane.

She laughed. "Silly! Chapter One! I think it's really *there* now. I'm on such a roll, thanks to you. The minute I got your fax with the corrections and queries, I set right to work. Your points were so helpful, Jane. I spent all day revising and incorporating everything you said. I can't wait to get started on Chapter Two!"

"Great," I said.

"Wow, it's no wonder you're an executive editor, Jane. You really know what you're talking about."

She'd promoted me from senior editor to executive editor. I appreciated that. Along with, grudgingly, the praise she was heaping on me. Gwen always offered positive feedback with constructive criticism, but without her around this past month, I pretty much had to rely on myself for gold stars.

I didn't know how I felt about getting an "A" from Natasha Nutley. I wanted to be above giving two figs about her opinion. Once, during my junior year at Forest Hills High, she'd complimented my new ruffled chiffon blouse, which my mom had bought in duplicate for me and Dana. I'd sat through English feeling stylish and cool and elevated in the eyes of the girls who'd overheard. I'd worn that blouse on every (rare) date I had after that, and whenever I woke up feeling ugly and boring. That had been the kind of stupid power Natasha Nutley had had over me.

"So, tomorrow I'll work on revising the outline for Chapters Two and Three, and I'll fax that back with the revised Chapter One, plus whatever I end up with on the draft of Chapter Two. Sound good?"

"Great. I appreciate the hard work, Natasha."

"Well, it's all thanks to you!" she trilled. "Bye!"

I hung up, irritated at her generosity. The phone rang a second later.

"Hey, how'd it go?" Eloise asked. I could hear the television in the background.

"Are you watching *Annie Hall* again?" I asked. The unmistakable sound of Alvie Singer's voice was whining a monologue.

"Serge can't get enough of it," she said. "Which gives me the perfect chance to hear all about Andrew. Think you'll see him again?"

"God, I hope not."

"That bad?"

"Let's put it this way. The trendoid *thing* your hot dress went to turned out to be his nephew's thirteenth birthday party. I think they thought I was meant to jump out of the cake or something. But I just got a message from Thursday night's guy. Ben Larson. We're doing MOMA."

"Ooh, sounds good," she said. "El-weeze, you are missing best part!" came Serge's accented voice through the receiver.

I laughed. "I'll see you tomorrow, El-weeze."

I had an entire day and night to recover from the effects of Blind Date #2. By Thursday night I'd surely have the energy to make small talk about being an editor while strolling around an air-conditioned museum.

Right now I couldn't imagine summoning the energy to pound on the wall as the *oh*s started making their way through the plaster. I'd started out wanting a date for a wedding. A fake date, no less. But suddenly, it was turning personal. The worse the dates were, the more I wanted something to work out for real. That was so stupid! Two awful blind dates in a row didn't mean anything. There was a whole city full of good guys out there. My two best friends had good guys. My aunt Ina was married to a good guy. My dad had been a good guy. So why was I two for two on the bad-guy scale?

## Six

Morgan Morgan nodded, nodded again, then nodded. If she agreed with my comments on her two revision letters, I had no idea. She sat next to me in my guest chair, which was wedged between my desk and the wall. I had more important things to do on a Wednesday afternoon than deal with Morgan Squared if she wasn't even going to appreciate my help.

"And I would take out this last sentence," I said, pointing at it with my pencil, "because it'll make the author think you really want to see his manuscript revised, when you really don't."

Morgan eyed me, then drew her gaze back to her letter.

I took a sip of the horrible office coffee that Morgan made every day. "Better to write, 'If you'd *like* to revise it, I would be pleased to take another look.' That gives the writer the tidbit of hope without outright saying *you* suggest he revises it."

Morgan kept her brown eyes on the letters. She nodded again. "Thanks, Jaaane," she said. "I'll be sure and tell Williaaam and Jeremy how helpful you were."

She'd said that with the air of someone who believed that was all I was after. Actually, it wasn't. I'd been ordered to help her. And anyway, I liked being put in the role of "supervisor." It made me feel as though I were worthy of offering my opinion around here.

I stole a peek at Morgan. She was studying my marks and changes, her suspicious eyes taking in everything. I had a moment of sympathy for her. She was so articulate and poised that I often forgot she was only twenty-two. Her nastiness was probably just insecurity. Because I was me, it was hard to even imagine that Morgan might be intimidated by me. She simply had her guard up, that was all. If I wanted to be nice, I *could* cut her a break. After all, wasn't that what we all wanted and needed?

"So, um, I'd be happy to look over the next letter you write," I offered.

"Gwen didn't say you had to look at them all," Morgan snapped. "I think it's perfectly clear that I know what I'm doing." She snatched the letters from my desk. That was the last time I'd let down my own guard around Morgan.

Jeremy Black appeared in my doorway. I almost sucked in a breath. He was wearing black pants, a black dress shirt and a black tie. The slightest hint of five-o'clock shadow kissed his sculpted jawline. Those long, sooty eyelashes rose and fell, rose and fell as he blinked. I was eye level with his zipper.

Suddenly Jeremy was naked and sitting in my guest chair, leaning back the way he always did at editorial meetings…waiting for me—

"Jane?"

I blinked. Jeremy and Morgan were staring at me. "Um, what?"

"Good job on the Nutley back cover copy," Jeremy praised, his gaze moving from the copy in his hand to me and back again. "I made some changes, and the last line could be stronger, more of a killer cliff-hanger. Play around with it and get it back to me tomorrow morning. And come up with a new list of title suggestions. They're okay, but not extended-list worthy."

"Oh, um, thanks, I will," I said to the light switch, which I focused on instead of his face.

"Great. Thanks." And with that he disappeared.

Morgan stared at me. I stared back. She was giving me that *Look all you want, honey, but he'd never even* use *a Ms. Average like you* expression. Then she stood up, turned on her sensible one-and-a-half-inch heels and left.

Well, at least Jeremy liked my back cover copy, which I'd worked very hard on. Remke had marked up my first attempt with his signature scrawl. Lots of question marks and *so?* How helpful. A *so?* from Remke meant it didn't "say" anything. I read over Jeremy's comments on my revised version. I'd gotten one exclamation point, two *good*s and one question mark, plus a cross-out of the last line with a scrawled *Come up with something stronger* in the margin.

Morgan returned with a stack of paper-clipped papers, which she dropped in my in-box, and then she trotted off. The Gnat had faxed her revision of Chapter One and a scene-by-scene, blow-by-blow description of Chapters Two and Three. That was fast. Didn't the woman have anything else to do but write and think about her stupid life?

It was now three-twenty. I'd spent the morning finishing up a preliminary line-edit for Jeremy about a teenager's climb up Mount McKinley with his father. Since I'd had only the last two chapters to go, Jeremy had okayed my working on it. Both Jeremy and Remke were sure that the American public was sick to death of Everest and its boring big-deal summit. A smaller, more attainable mountain was refreshing, they'd said. Plus, the memoir focused on the boy's relationship with his domineering father. It was about how the mountain and the struggle to climb it dominated even the most controlling person. It was a total tearjerker. Personally, I didn't get why anyone would want to climb a mountain, Everest or otherwise. The whole thing was idiotic. You spent all that time and money to be cold and miserable with the very good chance that you wouldn't even reach the top.

Anyway, between photocopying the McKinley manuscript and reworking my back cover copy for the Gnat's book, I'd never be able to think up new titles and read her revised chapter and the outline for Chapters Two and Three. I'd have to bring the Gnat home with me. Again. Where was *my* sanctuary? I'd been looking forward to a night of pure relaxation and de-stressing between dates. So much for that. I'd be spending the night with the Gnat.

My phone rang. "Jane Gregg."

"I expect to be called back when I leave you a message."

Aunt Ina. Guilt socked me between the eyes. "I'm sorry, Aunt Ina. I got home late last night, and today's been crazy and—"

"I have news for you, Jane," Aunt Ina snapped. "You're not the only person on this earth. Are you listening to me? Karen is nice enough to plan the shower, and you have to turn your sarcastic mouth on her?"

"I'm sorry, okay? She got me at a bad time. I'll apologize on Saturday."

"That's right, you will," Ina said. "What time are you coming? Karen's serving breakfast, so don't eat."

"I was thinking of getting there at eleven-thirty."

"The *meeting's* at eleven-thirty, Jane." Deep sigh.

Now it was time for my own deep sigh. Silent, of course. "Eleven twenty-five?"

Aunt Ina breathed heavily. "I'll meet you in front of Karen's building at eleven-fifteen on the dot. Do you hear me? *Eleven-fifteen.* By the time we get buzzed in, walk to the elevator, wait for it, then ride up and walk down the hall. We'll be a few minutes early."

I'd forgotten that early was fashionable in Forest Hills. "Okay, okay. Eleven-fifteen. See you then."

"You're taking a car service, right?" Aunt Ina asked.

"Um, yeah," I lied, mentally weighing the thirty-dollar car service tab against the dollar-fifty subway. I'd have to tell Ina that I'd gotten out of the cab on the corner to save money. She'd like that.

I hung up and did what I always did when super-busy and pressed for time. I checked my e-mail for personal messages from friends. There was a message from Natasha. I thought about skipping it, then remembered she was my ticket to a bigger office.

*Hi, Jane! Just wanted to let you know that I faxed over the revision of Chapter One and the scene-by-scene for the next two chapters. Can't wait to hear what you think! I'd like to schedule another meeting with you for next Monday, after your editorial meeting, to go over the first draft of Chapter Two. If that's no good, just let me know. Talk to you soon! —Natasha.*

I was sick and tired of the woman's exclamation points, energy and enthusiasm. Was I going to have to deal with her every Monday morning for the rest of my life? I sighed and closed her message and opened Amanda's. *So*

*I heard you and Andrew didn't have much chemistry. Oh well—because I also heard you're going out with Ben tomorrow night! He is so cute—you're definitely going to hit it off with him.*

I wouldn't mind *hitting* Andrew. How dare he reject me before I got the chance to reject him! Didn't have much chemistry. Grr! Try he was totally cheap! Try he took a blind date to a kiddie party at his parents'! Jerk.

The Blind Date Excitement Energy had just plummeted from negative one to negative one hundred. How was I supposed to keep up this pace of serial dating when each date was sure to report the same lack of interest back to Jeff and Amanda? Ben Larson was cute? Big deal. They were all cute. What I was looking for at this point was *tolerable*. And just a tiny hint of attraction. On both our parts.

Ben Larson had become too important. I had a miserable feeling that he was my last shot at a date for Dana's wedding. There was no way in hell that Saturday night's date, a doctor, mind you—who also lived on the Upper West Side, though not in a brownstone—was going to work out. The Fates of the universe were not going to bless me—a woman who wouldn't visit her grammy often enough, was sarcastic to her cousin, and disappointed her aunt Ina on a regular basis—with a doctor who lived on the Upper West Side. Life just didn't work that way. I'd learned that a long time ago.

Doctor Guy was going to be an asshole. I knew it already. And my very last scheduled blind date next Tuesday couldn't possibly work, because it was the very last. Which meant that tomorrow night's stroll around the Museum of Modern Art was my only hope. And so far, I was 0 for 2. Not good.

I typed a message of my own to Amanda and Eloise:

*How about a hometown FNRT? Big Sur, 80th & Third, same time.*

This would be a departure from our usual routine. We usually tried to pick interesting places in varied neighborhoods, especially neighborhoods we had no reason to ever be in otherwise. Like Tribeca. Twice I'd spent over a week in the huge Supreme Court building on Centre Street for jury duty without ever knowing I *was* in Tribeca. The West Village was another unexplored neighborhood, except for the area right about NYU, where I'd taken two classes in the school of continuing education (I hadn't met a guy, of course). But I wasn't even so sure that NYU *was* in the West Village. Maybe it was just Greenwich Village. When it came to the island I'd lived on for the past six years, I was as knowledgeable as a tourist. I hoped Eloise and Amanda wouldn't mind a Flirt Night Roundtable in our own overly explored neighborhood. I doubted they would; secretly, I thought we'd all be quite content to stay a few blocks from home. It was just that no one wanted to admit that.

I packed the Gnat's revised chapter and outline into my tote bag, along with my disk of back cover copy and title suggestions. I'd surely have to give myself another oatmeal facial tonight; the Gnat's porno would have hives on my face by paragraph five. The McKinley manuscript in my arms, I headed down the hall to Jeremy's office to let him—or the window behind his head, more accurately—know that he'd have my preliminary edit in ten minutes.

"If the copier doesn't break down in the middle of it," he joked, flashing that Pierce Brosnan smile at me for a half second.

I pictured Jeremy twirling me around for a slow dance at Dana's wedding, his Caribbean eyes focused on me in my lovely peach dress. That image alone would keep me happy for the twenty minutes I'd have to stand in front of the photocopier and the twenty minutes I'd have to spend clearing the nonexistent paper jams from area F.

Thursday night, 5:40 p.m. I'd timed my arrival at the Museum of Modern Art twenty minutes too early. But, considering that it was a hundred degrees and a hundred percent humidity tonight, I was grateful for the extra time to duck into the bathroom to mop myself off and clean myself up. Posh was located only a few blocks and one avenue from MOMA, and I was already completely wilted. Not the way to arrive for a blind date with my only real wedding escort possibility.

Dry and freshly powered and lipsticked, I headed upstairs in the thankfully cold museum, my favorite in New York, by the way. I still had ten minutes to kill, so I figured I'd meander around the bookstore and gift shop and check out the posters.

As usual, the gift-bookshop was packed with people. The museum was even more crowded than usual tonight because of the special late hours. I couldn't tell the New Yorkers from the tourists. Everyone was wearing black, even in June. I headed down the steps to the poster shop and waited for three blondes to finish flipping their way down the line of oversize posters (the least crowded area at the moment), then I zoomed into place and began flipping myself. Maybe a huge poster would cover up the coating of smoke grime that I'd suddenly noticed on the walls last night. I'd needed a break from the Gnat's outline—which I'd been loath to admit was developing very well (how had she become a good writer?)—so I'd gone on a little cleaning frenzy in my apartment. I'd lifted a framed black-and-white poster that Eloise had given me for a housewarming six years ago so that I could dust the bottom of the frame; the space underneath the picture was white. I hadn't realized or remembered that the walls were *white*. I'd thought they were the typical New York tenement beige. I'd been a little grossed out to realize that my beige walls were the result of my exhaling cigarette smoke on them for six years.

"What do you think of this?"

Startled, I turned around into the warm, open face of a cute, tall guy. He had something of a game-show host's too-big smile, but otherwise, he was good-looking, nicely built and well dressed. He appeared to be in his early thirties. I sensed he was a New Yorker.

"Do you think it's too much?" he asked. "I've got a bare wall in my bedroom, so I was thinking maybe."

"It's great," I said, nodding. *And so are you.* His eyes were hazel and fringed with dark lashes. His brown wavy hair was thick and lush.

So it was happening. Just like all those guidebooks and women's magazines said. If you were minding your own business and going about your life, you'd meet someone.

He aimed the game-show-host smile at me. "I'll have to come back for it. I'm meeting someone. Blind date," he said, rolling his eyes. "Like I'm really in the mood to make forced small talk for an hour with a total stranger."

I would have laughed and agreed if I hadn't been getting the sneaking suspicion that I was talking to Ben Larson. The coloring and age matched.

"My friend said she was cute," the Maybe Ben Larson continued, "but you know how friends lie about blind dates. I mean, if a woman needs a blind date, she can't be too hot."

*That goes double for a guy, you moron.* I smiled my sort-of smile. My ears started to burn.

"So, um, you live in the city?" he asked.

I nodded. "Upper East Side."

"Really? Why?" He laughed. "Isn't it boring up there?"

"I like it," I said, immediately bristling. "Where do you live?"

"West Village. I don't go above 14th Street."

Now there was a cliché that I hadn't heard in a few years.

"Hey, so it's too bad I'm meeting someone," the Maybe Ben said, "because I'd really like to talk to you some more. So, unless you're seeing someone, perhaps we could meet for a drink sometime."

Why would a guy who'd just insulted me—and who was about to go on a blind date with another woman— think I would be remotely interested in ever going out with him? Were guys that egotistical? Scratch that. Was *this* guy that egotistical?

More importantly: "Are you by any chance Ben Larson?"

He straightened, and his smile faltered. "Yeah, how'd—oh, man, oh hey, wow, are you Jane Gregg?"

I nodded and looked away from his embarrassed expression to the huge Picasso poster he'd been debating buying.

"Wow, so this is awkward," he said, game-show-host smile fading.

I offered up my a good-sport grin. "Well, we can always tell our grandchildren the great story of how we met before we met on our blind date."

He looked at me quizzically with the horror of a guy who'd heard the words *our* and *children* in the same sentence.

"I'm kidding?" I offered.

He sort of giggled. "Uh, I'm really sorry about trying to meet you. I guess I don't look so good anymore, huh. Well, it's kind of funny, right?"

Hysterical. "Totally," I said. *Like your jagged bottom tooth and your small hands.*

Those small hands gave me some consolation. You knew what they said about small hands. If Ben Larson turned out to be the jerk he was rounding out to be, he'd have to live with those small hands for life. *I* wouldn't.

"So, uh, should we check out the French painters?" he asked.

"Sure," I said, picturing the empty seat next to me at Dana's wedding. Picturing Natasha Nutley nuzzling Mr. Houseboat and dancing all night. What excuse could I possibly make for why my adoring boyfriend couldn't make it? Emergency brain surgery? Urgent rocket trip to Neptune? Meeting with the Pope?

The Gnat would know. Dana would know. And Aunt Ina would know.

Plus, as I've stated for the record, the brain surgeon I was scheduled to meet on Saturday was sure to be the biggest jerk of them all. (Okay, he was really just a *resident* at New York Hospital.) But that left Ben Larson as my only blind-date shot at dignity. Especially given the sad fact that if three in a row went bust, my blind-date bookie was sure to cut me high and dry before I even got to meet next Tuesday's guy.

As Ben and I smiled awkwardly at each other on the escalator to the second floor, I realized that I might have judged him too quickly, as I was prone to do. Okay, he'd made that crack about the Upper East Side, but then again, so did *everyone* who lived in New York City. Even people who lived on the Upper East Side tended to apologize for living in a nice neighborhood. And, so what that he'd tried to pick me up before knowing I was his blind date. Hadn't I been all too happy to be picked up by the cute stranger I'd thought he was? Hadn't I myself planned to be picked up by T-shirt Guy before I knew he was Kevin Adams? Did I have a double standard for guys? Well, did I? Okay, I sounded like I was rationalizing a bit. But not really. Dating was complex. Anyway, my point was that Ben Larson had been right about one thing: Blind dates *did* suck. That gave us a sensibility in common. It was something to go on.

Ben turned the game-show-host pearly whites on me. "So, later I thought we'd check out the sculpture garden, once it cools down a bit out there. A little hot out, huh? It's good you dressed scantily. I wish *I* could wear a little tank top."

I peered past Ben to the garden to cover my surprise. Had he insulted me? Or not? I couldn't tell. The sculpture garden was dotted with stone benches on either side of a narrow rectangular pond. Sitting out there seemed incredibly romantic. Unless he *had* just insulted me. *Chill out,* I yelled at my brain. *Just because the last two guys were nightmares doesn't mean you should read something into everything Ben says. You just met him. Give him a minute. Maybe he's nervous.*

"You're not cold?" he asked as we neared the second floor landing. "The AC is *blasting.* I'm cold and *I'm* in a dress shirt." He pulled at his light blue Oxford.

Who was he, Al Roker? What was with the weather commentary? "Not at all," I said, smiling. Was he insinuating that it was more important to me to dress sexy and show a little skin than to be comfortable, or was I being paranoid? *You're being paranoid. The guy can't ask a question?*

I had worn one of my many Ann Taylor jackets to work today, but Eloise had insisted I leave it draped around my office chair. "You want to *say* to Blind Date #3—if you're lucky you'll get to see more," Eloise had told me, laughing at her own cheesiness. "So the jacket stays here." That, even after I'd explained how it felt to face a blind date's mother with a Miracle Bra pushing up everything you had in a clingy, low-cut matte jersey dress.

"I can't wait to see the Modiglianis," I told Ben as we stepped off the escalator and headed straight ahead for the French Painters exhibit.

"Oh, you like him?" Ben asked. "I find him sort of, I don't know, cartoonish."

I stared at my black slingbacks. If Modigliani was good enough for the Museum of Modern Art...

"Will you excuse me for a few minutes?" I said as we reached the entrance to the exhibit. "I'll meet you inside."

"Everything okay?" he asked, raising an eyebrow.

"Yeah, I just drank a lot of water today." I cringed. Why did I say that? That was grosser than admitting I needed to sneak outside for a cigarette.

"Oh. Okay. I'll be in here." He pointed straight ahead. I could see a Modigliani's long neck across the wall.

I watched Ben Larson's back walk away, then I turned tail and bolted back down the escalator as fast I could in a crowd. It took me five minutes to weave around the mob of people in the lobby and get out the door. Warm, muggy air greeted me. I lit a Marlboro Light and sucked in a deep, oh-so-necessary drag, then exhaled. My equilibrium was now restored. Puff, puff, puff. One more drag, and I dropped the cigarette on the curb, ready to crush it.

"Hey, don't waste that perfectly good cigarette, young miss."

A homeless man was zigzagging toward me. He bent over to pick up the discarded cigarette.

"Here," I said to him, handing him a fresh cigarette. He grinned, revealing a need for dentistry. I lit the Marlboro for him, then ran back inside. I often plucked day-old butts out of ashtrays in my apartment when I ran out of cigarettes and was too lazy to go out for a pack. But I'd never stooped to picking one up off the street. It was so hard not to feel for the homeless in New York, to want to help them, to offer them change. They reminded me on a daily basis that it was possible to end up with nothing and no one if you weren't careful.

I popped a Certs in my mouth, figuring it would dissolve by the time I made my way upstairs and found Ben. I wondered if I'd interrupt him in the middle of chatting up some woman. But there he stood, in front of a Picasso, arms crossed. He eyed me as I joined him and wrinkled his nose. "Did you just smoke a cigarette?"

*Busted.* "Um, yeah." I couldn't even use my *I always smoke when I drink* lie. Which was the usual baloney I gave guys when I lit up on a date in a bar.

"Smoking's really bad for you," Ben said.

Really? That was another one I'd never heard before.

"I only smoke a few cigarettes a day." Liar. "I guess when I get a little nervous, I get a craving." I was trying for coy.

Ben nodded and returned his attention to the Picasso. "Of course, Picasso was Spanish, not French. But he lived in France, where he did most of his best and most admired work."

"Of course," I said in the same pedantic manner. Coy didn't seem to have any effect.

We moved on to a Chagal. Ben glanced at it, then moved on to the next painting, adding, "He's a little too religious for me."

I stayed put in front of the Chagal, staring at one of the paintings I loved most in the world.

"Now, this, this is more my speed." His game-show-host smile was aimed straight ahead.

I stared up at a giant square of black paint with three short orange lines on it.

"Isn't it violent in its expressiveness?" Ben remarked, his arms crossed over his puffed-out chest as he gazed at the painting. "It's so in-your-face. I love it."

I remembered a family trip to the Metropolitan Museum of Art with my parents, Aunt Ina, Uncle Charlie and Dana, who'd been in a stroller. I must have been six or seven. I'd been bored beyond tears and resented Dana, who not only got to be wheeled around in a stroller, but got to nap through the most boring day of our young lives. Uncle Charlie had just finished blabbing on about how much he loved a painting, and then he'd asked me what I thought of it. I rolled my eyes and said it was ugly. My mother had grabbed me by the arm and led me to a corner and told me that I was never to criticize something when someone had just finished saying he liked it. I was to keep my negative opinions to myself and nod. I wasn't sure whether or not I agreed then or now, but I'd listened. Other people offered their differing opinions all the time, usually to hurtful consequence, as Ben Larson had moments ago done to me over the Modigliani.

"Jane!"

I'd know that voice anywhere, even without the crackle of the speakerphone. I turned around to see Gwen Welle and her husband smiling at me. Groan. I thought I wouldn't have to look at her phony face for three more months. Now I had to talk to her and her phony husband on my own time. The problem with New York was that for a city with eight million people, it was really a small town where you ran into people you knew everywhere. In museums, stores, the subway, the street. And because of Murphy's Law, you generally ran into familiar people at the worst possible moments. When you either looked like absolute hell or were playing hookey.

"Hi Gwen," I said, my own phony smile plastered on. "You look great." That wasn't phony. She really did look good. She was glowing. Her husband had his arm around her shoulder.

"Thanks! I think it's because we left Olivia with a baby-sitter—for the first time. This is the first evening Ron and I have had to ourselves in four weeks!" She squeezed her husband's hand. "You remember Jane Gregg, from the office, don't you, Ron?" Ron and I produced the requisite smiles and handshakes. Gwen's eyes were on Ben; she was waiting for an introduction.

"This is Ben Larson," I said. "Um, this is Gwen Welle, my boss, and her husband, Ron."

Handshaking. Smiles.

Gwen turned her glow on me. "I'm so glad to see you out having a good time, Jane. I figured you'd be sweating it out in the office at—" she glanced at her watch "—6:20 on a workday. It can't be work, work, work all the time!"

Anger, hot and sharp, burned in my gut. "Well, considering that I *worked, worked, worked* till one o'clock last night on the Nutley outline, I thought I deserved a walk around a museum."

Gwen had the decency to realize she'd stung me. "Oh, well, I mean, I didn't mean that you weren't working hard, Jane. Oh, silly, you know what I meant!"

The husband looked at his watch. "Gwen, we'd really better go, or we'll be late for dinner with the Hudsons."

"Busy, busy, busy!" Gwen trilled. "Well, see you in a few months, Jane. But we'll have a chance to chat on Monday at the ed meeting when I call in." She eyed Ben. "Nice to meet you." She flashed me a *Good job on him* look, and then, after the typical goodbyes, they were gone.

"Whoa, a little defensive, Jane?" Ben Larson commented, game-show-host smile even bigger and wider, if that could be believed.

Just a few days ago I'd been driven to fantasies of pouring boiling water on a guy's head. Now I wanted to take that hideous black painting off the wall and break it over Ben Larson's game-show-host face.

"You know what, Ben?" I began, trying to keep a check on my anger. "My boss was right. Who do I think I am, walking around a museum at six-twenty at night when I should be working, working, working! I'd really better get back to the office."

Ben's smile fell. "Oh, but, well, I mean, you're already here, and she already caught you, so what would be the point of going back to work? She wouldn't even know."

"*I'd* know, and that's what's really important, don't you think?"

Ben Larson peered at me. "I guess." Ha! I'd deflated the smug bastard! "So, how about a rain check?"

I smiled to myself. "I'm going to be really busy for the next couple of weeks. I've got this major deadline looming, so…"

The smile fell further. "Uh, okay, so why don't you give me a call when things slow down?"

I put on my own game-show-host smile. "I will." And with that I fled down the escalator and out the doors of MOMA.

Twice in one week I'd fled a date. I'd never done that before in my life, and now twice in a matter of days I'd made an excuse and bolted.

The homeless man who I'd given a cigarette to was zigzagging up and down in front of the museum. I headed toward Madison Avenue. I didn't want to go home, but I had nowhere else to go. Amanda was working late, the way a good girl should, and Eloise was off to a free classical music concert in Central Park. There was no way I'd find her and Serge among the thousands sitting on blankets for that mosquito fest. And there was no way I was going back up to Posh to work.

I was only six blocks away from Crate & Barrell, which was on 59th street. I figured I might as well head over and buy Dana's bridal shower present, not that there was anything remotely French-inspired in that store. Maybe I'd buy myself new kitchen stuff I couldn't afford. After all, a spinster-in-training needed to buy these things for herself.

The walk home from Crate & Barrel was doing me good. I was now on Park Avenue and 63rd Street, facing a straight line of the most stunning avenue in the world. One majestic limestone apartment building after another, a formally dressed doorman at each entrance. Park Avenue was divided in the center by island after island of flower beds as far as the eye could see. Like Central Park and the Botanical Gardens and the skyline itself, Park Avenue was free. The brokest assistant editor could stroll up Park Avenue and immediately feel as though she'd bought the world. On a certain long stretch of Park, the stretch I was on at the moment, a person could easily stroll past Madonna or Katharine Hepburn or George Clooney. That was the most amazing thing of all about

New York. A walk home was free and came with the bonus of possible celebrity sightings.

Crate & Barrel had been even more depressing than my date with Ben. The store had been full of young couples wandering around, the men as interested in silverware and place settings as the women. It had taken me about four minutes inside the store to realize I was perilously close to tears. And Madison Avenue and 59th Street was no place for a crying woman. It was also no place to find a taxi, which was why I'd decided on the long walk home.

Sixty-fourth Street. The Gnat's block. I peered west up the unusually short block between Park and Madison. I wondered which amazing town house her "darling sanctuary" was in. Suddenly I realized I could run into her at any moment. I didn't like the idea of her thinking I was checking out her digs. I scurried away, then ducked down E. 65th Street.

Suddenly I felt like the brokest assistant editor again. How could just thinking about the Gnat do that to me? But somehow it didn't seem like all her doing. Something else was bugging me, pricking at the backs of my eyes and causing that stinging sensation. But what? I didn't have a date to the wedding, but was that enough to ruin my life? I still had two months to find someone to go with me. Two months. Anything could happen in two months.

But nothing ever did. And that was the problem. The one guy who'd approached me in months had turned out to be my own smarmy, critical blind date. Left to my own devices, I was a total flop. I couldn't get my own wedding date. And I couldn't even earn my own promotion without the help of the woman who'd caused every insecurity I had.

Something was wrong. Wrong, wrong, wrong. Yes, it was the dates and the whole notion that my love life was in the toilet and about to be flushed into the New York City sewer system. But it was something else. Something I couldn't put my finger on. Something that there were no quick fixes for. What? What was it?

"Hey, watch where you're going!"

"Sorry," I managed to croak at the woman I bumped into.

The stinging sensation at the backs of my eyes threatened. The worst thing about those free walks in the most la-di-da sections of New York was when you were sobbing down the street, surrounded by a million people you didn't know and who didn't care about you at all.

## Seven

The Flirt Night Roundtable was now in session, the honorable Amanda Frank currently being attacked for the inflammatory statement she'd just uttered.

"I'm just telling you what Jeff told me, Jane," Amanda insisted. "They *all* said it. All three of the guys he set you up with. I couldn't *not* tell you, could I?"

Eloise slammed our table with the palm of her hand. The people on either side of our table at Big Sur peered over, then withdrew their attention when it was obvious there wasn't anything interesting going on, like a hysterical breakup or a catfight. "So Jane's supposed to quit smoking because her blind dates didn't like it? Tough shit!"

Amanda bristled. "Well, tough shit when Natasha Nutley introduces her billionaire boyfriend at Dana's reception and asks where Jane's wonderful boyfriend is."

Amanda had a point there. Eloise and I blew smoke at

each other. I stared at the crowd lining the bar; the *non*-smokers were few and far between. Why did all those people get to smoke if it was so vile and disgusting and socially unacceptable?

"Jane, guys who don't smoke don't want to date a smoker, plain and simple, hon," Amanda said, sipping her Amstel Light. "And most guys in New York don't smoke. So unless you want to hide your little habit, you've gotta quit."

I turned beseeching help-me eyes to Eloise.

"Sorry, Jane, but I think she might be right." Eloise inhaled her Marlboro, then exhaled away from Amanda's direction. "Serge smokes—it's one of the main reasons I'm with him."

Amanda turned her offended blue gaze on Eloise. *"What?"*

Eloise sipped her Cosmo. "It makes it easier. Just like it makes it easier to date a nonsmoker if you don't smoke."

Amanda's mouth was still open. "So the only reason you're with Serge is because he smokes and therefore it's a hassle-free relationship? Eloise!"

"Well, not when you make it sound like that," Eloise defended herself. "I adore Serge. That he doesn't bug me about smoking is just a bonus, okay?"

"Do I really have to quit smoking to find a boyfriend?" I asked, inhaling an extra-deep drag of my Marlboro Light. "A *fake* boyfriend?"

"You're not looking for a fake boyfriend, Jane, and you know it," Amanda said. "And trust me, Timothy doesn't smoke and wouldn't touch a smoker with a ten-foot stethoscope."

Timothy Rommely was the doctor. Tomorrow night's doctor—the one that promised to be the worst of them all. He was a friend of Jeff's from college. Thirty-two. Upper West Side (but not in a brownstone). I'd long gotten over linking the Upper West Side and a blind date to fate. He supposedly looked like Greg from the television show *Dharma and Greg*. I doubted that. Doctors weren't *that* hot.

"A doctor might be worth quitting for, Jane," Eloise noted, exhaling a stream of smoke at me.

"*Anything* that can motivate you to quit is worth quitting for," Amanda cut in. "If it has to be a guy, fine. But I'd like to see you quit for self-love, Jane. You too, El. Your health, your future children, the people around you. Those are three very good reasons to stop smoking."

Amanda was one of the few people I knew who could get away with making references to "self-love." Eloise made a face and held her cigarette under the table.

I gnawed my lower lip and stared at the pack of Marlboro Lights on the table. The red Bic lighter next to it. The ashtray, full of ashes and butts. These things were as familiar and as comforting to me as the meat loaf, tuna sandwiches and Tang my mom used to make. When I looked at a pack of cigarettes, especially a fresh pack, I felt instantly comforted. Everything in the world was as okay as it was going to get when I had a full box of Marlboro Lights in my purse. When I looked at a pack containing just a few cigarettes, I felt panicked—a feeling that was never settled until I bought a new pack.

I didn't start smoking from peer pressure in junior high the way everyone else did. I hadn't taken a puff of a cigarette until I was nineteen, until the day Aunt Ina surprised me with a knock on my dorm room door that February morning almost ten years ago, her expression one I'd never seen before. The moment I'd seen that expression, I'd known my mother was dead. I'd spoken to my mom the day before. She'd mentioned she hadn't been feeling too well the past couple of weeks; she thought she had a nasty case of the flu. But she'd had ovarian cancer. And one moment she'd been alive, and the next, she was gone. My mother was gone.

My expression alone had been enough for Aunt Ina; she'd simply nodded in confirmation. My knees had given out and I'd dropped fast onto the floor. Aunt Ina picked me up and held me against her on the thin dorm bed. Neither of us had said a word for a half hour. Then Aunt Ina had told me that my mother was with my father now, her beloved husband who she'd loved so much. They were together at last. They were at peace. And they would always watch over me. It was then that I'd cried and couldn't stop.

A half hour later, Aunt Ina had gone down the hall to tell Uncle Charlie and Dana that I was ready to leave. (Grammy had been too inconsolable to make the trip up to Albany; she was staying with her best friend until we returned.) I'd picked up my roommate's pack of Marlboro Lights and slid out a cigarette and sniffed it. I'd seen the way Michelle would take a drag and let out a satisfying *ah*. I lit the cigarette and inhaled a small puff. I hadn't coughed. I'd sat on the bed, inhaling, exhaling, inhaling, exhaling, comforted by the *do-this, do-that* thoughtlessness, pleased by the methodical need to click the cigarette ever so gently against the rim of the ashtray so that the ashes would fall inside. From that cigarette on, I was a smoker.

Aunt Ina had knocked on the door, called my name, and I'd slipped Michelle's cigarettes into the pocket of my down jacket, along with a book of matches. Dana had packed a suitcase for me. Uncle Charlie had gone to the Registrar's to withdraw me for the semester. And Aunt

Ina wrapped my mother's favorite scarf, the one my dad had helped me buy for Mother's Day years back, tight around my neck. Then, once we were all together again, we'd bundled into Uncle Charlie's Buick, and I'd toyed with the pack of cigarettes in my pocket.

No one had said a word or shaken their heads when I'd openly smoked in front of them at rest stops, or in Aunt Ina's apartment, or outside the funeral home, or after the cemetery. I had watched as my mother's coffin was lowered into the plot right next to my father's. No one was going to tell me I shouldn't smoke. Ironically enough, perhaps, I hadn't viewed cigarettes as something that took life away. I'd only registered that they took *feelings* away. And so I smoked, constantly. I immediately became a pack-a-day smoker. Now, I was a pack-and-a-halfer, sometimes even a two-packer, depending on my stress level, which thanks to life, was always high.

Amanda waved away our smoke and mock-coughed. "Jane, did I mention that Timothy has a Jack Russell terrier named Spot? Isn't that adorable?"

Yes, it was. Suddenly, I wanted a Jack Russell terrier named Spot. I wanted a boyfriend who had that dog. I wanted a boyfriend and a dog. I wanted a boyfriend who supposedly looked like the actor Thomas Gibson. I wanted to be able to date Timothy Rommely. I wanted him to fall in love with me and never leave me. And if that meant quitting smoking, so be it. I crushed out the half-smoked cigarette and gnawed my lower lip.

Amada beamed.

"You're really gonna quit?" Eloise asked.

"Tomorrow morning," I said, lighting a fresh cigarette.

Eloise and Amanda laughed.

The waitress came by to ask if we wanted another round. We most certainly did.

"You know what, Jane?" Eloise said. "If you quit, I'll quit."

My mouth dropped open. "But you're seeing a guy who smokes more than the two of us combined."

"So I'll tell him he can't smoke around me or in my apartment," Eloise said. She took the last sip of her Cosmopolitan. "He's around too much anyway. I don't know what I'm gonna do about him. He keeps hinting about moving in, but I don't know. I like him so much, but..."

"But he's not the one?" Amanda offered, tucking a strand of long, blond hair behind her ear. "I mean, if smoking is one of the main things you have in common..."

"I don't know," Eloise said, exhaling a stream of smoke. "He is and he isn't. Sometimes I think I love him, sometimes I think we're just meant to be friends, and sometimes I wish he'd go back to Russia so I'd never have to see him again. Sometimes not being hassled about smoking is all I think there *is* between us."

"Sounds to me like you're not meant to make any decisions about him right now," I said. "You don't know how you feel."

Eloise nodded. "He's so cute and sweet. I wish I knew why some guys feel like the one and others don't. I would be so happy if Serge were definitely it."

The waitress set down our round of drinks. Amanda sipped her beer. "I know what you mean. If he *were* the one, everything would be so easy. You'd have your guy right there."

"But it's true, isn't it?" I asked. "You do just *know*, right?"

"I think so," Amanda said. "Although, remember how I felt about Jeff when I first met him? I thought he was too immature, but it turned out he was just insecure and nervous, which lasted only a few weeks. He's not immature at all. I'm so glad I gave him the chance to be himself. And for me to be myself.''

Huh. I remembered Amanda wondering out loud about whether or not to go on a second date with Jeff Jorgensen. She'd said he'd made stupid jokes and turned her off. When I'd met Jeff, I'd instantly liked him, well, except for his too-hearty laugh and penchant for screaming at the television while watching sports. And granted, he was definitely into hanging out with packs of guys who liked to make vulgar jokes, but wasn't I currently benefiting from his frat-boy ways? Meaning: lots of buds to fix me up with.

''Let's do it, Jane,'' Eloise announced. ''Let's lose the bad habit.''

''Yeah!'' Amanda exclaimed. ''You have to give up something to get something. That's the way life works. That's the way life is.''

''She's right,'' Eloise agreed. ''And you know what, Jane? We're stronger than cigarettes.''

I raised an eyebrow. ''We are?''

''Of course ya'll are!'' Amanda insisted.

''Excuse me,'' said a semi-good-looking guy to Amanda. Behind him at the bar stood his crew of other semi-good-looking guys, watching to see how his friend did with the table of ladies. ''Are you from Texas? I heard your accent.''

''Nah,'' Amanda said in Brooklynese. ''I'm a Noo Yawka. I was just kidding about the ya'll.''

''Oh.'' He turned back around.

We leaned forward and giggled. ''Well, I guess it's just the accent they want,'' Amanda said.

I took a long sip of my Comso, then lit another cigarette. I watched the smoke rise up to the high ceiling and mingle with the smoke from everyone else's cigarettes. If smoking was so alive and well in New York City's hottest nightspots, why did I have to quit? Why couldn't I find a smoking date right in here?

*Because you tried that for years, you fool. You haven't met a smoker since Max Reardon.* And now his new wife got to smoke away with him in bed after sex....

Was I ever going to get married? If I couldn't even make a date last longer than an hour and a half, how could I hope to share my life with someone? Was I supposed to mellow out and chill out and be more accepting of the little hurts guys inflicted during dates when they were supposed to be on their best behavior? Figure they were nervous and insecure? That they'd turn into princes on date four? Arg. As I'd already said, dating was complicated stuff.

So maybe you didn't always know for sure about a guy when you met him. But you did get a *sense* of him. And the same went for the guy. Did I really want a guy to label me as a smoker and get his sole sense of me from that? Nonsmokers simply didn't understand that smokers had gone through their entire adult lives puffing away— cigarettes had been a part of every single emotion and event, good and bad. Never smoking again was equal to terror. How did one do anything without a cigarette?

I'll bet if I hadn't been a smoker, I'd have poured that boiling water on Kevin Adams's head. I'd have flung back tortellini at Andrew Mackelroy's nephew. I'd have broken that stupid black canvas over Ben Larson's game-show-host face. I would rage out of control unless I could smoke away my feelings. Wouldn't I? What would I do instead of smoking?

And what would I get if I gave up cigarettes? That was the question. If it was a date to cousin Dana's wedding, if it was a guy who'd make me feel okay in Natasha Nutley's privileged presence, then it was worth it, pathetic as that sounded. That was my only real motivation to stop at the moment. I supposed I'd also win accolades from my friends and return my lungs to their original pink color. That would be cool. Smoking cost me a fortune, sent me outside in the pouring rain, the freezing snow and the unbearable heat. It made my clothes and hair smell bad. It made blind dates break out in hives and little kids unable to breathe. And, um, it caused cancer.

"You know, you two," Amanda began, "you'll have to quit one day, anyway, when you get pregnant, so you might as well quit now."

Eloise and I looked at each other and laughed. "According to Jeff, if Jane doesn't stop smoking now, she'll never even have *sex* again," Eloise pointed out. "So, she doesn't have to worry about getting pregnant."

I raised my Cosmo. "Okay," I declared. "I will smoke my last cigarette before I go to bed tonight, and when I wake up, I will join the proud ranks of the former smokers."

Eloise lifted her own Comso and clinked it with me. "I'm with you."

"It's gonna change your whole life, you guys," Amanda said. "Just you wait and see."

I emerged from the low-lit subway station at Continental Avenue to find myself in the middle of the very crowded outdoor mall otherwise known as Forest Hills, Queens. The affluent neighborhood was a shopping mecca for the middle class. Everyone's favorite stores were packed next to each other on the mile-long Austin Street, including every type of store you might have to run an errand in. On the same block, you could buy everything you'd ever need for a lifetime, from a prom dress to a lamp shade to a hamburger.

Every type of human being imaginable, every age, every race, headed slow and fast up the streets of Forest Hills. To avoid the crowd, I walked in the street itself, alongside the cars. Up at the corner, I could see Boston Market and farther down, toward Ascar Avenue, Aunt Ina's familiar strawberry-blond head. She stood in front of a luxury apartment building, between beds of red and purple impatiens. She was reading the *New York Post* and popping something into her mouth from a little plastic bag around her wrist. A few women walked past her through the double glass doors, held open by two uniformed doormen. Members of the esteemed Dana Dreer bridal party. I recognized them from the wedding shower planning meeting and the first bridesmaids' dress fitting.

I instinctively reached into my purse for a cigarette, then remembered I'd quit at midnight. I was no longer a person who smoked. It was very strange to head into nonsmoking territory without storing up reserves of nicotine. And this ridiculous "finalization meeting" would have me itching to smoke. Cigarettes had allowed me to postpone entering places I didn't want to go—Sorry, need a smoke! And they'd allowed me to sneak out for a nic fix—Sorry, need a smoke! Now I'd have no excuses. No postponing. No leaving. I wondered if I'd start twitching the way everyone said would happen during nicotine withdrawal. Then again, I wasn't quite off nicotine yet; Eloise and I had each bought the patch last night on our way home. I'd slapped one on at midnight and hoped for the best. The good news at the moment was that so far, so good. And, at least I didn't have to suck on a breath mint to hide my smoky breath from Ina. I was smoke-odor-free for the first time in ten years.

"Aunt Ina," I called as I neared her.

She spotted me and waved. "Did you bring the shoes?"

I held up my tote bag. "They're in here."

Ina enfolded me in her arms and squeezed me. She looked me over with her pale blue eyes. "Did you take a car service or the subway?"

"The subway," I admitted, wondering how she could tell just by looking at me. Lying over the phone was one thing. Lying to my aunt's face was another. I prepared for the lecture.

"Jane!"

"It's very crowded during the day," I insisted. "It's safe."

Aunt Ina narrowed her eyes. "So nothing weird happened down there? No one bothered you?"

"Nope," I said. "I keep telling you. It's not like it used to be."

Ina folded her newspaper and shoved it in her Bloomingdale's Big Brown Bag. "*It's not like it used to be,*' she tells me. What do you think I've been standing here doing?" The doorman held open the door for us. "There were three articles in the newspaper about people getting pushed in front of trains by crazy people. So don't you tell me it's safe, young lady."

I sighed. "We're here to see Karen Frieman," I said to one of the doormen.

He smiled and asked our names. I told him and he consulted a list, which made me roll my eyes. How pretentious. The doorman approved us, and we were ushered into the gold-and-brown marble monstrosity of a lobby. Mirrors everywhere. I stabbed the buttons to the three elevators.

"Your hair looks nice," Aunt Ina commented. "More

natural. I don't like it when you make it all pin straight. God gave you bouncy hair with a nice wave, and what do you do? Attack it with all that goo and a blow dryer.''

It was the summer humidity—magnified a thousand percent by the subway—that had *attacked* my hair and made it all bouncy with the dreaded wave.

Why did I have to quit smoking *today?* There was nothing I wanted more at this moment than a good, long drag of a Marlboro Light. I hadn't done anything without a cigarette in ten years. Yet somehow, I was supposed to get through Dana Dreer's bridal shower finalization meeting, a bridesmaids' dress fitting *and* a blind date with a doctor named Timothy Rommely.

''Here we are. Tenth floor,'' Ina said.

One minute later I was inside Karen's huge apartment. The hostess and maid of honor herself opened the door for us; she looked me up and down as usual. For Aunt Ina and Grammy I'd worn a cute sundress I'd gotten on sale at Zara International last week. If I'd worn my usual summer weekend outfit of cargo pants and a white T-shirt, I'd never hear the end of it. How did I expect to get promoted or meet a guy if I dressed like a teenager—a teenage boy, no less? That sparkling gem of a comment always came from Dana.

In Karen's huge living room, which was, I had to admit, very nicely furnished, I counted thirteen women, including myself. Seven were bridesmaids, plus Karen, the maid of honor. Two were Aunt Ina and Grammy. And three were Larry Fishkill's mother and his two grandmothers. Larry's sister, Penny, had been included in the bridesmaid tally. I spotted Grammy chatting with Larry's grandmothers by the cream cheese selection. Karen announced that we were to enjoy the bagel buffet and coffee, and then we'd get down to business.

Grammy came over to me and Aunt Ina. "Give your grandmother a hug," she ordered with a big smile. She practically squeezed the life out of me. "You're looking a little thin." Grammy turned her attention to Ina, who she hugged also. "Doesn't she look a little thin?" she asked her daughter.

"Young women and their diets," Aunt Ina dismissed with her trademark sigh.

Sometimes when I looked at my grandmother I could see my own mother. Virginia Gregg had had the same elfin chin and the same dark brown That Girl eyes, which I'd inherited. And we all had the same straight, small nose. I had my father's hair, though, very dark and thick. My mom's, like Grammy's, had been light brown and pin straight. Aunt Ina and Grammy still got what they insisted on referring to as "permanents." I'd tried to tell them that no one got perms anymore, but they told me what they always told me: *What do you know from everyone does or doesn't do, big shot?*

"So who's this I hear you're dating?" Grammy asked, leading me over to the buffet Karen had set up on a credenza against a wall. In front of us was every imaginable kind of bagel, four kinds of cream cheese, butter, fat-free margarine and three platters of mouthwatering lox. "Don't take the light cream cheese," Grammy said. "You really look too thin, especially in the face. Do you see how skinny her arms are?" she asked, directing this toward Aunt Ina. "You probably can't even open a bottle of soda."

I definitely wasn't looking too thin. But I appreciated the sentiment and the freedom to heap lox and vegetable cream cheese on a poppy-seed bagel without the slightest bit of guilt over how many fat grams I was about to ingest. Carrying my bounty to a group of hard-backed chairs by the windows, I joined Grammy and Aunt Ina.

"So what's his name, this new boyfriend of yours?" Grammy asked.

I cringed. Lying about a phony boyfriend was one thing; giving him a name was another. Somehow, naming him gave weight and depth to what was really just a fib, at least in my semi-guilty mind. What was I supposed to say? If I said *Timothy,* which was the name of tonight's date, that would only work if he worked out. And he wouldn't. No one would. There was one blind date after Timothy for next week, an investment banker named Driscoll Something-or-other. I couldn't very well tell Grammy and Aunt Ina that my new boyfriend's name was Driscoll. I'd save that if he worked out. Which he wouldn't, either.

My ego was really getting way too big.

"Um, Timothy," I said. At least I liked the name. When I brought no one to the wedding, I could always say that Timothy had been called out of the country on an emergency. Or that we'd broken up. At least then I'd get the sympathy I hadn't gotten over Max's wedding announcement. I had to suppress a smile at the irony of the Timothy situation. We hadn't even met and I was already planning our breakup.

"Timothy? So formal?" Aunt Ina criticized. "Why not Tim?"

Why not, indeed? "Well, you know, Aunt Ina, guys like to sound older than they are, more professional, so they all tend to give up the nicknames."

Both Grammy and Aunt Ina nodded. I'd said the right thing. "So does this Timothy have a last name?" Grammy asked.

"Um, Rommely," I said.

"Rommely. Where do I know that name from?" Grammy asked.

"It's from this month's book," Aunt Ina told Grammy. Aunt Ina sipped her coffee, leaving a red lipstick stain on the mug. She turned to me. "We're reading *A Tree Grows In Brooklyn* for our book club at the senior center."

*A Tree Grows in Brooklyn*. It was the only book that had ever made me cry. I always sobbed in movies at emotional moments, even at Hallmark commercials and those Seventh Day Adventist spots on television about lonely, misunderstood teenagers. But never had words on a page made me cry until *A Tree Grows in Brooklyn*. Until a scene in which adults had carelessly tried to take something from young Francie Nolan that she would never, ever give up: her dignity.

"Whose last name was Rommely?" I asked, swallowing a bite of lox and cream-cheese slathered bagel. "I thought the girl's last name was Nolan."

"No, not her," Grammy said. "The mother. The mother's maiden name was Rommely. She was a strong woman. She did what was right, not what was fair. That's the mark of a strong person."

Hmm. Perhaps there was some cosmic, karmic significance to the fact that my date for this evening was named Rommely. Doubtful.

"So we have to wait till Dana's wedding to meet him?" they asked in unison.

"I think so," I said, again feeling guilty at the lie. "I've got this and that, and he's got that and this, and with all there is to do before the wedding, I doubt I'll ever be able to get us all in the same room."

They sank their teeth into their bagels, nodding. Again I'd said the right thing. That was twice in the same fifteen-minute span. Unheard-of. A busy, hardworking boyfriend with this and that to do was all right by them.

"You're *sure* you don't want to meet Ethan Miles?" Grammy asked. "I can see the two of you together. He's such a nice young man. So polite. He's from Texas, did Aunt Ina tell you that? Isn't that something?"

Grammy was romanticizing Texas, a state she knew only from television, books and movies. When I thought of Texas, I thought of Clint Black or the Marlboro Man or the image of a cowboy and a horse. I'd never been on a horse. The only horses I was familiar with were the ones who lined up miserably in front of Central Park and took people on hansom cab rides. But those didn't count as Texas horses; they didn't trot on grass and dirt paths or run wild through meadows—they moved alongside taxis and speeding ambulances and messengers on delivery bikes. There weren't even horses in the Central Park Zoo, unless you figured in the two or three ponies in the Children's Zoo. What would I ever have in common with someone from Texas?

"Ma, she's seeing someone," Aunt Ina said, smacking her lips. "Let her be. This Timothy Rommely sounds nice."

It was interesting how all it took for someone to sound nice was a nice-sounding name. For all Grammy and Aunt Ina knew, Timothy could be a psycho killer. Thank God they hadn't asked what he did for a living. I had a feeling they assumed he was an Internet genius. Larry Fishkill had bored all of us to death for three years about the Internet and how it had once made millionaires out of ordinary people. Grammy and Aunt Ina believed every word that came out of Larry Fishkill's mouth. If I were to be honest, I'd have to admit that I sort of liked Larry, a little. He talked too much and he could be pedantic, but there was something real about him. He was far more down-to-earth than his fiancée.

Anyway, I couldn't tell Grammy and Aunt Ina that Timothy Rommely was a doctor. If he didn't work out—which he wouldn't—then whoever I brought to the Plaza would have to be a doctor—or at least play one at weddings. Why hadn't I realized how widespread one stupid pride-saving lie could get?

Grammy sipped her coffee. "All right, all right, she's seeing someone." She leaned in close to me, her dark eyes on Karen, who was consulting a legal pad on a clipboard, then returned her gaze to me. "This coffee's too strong. And the bagels are hard. Probably from the supermarket."

I smiled. I loved when Grammy and Aunt Ina ragged on people I didn't like.

Karen Frieman clapped her hands together. "Okay, girls! Time to get started!"

And I hated when anyone referred to women as "girls." Especially when women did it.

"It's hard to believe," Karen said, "but next Saturday is the big day. Dana's bridal shower. Which will be possible thanks to the help of everyone in this room. Let's all take a minute and give ourselves a hand. Come on, everyone, give yourselves a hand."

Oh God. How cheesy was this? I clapped twice, then a third time when Aunt Ina shot me a you'd-better-watch-it look.

Karen eyed her clipboard. "Our first order of business is to make sure that the final details are covered. At this point, it's all about picking up items and ensuring they arrive here in a timely manner. Let's go down the list and make sure everyone knows what she's responsible for taking care of."

Two months ago I'd been assigned the enviable task of getting the bridal shower invitations printed. My publishing credentials made me the "perfect person!" to walk into a printer's shop and order one hundred invitations. Of course, the invitations were adorned by tiny Eiffel Towers. Karen had wanted French phrases, too; I'd convinced her that RSVP was enough. The invitations had been sent out four weeks ago. Grammy, who'd taken a calligraphy course, had been responsible for addressing the envelopes; she was also in charge of making the Congratulations banner. Aunt Ina had paid for the invitations and the stamps.

Karen went down her clipboard. There was the French feast, catered by the local French restaurant. There was the French music, which one of Dana's bridesmaids was in charge of since she was the only one of us who'd been to Paris. No one, it seemed, knew anything about French music. We'd all heard of Edith Piaf, but that was about it.

The bridal party had to show up for the shower wearing stupid boat-neck tops with black-and-white horizontal stripes and black or white capris with little black or white Keds. Oh, and if we had a little black or white scarf to tie around our necks, "that would be great!" I didn't. And I wasn't borrowing Eloise's. Aunt Ina was in charge of the Registry; she and Dana had spent three days traipsing around Bloomingdale's, Crate & Barrel and Williams-Sonoma to choose everything a new bride could want for her shower and wedding. Grammy was in charge of noting down who gave what gifts at the shower; one of the bridesmaids had to create the stupid bow hat, a tradition I'd never understood. Every time Dana ripped a bow off a gift, the bridesmaid was to stick the bow onto a paper plate to make a hat that Dana would then cherish forever.

Larry Fishkill's sister, Penny, was in charge of taking official photos of the shower. His mother and grand-mother were in charge of catering. The other bridesmaids were responsible for this and that. And Karen was in charge of telling everyone what to do and keeping her ugly little fuzzy dog in the bedroom.

I poured myself another cup of coffee and watched Aunt Ina chat away with Larry Fishkill's mother. For the first time, I realized that my aunt's family was growing. She and my Uncle Charlie were getting a son-in-law, who came complete with relatives of his own. Dana was getting a husband. Someone was joining their family. Someone new. I shivered in the air-conditioned room. I'd never felt separate from the Dreers before. They were mine, my family. But I was just a relative, a granddaughter, a niece, a cousin. I wasn't the main thing, not to anyone. And I was the only Gregg left in the world.

A Fancy Affair was owned and operated by a tiny German woman built like a tank. She never smiled and walked around with a yellow tape measure draped around her thick neck.

"Let's line up by size, girls, since that's how the dresses will be kept in order."

Another woman who liked to call women *girls*.

The bridal party surveyed one another. No one moved. Women knew better than to even suggest that another woman was bigger or smaller or even the same size. You just didn't do it.

Ms. Fancy sighed like Aunt Ina and called out our names. We were handed our dresses and told to change into them.

My dress was a bit loose, I was surprised to see. Perhaps I had lost weight in the past month? Ms. Fancy wrapped the tape measure around my waist, then went down the line, whipping it here and there and writing down measurements in her little pink book.

"In my day, women had twenty-two-inch waists!" she bellowed. "Today, we all eat too much, eh?" She let out a hard burst of laughter.

The eight of us each stood on a circular platform in our peach peau de soie shoes in front of a wall of mirror. We all wore the same peach sleeveless dress with a high neckline and an empire waist. There was something very Audrey Hepburn about the dress. It was utterly simple yet elegant. I still thought the color was weird. Why peach? It wasn't even a color. It was in between pink and orange. Karen, the maid of honor, was in the same dress with a different neckline, showing off her ample cleavage.

Aunt Ina and Larry Fishkill's mother stood smiling on their little perches in the corner. "You all look so beautiful," Aunt Ina said.

"Just beautiful," Larry Fishkill's mother agreed.

Ms. Fancy's assistants and seamstresses pinned and tucked and turned us around.

As a few other women let out little shrieks when they were stuck with pins, I was busy being annoyed that Dana had so many friends to make bridesmaids. Granted, out of the eight, one was her cousin and one was her sister-in-law-to-be, but that left six others who were honest-to-goodness good friends. Good-enough friends to stand up for her at her wedding.

I recognized four from Forest Hills, women she'd grown up with. So not only had Dana managed to find true love and book a ballroom at the Plaza Hotel, but she'd also managed to hang on to her friends. Again I wondered what my cousin knew about life that I didn't.

Today Dana and Larry were meeting with their photographer, then visiting the florist to confirm their order. Dana had already had her final wedding dress fitting last week. I'd been invited by Aunt Ina, but I'd made some excuse. I wasn't ready to see Dana in her white gown. I doubted I ever would be.

Ms. Fancy announced a five-minute break to stretch. I immediately reached for my purse, planning to escape outside to smoke. And then I remembered. I sat down on my platform and twitched.

"Omigod," declared bridesmaid Julie. "My waist has gone up an entire inch! I am *so* going on a diet starting tomorrow."

"Shut up!" sing-songed the other bridesmaid named Julie. "You're a size two!"

Julie number one smiled in the mirror. You'd think the size of her dress would have been enough proof, but no, she needed her friend to remind her and the entire room. The two Julies were from Forest Hills; Dana had known them from grammar school. I remembered my parents' delight in their little niece having two best friends named Julie.

Maid of honor Karen was admiring her cleavage; she still stood on the platform next to me, turning slightly to the left and to the right.

"Um, Karen?" I began, eyeing her in the mirror. "I just wanted to apologize for pulling an attitude the other day, on the phone. I know you're taking on a lot as maid of honor, and—"

"Forget it," Karen said with a smile. "So tell me about Natasha Nutley! What's she like? It's so cool that you're editing her autobiography."

*Memoirs,* I wanted to correct her. Autobiography always sounded so official to me. And who was Natasha

Nutley to be writing down her life story at age twenty-eight as though she had anything to say to the world?

"She's, um, like you'd expect," I said, not even sure what I meant. "She's very glamorous."

"I'm so psyched that she's coming to the wedding. Dana says she has an amazing boyfriend who lives on a houseboat in Santa Barbara. Is that the life or what?"

I smiled, not sure what to say. It was bad enough that the Gnat had encroached upon my life at work and at home. Now she'd managed to become the topic of conversation at my bridesmaid dress fitting.

"So Dana mentioned that you're bringing your new boyfriend to the wedding too," Karen cooed, checking out her butt in the mirror." She smiled that *ooh, tell me all about it* smile. "Is it serious?"

"Uh, yeah, it's getting there," I said. "I don't like to talk about it too much. You know how it is. You can jinx a new relationship by talking too much about it."

Karen nodded sagely. "I know. I talked so much about my fiancé that it took him almost eleven months to propose. It's a year or forget it."

A year or forget it. I'd been with Max Reardon for a year, and he hadn't even thought about proposing that we move in together, much less get married. I wondered what it was like to have the luxury of tossing aside a guy because he hadn't proposed after the big year mark.

"So were you and Natasha friends in high school?" one of the Julies asked me. "I remember her. My older brother was a year behind you guys. He was totally in love with her."

"Him and every other guy," I muttered. "We weren't friends then."

"But you are now," Karen put in. "Dana said she ran into you and Natasha having lunch in a really nice restaurant in the city. You and your boyfriend are sitting with her and her boyfriend at the wedding, right? I'll bet her boyfriend is an actor too. He's probably *gorgeous.*"

"Natasha is only a professional acquaintance, nothing more," I snapped. "We're not *friends.* I don't even like her. Don't forget that she's an *actress.* Just because she was on television doesn't mean she's a nice person."

"Okay, *whatever,*" Karen said, eyeing her friends in the mirror.

"Who is this Natasha, the actress?" Larry Fishkill's mother called from her perch in the corner.

"Only a famous actress who's going to Dana and Larry's wedding," Aunt Ina explained. "Natasha Nutley. She used to baby-sit Dana for years. She was a raving beauty even back then, a pipsqueak of a girl around twelve, thirteen. Homecoming queen, prom queen...Jane," Aunt Ina called to me, "didn't Natasha win some local beauty pageant, too?"

According to the outline of her memoir, she'd won two local beauty pageants and was third runner-up for Teen Dream New York. But I'd known that then. I'd read all about it in the Forest Hills High newspaper, which covered every little and big thing the Gnat had done.

"She became an actress, commercials and one of the hospital dramas," Aunt Ina continued. "I can't watch those—all the blood and guts, ugh. Jane, which was the program?"

"She was on two of them," I said, stepping back onto my platform. "She had bit parts for a couple of days on each one."

"Oh, so that's why no one knows who she had the affair with," the other Julie said. "Because she was on two different shows."

"Right," I said. "She had bit parts on both." I emphasized the *bit parts*.

"I saw her on Sally Jessy Raphael last winter," Aunt Ina said. "She almost brought me to tears! What that poor girl went through over that actor. I wonder who he is. Do you know, Jane?"

"How would she know?" Larry Fishkill's mother asked. "She said she's not even friends with Natasha."

"Oh, Jane's her editor," Aunt Ina announced, pride in her voice. "She's helping Natasha write her autobiography. Jane knows everything about her."

All eyes swung to me. "I don't really," I said. "Just what she chooses to reveal in her manuscript. I swear I don't know who The Actor is."

I didn't. But I had an idea. It was almost too unbelievable to conceive. He was too stunning, too movie star. Too *everything* to have had a relationship with the Gnat, even for seven weeks. What was so special about a two-bit actress like Natasha Nutley when he could have had any woman in the world he wanted?

That was the only answer I wanted. The only answer I'd ever wanted. It was about her looks, yes, but it couldn't be just that. There was something else the Gnat had. *What? What* was it?

"Break time is over, girls!" Ms. Fancy announced. "Step back on your stools, please."

"Did you know that one of your hips is higher than the other?" the seamstress asked me in a totally conversational tone.

The bridesmaid to my left eyed me in the mirror, then her gaze dropped to my hips.

"I didn't," I said. "I never knew that. But I'm glad you told me."

The seamstress had the decency to look embarrassed. She ducked her head back down and continued pinning.

Perhaps that had been the reason why Blind Dates One, Two and Three hadn't been interested. It wasn't the smoking, after all. It was my Hip Issue. And just my luck that Blind Date Four was with a doctor, whose business it was to notice such deformities.

## *Eight*

"Me too!" I said for the fourth time in twenty minutes to Timothy Rommely.

He smiled, revealing one perfect dimple in his left cheek, which I wanted both to pinch and kiss. "I can't believe how much we have in common," Timothy said, taking a sip of his sangria. "I've never said or heard 'me too' so many times on one first date. Jeff must have really put some thought into fixing us up."

I laughed. If only he knew.

Timothy Rommely was, in a cliché, the man of my dreams. And for the past half hour, he'd been as perfect a blind date as you could get. Amanda hadn't been lying when she'd told me he looked something like Greg from *Dharma and Greg*. Six feet, lanky yet broad shouldered, with a shock of semi-short dark, dark hair and dark, dark eyes. We had similar coloring, actually, except that I was fair skinned and he was more golden. He wore cool black pants and a black T-shirt and black shoes. Way too cool for a doctor, I thought.

A *doctor*. This perfect specimen sitting across from me at the bar of a Spanish restaurant, this guy with the sparkling almost-black eyes and irresistible dimple and sweet smile, was a certified M.D. And he hadn't even brought it up. In fact, we hadn't even gotten to the subject of our careers. We were still on favorite movies we'd seen recently, favorite books and favorite foods.

Timothy Rommely didn't glance around the bar to check out other women. He didn't belch. He didn't order cheap carafes of wine. He didn't treat me as though I weren't worth his time or energy. *Au contraire.* Timothy Rommely was gazing at me as though I were a beautiful princess.

"So, how about we head over to the restaurant? I made reservations at Café des Artistes, if that's all right."

Café des Artistes. Only one of the most romantic restaurants in Manhattan.

I peered into those dark, dark eyes of his and wondered when he was going to reveal his Fatal Flaw. I was being set up, literally; at any moment, he would either insult me, emit a strange sound from his body, start crying, or run out of the bar. Or, he'd tell me he forgot to mention to Jeff that he'd gotten married last weekend.

*Please, please, please let me have this guy,* I prayed to the Fates of the universe. Eloise and Amanda had said you *knew.* Sometimes you had to wait to find out. But right now, I *knew.* For the first time since I'd seen the movie *Jerry Maguire,* a guy had *me* at "hello." I'd known right then and there that Timothy Rommely was a keeper.

The good doctor and I had played phone tag for the past couple of days; eventually he'd left a message asking me to meet him at a new Spanish restaurant downtown at seven-thirty for drinks. I'd liked his voice immediately. There was warmth in his voice, and not a trace of impatience. I'd expected the opposite from a doctor.

I still had half a glass of sangria. I sipped the sweet, fruit-filled wine, a very pleasant buzz beginning to come over me. I was sure that a half glass of sangria hadn't relaxed me; my date had.

"You have really sexy toes," he said playfully, peeking down at my Jackie Onassis red-hot toenails.

*I* had sexy toenails. Who knew there was anything remotely sexy about me? My cheeks turned pink. That earned a delighted small laugh from my date. I had a feeling that if Timothy did notice my uneven hips, he'd find them interesting.

"So did you grow up in New York?" Timothy asked as he signaled the waiter for our check.

I nodded. "Queens. Forest Hills."

The dimple appeared. "I can't believe this—another *me too!* I'm from Bayside."

This perfect specimen of manhood had grown up in Bayside, Queens?

He sipped his sangria. "So are your parents still in Queens, or did they—like mine—move to Florida the minute you graduated from high school?"

Ah. There it was. The Date Destroyer. There would be no Café des Artistes. He'd suddenly pretend he got beeped and had an emergency at the hospital.

*They're still in Queens, and in fact, when you propose marriage, my dad will throw us a wedding at the Plaza Hotel. He said he would if he could, honest.*

"I lost my parents," I said, staring at my sangria glass. I didn't know where to look. I tried to envision the expression on my face and hoped it wasn't too unnatural.

I felt his gaze on me. "I'm so sorry," he said. "I can't begin to imagine how hard that must be. How old were you? How did it happen?"

I looked up at Timothy Rommely and fell in love.

Timothy Rommely had a deep, real laugh, the kind of laugh that told you he really found funny what you just said. I'd been telling him about Posh and my job, and I'd gotten up to Morgan Morgan. He hadn't gotten past her name.

"There's a Morgan Morgan with a similar name and attitude in every job," Timothy said, that dimple taunting me. "I've got one on my rotation—Phillip Phillips the third. He actually has the stupid roman numerals on his hospital ID."

The waiter appeared with dinner. Timothy had ordered the mahi-mahi, and I'd ordered the grilled salmon. He forked a piece of mahi-mahi and reached across the table with it to my lips. "Ladies, first."

He'd surprised me. My lips parted and he slid the mahi-mahi into my mouth. His eyes were on my lips. My eyes were on *his* lips. "Mmm," I murmured. "That is so good."

I forked a piece of salmon and held it up to his lips.

"Ladies first," he reminded me, flashing that dimple.

His expression darkened just slightly as he watched me slip the salmon into my mouth. I closed my eyes for a second, savoring the perfect flavor and texture. "Incredible."

And then we dug in, eating, drinking, talking, laughing, sharing bites. Timothy Rommely had graduated—barely—from Princeton. He'd been premed, but he'd really wanted to be a rock star, well, a star rock bassist. His band had been named Anatomy; all the guys were premed and headed for different medical schools, so Anatomy had broken up. He'd gone to med school in New England, and now was doing his residency at New York Hospital, which was on the Upper East Side.

"I've got my own personal William—" He paused. "What was his last name, again. Something funny…"

"Remke," I said.

He snapped his fingers and laughed. "William Remke. That's it. The William Remke of New York Hospital is an Attending named Mark Lashman. Intimidates the hell out of everyone. Yesterday, one of my fellow residents got his head bitten off for asking a question thirty seconds before he was allowed to."

"How did you know you wanted to be a doctor?" I asked him, sipping one of the best glasses of red wine I'd ever had. "Was it because of Sardine?" Timothy had told me that his only personal experience with loss had been the death of his beloved dog, a Border collie named Sardine. He'd had the dog since he was three years old, a Christmas present from his parents. He and his older brother had been at summer camp in the Catskills when Sardine had been hit by a car. Timothy was fourteen, his brother twelve. They'd been summoned to the camp office in the middle of a regular, average day, in the middle of lunch, which meant that something bad had happened. His parents had driven up to tell the boys about Sardine face-to-face.

Timothy nodded. "You're probably wondering why I didn't become a vet. That had always been the plan, actually. But when my brother heard about Sardine, he ran off into the woods, and no one could get him to talk for two weeks. It was really weird. We had to leave camp. After that, I'd planned to become a psychiatrist, but when

I started my internship, I found myself more interested in internal medicine. So here I am.''

Here he was indeed. ''So what made your brother start talking?'' I asked, spooning the tastiest, softest rice I'd ever had into my mouth.

Timothy smiled. ''My dad promised my brother and me he'd help us build a tree house with separate small rooms for the both of us. That was going to be our summer project. And we built it, but we forgot to leave an opening for the doors. My brother was the one who'd told us there was no way to get in. He hasn't shut up since.''

I laughed, and so did Timothy. We smiled at each other. I suddenly wanted to tell him everything, about my last day with my father, about the Plaza and the ballroom and my wedding and the guy I was supposed to find. But I couldn't. *That* you didn't tell a guy no matter how connected you felt to him.

''Dessert?'' asked the waitress as she wheeled a cart piled high with the most exquisite sugary creations I'd ever seen.

Timothy leaned close. ''I know an amazing dessert place in the Village.''

Our date was going on its third round. Drinks, then dinner and now dessert. And perhaps afterward, a long walk. I couldn't imagine leaving Timothy's company. At the end of the night, when it was time to say goodbye, someone was going to have pry me away with a crowbar. Or pinch me. Because this had to be dream.

As Timothy and I walked north along the East River promenade, even the ugly Triborough Bridge managed to appear romantic. The Roosevelt Island tram was swinging its way high above our heads toward the little island between us and Queens. We moved out of the way of a pack of nighttime joggers wearing reflective socks. A few couples walked slowly in each direction.

And now I was one of them. I was one of the couples that I used to look wistfully at, wishing I could be walking hand in hand down the street, down the promenade, in the park, wherever.

Timothy and I weren't holding hands, of course. Not yet, anyway. I suddenly wished I had telepathy. I wanted to know what he was thinking—of me, of our date, of whether he wanted to see me again.

The couple in front of us had lit cigarettes; we were hit full in the face with the heavy stink of exhaled smoke. Timothy grimaced and waved it away. All I could do was smile. I wasn't a smoker. Not anymore. And not once had I twitched tonight.

"I asked Jeff if you smoked," Timothy said. "But he told me he wasn't sure. I usually wouldn't go on a blind date unless I knew for sure the woman wasn't a smoker, but something about the way he described you made me think there was something there. Something, I don't know…"

I wanted to finish his sentence. Something *special*. I hadn't been a special anything to anyone since the days when Max Reardon had still loved me.

And I wouldn't be anything to Timothy had Jeff been either unkind enough or aware enough to recall that I smoked. Or used to. Last night's decision to quit might very well get me much, much more than a date to a wedding.

"So this is you, right?" he asked as we neared the steps leading up to the 81st Street crossover.

I nodded. How had we gotten here so fast? It wasn't time for this date to end. It would never be time. But it was two o'clock in the morning.

"Are you free Tuesday night?" Timothy asked. "If you want to see me again, that is," he added, the dimple flashing.

I felt like doing cartwheels. "Tuesday?" I repeated, pretending to mentally consult my datebook. "Yes. I'm definitely free."

That was actually a lie. Blind Date #5, the very last one, was scheduled for Tuesday. Driscoll Something. But he could be unscheduled. Pronto.

"Tuesday, it is, then," he confirmed. He reached out his hand and I slipped mine into his. His hand was soft and warm and big, his fingers strong and steady as a doctor's should be.

We stood on the concrete overpass between the East River and East End Avenue, the FDR Drive and its nonstop traffic whizzing directly underneath us. Timothy looked at me. And then, ever so slowly, he tilted his face and kissed me, in front of everyone who was driving south. Then he took my hand and we walked across East End Avenue to my apartment building. And with one more warm, sweet kiss, Timothy Rommely was gone, speeding away in a yellow taxi.

"Ooooh! Oh yeah! More, more! Yeah, Ooooooh!"

As Opera man gave it to his *Oh* Moaner, I envisioned taking a shower with Timothy Rommely. Envisioned his thick, dark hair wet against his head, his golden chest glistening and soapy, his—

"Harder. Harder! Oooh! Yeaahhhhhhh!"

I stretched out, my hands behind my neck and strained to hear Opera Man's girlfriend over the opera.

*"Ooh! Yeah! Yeah!"*

The phone rang and I snatched it. It had to be Eloise. Or maybe it was Gnatasha. I wouldn't put it past her to call this late. She probably wanted to let me know she'd be five minutes early for our meeting on Monday morning to go over her revisions.

Nope. It was Eloise. "How'd it go?"

"I'm in love," I breathed into the receiver.

"Tell me everything!" Eloise said. "Serge is sleeping, and I'm wide-awake."

Opera Man turned up the volume, then lowered it a few minutes later. He always blasted the music just when the Oh Moaner was about to reach orgasm. I wasn't sure if he did it so that no one would hear (as if I couldn't hear everything leading up to it) or if it turned her or him on further.

Starting with the sangria and ending with the kiss in front of all those witnesses driving by on the FDR, I explained why I was in love with a guy I'd met eight hours earlier.

"Wow," Eloise said. "Wow!"

"Yeah," I agreed. "Wow."

"Don't forget to call Driscoll and cancel Tuesday's blind date," she reminded me.

I couldn't wait. That would be the happiest phone call of my life.

"Oh, I almost forgot!" Eloise said. "Guess what I signed us up for today? A SmokeNoMore session at the Learn It Center."

"You're kidding," I said. "How much?"

"Sixty bucks," Eloise said. "But if you don't quit, you can come back for free, so it seems worth it." Eloise then confessed that she'd ripped off the patch last night and smoked an entire pack of cigarettes by three o'clock today, mostly out of guilt that she was smoking. "It's Monday night at six-thirty in our neighborhood. I'm gonna smoke my heart out till then, then quit on Tuesday."

"El, you don't have to, just because I am. You have to really want it."

She laughed. "You don't really want it."

That wasn't true, not anymore. I hadn't realized it until now. For the first time, I wanted something more than I wanted to smoke. "I want the guy, though. Who cares what the motivation is, El? Whatever gets you where you're supposed to be, right?"

"I guess," she said. "Well, I'll quit in the name of solidarity."

"I love you, Eloise."

"I love you, too."

For the first time in five years, I drifted off to sleep fantasizing about a real possibility as the Oh Moaner moaned. Not Max, who I couldn't have. Not Jeremy, who I'd never have. Timothy. Someone who I *could* have. Someone to whom *I* could be the main thing.

## Nine

The Learn It Center was housed in an ugly junior high school on 92nd Street, off Lexington Avenue. The one and only SmokeNoMore session was in Room 214. Eloise and I sat down in the second row. Twenty people or so were dotted around the room. Everyone looked miserable.

"If I gain weight, forget it." This from a very thin, gorgeous blonde.

"You might as well be fat if you have lung cancer." That from the jealous chubby next to her.

"My dad's giving me a thousand bucks if I quit for a month." Teenager.

"I asked my six-year-old what he wanted for his birthday, and he said, 'Mommy, I only want you to stop smoking.'" Mommy.

"Who can afford to smoke? They're, like, $4.75 a pack!" Britney Spears look-alike.

*I'm quitting so I can score a date to a wedding with*

*the guy of my dreams.* I wasn't offering that tidbit. I'd prefer to wax health conscious and talk about the effects of tar on the delicate cilia of one's lungs.

Eloise was fidgeting in the uncomfortable little chair-desk combination that we were forced to sit in. She was quiet. She hadn't said much on the subway ride up to the Learn It Center. I figured she was nervous. I'd smoked more than she did, but giving up cigarettes when your boyfriend smoked like the clichéd chimney was a major nightmare.

"I wonder why the Gnat missed our meeting this morning," I said to Eloise for the third time today. "I just don't get it. It's so uncharacteristic of her. I left her three messages today, and she never called me back."

Eloise gave me the I'm-not-really-listening smile and continued fidgeting.

Why hadn't Natasha shown up for the meeting? Or called? She herself had arranged the ten o'clock meeting with me days ago, then confirmed it with me on the phone yesterday—at home, of course. I'd been in the middle of a very important brainstorming session with myself over which name I'd go by if I married Timothy: Jane Rommely. Jane Gregg Rommely. Jane G. Rommely. Jane Gregg-Rommely. Jane Greggely.

Morgan, who'd ordered the Continental breakfast for this morning's meeting, had buzzed me every twenty minutes to ask if she should put the butter for the bagels in the little refrigerator in the kitchen. I'd heard the usual triumph in Morgan's voice, the *you're toast* glee. If Natasha started missing meetings, Remke and Jeremy would pull me from the project. I'd never get promoted.

"Hello everybody!" A thin woman wearing a ton of chunky jewelry and carrying a bunch of pamphlets strolled to the small metal desk at the front of the class.

"I'm Dinah, and welcome to SmokeNoMore!" She put her hands on her hips. "Okay, I'll cut the crap. None of you is happy to be here. In fact, you all probably got here kicking and screaming. You're dreading even the thought of quitting smoking."

A lot of nods, laughs, and one "You got that right, sister."

"Well, I'm here to tell you," Dinah went on, "that quitting smoking *does* suck. It sucks as bad as you imagine it does. But—" she held up a hand "—quitting doesn't suck as much as smoking does. And it's not impossible. You can do it. I did it, and so did countless other addicted smokers. I didn't gain twenty pounds. I didn't murder my mother-in-law. I didn't burst into tears at my job. Okay, maybe once or twice. But I'll tell you what did happen when I quit. I gained self-respect, whiter teeth and about two thousand bucks in savings. I have been smoke free for two years, eight months and four days."

Everyone clapped.

Eloise burst into tears.

I put my hand on her arm. "El? It'll be okay. We're doing it together."

As Dinah began handing out the pamphlets, Eloise covered her face with her hands. And that was when I noticed the teeny, tiny diamond ring sparkling on the third finger of her left hand.

My mouth fell open. "El? What's that on your finger? It looks suspiciously like an engagement ring."

"It is," she whispered, and then burst into tears again.

"Wow, you must really be a heavy smoker," said the redhead sitting to Eloise's left. "I only smoke a pack a day and I'm sort of excited about quitting. It'll be okay, hon."

Eloise fled the room. Dinah gnawed her lower lip.

"I'm sorry," the redhead said to me. "I didn't mean to upset her even more."

"The poor dear," Dinah murmured, her expression full of empathy. "Class, excuse me one moment. We have a very nervous quitter apparently—"

I shot up and grabbed our pamphlets. "Oh, um, no, Dinah, she's nervous about something else. I'll go talk to her."

Dinah nodded. She held up a ten-by-twelve glossy of a blackened lung. "Who knows how many cigarettes it took to turn this once-pink-and-healthy lung into this cancer-waiting-to-happen? Huh? Who can tell me? Anyone?"

I slipped out the door and found Eloise slumped down against a locker, her hands still covering her face, the tiny diamond gleaming against the cool metal gray of the locker.

I slid down onto my butt next to her. "So I guess congratulations aren't in order?"

She dropped her hands. "I'm happy, I really am." She turned her tearstained face to me. "I'm just nervous, I guess. Being engaged, getting married. It's just so overwhelming."

Yeah, especially when you: A) didn't want to get married and B) didn't love the guy.

"Eloise, I don't understand. You don't even want Serge staying over too often during the week. Now you want to spend every night with him? For the rest of your life?"

She stared at the diamond. "I love him, Jane. I really do. Serge is a great guy. He's sweet, he loves me to death, he's fun, he'll be a good father." She burst into tears, the hands flying up to her face.

"And you're crying because…?"

She dropped her hands and wiped her eyes. "I don't know. I'm just nervous. Overwhelmed."

"El? Can I be honest with you?"

She nodded and pulled a tissue out of her purse.

"I think you're crying because you said *yes* when you mean *no.*"

"That's not true," she insisted. "I did mean yes. I'm engaged. That's something to be really happy about."

"It is, yes. But do you want to marry Serge?"

Eloise leaned her head back against the locker. "He proposed, Jane. He told me he loved me more than anything in the world. And I know he does. He treats me like I'm a princess. Not one guy I've ever been with has treated me even close to how Serge does. He makes me feel like I'm the greatest thing since fat-free cookies."

"Yeah, but do you want to marry him?"

"What I want, Jane, is to go home, okay?" Eloise stood. "Go back inside. I'll be fine."

I stood up too. "Let's go get something to eat. I'm starving."

"'Kay," Eloise said in a shaky voice, staring at the dirty gray floor.

I put my arm around her and led her past the long display case of sports trophies against the pale green cinder-block wall.

Eloise needed an EngagedNoMore seminar. And I, the person least qualified to teach it, was all she had at the moment.


"I'll have a bacon and American cheese omelette with a toasted bagel, just a little cream cheese, and a Coke," I told the waitress at the Comfort Diner.

"I'll just have dry toast and a chamomile tea," Eloise said.

"That's all you want?" I asked her.

"I don't even think I can eat that much," she replied.

The waitress put her little pencil behind her ear and left; a busboy plunked two glasses of ice water on our table.

"So when did this happen?" I asked. "And why didn't you tell me?"

"Saturday night."

"El—we talked on the phone Saturday night! I told you all about my date with Timothy, and you never mentioned it. You didn't mention it last night either."

Eloise gnawed her lip. "I just wanted to sit with it for a while, you know, get used to it myself before I told anyone."

"What did your grandmother say?" I asked her.

Eloise sipped her water. The waitress delivered our drinks.

"El?"

"I haven't told her."

Of course she didn't tell her grandmother. Because she herself couldn't believe it was true. "So tell me about his proposal," I said. I had to tread lightly here, I knew. If I started squawking at her, she'd run out. What Eloise needed was support, someone to talk to, someone she could be honest with who wouldn't judge her. Then she'd see that she couldn't marry Serge.

"He came over to make me dinner, an American feast. He learned how to make meat loaf, mashed potatoes and apple pie in his citizen class. So he made me dinner, and then he wanted to go for a hansom cab ride in Central Park, so we did, and we were just going past Tavern on the Green when he took my hand, told me he loved me more than the world itself and asked me to be his wife. Jane, it was like a dream. It was everything I'd ever wanted to hear. And in that moment, I realized that it was everything I wanted. I do love Serge. I do. And I said yes. I didn't even hesitate, Jane. That's how I know I really want to marry him.''

The waitress slid our food on the table. I didn't know what to make of what Eloise had just said. Who was I to tell her how she felt? No one had ever proposed marriage to me. How did I know how that felt? Or what went through a woman's mind? Who I was to tell Eloise that she didn't love Serge? If she said she did, maybe she did.

She burst into tears. The diamond twinkled over her eye.

But she didn't. She didn't love Serge. And she didn't want to marry him. We both knew it.

"I'm engaged, Jane. I want to be engaged. I want to be getting married. And Serge is a great guy. No one else is ever gonna love me the way he does. No one."

I forked a cheesy bite of omelette into my mouth. "You don't know that, Eloise. That's like saying if you don't marry Serge, you'll never marry anyone."

"I'm thirty years old," she snapped. "I haven't married anyone yet. By the time I meet someone else, go through a relationship and he proposes, I'll be who knows how old. Thirty-two? Thirty-five? No thank you. Who needs that kind of embarrassment or pressure to find somebody."

"Eloise…"

"I love him, Jane. If I didn't, I wouldn't have said yes. I want to get married."

Did she realize that she kept saying *I want to get married* but that she never once said *I want to marry him?* I believed that Eloise loved Serge—the way you loved a dear friend. But she didn't love him the way you loved the man you wanted to marry.

"Do you love Serge the way you loved Michael?"

"That's totally different," Eloise said, biting off a piece of toast. "I was twenty-five and stupid. And everyone knows romantic love isn't the same as love-love. Every woman goes through a Michael who breaks her heart. You did with Max, Amanda did with Gary from college. You don't marry those guys. You don't marry the ones you're madly in love with. You marry the guy who's gonna love you, the guy you don't have to worry about, the guy who'll make you feel safe and secure. You know what I'm talking about, Jane."

*Who cares what the motivation is if it gets you where you're supposed to be....*

I did know what she was talking about. I knew very well. But it still sounded wrong. It *was* wrong. Wasn't it?

"Serge is a great guy. And I'm ready to settle down. End of story. Be happy for me, okay?"

I would be. I really would. If only *settle* weren't the key word.

"Morgan, I'm just saying that the revision letter is a little harsh. A few words of praise for the guy's style would go a long way—"

"Well, I thought his style staaank," Morgan said.

"So why are you asking him to revise his memoir?" I asked, losing patience with Horse Face. I had a lot of work to do this afternoon, and Morgan had taken up way too much of my Tuesday as it was. I'd spent the entire morning reading over her rejection and revision letters and making very thorough and thoughtful comments. Fifteen minutes after I'd returned the stack to her, she'd trotted into my office, more defensive than usual.

"The guy has dyslexia, Jaaane. That's what his memoir is about. I'm not going to lie and tell him he can write when he can't. That doesn't mean the memoir itself wasn't moving and worthy of being published. But he has to work harder or make it 'told to.'''

"Morgan—"

"Look, don't tell me like you know, Jaaane. I grew up with a learning disa—" Morgan clamped her mouth shut. I could see the pink tinges coloring her cheeks, and the anger in her eyes. She hadn't caught herself in time.

"Morgan, there's nothing wrong with—"

"I don't need your words of wisdom, Jaaane. All I care about is that you keep that to yourself."

Sympathy hit me in the stomach. Morgan had grown up with a learning disability and had clearly overcompensated with her attitude her entire life. I pictured her as a little kid getting picked on and teased by mean kids in her class. Teachers and parents constantly looking at her with concern. You had to develop a thick skin to deal with a learning disability. That was all Morgan's insecurity and bitchiness was: self-protection. Didn't I know a thing or two about that very subject? "Morgan, you can trust me."

"Yes, I know I can, Jaaane." She leaned back and toyed with her pearl necklace. "Because if I can't, you just might find something very embarrassing revealed about yourself."

What was this, high school? "Like what?" I asked through clenched teeth.

"Like that you're in love with Jeremy Black. I'm sure he and everyone else would find that just adorable—and more than a little pathetic."

This wasn't high school. This was a soap opera. "First of all, Morgan, you're dead wrong. I most certainly do not have feelings for Jeremy. And second of all, I have a boyfriend." Well, I almost had a boyfriend. I had a second date tonight with the guy who was sure to become my boyfriend.

"Whatever," Morgan said. "That doesn't mean you don't drool over Jeremy. I've seen you stare at him like you're in love. You can't even look him in the eye. It's so obvious."

"Well, if it's so *obvious,* then I guess everyone already knows about my supposed love for Jeremy. So I don't have anything to worry about, now do I?" That comeback was an A+. It was the kind of thing you usually could only wish you'd said when you were kicking yourself late at night, torturing yourself over how you lost the conversational war.

"Oh, I think you do," Morgan said. "I think Williaaam would get a big kick out of it. Gwen too. Plus all the guys in production. They might even feel sorry for you. Take your high-profile project away. After all, who could expect you to concentrate on your work when you're suffering from unrequited love for your supervisor's supervisor?"

I'd have to think of a snappy comeback to that one when I was torturing myself tonight instead of sleeping. Was she kidding with this stuff?

She was kidding, right?

"If you're discreet about me, I'll be discreet about you." And with that, Morgan snatched her letter from my hand and galloped out of my office.

Jeremy's face floated into my mind, his sooty lashes blinking over his Caribbean eyes in the usual slow motion. I hadn't thought about him in days. I'd been fantasizing daily about Jeremy Black for five years, ever since Max and I broke up. Yet two and a half days had passed without the thought of his lips and fingers passing once through my mind. The only guy I could think about was Timothy.

Ha. Morgan was too late. My drooling days were over. I didn't have anything to worry about. If I didn't have so much to do, I'd go tell her too.

I checked my e-mail, hoping the Gnat had dashed me off a message explaining herself for blowing me off yesterday and not returning my phone calls. Her revised version of Chapter One was good, but it still needed a few tweaks before I could condense it for the *Marie Claire* excerpt. This just figured. The Gnat was nowhere to be found at exactly the moment I needed her to harass me with her voice and presence. She hadn't returned my phone calls from yesterday or today. And Jeremy expected the excerpt, polished and perfect, on his desk Friday morning.

No e-mails from the Gnat. There was one from Eloise though. *Don't worry about me okay? I'm really, really, really happy. —E*

That was three *really*s too many for a declaration of happiness. Eloise had looked anything but happy as we walked home from the diner last night. And she'd looked anything but happy as we rode the M31 bus to work this morning. Eloise had spent the ride staring at her diamond and staring out the window. She'd asked me not to mention the engagement to Amanda before Friday; she wanted to tell her in person at the Flirt Night Roundtable.

I punched Natasha's telephone number into my phone; her voice mail floated over the speaker. "Hi, it's Natasha! So sorry I missed your call. Leave a message at the beep. Bye!" I left message number five. Where was she? What was she doing that she couldn't return repeated phone calls from her Very Important Editor? Maybe Mr. Houseboat had flown in early from "the Coast." Maybe they

were having sex all over New York City. Like under the
low-sweeping trees in the Shakespeare Garden in Central
Park, or in the elevators in Bloomingdale's or in the back
of a taxi. Or—

"So did Natasha explain why she didn't show up yesterday?"

I turned to find Jeremy filling up the doorway to my
office, a thick manuscript against his chest.

"Morgan mentioned you're having trouble reaching
her," he added.

That little bitch. So this was her way of letting me
know she meant business.

"Oh, um, I've spoken to Natasha," I said to the light
switch. Maybe I did have something to worry about. I
still couldn't look Jeremy in the eye, new guy to obsess
over or not. "Everything's fine. She got so into writing
that she lost track of time and didn't want to be interrupted from the creative process. Celebrities!"

Jeremy nodded in slow motion. "Well, they pay the
bills," he agreed ever so good-naturedly. "Glad things
are going well, Jane. I'll have the excerpt Friday morning,
right?"

"You bet."

I waited until I heard Jeremy start arguing down the
hall with Paulette before I punched the Gnat's number
into my phone again. "Hi, Natasha, it's Jane Gregg again.
I just wanted to make sure I got across how urgent it is
that you call me back. Hope everything's okay."

*Could* something be wrong? Had she nicked herself
shaving and headed straight for her plastic surgeon's office in Beverly Hills? Was she under the knife right now?

Cavalier, huh? That was because I knew exactly what
Gnatasha Nutley was doing instead of calling me back
and showing up for meetings and tweaking Chapter One

and making an associate editor of me. Besides screwing a delivery boy or buying out Manolo Blahniks at Barney's or meditating, the Gnat was busy making me feel like the invisible Jane Gregg again.

## Ten

My cute outfit from Banana Republic—pale pink structured shell and pale gray bootleg pants—was absorbing the odor of Indian food as Timothy and I walked down East 6th Street, aka Little India. At least my jacket was spared from smelling like curry. Once again, I'd left it draped over my chair at work in the name of showing a little skin. My sleeveless top was corporate cut, meaning: boat neck. Which ensured no comments could possibly be forthcoming from dates, children or mothers.

Eloise had called in sick today (Mental Health Day, actually), so she hadn't been around to help me get ready for big date *numero dos*. I'd tried to reach her a few times to make sure she was okay, in the Serge sense, but either I hadn't made it past Screening or she was out, wandering the East River promenade and staring out at the ugly water. Whenever Eloise disappeared, it meant she was thinking and wanted to do it alone.

Timothy's presence was so strong. For a second I fantasized that we were married and on our way to dinner with friends or relatives or in-laws. Jane Greggely. The name filled my head and repeated itself over and over. Was my subconscious trying to tell me something? That Timothy Rommely was going to be important in my life? That he—including his name—was my other half?

Okay, okay. I was getting a little ahead of myself. Per every article, book or piece of advice anyone had ever given me, you were supposed to "just have fun," "enjoy yourself," "take it one date and day at a time." *Please.* Anyone who ever went on a date with a guy as perfect as Timothy Rommely imagined herself married to him. Perhaps that was why I never fantasized being married to Jeremy. There was no chance of a date.

"Mmm…" Timothy murmured as he took a deep breath with his face pointed upward. "Does that smell amazing or what?" He'd told me on the phone earlier today that he loved Indian food, loved the tiny, dark, ridiculously cheap restaurants that were crammed into every nook and cranny on the block between First and Second Avenues. There had to be twenty on the south side of the street alone. According to lore, the restaurants supposedly shared one kitchen. "This is the one," Timothy said. "Little Bombay. It's supposed to have the best tandoori in New York."

Three smiling waiters hovered the moment we entered. The long, narrow restaurant was crowded, despite all the others to choose from on the block. Strands and strands of multicolored lights adorned the walls and ceilings, as though it were Christmas. An elderly man in a white robe with gold tassels sat cross-legged on a platform in front of the picture window, playing a sitar. Everywhere were couples. Talking, laughing, sharing exotic food, sharing themselves. How good it felt to be one of them.

Timothy and I spent longer choosing our feast than we probably would spend devouring it. Vegetable samosas, potato-and-peas-stuffed bread, tandoori chicken, Biryani rice, lamb tikka, spinach and cheese in a mysterious sauce. And Indian beer. I loved Indian food, which was another *me too* for Timothy. An ex-boyfriend of Eloise's had introduced me to Indian cuisine. It was as though all the bland chicken and boiled vegetables I'd grown up eating had run away from home and gotten a life. I'd never known that food could taste that way. When I ate Indian food, I felt as though I were somewhere exotic and interesting instead of New York City on the Entry-Level Salary Plan. Once I'd tried to convince Aunt Ina to try Indian. She told me she was too old for that kind of nonsense.

The waiter set down a plate of flat, crisp bread and three shallow bowls of different sauces, then poured Taj Mahal beer into two frosty, tall glasses. Timothy lifted his glass and looked me in the eye. "A toast. To the beginning of something good."

I clinked, and we smiled the same happy, shy smile. A smile that said there would be a third date. A smile that told me I might be able to ask Timothy to attend Dana's wedding with me. My heart moved in my chest. *Please, please, please,* I prayed. *Let this work out. Let me have this. Let this guy sit next to me at Dana's wedding. Let him discuss the latest surgical technologies with the Houseboat Dweller, who'll be fascinated. Let Natasha eye Timothy appreciatively and whisper, "You really did good, Janey." Let me dance with Timothy to every slow song in the mini-ballroom of the Plaza Hotel, his dark eyes only on me.*

"So how was work today?" Timothy asked.

He had no idea how much that banal question meant to me. Max had hated that question. He'd thought it was meaningless small talk, that no one really cared how someone's day was, and you couldn't really "get it" anyway, since you weren't there. Max hadn't understood the concept of commiseration. Or of having someone to ask in the first place. I hated remembering that Max Reardon wasn't Mr. Perfection. He'd become exactly that the moment he'd dumped me. And whenever something reminded me that he had some annoying spots, I'd get irritated.

"A little weird, actually," I said, sipping the strong beer. "My star writer is missing."

Timothy raised one perfect dark eyebrow. "Missing?"

"She arranged a meeting with me yesterday morning and never showed up," I explained. "I've called her five or six times between yesterday and today, and she hasn't called me back. She knows we're on deadline."

"Do you think she's okay?" he asked. "Maybe something happened."

"Nah, no chance," I said. "She leads a charmed life. Nothing bad happens to people like her."

Timothy dipped a piece of flatbread into the spiciest of the sauces. "I know the type. I have a cousin like that. He looks like Brad Pitt, graduated summa cum laude from Harvard, made his first million on the stock market and he's not even thirty yet."

I laughed. "I have a cousin like that, too. She has a closet full of Chanel and she's getting married at the Plaza Hotel in two months. Her fiancé made his first million on the Internet."

"Another *me too,*" Timothy said. "How many has that been for us?"

I was smiling so hard I thought my face would burst. "At least fifty."

"And this is only our second date. By the end of the third, there'll be hundreds. Unless I'm *presuming* there'll be a third date." Charming. Very charming.

*Ba-boom, ba-boom, ba-boom* went my heart in my chest. Really fast. "I hope there will be," I barely managed to whisper.

"Well there's our fifty-first *me too,*" was Timothy's perfect response. "You know, Jane, I'm surprised you yourself don't have a fiancé making millions on the Internet."

"Me? Why?"

"Are you fishing for compliments?" he asked, dimples popping.

Huh? My face must have registered my complete innocence because he laughed.

"Wow. You're not exactly a diva, are you?"

The Gnat came to mind. "I wish. Just for twenty minutes I'd like to know what it feels like to look like a supermodel and say and do whatever I want. Have everyone fawn all over me."

"I'll bet it's not as great as it sounds," Timothy said, leaning back. "A famous rock star ended up in the emergency room at the hospital last week. He'd swallowed around seventy sleeping pills. Everything he had wasn't enough to make him feel okay to even be alive. That's bad. Real bad."

Two waiters wheeled a cart full of steaming shallow silver pots in front of our table. Our plates heaped with the most aromatic, colorful food I'd ever seen, Timothy and I dug in.

"So I was serious, by the way," Timothy said, his fork

poised halfway to his mouth. "I'm really surprised someone hasn't snatched you up."

I felt my cheeks turn pink. I was glad I could blame it on how spicy the food was. I wasn't exactly used to compliments. Especially not from someone who made funny things happen to my stomach. I wanted to kiss him so bad. For one long kiss from Timothy, I would gladly lean across the table and stain my eighty-seven-dollar Banana Republic structured shell with lamb tikka and creamed spinach in cheese sauce.

"I did have a serious boyfriend, but it ended a few years ago."

Timothy cut a piece of stuffed bread for both of us. "Broke his heart, huh?"

"Other way around," I said, staring at a raisin in my Biryani rice.

"Fool," he said with a smile.

Wasn't it amazing that you could actually feel your eyes twinkle?

"So what about you?" I asked. "An available good-looking doctor? Unheard-of."

"I've had a few serious relationships," Timothy said as the waiter refilled our water glasses, "but nothing worked out. Moving to Rhode Island for med school killed a serious college romance, and then med school itself killed another one, and since I've been a resident, I haven't had a girlfriend. I'd need someone who's just as busy as I am, someone totally dedicated to her career. Like you. Jeff told me you're known for working around the clock."

I sent Amanda a silent thank-you over the airwaves. "You have to, if you want to get anywhere. I'm dying to get promoted. This project I'm working on now—the one the missing writer *isn't* writing at the moment—everything's riding on it. Everything.''

''Like what?'' he asked, spooning spinach from the pot onto his rice.

''Like a raise. Like a more impressive title. Like recognition for the six years I've been working my butt off. Associate editor means you're out of the assistant trap. I can't wait to get that word out of my life.''

''Does that mean you won't *assist* me in finishing the chicken tikka?'' Timothy asked, waving a fork-speared piece of red chicken in front of my lips.

This had to be a dream. Like on that old TV show *Dallas* that my mom and Aunt Ina had been addicted to. Any second I'd wake up and smell the chicken tikka and realize that perfect guys and perfect dates didn't exist for me. But unless this was a very long dream, an hour and a half had passed since Timothy had picked me up in front of Posh. And he and I were still here.

''No. No. And no. But thank you,'' Timothy told me as he handed the concession clerk at the Union Square movie theater a ten-dollar bill for the Value-Combo: a huge bucket of popcorn and the biggest plastic container of Pepsi I'd ever seen in my life. His change was a quarter.

He'd refused to let me contribute to the check at Little Bombay or for the movie tickets or popcorn and soda. Aunt Ina would like that. So would Dana. I'd never admit it, but secretly I was more than a little pleased at his respect for the traditional date. According to polls in *Mademoiselle* and *Glamour,* only slightly more than half the women under thirty-five expected the guy to pay for at least the first date. The whole subject made me feel queasy. In this day and age of paternity leave and women

CEOs of Fortune 500 corporations, the idea that a guy *should* pay for dates was bizarre. So why was "Did he pay?" so many women's first question after a date?

Bucket of popcorn in my arms, tub of Pepsi in Timothy's, we waited in the ticket holders' line inside the huge, multilevel movie theater. I couldn't help but notice how perfect we were for each other height-wise. With one effortless tilt of my head I could lean it on his shoulder. Timothy and I had agreed on a movie in twelve seconds flat. Turned out we were *me too* over Arnold Schwarzenegger also.

"I'm so sick of this!" hissed the young woman in front of us.

The tall guy in the backward baseball cap standing next to her peered around with an embarrassed look on his face. "Debbie, this isn't the time or the—"

"Oh, really?" Debbie snapped, her hands on her hips. "What *is* the time or the place? It's never the time or the place with you, Rob."

Timothy and I looked at each other and smiled. A couples fight in line was more entertaining than any movie could ever be.

"Debbie, can we just see a movie and enjoy ourselves?" Rob asked with the same weariness I often heard in my uncle Charlie's voice.

"No, we cannot," Debbie replied, crossing her arms over her chest. "I want an answer now. Are we moving in together or not?"

Rob turned red. Timothy and I both glanced down at the floor. Suddenly our front-row seats to Debbie and Rob's intimate fight were a little too close. This was getting serious.

"Deb, we're in a movie theater! Gimme a break."

"I'll give her to five," I whispered to Timothy. He looked at me quizzically. "One, two, three—"

Debbie fled on three. Rob glanced after her, rolled his eyes, shook his head and dug into his popcorn. I could hear him crunching.

"You're not going after her?" asked the woman behind Timothy and me. Timothy and I both turned around. The young woman, around twenty-two or twenty-three, stepped out of line so she could glare at Rob, who was now staring at her as though she'd beamed down from Planet Freak. "I can't believe you."

"Do I know you?" Rob bit out. "Mind your own business." He turned back around and continued crunching his popcorn.

Business-minder made a sound I often heard pass Aunt Ina's lips, then she slipped back into line. Rob made a similar sound and stomped out, leaving a popcorn trail. I turned around and shot Business-minder a good-job smile.

"Guys are such assholes," Business-minder said. I whipped back around and stared at my feet.

"Not all of us," Timothy said, looking at me.

I grinned at him, and we moved up to fill the gap that Debbie and Rob had made. I was about to say something clever, but the loud woman now in front of us beat me to it.

"Arnold Schwarzenegger is so eighties," insisted the woman. "He's, like, fifty years old or something. He's totally over."

"He is not," said her male companion. "Arnold is age-less."

"Like men and women and relationships," Timothy whispered to me.

Okay. This had to be it. Was Aunt Ina going to pop out of line and pinch me? Would I wake up in my bed alone at any minute to the squeaks and *oh*s of Opera Man? Or was I really here, on this date with the most perfect human being alive?

The line shuffled forward; the woman behind me bumped into me. That was as good as a pinch. I was still here.

Timothy and I beelined for center seats, dead in the middle of the theater. "Compatible movie-seat preferences," Timothy said. "That's a biggie." He waved a piece of popcorn in front of my mouth and smiled at me.

I opened my mouth. Timothy pulled back the popcorn and kissed me.

"Are you guys gonna make out all night?" demanded a grumpy-voiced older woman behind us. "I can't see over his head."

Timothy and I both turned around. Grumpy was the only person sitting in her row. "Yes, ma'am," Timothy said, dimples popping everywhere. "We are going to make out all night."

The woman smacked her lips and made a noisy show of moving exactly one seat over to the left.

"You're not going to make a liar out of me, are you?" Timothy whispered to me just before the theater lights dimmed. He slid lower in his seat, took my hand in his and looked at me.

My heart pinged in my chest and I slid lower, too, unable to take my eyes off his face. I was too overwhelmed to shake my head or utter a no, so I puckered up instead. And through the annoying reminders in Dolby digital sound not to talk, litter or smoke in the theater, Timothy Rommely and I made out.

*Buzzzzzz!*

Was that Timothy, come back to say he couldn't bear

to be away from me? Given how great tonight had gone, that fantasy wasn't entirely out of the question. But I had a feeling my midnight buzzer was one of the tenants who'd lost the downstairs door key or someone's boyfriend trying to get into the building. I ignored it, figuring they'd buzz everyone else.

I pulled the blanket over my head and flipped onto my stomach, eyes closed. I traced my lips with my finger. I could still feel Timothy's good-night kiss. Kisses, I should amend. Two whoppers. In between whoppers, he'd asked me out for Saturday night. *Saturday night.* When a guy asked you out for Saturday night, especially when it coincided with the all-important third date, you knew you were headed somewhere.

*Buzzzz!!*

I threw off the comforter and stomped to the intercom by the door. "What!" I snapped.

"Jane? It's me, Natasha."

*Natasha?*

I buzzed her in. What was she doing here? It was twelve-thirty a.m. on a weeknight. She had so much nerve! First she disappeared for two days, then she woke me up in the middle of a perfectly good dream to—to what? What could she possibly want? I took inventory of the mess in the room and straightened up as best I could. I didn't want her here. What would she think of my pathetic little studio? At least she was under the very false notion that I didn't spend much time here. I would be mortified if she knew this was my home. Even if I was perfectly proud of it myself. But I wasn't sure if you could really be proud of something you were embarrassed to show someone.

I unlocked, opened the door as far as the chain latch would allow and peered down the stairwell. I could hear her delicate thumps as she made the trek up to the sixth floor. She sure was taking her time, six flights or not. Suddenly came the jangle of bracelets, then the red ringlets appeared. I slid off the chain latch and opened the door wide.

"Natasha? Is something wrong?"

She smiled as she reached the landing, a weak sort-of smile. She wore a white tank top and white jeans as though she were in Arizona. And lots of silver jewelry, as usual.

"No, no," Natasha said. "Nothing's wrong. I was out taking a midnight stroll down to the river and I realized I was passing right by your building, and there was your name on the buzzer downstairs so I figured…"

No one took a midnight stroll to the river. Certainly not on a weeknight. And certainly not alone. Not a woman alone, anyway.

"Can I come in?" Natasha asked.

I pulled the door open wide. "Do you want something to drink? I have herbal tea and instant coffee and maybe some orange juice. I wish I had more to offer you, but I'm never here, so anything would just go to waste…"

"Herbal tea would be great," the Gnat said, tossing a ringlet behind her shoulder. She peered around. "You and your boyfriend didn't get into a fight, did you?"

My boyfriend. I was so close to owning those words. "Uh, no," I said. "We spend nights apart when he has an early rotation in the morning, so…"

"Rotation?" Natasha asked. "He's a doctor?"

"Resident. New York Hospital."

"Wow, a doctor," she exclaimed. "Your parents must—" She stopped short. "I mean, your mom must be so proud."

"I'll just go get you that tea," I said, heading down

the little hallway. Actually, I didn't think my mom would have been impressed by my dating a doctor. My mother had been a true believer in ''pretty is as pretty does.'' And if a mechanic did prettier than a doctor, she'd have preferred I dated the mechanic. I was a little surprised that the Gnat didn't know my mother had died. Her mother had been friendly with mine. Wouldn't Mrs. Nutley have mentioned something about it when the Gnat had told her I was editing her memoir? Then again, I doubted I'd come up in conversations Natasha Nutley had with anyone.

''If it's no trouble,'' Natasha called after me.

''Go ahead and sit down on the bed if you want,'' I said from the kitchen. I hadn't had time to fold up the futon into the couch look. I wondered what she was thinking about my apartment. Was she looking around with a horrified look on her face, wondering if a water bug would crawl on her shoe at any second? Was she thinking how strange it was that a big-deal senior editor like me had a fuchsia Parsons table and plastic Venetian blinds?

I set the water to boil, then opened the cabinet under the sink and listened for sounds of Eloise and Serge. I hadn't heard anything since I got home. I'd wanted to tell Eloise all about tonight, from start to finish, and hear about what was going on with her. Maybe she and Serge were out at a nightclub.

''You're sure it's no bother?'' the Gnat called out.

What was she, Southern? Better question: What was she doing here?

Bamboo tray loaded, I came back into the main room to find the Gnat sitting on the futon, bent over, her face smushed in a pillow on her lap. ''Natasha? Are you feeling okay?''

She sniffled and glanced up. She was crying. I stood there, holding the heavy tray, not sure what to do.

"I'm sorry," she said, bolting up and wiping under her eyes. "I should probably go." But instead of going, she burst into tears and sat back down on my bed.

Gnatasha Nutley was sobbing in my apartment.

"Are you having writer's block or something?" I asked, setting down the tray on the Parsons table. "I can help you through it. Sometimes it's just a matter of finding the muse again, unblocking what it's stuck behind—"

She looked up at me, her tearstained face still absolutely beautiful. Her nose wasn't even red. "I'm pregnant."

Oh. Huh. "And, um, so, um—"

"I'm happy, really happy," the Gnat said. "And Sam, he's just thrilled. I had to tell him long distance, of course, but you should have heard him whooping! He was so excited, I had to hold the phone away from my ear."

And she was crying because...?

"It's just that—" The Gnat squeezed her eyes shut, and her face crumpled. "I don't know if I want to marry Sam. I love him and all. I love him so much, but I don't know."

Was there something in the water? Water I hadn't drunk? What was with all these Proposing Men and I'm Not Sure Women?

I had no idea what to say. "I'll, uh, go get you some tissues." Well, it was *something*. And she did need tissues. She was slobbering all over my pillow.

"I've made so many mistakes," the Gnat continued as I dashed into the bathroom for a roll of toilet paper. It was the best I could do, unless she wanted to wipe her eyes and blow her nose with scratchy paper towels. I handed her the roll, and she unwound a wad. ''I just don't want to make another one and—'' She covered her face with her hands. Her ringlets were tossed everywhere. For a second I had the slightly maternal instinct to brush her hair out of her face. But I couldn't. This was Gnatasha Nutley. Who was I to touch her? It was as though Madonna or Sharon Stone or Julia Roberts was crying in your living room. I felt as though I were intruding, somehow, even though this was my apartment. ''I want to do the right thing for the baby,'' she said in a tiny voice.

''I'm sure you will, Natasha,'' I said. After all, wasn't motherhood instinctive? Even faux celebrities could be good mothers. ''You just need some time to get used to the idea of marriage, that's all. Your whole life will be changing.''

She blew her nose and sniffled. ''I guess.''

I sat on the opposite side of the bed, as far away as I could get from her on a full-sized mattress. ''I have a friend in a similar situation. She's not pregnant, but her boyfriend proposed and she said yes, but she doesn't really love him. Not the way she should for marriage, anyway.''

''So is she gonna marry the guy?'' Natasha asked.

Sweet, generous, funny, original Eloise Manfred marrying a man she didn't love just to get married? No. She wouldn't do it. Would she? ''I don't know. I hope not.''

''Every woman wants to get married,'' Natasha said. ''It's hard to say no when someone's proposing. Especially when you're facing thirty. No one understands that better than me.''

I nodded. Eloise was facing thirty-one. ''But if you love Sam, why don't you want to marry him?'' I asked.

Natasha stared at her feet, which were encased in pale pink suede platform clogs. She covered her face with her hands again. "I don't know. Maybe I'm just scared about being a mom. I've never been a mother before, and I don't know how...I might not be good at it and..." She dissolved into tears again.

I was squirming. I wasn't sure how to comfort her. "I'm sure you'll be good at it, Natasha," I told her again. "It's, um, instinctive."

She sniffled and blew her nose a few times. "Can I have a cup of tea?"

I poured us two cups and handed her one. She ripped open a packet of Sweet'n Low and shook it in.

"I guess this must seem pretty weird, huh?" she said, cradling the mug with her hands. "Me crying on your doorstep at this hour of night. I just didn't know where else to go. I mean, I don't really know anyone in New York anymore."

"What about your parents?" I asked, then regretted it the second it was out of my mouth. She'd written briefly in her outline about her strained relationship with her parents. I'd figured a lot of what she wrote had been embellished for drama's sake. But maybe not? Perhaps that was why she didn't know about my mother.

"They don't like me much," Natasha said in such a low voice I wasn't sure I'd heard her right. She sipped her tea.

I remembered her parents. The Nutleys weren't the warmest people in the world. Back in Forest Hills I'd never thought much about Natasha's parents. They were parents like all parents. They yelled and fussed and annoyed. And at least she had two of them. When I'd known the Gnat, I'd had only one parent. Anyway, woe is her. If her parents didn't like her, it was because she'd been mean to them or done something awful to them.

"I remember how nice your parents were," Natasha

said. "A few times when I was baby-sitting Dana, the Dreers would come home with your parents and they'd set out cake and coffee. Your mom always smiled at me and told me how pretty my hair was, and your dad used to slip me an extra dollar. They were so kind."

My mom always did comment on Natasha's hair, every time she saw her. I'd forgotten that. And I could picture my dad slipping her dollars. He used to give me dollar bills all the time. Every morning when I got to school, I'd find a dollar hidden somewhere—in my pocket or jacket or lunch box or notebook. And then came the day I knew I couldn't look for one.

"My mom died," I said, staring at my teacup. "A long time ago now. My sophomore year in college."

I heard her gasp; it so surprised me that I glanced at her, and our eyes met for a moment. "I am so sorry," she said. "I didn't know."

"You'll be a good mom," I told her quickly, so she couldn't ask me how or when or why about my mother. "I'm sure of it."

She regarded me, and I got the sense she knew I didn't want to talk about my mother. She sipped her tea, then smiled weakly at me. "Do you really think so?"

"Yeah," I said. But I wasn't. I had no idea if she'd be a good mother or not. Although I figured that if you were worried about your maternal qualities in the first place, your chances were pretty good.

"So what's your boyfriend's name?" she asked.

"Timothy."

"Timothy," she repeated. "I've always liked that name. Think he's the one?"

"Maybe." And that was true.

"I'm sorry I didn't call you back yesterday or today," Natasha said. She stood and placed her cup on the bamboo tray. Then she walked to the window and peered through the faux Venetian blinds. "I was freaking out about the news about the baby, so..."

"That's okay, Natasha. I understand."

"I worked today, though. I polished my draft of Chapter Two. I'll fax it tomorrow. I read your notes on the outline for Chapter Three, and I completely agree with you. Focusing that chapter on my romantic history is perfect. Give readers a sense of where I come from emotionally, why I ended up selling my soul. I think that'll be interesting."

*Sordid* was more the right word. "You can start with Jimmy Alfonzo."

Natasha sat down. "Jimmy Alfonzo. You remember him?"

"Of course," I said. "He was Homecoming King. Well, the only Homecoming King who refused the crown. He was your boyfriend forever. From, like, the sixth grade through graduation, right?"

"On and off," she said, reaching for her tea. "Off when he was cheating on me and on when I was stupid enough to forgive him."

I almost spit out my mouthful of tea. "He cheated on you?" It was hard to imagine a guy cheating on Natasha Nutley. Why would he? What girl could possibly be more attractive than she was? Especially back in high school.

"All the time," she replied.

Huh. "So why'd you keep going back with him? You could have had any guy you wanted in high school."

"I loved Jimmy," she said. "Simple as that. Looking back, I guess I'd ask myself how I could love someone who treated me like shit. But he was everything to me, and he knew it. So he took advantage of that."

Huh. Whodathunk?

"Did you have a boyfriend in high school?" Natasha asked.

Robby Evers's face flashed before my eyes. "No." I leaned my head against the wall and pressed my knees to my chest.

"'Cause you were always studying, probably," she said. "Weren't you buddies with Robby Evers? I remember you guys were always walking around together. Did you know I almost went to the junior prom with him?"

Yeah, I knew.

"I thought it would be something if a guy like Robby liked me, you know?"

I stared at her. "What do you mean? *Every* guy liked you."

"Every guy wanted to screw me," Natasha corrected. "But Robby was different. You probably knew that better than anyone since you were such good friends. He was so smart and poetic. And nice-looking, to boot. He really cared about things. I figured if Robby liked me and wanted to go out with me, I was probably okay, you know? Because he was Mr. Integrity. He wouldn't date a girl just because she was pretty or had big tits."

Huh again. But I wasn't so sure about that. Robby was Mr. Integrity, yes. But he wasn't attracted to Natasha because she was a good person. Who knew if she was? It wasn't as though the Gnat was famous for saving the whales or selling more magazines for the school newspaper than any other kid in school. Robby had fallen in love with her because she was gorgeous and had huge breasts. Whether the Gnat wanted to believe it or not. She was fantasy girl, and for a second, he'd had her.

"So why didn't you go with him to the dance?" I asked. "Why'd you get back together with Jimmy?"

"Because Jimmy said he was sorry and whispered a

bunch of sweet junk in my ear and told me I couldn't possibly go to the junior prom with anyone but him, and I fell for it again.''

"You broke Robby's heart," I told her.

And that was when it hit me. She *had* broken his heart. So he must have liked her for more than just her face and body. He hadn't been mourning a hot date with Miss Popularity. He'd been mourning a lost dream.

"I was so sorry about that," Natasha said. "I wrote him a letter and tried to explain the hold Jimmy had on me, had on me since the sixth grade. But Robby wouldn't talk to me after that.''

There didn't seem any need to tell the Gnat I'd been in love with Robby. That she'd stolen him out of my fragile grasp. Not because she'd already won. But because it turned out that she hadn't. She hadn't won much at all. In fact, she'd lost. Lost knowing what a great boyfriend she could have had in Robby. And lost so much by loving an asshole like Jimmy Alfonzo.

"So what happened to Jimmy?" I asked. "Do you two still keep in touch?''

Natasha shook her head and smiled. "After high school, he moved to Las Vegas to work in the casinos. I got a postcard from him saying he'd married a showgirl. Never heard from him again, which was fine by me, and—''

"Oh! Oh, yes! Oh, Ohhhhhh!''

Natasha looked at me, her green eyes wide.

"Yes! Yes! Ohhhhhhh!''

She giggled and covered her mouth.

"Give it to me. Yeah! Oh! Oh! Oh!" *Squeak. Squeak. Squeak.* "Ohhhhhhh!''

Natasha Nutley and I doubled over in laughter.

"You can't stay here with that going on," she said,

catching her breath. "Wanna stay at my place? I have a really comfy pullout sofa and central air-conditioning."

She was inviting me to a two-person slumber party? I wasn't sure I could handle that. I wasn't sure I liked this new friendly thing happening here.

Opera Man turned up the volume. I didn't recognize the opera.

"Come on, Jane," Natasha said, smiling. "It'll be fun. Plus, it's really nice to have someone to talk to. Someone who knows me from back when, you know? Your life is so together and mine is such a mess—"

"Oh yeah! Oh! Oh! Ohhhhhhhh!"

"Let's get out of here," I told her. And we both burst into giggles as the wall started to vibrate.

## Eleven

How could I have resisted an invitation to check out the Gnat's lair? I'd never been in an apartment between Lexington Avenue and Central Park, and I wouldn't have been surprised to find the walls encrusted with diamonds. Turned out that the Gnat's small but gorgeous apartment was built originally as servants' quarters in a town house. No diamonds in the walls. In fact, her apartment was belowground, which meant she had decorative black iron bars on her windows and a view of people's feet. My pathetic studio had a better view—and sunlight.

"Jane, do you want pecan pancakes or regular?" Natasha called from the kitchen.

I glanced at my watch. It was eight in the morning. I had enough time to wolf down a homemade breakfast I didn't have to make myself before leaving for work. "Um, pecan would be great," I called back. It was trendy to cook and take too-expensive cooking classes, so it was no shocker that the Gnat knew her way around a spatula and some Bisquick. I finished folding up the sofa bed and put the cushions in place. "Can I help with anything?"

"Nope," she yelled. A minute later she appeared with a platter stacked with pancakes. They smelled amazing. She set down the platter on the tiny dining room table in the tiny dining nook by a window. She'd laid out a whole feast. A carafe of hazelnut coffee, orange juice, fruit salad and now the pecan pancakes.

"Ooh, so we might as well work over breakfast," she said, hopping up from her seat. "Oh, and I'll do those final revisions on Chapter One today and fax the revised version to you by three. Is that okay?"

I nodded. "That'll give me today to condense it, tomorrow to polish it and then I'll have it on Jeremy's desk first thing Friday morning."

"Jeremy's a hottie, isn't he?" Natasha asked, refilling my coffee cup. "Don't you think he looks like James Bond? What's that actor's name again?"

"Pierce Brosnan," I said through a suddenly cardboard tasting mouthful of pecan pancake. Then I realized I had nothing to worry about. Natasha couldn't make a play for Jeremy: she was already taken. Whew.

"Right! Pierce Brosnan! Mmm—what a dreamboat. It's a good thing I'm practically married," she trilled. "Or I'd go after him in two seconds."

Yes, it was a very good thing she was taken. Timothy Rommely in my life or not, I'd die if Gnatasha Nutley ended up with Jeremy Black. Could you imagine if she got her hands on the only other man I'd fantasized about for years?

"Did you want cream for your coffee?" Natasha asked. "Or is milk okay? I have both."

"Milk's fine," I said.

"I'll just go get my draft of Chapter Three," she said. "Be right back." She disappeared into her bedroom.

Even at eight in the morning she looked incredible. She had on no makeup, and her hair was pulled back in a low bun, some delicate strands of ringlets falling free around her face. She wore an ice-blue microfiber tank top and perfect-fitting Levi's. She was barefoot and had a silver ring around one of her toes. If I bought every single thing she was wearing and put it on, I'd never look the way she did.

When we'd arrived last night, she'd fussed over me the same way Aunt Ina always did when I came to visit. *Are you comfortable, do you need anything, are you sure, is that blanket warm enough, do you want to borrow socks?* Maybe the Gnat was being so nice to me because she thought I held the fate of her memoir in my hands. If only she knew it was the other way around—her memoir held the fate of my life in its hands. We'd talked a bit last night in her living room, mostly about how well Dana had turned out, how exciting it was that she was getting married, that her bridal shower was this Saturday, blah, blah, blah. Talking about Dana and her wedding was as good as a sleeping pill; I'd started yawning like crazy. So the Gnat had set up my bed in her living room, which was more folksy than I'd expected. By the time my head hit the pillow, it was close to two o'clock. I'd fallen asleep right away. The next thing I knew, the Gnat was mixing pancake batter.

Maybe she was being so nice because she'd told me more than she wanted to. Did she regret her midnight breakdown? Her pregnancy confession? The admission that Jimmy Alfonzo had cheated on her?

Her phone rang and she reappeared in the living room, the chapter in one hand and a cordless phone in the other.

"Hi, Mom!" she said in a super cheery voice. "I'm glad you called back. No, that's not what I meant. I know you and Dad are really busy, too. I was just saying thanks for returning the call, that's all. So, the reason I called was that I thought I'd come over on Saturday and visit with you and Dad. I have a gift for you guys. Oh, well, that's okay. I could come later on, around three-thirty, then. No, I don't mind. A couple of hours is fine. No, it's no big deal. It's just a short train ride."

I poured maple syrup on my pancakes and pretended not to notice the Gnat's voice was catching in her throat. It was easy to ascertain that her parents did not want her to visit them. So she had been telling the truth. Her parents didn't like her. I wondered why. Her outline didn't get into the details, just that she and the Nutleys didn't speak or see each other very often.

"Hey, so guess who's here right now?" she exclaimed overbrightly into the phone. "Janey Gregg. Remember her? Yes, that's right, Dana Dreer's cousin. Right, you were friendly with Jane's mom. Maybe. I don't know. I guess I could ask. Will you hold on?"

Ask me what?

"Jane, my mom wants to know if you'd like to come visit with me on Saturday. I know you have Dana's shower, so maybe afterward you could join us?"

I suddenly wanted a cigarette. No. Not just one. A whole pack. I'd been fine for days, and now the desire to smoke hit me so hard that my knees almost buckled. I was supposed to visit the Gnat's parents with her? After suffering through Dana's shower? All I wanted to do on Saturday afternoon was zone out and wonder what I would wear that night on my date with Timothy.

But Natasha was waiting for an answer. I couldn't tell

much from her expression, but I sensed it was important that I say yes. "Um, okay."

She beamed and took her hand away from the mouthpiece. "Jane can come, Mom. Yeah. Okay. So four o'clock. Can I bring anything? Are you sure. Okay. See you then. Bye." She clicked off the phone and tossed it onto the sofa. "My mom's really excited to see you," Natasha said. "She just adored your mom."

I smiled. "You know, I'd better get going or Remke will have my head. We have a meeting this morning, so…" That was a lie. But I had to get out of there. Had to get away from her. Suddenly I was going on family visits with her and listening to her tell me that her mom adored my mom? Who did she think she was? My new best friend?

Why had I agreed to go to her parents' with her? Why had I agreed to the slumber party? Was it curiosity? Morbid curiosity? A teeny part of me did sort of like my sudden status. Not only was I Natasha's editor, I was also her confidante. Being the editor of her memoirs already made me her confidante, but this was different. This was almost like friendship. And that wasn't happening. No siree. I'd help her out with her parents in the name of keeping her sane enough to write her ridiculous life story, and then she was on her own.

Ha. How on her own could she ever be with a baby on the way and a proposing houseboat-dwelling boyfriend?

At exactly 9:00 a.m. on Friday morning, I placed the excerpt of Chapter One of *The Stopped Starlet* on Jeremy's desk. That title had not been one of my suggestions. Remke came up with it himself. *S* was a sensual letter, he'd insisted, and you couldn't beat alliteration or the word *starlet*. Plus, *Stopped* would elicit sympathy from consumers and make them want to know what it meant. It hinted at conspiracies, Remke had said. Natasha had the surprising good sense to think the title was silly but super-marketable, and she gave it her blessing. Morgan had been shocked that her title suggestion hadn't been chosen: *Gag Order: I'm Talking Now.* Very sexy, Morgan. Anyway, Remke wanted to keep the title short so that a provocative full-body photo of the Gnat could take up most of the cover. Daisy, the art director, suggested placing a sophisticated-looking man next to Natasha and blanking out his face to represent the Mystery Actor and add to the cover's salability. I thought that was a great idea. Remke was mulling it over.

Lightning and thunder crackled outside Jeremy's window. Was that an omen? No. It was just rain. I'd spent the past two nights polishing and perfecting the excerpt of the Gnat's pornographic Chapter One, which was actually quite emotional and well-done, if I did say so myself. But Jeremy would be the judge of that.

I settled myself in my office and began reading the Gnat's revisions of Chapter Two. Or tried to. I could hear the unmistakable sound of a baby gurgling and cooing in the hallway. That could mean only one thing. Gwen had brought in O. Welle.

My computer let me know I had new e-mail. One was from Timothy, who wanted to make me dinner tomorrow night—his specialty. Or, if that wasn't okay, we could go out for Mexican instead. Hmm. Did that mean he was planning the Big Seduction tomorrow night? Date Number Three was often sex night. Was it too soon for sex? I wasn't sure. Timothy and I had clicked big time, and he'd called on Thursday afternoon to say hi. The third date was famous for creating relationships. But sex was famous for killing relationships. Someone always expected more. And that someone was usually me.

The next e-mail was from Eloise to me and to Amanda. Tonight's Flirt Night Roundtable was suggested to be held in Bloomingdale's, so that Eloise could register for wedding gifts, and didn't I have to buy my cousin a shower present, anyway? Huh. So Eloise was serious. She was marrying Serge. You didn't register for gifts unless you were getting hitched. Eloise had told me yesterday that she'd called Amanda and told her she was engaged. According to Eloise, Amanda was as surprised as I'd been. But Amanda had turned on the congratulations. I knew Amanda Frank. If Eloise said she loved Serge and was getting married, that was all Amanda needed to know. She wasn't a buttinsky. She took what people said at face value. And besides, Amanda had an annoying habit of treating people like adults.

Amanda had already replied to the suggestion with an enthusiastic *cool*. I sent back a ditto. I'd had lunch with Eloise yesterday and today, but she'd been quiet and off in her own world. So off that she hadn't even registered surprise when I'd mentioned I'd slept over at the Gnat's Tuesday night. She still hadn't told her grandmother about the engagement. The only people who knew were me and Amanda. She kept the little diamond turned around on her finger at work, so none of the Poshes had noticed it. She'd taken off by herself the past couple of nights, and I'd had to focus on the excerpt, so I hadn't spent much time with Eloise. Yesterday I'd asked her if she was mad at me, for my reaction to her news, and she swore she wasn't. Considering all she'd said about Serge before he proposed, she understood my worries. I missed Eloise. But I figured I might as well get used to the lack of her in my life.

I hadn't heard much from the Gnat, either, except to receive her polished draft of Chapter Two and her first draft of Chapter Three, which I'd read this afternoon. I wondered if I should buy her a baby gift tonight in Bloomies. What did you buy for a baby-to-be if you didn't know the sex? Maybe I should go to Baby Gap and ask the salespeople for help.

"There you are!"

Double ugh. That was Gwen's phony voice.

"Say ha-woe to nice Jane-Jane," baby-talked Gwen to Olivia, who was staring at me from her carriage. Olivia's eyes were bluer than seemed possible. She had long eyelashes and wisps of fine, blond hair. She truly was exquisite.

"Wow, she's getting so big!" I exclaimed in as interested a voice as I could fake.

"Livie smiled today, didn't she!" Gwen cooed to the baby. "I took her to her pediatrician today because I was worried about the color of her dark poopie, but the doc says everything seems okay. That's rightie, poopie-doopie, everything's okay," she sing-songed to Olivia.

Was there a response to that? I didn't think so.

"So how's that cute new boyfriend of yours?" Gwen asked. "What was his name?"

Museum Asshole. "He was just a friend. I do have a boyfriend though. His name is Timothy."

"Oh! Well, that's so great, Jane. It's so nice that you have friends and a boyfriend. Living it up in New York. You're really living the life. When I was your age, all I did was work, work, work! I'm amazed I got married at all!" She was looking at my desk, or trying to. My shoulders were blocking most of her view. What was her problem? And who was she trying to kid? Gwendolyn Welle had been with her icky husband since she was a sophomore in college. What was amazing was that the two phoniest people in the United States of America had managed to find each other.

My intercom buzzed. "Jaaane," Morgan whined. "Is Gwen with you?"

"Uh-huh."

"Could you let her know that Williaaam and Jereeemy are ready for their meeting."

"That's my cue!" Gwen trilled. "Say bye-bye to Jane-Jane," she baby-talked to Olivia.

"Oh, hey, Gwen? What would you suggest getting a pregnant friend who's just announced her news? Someone who's not even showing yet."

"You can never go wrong with getting a mom-to-be the book *What To Expect When You're Expecting*," Gwen told me. "I must have read and reread that book three times while I was pregnant. See you later! Come on, Livie-loo. Time to play with Morgan while Mommy goes to a meeting." Gwen pushed Olivia's carriage down the hall to Morgan's cubicle. Morgan was baby-sitting until the meeting ended.

*What To Expect When You're Expecting.* Excellent idea and very appropriate, considering that the Gnat was worried about her mothering skills. I could stop at Barnes & Noble on my way to the subway tomorrow morning.

I began rereading the Gnat's Chapter Two and was into a juicy part about the number of men she'd slept with on the Hollywood "casting couch" when Morgan buzzed me and informed that my presence was requested in the conference room. When I arrived, Remke, Jeremy and Gwen were sitting in their usual seats. No one was looking at me. Remke was thumbing through memos, as usual. Jeremy was reading—gulp—my excerpt. And Gwen was pretending to be checking threads in her skirt.

Oh, God. Was I getting fired?

"Let's go, let's go," Remke said, eyeing me over the rim of his glasses. "Sit down."

I sat. And waited.

"Gwen wants to discuss the Nutley project," Remke prompted.

"Well, I just want to make sure everything's going all right," Gwen added. She turned to me. "I'm worried that you're all alone on this project without any support."

"Things are going really well," I said. "Natasha's working hard, and I'm getting some great stuff out of her...."

"I'm sure you're both doing your best," Gwen offered. "And by keeping up the hard work and with additional experience, you'll be a very strong editor. But right now, you're really just learning." She directed her phony concerned expression to Jeremy and Remke. "I'd be happy to act as a support system for Jane and approve her work as she goes. Perhaps I could even give Natasha a call and let her know she has a senior editor behind the scenes who's—"

Jeremy stopped reading my excerpt and slapped it on the table. "Gwen, Jane's doing just fine. This excerpt she wrote from Natasha's first chapter is excellent. Absolutely excellent. There's not a thing you could have contributed to make it stronger. Jane has a long history with Natasha, and she's clearly guiding her very well."

"We're done here then," Remke said. "Good job, Gregg."

"I'm impressed," Gwen exclaimed. "I've trained you well, Jane!"

I'd done it. I'd actually done it. I'd *arrived*. Gwen Welle was threatened by me!

"Black, stick around," Remke said. "Let's talk about

that Backstreet Kid. Gwen, if you'd like to stay, I'd love to have your thoughts on this.''

"Oh, great!" Gwen exclaimed. "Let me just make sure Livie's settled.''

Gwen followed me out. As I passed Morgan, who was cooing at Olivia, she shot me a good-job nod. Clearly she'd heard every word in the conference room and was impressed that Gwen was threatened by me.

Gwendolyn Welle, senior editor extraordinaire, threatened by *me*. After six years of hard work, I'd made it. I couldn't wait to tell Eloise. I ran to her office, but she was deep in conversation with Daisy. I thought about calling Timothy, but it seemed too early in the romance for that. We weren't at the call-each-other-for-anything stage yet. I might as well tell him tomorrow when he was feeding me his homemade enchiladas. That would be celebration enough. I skipped to my office and reveled by swiveling around on my desk chair.

The intercom buzzed. "Jaaane," Morgan whined. "You're wanted in the conference room for a staff meeting.''

A staff meeting? Was I getting promoted? I was. I was getting promoted! Why else would Remke call a staff meeting on a Friday? Remke, Jeremy and Gwen hadn't stayed after our little meeting to discuss the Backstreet Boy. They'd stayed to discuss my promotion to Associate Editor!

Deep breath, deep breath. Affect the poise of an associate editor. I pulled out my compact and de-shined my nose, then touched up my lips with my trusty Clinique Black Honey lip gloss. A fluff of the hair, and I was ready to be congratulated.

The editorial staff and the art department were gathered in the conference room. Two champagne bottles and a bunch of plastic cups were on the table, along with a platter of cookies. Omigod. Omigod. Omigod. I was getting promoted. This was it.

"Since we're all here today, including Gwen," Jeremy began, "I thought it would be a good time to announce some wonderful news."

My heart was ba-booming so fast. What if I couldn't speak when Jeremy announced the promotion? Deep breath, deep breath.

Jeremy cleared his throat. "I'm very happy to announce my engagement to Carolyn Klausner, an executive vice president at *Vogue*."

The ba-booms stopped. I felt eyes on me. Four eyes, to be exact. Morgan's and Eloise's. Everyone was clapping. I forced myself to clap, too.

"Let's go, let's go," Remke said. "Let's make a toast."

As the champagne popped and poured, Eloise snaked her way over to me and squeezed my hand. "Are you okay?" she whispered.

I nodded and squeezed back. I wasn't upset over Jeremy. *Quelle surprise,* but I wasn't. Yes, a Heidi Klum look-alike-slash-executive-vice-president-at-*Vogue* was marrying Jeremy. My Jeremy. The man I'd been dreaming about for five years. But the only thing I was upset about was that I'd been stupid enough to get my hopes up about the promotion. Maybe Gwen hadn't been threatened by me, after all, Maybe she simply thought I wasn't up to the task.

What Tiffany's was to Holly Golightly, Bloomingdale's was to me. Nothing very bad could happen to you in Bloomies. Except for maybe having your credit card revoked for exceeding the limit or getting sprayed with five different perfumes by aggressive floor models. Granted, Bloomingdale's wasn't exactly *the* elite of New York City department stores, but bad things *could* happen to you in Barney's or Bendel's or even Saks or Bergdorf's: Saleswomen could appraise your clothes and shoes and purse and hair and makeup and raise their noses in the air and not even bother asking if they could help you.

My favorite part of the store was the main floor, with the cosmetic counters and accessories and jewelry and hosiery. You could spend an entire afternoon in Bloomies without spending a penny: getting a free makeover, trying on stylish clothes and shoes you could never afford, imagination-decorating your entire apartment. And the bonus was people watching.

The Flirt Night Roundtable was meeting in front of the MAC counter to try on lipsticks before heading up to the registry to fill out the paperwork for Eloise. Eloise was busy asking the MAC beauty advisor about bridal makeup for the big day. For a woman who'd burst into tears when telling her best friend she was engaged, she sure was going full steam ahead.

"Hey, ya'll!" Amanda called with a wave as she weaved her way over. She beelined for an empty spot in front of the lipsticks and applied a shimmery pink. "What do you think?" She puckered up.

Eloise kissed her on the lips. "There. Now you can see how it looks on me."

"I think it looks different on an engaged woman," Amanda said. "You know, when your skin's glowing, pink looks pinker."

But Eloise wasn't glowing. She was fake-happy, and I knew it. I wondered if Amanda knew it, too. I'd been tempted a few times yesterday to call Amanda and get her perspective about Eloise's engagement, but I hadn't wanted to talk about El behind her back. Anyway, Amanda didn't know Eloise the way I did. And I didn't want Amanda to get the wrong idea, that I was jealous or something. That was what I was afraid she'd think. I wasn't sure why. Maybe because they both had serious boyfriends, and I had two dates under my belt.

"So Jane! Looks like you and Timothy are gonna be getting engaged soon, too!" Amanda said. "He told Jeff he owes him big—like a Porsche—for fixing him up with you!"

The smile burst out of me. "He said that?"

"Hey, who knows," Eloise said. "Maybe we'll have a double wedding! Wouldn't that be amazing?"

"Can I help you ladies?" asked a male beauty advisor.

Saved. Amanda and Eloise lunged for the lipsticks and an available mirror and the advice of a guy with pink hair. A double wedding. Dana's wedding was enough wedding for a long time to come. Okay, okay, I wouldn't mind an engagement ring twinkling on my finger. I wouldn't mind a wedding in a mini-ballroom at the Plaza Hotel. I wouldn't mind being married to the man I loved.

Was I jealous of Eloise? I suddenly felt like Ally McBeal when she shrank to teeny-tiny size on her chair after she was made to feel small, small, small. I didn't think that was it, but maybe it was. Maybe I was simply jealous that I was being left behind. Losing my best friend.

After a half hour of makeovers that cost us each over fifty bucks in cosmetics we didn't need, we descended on Registry Lady. Forms in hand, Eloise, Amanda and I hit my second favorite part of Bloomingdale's: the bed and bath department. We wandered around the entire department to look at everything, and then Eloise started making selections. We decided to put one of each thing she chose in our shopping baskets so that she could immediately see if colors matched or if she didn't like something fifteen minutes later.

Eloise chose thick dark purple towels (twenty bucks for a bath towel!) and a very cool bath mat with tiny cartoon moose. Art Deco-y accessories, and a shower curtain that was a movie poster of *Casablanca* with Bogey and Ingrid Bergman in a heated, tense embrace. A down comforter thicker than my winter coat. A duvet cover more expensive than my winter coat. Pillows, thick and thin, down and synthetic. Calvin Klein sheets and pillowcases in a three-hundred-thread-count. Flannel Ralph Lauren sheets. A feather bed. A talking scale.

Two hours later, Eloise announced she'd changed her mind. She wanted a paler color scheme. Who even knew if Serge would like any of this? she'd worried aloud. Maybe she should come back some other time with him and they should choose together, she'd said. And so the three of us took our baskets and dumped everything on one of the display beds when the salesclerks weren't looking.

"Let's move the Flirt Night Roundtable to a round table," Eloise said, looking a tad grim. "I need a drink."

Amanda and I looked at each other and nodded. And ten minutes later we were sitting at one of the low round tables near the fireplace at Arizona 206, a Southwestern restaurant across the street from Bloomingdale's. Three frozen margaritas, Eloise's Marlboros Lights and a book of matches were before us. Eloise had decided this wasn't the time to give up her favorite bad habit.

"So you haven't had a single puff since last Saturday?" Amanda asked. "Wow, Jane! That's so great!"

"Let's toast to Jane's one-week anniversary as a non-smoker," Eloise said, raising her margarita.

We toasted, my eyes on the familiar light-brown-and-white pack of cigarettes. She'd admitted she'd sneaked more than a few cigarettes over the week; it was one of the reasons she'd avoided me. I'd told her she should feel comfortable puffing all she wanted in front of me. I was stopping in the name of love. She already had smoking love.

And that had made the three of us crack up. The tension had been cut, and the Flirt Night Roundtable was in full session on East 59th Street.

"Oh shit!" I said. "I forgot to buy Dana her shower present."

"Just give her money," Amanda said. "It's what couples want anyway. No one wants another hideous Mikasa vase."

"But they're gazillionaires," I reminded her. "What does she need my hundred bucks for?"

"Rich people are obsessed with money," Amanda said. "They can never get enough. Because they *spend* so much. Trust me, your measly hundred bucks will help pay the Plaza bill. Why do you think they're inviting so many people?"

She had a point there. "Still, you don't think Dana will find money from her cousin too impersonal?" Dana was definitely money and status obsessed, but we were family, after all.

"No way," Eloise said. "She'll think it's ever so appropriate."

I raised my margarita. "Okay, if you guys say so."

"Jane, are you sure you're okay about Jeremy?" Eloise asked.

Amanda looked from Eloise to me. "What about Jeremy?"

"He announced his engagement to some *Vogue* VP,"

Eloise said, exhaling a stream of smoke up toward the ceiling.

"Yeah, instead of announcing my promotion."

"Ooh, sorry, Jane," Amanda said. "*Are* you okay?"

I was. And I didn't know why. Why wasn't I a blubbering mess? The man I'd been obsessed with for five years had gotten engaged to another woman, and all I could think about was whether or not Gwen was truly threatened by me or not. Where was my broken heart? Where were my tears? Where were tissues and pints of Häagen Dazs? Perhaps I was okay because I was actually happy for Jeremy. How could I not be happy for someone who'd stood up for me in front of Remke and Gwen? He'd praised my work at exactly the right time, in exactly the right place, in exactly the right way. Maybe I'd gotten what I needed from Jeremy after all. His approval. No. That wasn't quite it, either. I'd been nuts about Jeremy. I'd fantasized about him forever. I hadn't been after his approval; I'd wanted *him*. Was it Timothy? Were two promising dates enough to make me forget about Jeremy Black? I didn't think so. So what then? What, what, *what?*

Maybe it was hard to be upset about Jeremy's engagement when things were going well in my life. I had earned Jeremy's praise on the excerpt; that had done a lot to fill me up inside. And I had made Gwen nervous; I was sure of it. I thought of the Gnat, sobbing all over my pillow. All but begging her mother to accept a visit. At least I had Aunt Ina and Uncle Charlie and even grumpy Grammy. They'd do anything for me. And I had Eloise and Amanda, who'd also do anything for me. And I might even have Timothy, who in a mere twenty-four hours would be folding over tortillas with my name on them. Maybe I was simply in a "good place," as they said in the self-help books. What other explanation could there be for my lackadaisical response?

"I'm totally okay," I insisted. "I really am. I'll get promoted when the Gnat finishes her book. When I turn in that baby, edited brilliantly, I'll be an associate editor the next day."

"A toast to Jane's much-deserved and forthcoming promotion," Eloise declared, raising her glass. We clinked. Eloise lit another cigarette and was careful to blow the smoke away from both Amanda and me.

"Are you really going to the Gnat's parents' tomorrow?" Eloise asked.

I nodded and explained the whole story to Amanda. The midnight visit. The crying. The slumber party. The pancakes. Her conversation with Mommy Dearest.

"You mean her mother's conversation with Daughter Dearest," Eloise said with a laugh.

Eloise caught me off guard. I hadn't meant that at all. Somewhere, somehow, a smidgen of sympathy had developed in me for the Gnat. Probably because her hard work had enabled me to condense her chapter into that "excellent" excerpt so easily. She'd saved my butt from Gwen's claws. I owed her one, now. That was all.

"She's not going to Dana's shower, is she?" Amanda asked.

I sipped my margarita. "No. We're taking the subway to Forest Hills together, though. The Gnat thinks it'll be fun to go slumming on the F train instead of taking a car service, but she's afraid to go by herself."

"What's she gonna do all day while you're eating bad deli and watching Dana open present after present?" Eloise asked. "I can't see Natasha Nutley shopping in Banana Republic or Bolton's on Austin Street."

Me neither. "She wants to spend the morning and afternoon walking around the old neighborhood, check out her old route to the schools we went to, where she used to hang out, that kind of thing, and then we're meeting in Starbucks at three forty-five to head over to her parents'."

"That is one long day," Amanda pointed out. "How are you gonna have energy to hook up with Timothy for your big third date?"

I smiled. Eating and having your clothes removed required absolutely no energy at all.

## Twelve

"So, um, I have something for you," I told Natasha as we settled ourselves on the hard orange seats of the F train bright and early Saturday morning. I handed her a Barnes & Noble shopping bag. I'd toyed with the idea of getting her a card while I was at the bookstore, but that seemed to be going too far. The book seemed to be a card and a present in itself.

"What's this?" Natasha asked, surprised. "You didn't have to get me anything."

"Well, um, I was in the bookstore this morning, and I noticed it on a display, and I thought it might be useful. Unless you have it already."

She pulled out the heavy paperback of *What To Expect When You're Expecting*. She glanced at me, her face breaking into a huge smile, then she started flipping through the book. "Jane, this is so thoughtful. Thank you so much! I was meaning to buy this book."

She was pregnant. Right here, right now, a life was growing inside of her. I wondered what that felt like. I couldn't just ask her; she'd probably think that was the strangest question she'd ever heard. I couldn't imagine what it was like to know you were carrying life inside you, that a little baby version of you and your man was developing in your womb, growing every second. What did that feel like? Maybe you couldn't physically feel the baby growing at this point, but the knowledge of it must be wild. You probably never felt alone.

"Jane, I can't tell you how much I appreciate this gift," Natasha said.

I smiled. "You're wel—"

"Can I have your autograph, dear?" a woman interrupted.

Natasha and I glanced up from *What To Expect When You're Expecting*. A middle-aged woman was beaming at the Gnat, a piece of paper and a pen extended toward her.

"I hate to bother you," the woman gushed, "but I just love you and all your movies. I didn't know you took the subway! This is so exciting! You're so beautiful!"

What movies? The Gnat was strictly small screen.

"I'm so excited!" the woman exclaimed. "It'd mean the world to me if you'd sign your autograph."

What a fool I was. I was feeling sorry for the Gnat last night? Ha! She didn't deserve an ounce of my sympathy. She was *famous*. Faux celebrity or not. She'd been on so many talk shows earlier this year that she was recognizable to the stay-at-home set. The whole thing seemed so sleazy. This woman—and countless others—wanted Natasha Nutley's autograph because she'd slept with a famous actor? A famous actor who made his women sign documents while screwing them? Why did that merit fame?

Now I knew why the Gnat had wanted to take the subway instead of a car service. So she could whip around her ringlets and have strangers fawn all over her for her autograph. It was a good thing the subway was practically empty. Like I needed to spend the forty-minute ride watching the Gnat sign her name?

Natasha smiled at the woman and took the piece of paper and pen. She leaned the paper against the book, which rested on her unusually conservative dress-covered thigh. The Gnat typically wore skimpy tank tops and tight bootleg pants and high-heeled sandals. Today she sported a pale blue linen dress with a high round neckline, cute cap sleeves and a hem just past the knee. It was very Audrey Hepburn. A pale blue thin cardigan was tied around her neck. She wore sandals, but with a reasonable heel. Instead of her usual Prada or Gucci or Louis Vuitton purse, a pale pink straw tote bag was slung over her arm. She looked like a fourth-grade teacher on a class trip to the White House instead of the infamous Gnatasha Nutley on a Saturday morning.

I glanced at the autograph as the Gnat handed the paper and pen back to the woman. My mouth dropped open. Signed in black ink in a slightly illegible scrawl was: *Nicole Kidman.*

The woman beamed as she stared at the autograph and pressed it to the chest. "I can't wait to tell my husband!" she exclaimed, and scurried away.

Okay. Was I missing something here? I glanced at Natasha. "Nicole Kidman?"

"You didn't think she wanted *my* autograph, did you?"

Um, yes, I did. "Why not? You're famous."

"To you, maybe," Natasha said, eyes on her lap. "Not to your average person on the F train or walking down the street. I'm mistaken for Nicole Kidman all the time."

Woe is her for the hundredth time. How tough that must be. To be mistaken for one of the most beautiful actresses in the world.

"But how did you know that woman didn't want your autograph?" I asked. "She could have looked at the autograph, been totally confused and said, 'I thought you were Natasha Nutley.'"

She laughed and raised an eyebrow. "Well, she didn't, did she?"

"But—"

"Jane, after I'd been on television the first time, someone asked me for my autograph. I'd practiced my signature a thousand times for that very moment. The guy handed me a piece of paper, and I wrote 'Natasha Nutley' so proudly. The guy looked at it, looked at me, then looked at me closer and said, 'Hey, you're not Nicole Kidman!' Then he crumpled up the piece of paper and threw it on the ground."

The sympathy returned.

The Gnat's bracelets jangled as she brushed back a ringlet. "I picked up that autograph and smoothed it over and put it in my purse. I've kept it all this time, to remind me that I am someone. No matter what, I'm someone."

"Of course, you're someone," I said. "You *are* famous. You've been on TV and had your picture in so many maga—"

"No, I don't mean that," Natasha interrupted. "I mean, no matter what. Aside from The Actor, and the talk shows and the magazine articles and the memoir, I'm someone. Just me. Whenever that gets tested, I pull out that tattered autograph, and I look at it. And I'm reminded that I have to believe in myself. So what's the big deal if I make someone happy by signing Nicole Kidman's name? It doesn't cost me anything, and it makes someone's day, gives them a story they can tell for the next week.''

But it did cost her something. It had to.

She began flipping through the book. She clearly wanted to change the subject. Fine with me. But to what? She hadn't asked me if I'd read her draft of Chapter Three. Maybe she was waiting for me to let her know what I thought of it. But I was tired of talking about her. Tired of *her* sex life and *her* beauty and *her* unexpected problems.

''So guess who got engaged?'' I blurted out. ''Pierce Brosnan.''

''Really?'' Natasha asked. ''To that *Vogue* exec?'' At my nod, Natasha let out a whistle. ''Wow. The last of the most eligible bachelors in New York is off the list. I'll have to remember to pick up a congratulations card for Jeremy while I'm shopping today.''

''Wanna know a secret?'' I asked her. She looked at me and nodded. ''I used to have the biggest crush on Jeremy. A long time ago, I mean. When I first started at Posh. Isn't that funny?''

Oh, God. What was I *doing?* Now I really had diarrhea of the mouth. When Natasha and I had been reintroduced after ten years in the Blue Water Grill, I'd spouted non-stop lies. Now I was confiding the truth in her? Well, the half-truth. My crush on Jeremy had lasted until I'd fallen for Timothy all of a week ago. Why? Why? Why? I'd given it a lot of thought last night, but I still couldn't figure it out. How could I go from dreaming of Jeremy every night, hoping he'd notice me, hoping he'd ask me out, to being absolutely fine that he'd gotten engaged? I'd lost something here, hadn't I?

''You never went for him?'' Natasha asked as the train rumbled to a stop in the first station in Queens.

I laughed. "Are you serious?"

"Yeah, I'm serious. Why not?"

"Right," I said. "Uh-huh. Tell me another one."

"Jane! You're a beautiful, smart woman. Why wouldn't he go for you?"

Who was she, Aunt Ina? "That's sweet, Natasha, really, but I'm not an idiot. I'm not exactly in his league. You're the type he'd go for. Not me."

Had I just told Gnatasha that I most certainly was *not* a super-fabulous senior editor making one hundred thousand smackers a year? Yes, I had. *Not in his league.* What the hell was wrong with me? Maybe I could amend that so she'd think—

Natasha looked at me. "He's engaged to an executive vice president of the most respected women's fashion magazine in the world. I doubt he'd be interested in a whore who's a recovered alcoholic to boot."

My mouth dropped open. "Natasha!" I was allowed to think of her that way, but *she* wasn't. Come to think of it, even I didn't go *that* far. Did she really have so little self-esteem? How was that possible? She was exquisite. She was mistaken for Nicole Kidman, for goodness' sake! She'd had everyone wrapped around her ringlets from the minute she was born. She'd smiled her way through junior high and high school without a pimple and graduated with the Homecoming Queen crown. She had two parents, living and breathing in the home she'd grown up in. She had a getaway on 64th between Park and Madison and a marriage-proposing, houseboat-dwelling boyfriend in California. She had a book contract that would keep her wealthy for life (if Remke was right about its anticipated success). She had a publisher salivating to sign her to a sequel. And now she was pregnant. She had *everything*.

Fine, she'd had a few disappointments along the way, but who hadn't?

"Okay, so I'm monogamous now," Natasha corrected. "So I licked the drinking problem. But once a mess, always a mess. It's always there, just waiting to come out. Why do you think I'm so nervous about being a mother?"

"So you're saying people can't change?" I asked, the sympathy growing annoyingly stronger. She couldn't be serious. Yes, she'd been a bed-hopper with a penchant for vodka tonics, but now she was a sober, one-man woman who wanted to be a good mother.

That thought stopped me cold. She'd been an alcoholic slut, and now she *wasn't*. Beating both must have torturous. Beating even *one* addiction would have been hard enough. What the hell did I know about either world or what it must have taken to stand on her own two feet? She *had* changed. And she'd come through just fine. More than just fine. She'd come through her own personal hell a winner. So why didn't she know it? Why did she still think of herself as a loser?

"Natasha, you've already proven that people can change. You're walking proof. The outline for the memoir documents every word. You've overcome so much. How can you sit here and tell me that you haven't changed?"

"Just wait until you meet my parents, Jane. You'll see *how*."

Did I have to? I didn't know if I could take it. I didn't want to feel sorry for Gnatasha Nutley. I didn't want to like her. I didn't want to have conversations with her that were more intimate than the ones I'd had in the past week with Eloise. I wanted the Gnat to go back to being all hair and bangles and perfection. Gnatasha Nutley was morphing into a human being right in front of my eyes.

It wasn't fair. I wanted her ridiculous life story to go back to being ridiculous.

"Yo, excuse me, Miss Kidman?" asked a teenaged boy with an awestruck expression and a backward baseball cap. "Could I get your autograph?"


I could smell the hazelnut coffee the minute the elevator doors pinged open to the tenth floor of Karen Frieman's apartment building. Talking and laughing spilled out from underneath Karen's door. Oops. I wasn't late, was I? It was ten-forty. Which meant I was ten minutes late and twenty minutes early at the same time. The shower attendees were supposed to arrive at ten-thirty, and Dana was due at eleven for the big surprise. We'd been instructed to pipe down starting at ten-fifty and be prepared to shriek "Surprise!" at the top of our lungs when the doorbell rang at eleven.

Aunt Ina, in the fake French outfit we'd all been forced to wear, frowned at me the minute she saw me. "You're late, young lady." Her hands flew to her hips, which were encased in loose black capri pants. She wore her little white Keds. I had to admit that Aunt Ina looked pretty cute. She even had a beret atop her strawberry-blond curls. She grabbed my chin and kissed me on the cheek, then wiped off the lipstick stain she always left behind.

Karen's apartment was filled to capacity with people. The seven bridesmaids and the maid of honor were in the French outfits; of course, Karen had to stand out as the big cheese of the bridal party, so she was the only one allowed to wear a beret. Darn! I wanted to wear one! (Just kidding.) I'd ordered fifty-five invitations to the shower, and there must be that many women dotted around the huge apartment. Some were friends of Aunt Ina's from the neighborhood, but most were Dana's friends from

Forest Hills and college and the few jobs she'd held as an assistant buyer at Sak's and Bloomingdale's.

"You look nice," Ina said, surveying me. Thank God I'd remembered to wear the outfit: black capris and a black-and-white horizontal-striped boat-neck shirt with a stupid little white scarf around the neck. I'd forgot I had a little chiffon scarf. Amanda had given it to me with a pair of earrings for my birthday two years ago. "Your skin looks good. All dewy. Are you using something new?"

Yeah. It was called Finally Being Away From Natasha. That subway ride had been slightly too intense, slightly too surprising. I took a deep breath and tried to clear my mind of Natasha. It was bad enough I'd have to spend a couple of hours at her parents' apartment when it was clear there was tension in the family. And I'd have to take the subway back with her. It would be her, her, her, when I wanted to think about me, me, me…and Timothy. Perhaps he was the reason for my dewy complexion. The anticipation of tonight. Of those dark eyes smoldering at me. That dark hair brushing against my neck. That—

"There you are!" Grammy said, coming toward me. She handed me a cookie. "Don't let anyone see. We're not supposed to eat anything till Dana gets here." I popped the cookie into my mouth and smiled at Grammy. "So how's Mr. Rommely?" she asked. "Still dating?" Grammy wore the striped top and the little scarf, but she had on a white skirt instead of capris.

"Ma, of course they're still dating," Aunt Ina said. "It's serious. When it's serious, you don't break up every five minutes."

If only.

"Okay, okay," Grammy said. She pulled a compact and lipstick from her purse and applied a fresh coat of coral. "I can't ask? Ethan Miles is still available, you know." Yeah, no doubt. "He is such a nice young man. Do you know what he did just yesterday when your aunt and uncle were over? Your uncle Charlie was spraying air freshener in the hallway to get rid of the disgusting smoke smell from the Norwells next door, and who was coming home from work but Ethan. So your uncle Charlie asked if he'd mind playing a game of chess, and what did Ethan say? He said, 'Sure, love to.' And they played two games, leaving your aunt and me to have a nice visit and talk. Isn't that something? A busy young man like that entertaining your uncle Charlie."

Grammy was clearly missing the point: Ethan Miles apparently had nothing better to do.

"So when are you seeing Timothy again?" Aunt Ina asked. "Tonight? In my dating days, Saturday night was date night."

I nodded. "It still is date night. He's making me dinner." I regretted it the minute it left my lips. What was I, an idiot? You didn't tell your aunt or grandmother that a guy was taking you to his apartment for a date. It didn't matter if you'd been seeing the guy for months or years. Good thing they had no clue that this would be only my third date with Timothy.

"That had better be one of your smart remarks, Jane Gregg," Aunt Ina said, hands on hips again.

"It is," I confirmed. "Just kidding. Sorry. Um, we're going to a concert in the park and then he's taking me to dinner in a really nice restaurant."

"The Rainbow Room?" Grammy asked. "That's a nice restaurant. In my day, that's where all the young people went."

I'd never been in the Rainbow Room. It was a legendary restaurant, but it seemed to be on par with the

Empire State Building or a Broadway show: for tourists, not New Yorkers. Or, for tourists and *wealthy* New Yorkers.

"What does Timothy do for a living?" Aunt Ina asked. "Did you tell us? I can't remember."

I was now about to be elevated in the eyes of my aunt and grandmother with one word. "No, I don't think I mentioned it. He's a doctor."

Aunt Ina and Grammy stared at each other and broke out into huge smiles. "A doctor!" Grammy exclaimed. "Isn't that something. Surgeon?"

So, a regular old doctor wasn't enough, huh? I had my grandmother's number. "He's a resident, so he's not sure yet what his specialty will be. But he's leaning toward internal medicine."

"You're next," Aunt Ina declared, shaking her head, but now with a mixture of tearful pride and joy in her light blue eyes. "I just know it. Dana's already promised to aim the bouquet right at you, so be sure and catch it. You have a lot of competition. They'll all be clawing for that bouquet."

They could have it. "I'll try," I promised, my fingers crossed behind my back. There was no way I was lining up for that embarrassing display of singlehood. One of the Julies could catch it. I'd have to remember to time my trip to the bathroom moments before Dana got ready to throw.

Aunt Ina reached over to me and began flipping up the ends of my hair. "Why do you make your hair so straight, Jane? A little wave is nice."

"Everyone! Everyone!" announced Karen. "It's almost eleven. No talking from this minute on!" The lights were turned off. I could smell four different overpowering perfumes fighting for dominance over the hazelnut coffee.

"Everyone, shush!" hissed Karen.

The bell rang. "Who is it?" called Karen.

"It's me, Dana."

"Come in, it's open," Karen said as nonchalantly as possible.

Dana opened the door. The lights flipped on. "Surprise!" everyone shrieked.

"Omigod. Omigod!" Dana shouted. "I can't *believe* you! Omigod! The bridesmaids all look so adorable! Omigod!"

As Dana omigoded around the room, kissing and hugging fifty of her closest female friends and a few relatives, I peered out the window onto the Forest Hills streets from the tenth-floor view. People looked like ants from up here. I wondered if I could see the Gnat without realizing it. I was curious to know where she was, what old haunts were calling her name.

I knew what it was like to want to retrace your steps. To visit the sites you'd spent your best and worst times in. After Max had broken up with me I'd been drawn to a local playground that had been one of my childhood haunts. I'd swung on the too-small swings for an hour, smoking furiously, and by the time I'd left I'd felt comforted just enough to make it home. That playground had been the stage of happy times for so many years when I was a kid. My father had been alive while I'd swung there, when I'd climbed onto the jungle gym. Natasha hadn't yet moved to Forest Hills to introduce me to insecurity and steal the heart of the boy I adored. And Dana Dreer was just a pipsqueak, no cuter than I was until puberty turned her into a princess and me into a closet loudmouth too shy for a personality.

Three or four years ago, that playground had been torn down so that a new apartment building could be built.

When I'd stopped by one Sunday after a guilt-visit to Grammy and saw the construction site, I'd cried. There hadn't been anywhere to go for comfort after that. There was only Eloise and St. Monica's on the first Sunday of every month after services.

Edith Piaf began singing, and Karen announced it was time to dig in to the buffet. A line immediately formed as though no one had ever eaten before. I made myself a lox-on-vegetable-cream-cheese-slathered-bagel-sandwich and tried to make myself invisible by sitting on an ottoman in the far corner. Twenty minutes later, Karen announced it was time for Dana to open her gifts. Claps and shrieks. I tried to stay where I was, but Aunt Ina glared at me and pointed to the chair next to hers. I dutifully lugged myself over and plopped down.

Dana sat in a high-backed chair facing the crowd, a mountain of wrapped presents next to her. Oops. Maybe I should have gotten her a gift instead of slipping a hundred-dollar bill into a card. Nah. Eloise and Amanda were right. Who wanted another vase or coffeemaker? People wanted money to do what they wanted with. Grammy handed Dana a gift, and bridesmaid Amy picked up her little notepad and pencil to document who gave what for thank-you cards.

"So what did you get Dana?" Aunt Ina whispered to me as Dana carefully unwrapped. We were going to be here a long, long time at this rate.

"A hundred."

"Jane!" Aunt Ina scowled.

"What?" I whispered. "My friends told me to give money. They said that was what couples really want."

"From strangers!" Aunt Ina hissed. "You don't give your *cousin* money. You buy her a present, something personal." She shook her head.

"I'm sorry," I said. "I thought she'd appreciate the money."

"Jane, she's marrying a millionaire. She doesn't need your money."

"Why, because I live in a rattrap and make twenty-six thousand a year? Because I'm so pathetic next to her?"

Aunt Ina shook her head, more slowly this time. "Jane, I've just about had it with you," she whispered into my ear. "This isn't about *you*. It's about the difference between right and wrong. Family spends the time to buy a personal gift. You don't give your cousin money. I don't care how much or how little either of you has. Do you hear me?"

How could I not? She was hissing in my ear.

"Mommy, look what Karen gave me!" Dana exclaimed over Edith's mournful wail. "It's that gorgeous print I fell in love with at the museum!"

"How nice!" Aunt Ina said, big smile. She turned to me. "*That's* what you give your cousin. Something you know she'll cherish. That print probably cost all of twenty-four dollars and couldn't be more perfect a gift."

"Well, I guess I can't do anything right, can I?" I snapped into her ear.

"Mommy, look what Julie knitted for me!"

The Ally McBeal shrinker zapped me again. I felt so small. As Aunt Ina jumped up to feel the wool sweater and ooh and aah, I took the opportunity to slip away to the other side of the room under the pretense of pouring myself another cup of coffee. Okay, I screwed up. I should have followed my instincts and gotten her a real present. I shouldn't have waited until the last minute to go present shopping and then forgotten to buy anything. But I would have bought Dana a real present this morning if I'd thought it was such a big deal.

"Janey! Thank you so much!" Dana called, waving the money-stuffed card in the air.

I smiled big and mouthed a you're welcome. Was she secretly hurt, or was Aunt Ina just being Aunt Ina? I wasn't sure. I wasn't sure about anything.

All I wanted was to be in Timothy Rommely's apartment, eating chicken enchiladas and drinking homemade margaritas and licking salt off his lips. Instead, I had hours to go here, then a visit with the Nutleys—which sounded truly frightening—and then a subway ride back on the Nicole Kidman express.

God, I wanted a cigarette.

Starbucks was packed. I found Natasha sitting at the long counter along the window, wearing her sunglasses and reading *The Village Voice*. She saw me and waved, then jumped off her stool. I had the weird and unexpected sensation of being comforted by seeing her. Probably because I knew *she* wouldn't yell at me. What a relief it was to spend some time in the presence of someone who thought you could do no wrong. Whether it was fake or not. Maybe that was why the Gnat didn't mind signing someone else's name to autographs. For that four seconds, she was someone else.

"So how was the shower?" she asked, slipping the newspaper into her straw bag.

"Don't ask," I said. "The usual family nightmare."

"Can't possibly be worse than my family," she insisted as she led the way out.

How bad could the Nutleys really be? I was sure they were the same old annoying but lovable types as Ina and Grammy and Uncle Charlie. They weren't the same generation as Natasha and I, they didn't understand a word you said and they had no qualms telling you off. That was family. My parents had been a little different because they'd been so young and sort of hip. The Nutleys were square, which had to make things harder. Plus, when you were used to the whole world falling all over you, it was probably a little tough to deal with parents who knocked you down to size.

"So what did you do today?" I asked Natasha as we turned down the side street her parents' building was on.

"I mostly walked around, past P.S. 101, Sage, and the high school," she said, brushing a ringlet out of her face. "It was pretty nostaglic. Whenever Jimmy and I got into a fight or broke up or my parents yelled at me for something, I used to go to the little playground behind Russell Sage and sit under my favorite tree and cry. I sat under that nice old tree so much that I came to think of it as mine. I even tried to carve my name into the trunk, but I only managed to carve part of the *N.* I looked for it today, but the weather and the years must have obliterated it."

So she had her "place" too. Maybe I should have picked a tree. It would still be there today, unlike my playground.

"Here we are," she said, leading me down the steps into the courtyard of a building off Austin Street. "Do I look okay?"

I suddenly realized why Natasha looked like an astronaut's wife. Because she was visiting her parents and obviously wanted to come across in a conservative, good-girl way. The sympathy churned in my stomach. She sure was trying hard.

Natasha didn't say a word as we took the elevator to the fourth floor. When we arrived at 4K, she took a deep breath, smiled at me and knocked. When the door opened, Natasha attempted to hug and kiss her mother, but she'd caught Mrs. Nutley off guard, and the whole thing turned awkward. Natasha had ended up air-kissing her own mother.

"Jane! How nice to see you!" Mrs. Nutley exclaimed. "My goodness, you look so much like your mother, God rest her soul." I smiled. "So come in, sit down," Mrs. Nutley said. "Natasha, your father had to go out for a little bit. He should be back soon."

Natasha offered an *oh, okay* smile, but I could see she was disappointed. We followed her mother into the living room. The room hadn't changed in fifteen years. I'd been in this apartment once before, when Natasha had invited every girl in our sixth grade to a "beauty" party. From four o'clock to seven, we gave each other facials and manicures and pedicures. That had endeared Natasha and the Nutleys to the parents of every girl in Mrs. Green-man's class. Natasha was the popularity queen that every girl talked incessantly about at home, so invitations to her party made everyone feel important, and in turn, made parents feel their daughters were on the social A list. The Miner twins and I had been sure the Nutleys understood that and insisted she invite *all* the girls, or else no beauty party. The dynamic of the party was the same as it was in school. Cliques formed immediately. Lisa, Lora and I had found a corner and painted each other's toenails and sung along to the Go-Go's, just like everyone else. We'd refused to admit that we'd had a good time or that we'd been thrilled to be invited.

Natasha and I sat down on the sofa, which was covered in plastic like Andrew Mackelroy's parents' on Delancey Street. Mrs. Nutley sat in one of the hard-backed chairs on the other side of the coffee table, the strained expression never leaving her tight face. "Help yourself," she said, gesturing to the pitcher of iced tea and the plate of vanilla wafers on the table. "So, Jane, I understand your cousin Dana is getting married. How nice."

How monotone. I blabbed on about Dana's shower and the upcoming big day, more to fill the painful awkwardness than because I wanted to talk about Dana. Mrs. Nutley wasn't even looking at Natasha. And I seemed to be the guest here. I wanted to bring the conversation back to Natasha, let her have some of her mother's attention.

"Well, you must be so proud of Natasha," I said to Mrs. Nutley. "She's so accomplished at such a young age! And who knew she was such a great writer!"

Mrs. Nutley sipped her iced tea and turned the strained smile to me. "I understand you're the editor of the book. How did you get into publishing? Did you always want to be an editor?"

I glanced at Natasha. She had an equally strained smile on her face. I blabbed on for a minute or so about my career and again tried to turn the subject to Natasha, but her mother kept changing the channel. The tension in the room was almost unbearable.

"Daddy's not coming back, is he?" Natasha asked in a small voice. "Not till I leave, right?"

"Natasha, you made your bed," her mother said, looking at her for the first time. "I'm sorry, but you did. You're going to have to live with the consequences of your actions."

Natasha put down her glass of iced tea. Was she going to throw the tea in her mother's face? Storm out? "Mom, there was a special reason I wanted to come visit you and Dad today."

I let out a breath I didn't even know I was holding.

"Well, that's no surprise, Natasha," Mrs. Nutley said. Her voice was so cold. "Your father said there had to be a reason. How much do you need?"

Natasha turned white for a second. "No, Mom, I'm not here to ask to borrow money. Is that what you thought?"

Mrs. Nutley had the decency to color. "Natasha, I don't know what to expect from you anymore."

"Well, speaking of expecting," Natasha began, seeing her opening, "I have some really great news. I wanted to tell you and Dad together, but I guess you can tell him for me."

Her mother waited, the strain on her face never giving. She picked up her glass of tea and sipped it, more to have something to do than because she was thirsty, I surmised.

"You're going to be grandparents," Natasha announced. "I'm going to be a mother. Isn't that wonderful?"

Mrs. Nutley looked at Natasha with an expression of pure disgust. "I don't see a wedding ring on your finger. And I don't suppose there'll be one. I don't suppose you even know who the father is. What a piece of work you are."

"Let's go, Jane," Natasha said, bolting up. "I'm sorry I interrupted your day. Please tell Dad I'm sorry I'm embarrassed him by coming to Forest Hills."

"Don't you use that tone with me," Mrs. Nutley snapped. "As though *you're* the wronged one. You *are* an embarrassment to this family, Natasha. And you just keep it up, nonstop."

Natasha grabbed her straw bag and ran to the door. I shot up and glanced at her mother; she stood and turned her back. Suddenly I wasn't so sure which was worse: having no parents, or having parents who didn't respect you. Who didn't like you enough to just love you. Who kept a record of all your mistakes and shortcomings in indelible ink.

I ran after Natasha; I could hear the clatter of her sandals down the stairwell. I caught her at the landing to the first floor. She dropped down onto the bottom step and cried, her face buried in her hands.

"Come on, Natasha," I whispered, extending my hand. "Let's get the hell out of here."

She looked up at me, her face crumpled and tearstained. She took my hand. She didn't say a word as we walked the short distance to the Continental Avenue subway station and waited on the hot platform for the R train. She twisted her hair up into a bun at the back of head and put on her sunglasses.

The train roared into the station, offering a bit of wind relief. We settled ourselves onto two seats on the now crowded train. "You were right, Natasha," I said, once the train moved out. "Your family is a bigger nightmare than mine."

She let out a small laugh and reached a hand under her sunglasses to wipe away tears.

"How did you make your bed, anyway?" I asked.

She sniffled and reached into her bag for a tissue. "I've been a slut in their eyes since my mother caught me and Jimmy making out on my bed when I was in the seventh grade. I could never do a thing right as far as they were concerned. My grades disappointed them, the phone ringing off the hook annoyed them, Jimmy and his tattoo bothered them. My mother liked to say that my looks would get me places I hadn't bought a ticket to, and that I'd be in a for a rude awakening someday."

I could definitely imagine Mrs. Nutley saying something like that. I wondered if my mother had really liked Mrs. Nutley or if they'd only been acquaintances. I couldn't imagine my spirited, fun mother being friends with such a cold bitch, who clearly had serious issues. "I had no idea things were so bad back then," I told Natasha. "I thought your life was perfect."

Natasha shook her head. "My parents and I have always had a very strained relationship. They were horrified when I told them I wanted to be an actress. To them, Hollywood's like one big orgy, and when I dropped out of college to pursue the acting dream, they freaked out. When I went into rehab, they pretty much wrote me off. And then I went on national television and told the world about my affair with The Actor. That did it. I'd shamed them, and they told me they were washing their hands of me."

I was shocked. "But you're their only child. And you're pregnant!"

"They're weird people," Natasha said. "Cold and unforgiving."

"What is there for them to be ashamed about?" I asked. "It's not like anyone in Forest Hills thinks of you as anything less than a major celebrity. You saw how Dana reacted to you. She's proudly told everyone she knows that the famous Natasha Nutley is coming to her wedding. She's so thrilled."

Natasha smiled weakly and shrugged. The train lurched into the next station and flung me against her.

"Don't you have any other relatives?" I asked. "A doting grandma or aunt? Anyone?"

Natasha seemed to brighten for a second. "I do have an aunt Daphne—my dad's sister. We were close when I was young, but she's always sided with my parents. I'm afraid to even call her to say hi."

"I just don't get it," I said. "How could your entire family not appreciate everything you've accomplished? Don't they know how hard you worked to break into show business? How agonizing it is to deal with a broken heart? How difficult it is to conquer an addiction? Your parents should be applauding you.''

It was true. They *should* be applauding her. You'd think her parents would be hungry to forgive and forget, even if they were toughies. She was trying to keep the relationship alive, but if even a grandchild couldn't crack Mrs. Nutley, things truly might be hopeless. I had a feeling that Natasha wouldn't give up on them, though. It was becoming clearer and clearer to me that Natasha wasn't a quitter. No matter what, she wasn't afraid to keep trying, to keep forging ahead. I wasn't like that. I'd never been like that. The minute I felt defeated, I stopped. I gave up. I always figured there was no point in wasting time and effort and energy trying so hard for something that would never be.

Something occurred to me just then. Perhaps that defeatist mentality had something to do with why I wasn't upset about Jeremy's engagement. It wasn't that my crush hadn't been real. It was that it had been just that: a *crush*. A crush you have on a movie star, a rock star—from afar. You don't expect anything to really happen, so it's completely safe. And you expect stars to marry models. You don't get upset. Natasha had been right to express her surprise about my never making a play for Jeremy. Out of my league or not, I'd put the kibosh on even the possibility. I'd been doing that forever. Expecting the worst and acting accordingly. I'd focused on Jeremy Black for five years because I'd been afraid to focus on a ''real'' guy, a guy I might be able to have a real relationship with. ''Loving'' Jeremy from afar had kept me safer than I ever realized. I'd never make my feelings known, and he would never be attracted to me himself…no, there would never be a thing to worry about. I'd never have him—and I'd never lose him.

Natasha pulled a pack of tissues out of her bag and slipped one underneath her oversize glasses. She was crying.

"Natasha, they *should* be applauding you," I told her. "They should." I wanted to make her feel better, but I had no frame of reference for what she was going through. My parents had been so supportive, so loving, so good to me. I couldn't imagine what it felt like not to have my parents' love and respect. I only knew what it was like not to have them at all. But at least I knew that they'd loved me while they were alive.

"Applauding what?" Natasha asked. "Jane, I sign another person's name when people ask for my autograph, remember? No one knows who I am. *I* don't even know who I am—" Her hands reached under the sunglasses. "Let's change the subject, okay?"

"You *do* know who you are, Natasha. You make things *happen*. Your acting career. Your relationship with The Actor, getting around The Document, writing an outline for your memoir and selling it, your relationship with Sam. You're totally proactive. And when things don't work out, you pick yourself up and try something else, something better. You have so much to be proud of! And you *should* be proud of yourself. I can never make anything happen the way you do."

"That's not true," Natasha said. "You're an executive editor, you've got a doctor for a boyfriend, your family loves you, you have a circle of good friends. Your life is so enviable, Jane. You don't realize it because it's yours, but it is. Trust me."

I think I already did. A little. Maybe.

"Don't you see, Jane?" Natasha continued. "I'm just trying to *cope*. Everything I do is in reaction to something awful that happened, you know? I know this'll sound cli-

chéd, but it's like I have to write out where I've been to
see where I'm going. Does that make sense? That's why
I'm writing the memoir. People think I'm capitalizing on
The Actor's fame, but that's not it at all. I really loved
him,'' she whispered. Both hands sneaked under the sunglasses again.

"Natasha, I know what it's like to be heartbroken," I
said. "And it's not like my life is so perfect. I'm not an
executive editor—just an assistant editor." That was all
she was getting. There was no way I was 'fessing up
about my made-up boyfriend who lived on the Upper
West Side. No way. I didn't know Natasha. Not really.
She clearly had no trouble telling anyone her personal
business. She wasn't necessarily confiding in me. She was
simply yakking to an interested party—the editor of her
autobiography. How did I know I could trust her?

Natasha took off her sunglasses and blew her nose. She
looked at me. "Wow, girl. You deserve a promotion."

## Thirteen

Eloise and Amanda had insisted I wear my new black lace Miracle Bra with the matching itty-bitty panties for tonight's date with Timothy. I was glad I listened. Sex was everywhere in Timothy's apartment. In the kitchen as he spooned his homemade mole sauce into my mouth. Across the dining room table as he refilled my wineglass and told me stories about his first kiss when he was twelve. From Timothy's stereo speakers, softly playing Marvin Gaye. And now, on his living room sofa, where we were sitting so close to each other that I might as well have been on his lap. Which was where I wanted to be.

Was anything sexier than a man in faded Levi's and a white T-shirt?

After the day I'd had, tonight was like a soothing balm. I'd had just enough time to go home and change and make it to Timothy's apartment across town. I'd walked Natasha home from the subway station and ordered her to take a bubble bath and listen to some great music and think about all the wonderful things in her life now. Granted, she might not be able to change how her parents felt, but she could focus on how good things were for her despite them. She had the baby to think about, and Sam and her career as a writer. I'd gotten her cheered up enough to whip off the sunglasses and smile a tiny smile.

When I'd arrived at Timothy's apartment, a one-bedroom in a high-rise on 87th off Broadway, he'd welcomed me with a bouquet of red roses, a kiss and a glass of red wine. I hadn't been allowed to help with dinner; I was only allowed to "adorn his apartment and look beautiful." During dinner, I'd told him that Natasha wasn't missing anymore, that my boss was threatened by me, and I'd asked if he thought it was a faux pas to give your cousin money for a bridal shower gift. He toasted me to the first two, and assured me that giving money was never a faux pas. I'd told him he was an amazing cook, which was only half true. Who was I to expect that a doctor who looked like Thomas Gibson and was so sweet and funny and smart and irresistible and available could cook Mexican, too?

I'd relaxed after fifteen minutes in his presence. But I was nervous now. Every time Timothy moved a muscle, I mentally jumped.

"Nervous?" he asked, dimples popping.

"Me?" Coy, coy, coy.

And then he kissed me. Slow at first, then faster, harder. I slipped my arms around his neck and pressed against him. I could hear his intake of breath. He tasted slightly of red wine. He pulled back and looked at me, running a hand down my hair. "You are so beautiful."

I couldn't say a word. I could only kiss him. His hands stroked up and down my back, and then he pulled back from me again and opened the top button on my thin black cardigan. He looked up at me to see if I'd stop him. No way. He smiled, then opened the second button and kissed the little expanse of skin as he went down, button by button. I leaned my head back against the cushions and stared at the top of his dark head as he trailed kisses to the top of my stretchy black skirt. My hands were in his hair, stroking back the silky strands. And then he shot up and kissed me so hard, so passionately, I could barely breathe. He slowly took off my cardigan, his eyes never leaving the Miracle Bra. Then he trailed kisses from my stomach up to my neck. His tongue darted over my lips, inside my mouth, back over my lips.

I felt like a pat of butter melting over toast. Timothy sat back and pulled me on top of him so that I was straddling him. His eyes were on my bra. He glanced up at me for a second, then kissed me again. His hands were on the clasp to the Miracle Bra. He couldn't get it open.

He laughed and looked at me. "You'd think I'd be able to open this thing after all these years. Guys have been unhooking bras since they were fourteen."

"Maybe I should help," I said.

Timothy leaned back and smiled. "Maybe you should."

I unsnapped the Miracle Bra, glad my 34Cs would stand on their own. The second Timothy heard the little click, he took over. His hands and mouth were everywhere.

"So maybe we should move this party into the bedroom," he said.

"Maybe we should."

He laughed and took my hand and led me topless into his bedroom. I was glad to see a stray sock on the side of the bed; Timothy was humanized. We fell onto the bed,

Timothy half on top of me. I took off his shirt; he took off my skirt. Our hands, mouths, legs, arms were all over each other. He reached a hand over to his bedside table and pulled a condom out of a little wooden box. He looked at me and I smiled, which gave him the go-ahead. I didn't feel nervous. I felt ready. Ready to make love with Timothy Rommely, ready to give myself to him completely. I couldn't wait to feel him inside me, filling me up, his weight and hard body pressed against me. I settled myself flat on the bed, my head nestled on his soft pillows, the top sheet turned over on my chest. And waited.

And waited. Timothy was sitting on the edge of the bed, facing away from me. ''Uh, maybe we should just kiss for a little while,'' he said, sliding over to me. He lay beside me and began kissing my neck. ''Hiding that hot body under there isn't going to help.''

Oh. Oh! Duh. You'd think I'd never had sex before. I'd been with only three other guys. My first was Max. Twenty-two was a little late to lose your virginity, but that was me, queen of the late bloomers. After losing my mom, I couldn't imagine finding comfort in the conversation or arms of some college kid who was more interested in getting in my pants than getting in my heart. Well, actually, the truth was that I'd been afraid. Scared out of my mind. Why like a guy when it meant I might lose him? And then Max, handsome, wonderful Max, had taken the choice out of my control. I'd fallen in love. Next was Soldier of Fortune Guy. I'd slept with him because I was tired of Max being the only one. The sex hadn't been so great with SOF Guy. He'd been too fast and too clumsy and too interested in his own orgasm. Or maybe he'd just been nervous. Back then, I'd written him off as selfish. And then there had been Gorgeous Dumb Guy.

We'd met over lattes, gone on three dates—all at Starbucks—and he'd dumped me over lattes. He didn't think we were sexually compatible. Jerk. Try we weren't intellectually compatible!

Timothy peeled down the top sheet and again his hands and mouth were all over me. But I could feel that there was nothing going on down there with him. Was it me? Was it him? What was it? We'd been so hot and heavy, and now *nada*. I usually skipped all the articles about sex in *Mademoiselle* and *Glamour* and *Cosmo;* I never had sex, so what was the point of reading about it? Now I wished I'd paid more attention. Was I supposed to do something? Try to turn him on? Ignore it?

"Damn," Timothy said, flopping onto his back next to me.

"It's okay," I said, hoping that was the right thing to say.

Timothy smiled at me, grabbed my hand and squeezed it. "You sure?"

I nodded. "Maybe it's better not to rush it, anyway."

"That's true," Timothy said. "We do have all night."

That wasn't exactly what I meant, but it was good enough for me.

Ten minutes later, he tried again. Still nothing. And nothing ten minutes after that. Now Timothy wasn't quite as okeydoke about it.

"Maybe I should just take you home."

"Maybe you shouldn't," I said, hoping he'd get our little private joke.

"This really isn't funny to me, okay?"

Huh. Now what was I supposed to say?

"Look, maybe I should just take you home."

"Timothy, it's really no big deal."

"It is to me," he said, throwing off the sheet. He handed me my skirt.

There was nothing worse than a guy handing you your skirt with an expression like Timothy's. I suddenly felt very naked. What the hell had happened to my perfect night? So what if we couldn't have sex? Who cared? I just wanted Timothy.

My arms folded over my chest, I followed Timothy into the living room. He sat on the sofa, tying his sneakers. "Timothy, let's just watch TV or something," I said. "It's only midnight. I had this whole vision of us waking up together, reading the *Times,* eating bagels…"

"Jane, I'm really sorry, but I'm just in the mood to be alone, okay? Here's your bra." He tossed it to me, and I felt myself blush.

I didn't know if I was supposed to be mad or supportive. I didn't know Timothy well enough to know if he was always like this or if he was truly suffering from first-time-out syndrome. I found my sweater in a ball by the side of the couch.

Dating was costing me a fortune in dry cleaning.

"How about a nightcap?" I said to Timothy as we neared my apartment building. He'd been quiet during the cab ride here, but he was the only guy I'd ever been on a date with who had actually "taken me home." Most guys would hail you a cab and kiss you goodbye at the curb. But Timothy had insisted on taking me home the only way a guy could without a car.

"Sounds good," he said, dimples popping.

Finally. I'd been afraid I'd never see those dimples again.

"Cute place," he said as I opened the door to my apartment and switched on the lights. "Very cozy."

So cozy that three minutes later we were lip-locked on my futon. My cardigan had been flung over my television, and my skirt had tried to join it, but missed and landed on the floor. The Miracle Bra was draped over the Parsons table. Timothy's T-shirt and jeans were on the kilim rug. He had the most amazing body. His New York Sports Club developed chest was tanned and lightly covered with silky, dark hair. And what abs.

Once again, hands, mouths, fingers, arms, legs and breath were everywhere. And once again, Timothy ripped open a foil packet containing a condom. And once again, Timothy busied himself putting on said condom.

And at exactly 12:52 a.m. on Sunday, June 14, Timothy and I made love.

*Squeak. Squeak. Squeak.*

"Oh! Oh! Oh, yeah! Ohhhhh!"

That wasn't Timothy and me making all that noise. We'd both flopped onto our backs, sated and happy and breathing hard, our eyes closed, when Opera Man's girl-friend started moaning her *ohs*.

Timothy's eyes widened and he laughed. "Hey, that's *Carmen*, isn't it?" he asked, straining to listen to the opera through the wall. "Do you think they heard us?"

I blushed. We had been a little noisy. Well, just at the end, really.

"Oh! Oh! Oh!!! Oh yeah! Oh!"

"Are they married?" Timothy asked, his hands behind his head.

"Nope. He lives alone. I've never seen him, or her, but I think it's the same woman. She always sounds the same."

"Well, I can't let him put me to shame like that," Timothy said, trailing a line of kisses down my neck, down my chest, down my stomach.

Did I mention how much in love I was?

* * *

I was a nervous wreck the following week. Each day I waited for the big speech. The It's Not You, It's Me. Which really translated to It's Not Me, It's You, Because I Don't Like You After All. But one entire week later (it was now late Saturday afternoon, seven nerve-racking days since Timothy and I had done the deed for the first time), no big speech. No big anything, for that matter, but, well, Timothy was a doctor. I hadn't seen him since Sunday afternoon. Yeah, yeah, he'd let me know this past week would be a nightmare for him rotation-wise, but I was dying to see him. Oh, the pun I could make in this lovesick state! But I wouldn't. I had better things to do. Like whoop it up around my apartment because guess who had a date with a doctor named Timothy Rommely for Princess Dana's wedding!

I'd asked Timothy the big question last Sunday morning, after we'd made love the second time (yes, the second time *that morning*). The you-know-what issue that had plagued him the evening before had gone bye-bye. He'd stayed over on my too-small futon, which meant we'd slept cuddled together, our arms and legs flung over each other, our mouths *thisclose* for sleeping kisses. In the morning we'd gone out to pick up the *Times* and some bagels and cream cheese, then went back to my apartment to luxuriate in bed for a couple of hours. We'd had sex in at least three positions. And then Timothy surprised me by grabbing the Style section to read. "Hey, I know that guy!" he'd exclaimed, pointing with his bagel at a photo atop a wedding announcement. "This woman's related to Nelson D. Rockefeller!" was followed by "I can't believe this guy's getting married at twenty-four." And so it seemed the perfect time and place to mention that my cousin's twenty-four-year-old face would soon grace those very pages.

"Sure, I'd love to go. Do I need a tux?" was his response to the question I'd been terrified to ask.

It was that simple. One question, one affirmative answer and, suddenly, I had a real date to the wedding. No, not just a real date. Timothy was hardly just a guy to help me save face with Natasha and Dana and Aunt Ina and Grammy. *He* was real. He wasn't some too-good-looking, out-of-my-stratosphere man I could never have. He wasn't *safe*. He was the real thing. And there I was, going for it whole hog, as Amanda would say. I would have liked to smoke my way through how scary it all was— liking someone so much, wishing on stars the way I did when I was a kid that he'd fall madly in love, hoping, hoping, hoping that this little romance would blossom into something beautiful and big and mine, all mine.

Okay, back to earth. Things weren't perfect, but they weren't supposed to be. Wasn't that what I'd learned from my lack of reaction to Jeremy's engagement to Ms. *Vogue*? Loving someone you couldn't have was perfect. That way, you only hurt yourself, because you were having a very intense relationship with your own heart and dreams, instead of with another person. I'd already begun putting my little epiphany to use. For example, when Timothy had told me before he left early Sunday afternoon that "dating a doctor ain't all it's cracked up to be— sometimes I'm so busy that my closest friends don't see me for weeks," I didn't go ape and call Eloise and Amanda and ask for an analysis. My instincts had told me that a statement like that was cause for mini-alarm. *His closest friends?* What was I? Chopped liver (as Aunt Ina would say)? And, although I only had three dates and one sleepover to go on, I had noticed that Timothy could be a tad impatient, like the way he'd acted last Saturday night when we couldn't make love.

And, while I was going over his every flaw and fault and driving myself bonkers and triggering my own whopping desire to smoke an entire pack of cigarettes, I might as well throw the biggie into the fray: He didn't call me until Wednesday. Did I sound childish? Like a teenager? I wasn't sure if I was allowed to quibble about this. But it seemed like another warning signal. How much could he like me if he didn't call Sunday night to tell me what a wonderful time he'd had, that he couldn't wait to see me again and, in fact, how about a date Tuesday or Wednesday? He hadn't called Monday either. I'd thought about calling him on Monday night to say hello, but I didn't want to seem too clingy. Same for Tuesday. Eloise had instructed me to call him, that this wasn't the 1950s if I hadn't noticed, and since when did I give control of my life and my relationship to the guy? Why did he get to call the shots? I didn't know the answer to that. I just knew I couldn't call him. I wanted to be *called*. Did that make sense? By Wednesday I'd been jumping out of my skin, but then he'd called! I'd been reading Natasha's revision of Chapter Two, which was really juicy and well-done, when the phone rang. I'd said my mini-prayer that it would be him and not Aunt Ina, and God was on my side.

Sort of. Timothy told me he was so sorry he hadn't been able to call, but busy, busy, busy, rotation, rotation, rotation, the William Remke of the hospital was on the warpath, busy, busy, busy, blah, blah, blah, he didn't think he'd have a chance to get away from the hospital other than to sleep for the next week, maybe even two weeks, things were that bad, blah, blah, blah, he wished he could stop by even to say hi, but busy, busy, busy, blah, blah, blah.

There was nothing worse than being beyond disappointed and not being able to be upset at the source. How could I quibble with the working life of a resident? Everyone had heard the horror stories of interns and residents working thirty-six hours straight, four hours a day for sleep and barely half a day off. Who was I to complain that Timothy couldn't come over to watch *Who Wants To Be a Millionaire* with me? The guy was busy for real. He wasn't playing squash with his friends or going to strip clubs or watching televised sports. He was working. And I'd better get used to it if I wanted this man in my life. Which I most certainly did.

I'd been hoping to whine about these matters at the Flirt Night Roundtable this past Friday, but it had been canceled. Amanda had a ''thing'' to attend with Jeff (business related) and Eloise was fighting a cold. So I'd made myself busy by finishing up my comments for Natasha's revised Chapter Two (which needed only minor tweaking) and making marginal notes on the first draft of Chapter Three. I'd read Natasha's work with a very different eye than I had when I'd first taken her on as an author. And with a very different heart. A heart, period. After spending so much time with her, learning so much firsthand about her, witnessing her mother's coldness with my own eyes, I had a context for everything I read. Natasha had called in a few times to report on her progress on the outline, which she was developing into a chapter-by-chapter masterpiece. She was also on page 120 of *What To Expect When You're Expecting*. She'd sounded okay—not her usual effervescent self, a tad subdued, but not depressed. I'd called her last Sunday afternoon after Timothy left to ask how she was doing. She burst into tears at the sound of my voice. I asked if she wanted some company, I felt so bad for her, but she said no, she needed to be alone and try to work her mother's words out of her system. I believed she would be okay. She'd proved she could handle quite a lot. At least she had the House-boat Dweller. It wasn't like she was all alone in the world. She had the proposing boyfriend and the baby, and that surely brought her a large degree of comfort.

The phone rang. Timothy? *Please, please, please.* Nope. This time it was indeed Aunt Ina, checking in with her thrice-weekly hello. Uncle Charlie had a sore throat, Grammy was just fine and guess what that nice Ethan Miles next door did the other day? He was nice enough to hang up the new needlepoint duck-pond scene that Grammy had had framed. Dana was arguing with her florist, and Aunt Ina was the queen of her building now that the wedding was coming right up. "Marla in 4K wants to know how much the wedding is costing us," Aunt Ina tsk-tsked. "Do you believe her nerve? I was going to tell her that Larry's paying, but what is it her business? I told her it cost plenty." And of course Aunt Ina asked how things with Timothy were, to which I'd replied with an enthusiastic "Great!"

As Aunt Ina and I said our goodbyes and hung up, I realized that I wasn't breaking out in hives over the fact that the wedding was just over a month away. *Why* wasn't exactly a million-dollar question. I knew it was because of Timothy. In just four mere weeks, my life had changed so much. I'd gone from boyfriendless to boyfriendfull, smoker to nonsmoker, ignored by Jeremy and Remke to applauded for my efforts, and I'd even admitted my true status as lowly assistant editor to Natasha. And it didn't even hurt. Thanks to her, and to Gwen and Jeremy and Remke—and even to Morgan Morgan—my worth as an editor had been validated enough to make me feel appreciated. So title, schmitle. Well, okay, *not* title schmitle. I wanted to be an associate editor so bad I could—I didn't know what I could do. I only knew I wanted it. I'd have to wait until late January, when the complete manuscript of *The Stopped Starlet* was due. That was when Remke could read for himself just how much I deserved to be an associate editor—and deserved a big fat raise.

I was suddenly struck with the desire to clean house, to vacuum my rug with Carpet Fresh and Windex my windows and mirrors and fold all my underwear, which was currently strewn all over in the top drawer of my dresser. I wanted my apartment to gleam the next time Timothy came over, not that I knew when that would be. Perhaps this coming week? The following week? Anyway, I knew exactly where to begin my cleaning frenzy: by getting rid of my cigarette paraphernalia. I was ready to throw the ashtrays and lighters away.

The whole sorry mess in a D'Agastino's supermarket plastic bag, I opened the cabinet under the kitchen sink and tossed the bag in the trash. Goodbye, smoking career—

"But you said you love me, El-weeze!" Serge bellowed one floor below. "You wear my ring. We are engaged to be married!"

"Serge, I do love you, it's just that I'm not ready to get married."

"To me!" he shouted. "You mean you are not ready to get married to me!"

Silence.

"If you loved me, El-weeze, *me,* you would marry me."

"I'm sorry, Serge. I'm so sorry."

Silence. And then the door slammed.

I finally took the hand away from my mouth. I ran to the window and stuck my head out. A half minute later, Serge stormed out of the building and up the street. I flew downstairs to Eloise's. "El? It's me."

She opened the door, her face tearstained. She held up her left hand. The tiny diamond ring was gone. I pulled her into a hug and she collapsed against me.

"I'm not engaged anymore," she said through sniffles.

"What happened?" I asked, walking to the futon and sitting her down.

"I guess it started the night we held the Flirt Night at Bloomies," Eloise said. She hugged one of the red pillows to her stomach. "I'd been so psyched to pick out all the stuff I wanted for my apartment. And then I realized I wanted the *stuff*. I wanted the plush towels and hundred-dollar coffeemaker and a talking scale. I wanted to walk around waving my ring. And then I realized I wanted everything you got to have for getting engaged—" Eloise broke down in tears and crushed her face against the pillow.

"Except Serge?"

Eloise lifted her face and nodded. She reached for her cigarettes. "Now I really blew it." She lit a Marlboro and sucked in a deep drag. "Now I'm not only *not* engaged, I don't even have a boyfriend."

"But, El, now you'll be able to meet the right guy. The one you'll want even more than the stuff."

"I guess." She exhaled a stream of smoke away from my direction. "I miss the feel of the ring."

"Let's go shopping for friendship rings in the East Village," I suggested. "C'mon. Let's go right now."

"Okay," Eloise said in a small voice.

"And let's stop by St. Monica's and light a candle for your empty finger," I added. Eloise sniffled and nodded.

"It's gonna be okay, El." I handed her a tissue. "You're now free to meet the guy of your dreams."

"Is it really ever gonna happen?" Eloise asked. "Are either of us ever gonna get married?"

What was going on here? Eloise was the most independent woman I knew. Now she was focusing on marriage as an end? That wasn't like her.

"Of course it's going to happen," I told her. "For both of us. But I'm a little surprised to hear you talking like this, El. You've never been hunting for a husband. You're so your own person—"

"I'm full of shit is what I am."

"That's not true," I shot back. "You've built a career, you have this amazing apartment, you've dated so many different types of guys. You're finding what you want. By the time you're really ready to settle down, you'll marry exactly the right guy for you."

Eloise gnawed her lower lip, then she jumped up and covered her face with her hands. "The right guy? Who wants the *right* guy, Jane? Are you kidding me? You of all people should get it."

"Get *what?*"

"What's the fucking point?" Eloise shouted. "Who wants to love some guy who's just gonna leave you, anyway?"

Oh. Now we were on the same page. I got up and took Eloise's hand and led her back to the sofa. "El, you can't look at it like that. Your mother wouldn't want you to. How would she feel if she knew you were scared to commit to someone because you were afraid you'd lose him, too? She'd feel like that was her fault."

"It was her fault!" Eloise screamed. "She died on me. Just like yours did—after your father did on her and on you. You should know how I feel. Instead, you sound like some fucking therapist.''

I noticed she didn't bring her father into the equation, and that could only mean whatever had become of him was too painful to talk about. Had she been thinking of him when she'd said, *Who wants to love some guy who's just gonna leave you, anyway?*

I wasn't going to bring up her father, but I felt the need to say something, so I started in. ''But, Eloise—'' But, Eloise, what? She wasn't wrong. She wasn't right, either. But she wasn't wrong. ''I don't know what I mean, okay? I just know that if we don't try, we'll be alone. Isn't that worse?''

''No, because at least we'll be alone and *not* miserable instead of alone and heartbroken or grief stricken.''

''Alone and not miserable?'' I asked. ''Isn't that an oxymoron?''

''We can be happy and alone,'' Eloise said, blowing her nose. ''We have so much going for us. Both of us. Our careers are going really well, we're totally on our own, we're doing really interesting things, we live in the greatest city in the world—''

I laughed. ''Yeah, our lives *really* suck.''

''Stop making sense,'' she said, a small smile tugging at her lips. ''I hate when you do that.''

''Everything is really going to be okay. I'm beginning to think that everything will be okay when it's supposed to be. Does that make any sense?''

''Yeah. I think so.'' She tucked a Jennifer Aniston layer behind her ear and took a deep breath. ''Enough of this melodrama. Let's go shopping. We have to get you something hot to wear for July Fourth. You're gonna spend the Fourth with Timothy, right?''

I shrugged. "Maybe. He didn't mention it. He might have to work."

"Well, how about if we make plans right now," Eloise said. "If Timothy has to work, it's you and me. If he doesn't, I'll hang out with Amanda and Jeff and his six thousand friends."

"I've got a better idea. If Timothy doesn't have to work, you spend the holiday with us. I'd love for you to get to know him."

"So you really like this guy, huh?" Eloise asked, lighting another cigarette. "You're not scared shitless?"

"I'm more scared than I was during *The Blair Witch Project*."

Eloise laughed her head off.

## Fourteen

Monday: Waited for the phone to ring. It did, but was never Timothy. Natasha delivered her revised Chapter Two. Aunt Ina instructed me to walk around my apartment in the peau de soie shoes to break them in for the wedding.

Tuesday: Phone rang! Timothy was working double time all week, but how about if he came over tomorrow night. Might be late. *No problem!* Wrote revision letter to Natasha on Chapter Three and for the revised outline.

Wednesday: Timothy canceled—couldn't get away from the hospital. Could I pencil him in for July Fourth for the fireworks and a rooftop barbecue? Sure I could! E-mail from Natasha: She was gung ho to start revising, planned to send the revised, polished first three chapters and the final outline two weeks from today.

Thursday: Phone rang unexpectedly. Timothy working the Fourth, so sorry, but he would make it up to me with fireworks of our own next week. I was so depressed that I didn't 'fess up to Jeremy that I was free to take on new projects now that Natasha was set and writing.

Friday: Flirt Night Roundtable held at trendy Union Square Café. Amanda, Eloise and I toasted to Eloise's bravery at giving Serge back the ring. Amanda and Eloise insisted Timothy's disappearing act didn't mean a thing—it was just the life of a doctor-to-be.

Saturday: Eloise and I watched the fireworks from the FDR Drive. Got chocolate fat-free frozen yogurts and went home to watch *Dirty Dancing* on television for the hundredth time. Natasha called to wish me a Happy Fourth. She was on page 200 of *What To Expect When You're Expecting* and busily working on *The Stopped Starlet.* Timothy did not call to wish me a Happy Fourth. Discussion with Eloise on what that meant (she insisted in best-friend style that it meant zippo, that the Fourth wasn't Thanksgiving or Christmas or my birthday or even remotely a phone call holiday). Aunt Ina called to wish me a Happy Fourth. So did Grammy. And Amanda.

Sunday: Read the *Times.* Mentally wrote my wedding announcement. *Gregg and Rommely To Wed. The bride will be known as Jane Greggely.* Waited for the phone to ring. It did: Aunt Ina: Had I started breaking in my bridesmaid shoes? (No, I had not.)

Monday: Waited for the phone to ring. Told Jeremy I was workless until next Wednesday. Assigned a new memoir-to-be about a male virgin, age thirty, who was neither a priest nor all that religious. Got a stack of slush manuscripts. Morgan eyed me funny all day.

Tuesday: Called Eloise and Amanda for advice. Should I call Timothy? Or wait? Both said wait. The guy was a doctor, after all. Morgan eyed me funny again. Reminder call from Aunt Ina to pick up my bridesmaid dress.

Wednesday: Picked up the phone instead and put it down twelve times. Read one slush memoir. Left early to get bridesmaid dress. Stopped in on Aunt Ina and Uncle Charlie; Grammy was over. Had a pastrami sandwich and carried my dress home on the subway. Claimed I was just stressed out from work when Ina kept asking if something was wrong.

Thursday: What, I wasn't a person in this relationship? I was calling him. Was it a relationship? Did three dates make a relationship? Did sex? Did three dates almost three weeks ago with sex make a relationship? Answering machine. I left a message. Not too desperate. Just a hello and a "Call me, I miss you." Morgan eyed me funny again and asked if something was wrong, Jaaane. I told her everything was just fine, thaaank you very much. Wouldn't she love that.

Friday: Flirt Night Roundtable. Held, at this very moment, at Big Sur on the Upper East Side. Timothy hadn't called me back. Amanda was beside herself. Eloise was gnawing her lip. I was beyond depressed.

"I just don't understand what happened with Timothy," Amanda said. "Should I ask Jeff to call him and find out what's up?"

Eloise exhaled a stream of smoke. "No way. That's too high school. He'll call when he can. He's just busy, that's all."

For three weeks? "Yeah, right," I said. "Who's too busy to start up a relationship, eat out at great restaurants and have sex? That's all a couple does for the first month or two. What did I do wrong?"

"You didn't do anything wrong!" Eloise declared, her hazel eyes angry. "He's just a jerk."

"Hey, we don't know that yet," Amanda mediated.

"Maybe he's just really busy. The guy *is* a resident. They don't keep the same hours as normal people."

I sipped my Cosmopolitan. "But he kept the same hours for our first three dates," I reminded Amanda. "I saw him Saturday, Tuesday and the next Saturday. Now I can't even see him once a month? Please. I'm getting the big blow-off—I know it. I don't get it, but he's definitely blowing me off. I did something wrong. But what?"

"Jane, you did nothing wrong," Eloise said, pointing at me with her cigarette. "You know what? I'll bet it's the erection thing. Maybe he's embarrassed and—"

"Eloise!" I slapped her hand.

"What erection thing?" Amanda asked, blue eyes wide.

"He couldn't get it up the first time they did it," Eloise explained. "And he got kinda huffy about it."

"Amanda, please don't tell Jeff that," I begged. "If Jeff talks to Timothy and says something about it, I'll die. Timothy will never talk to me again."

"Honey, don't worry," Amanda assured me. "I won't say boo, I promise."

I let out a breath. "Anyway, it only happened that one time, the first time we tried. After that, we did it twice, no problem—and then twice the next morning. He doesn't have trouble in that department."

"Yeah, but guys are definitely sensitive about that," Amanda pointed out. "It happened with Jeff in the beginning. He would get so frustrated and embarrassed. It took a lot to make him see I didn't care."

"So what happened? Did it go away?" I asked.

"Not totally," Amanda said. "It doesn't happen all the time. But when it does, at least now he knows not to get upset. When it first happened, I thought it was my fault. But I read up on the subject and learned it wasn't.''

"So what makes it happen? I asked.

"A lot of factors in him that have nothing to do with us. In fact, one article said that the more attracted to you a guy is, the more trouble he can have getting it up the first few times, because he's so nervous."

Huh. I made Timothy that nervous? I liked that.

"Trust me, Jane," Eloise said. "With that Miracle Bra of yours, Timothy was definitely overheated by you." We cracked up and sipped our drinks. "Speaking of Miracle Bras, do you think the Gnat's chest is real?"

"Are her boobs huge?" Amanda asked, waving away Eloise's smoke.

"It's not that they're so big, they're just perky," I replied. "Everything on her body is perky."

"So I never got to ask you what her parents were like," Amanda said. "Were they too fabulous and pretentious for words?"

Mrs. Nutley's strained face popped into my mind. "Actually no. Her dad wasn't there, and her mom was pretty cold. I don't think the Nutleys are too pleased that their daughter is airing her dirty laundry to the world."

"Does she talk about them in the book?" Eloise asked. "I could see that pissing them off."

"Nope. She says she's not close to her parents and that she knows she's a disappointment to them, but she doesn't spend much time on the family dynamic. The memoir's not about that."

"So what are they getting all upset about?" Eloise asked. "She's an adult. If she wants to tell the world about some actor she screwed, that's her business."

"Yeah, but it reflects on her parents, doesn't it?" Amanda remarked. "She's telling the whole world the intimate details of a pretty sleazy experience. Her parents have a right to be embarrassed.''

I didn't agree with that. A month ago, I would have. But not anymore. A relationship that had left Natasha heartbroken wasn't sleazy. That she was choosing to write about it wasn't sleazy either. Many celebrities, no matter how they'd achieved that fame, wrote about their personal lives, as did many average Joes off the street. It was cartharthic. And that was because Natasha, like everyone else, wasn't writing the memoir to share her private life with the world; she was writing it for *herself.* Whether she was defending herself, learning about herself, documenting a period in her life in her own words for her grandchildren or just writing a very long diary entry, she was doing it for herself. And that she was getting a semi-decent advance to write it was just icing on the cake. I had a feeling Natasha would have agreed to write the memoir for free if guaranteed publication.

''You know,'' I told my friends, ''I don't think the memoir has anything to do with Natasha airing her dirty laundry. I think it's about her coming to terms with herself, with a painful period in her life. And writing a book isn't exactly easy.''

''Whoa, Jane,'' Amanda said, reaching for her gin and tonic. ''Since when did you become Natasha Nutley's defender?''

Huh.

*Squeak, squeak, squeak.*

''Oh! Oh! Oh!!! Oh, yeah!! Yeah! Yeaaaaaaah!!!''

I peeled open an eye. Had the Oh Moaner woken me or had the phone rung?

*Ring!*

Didn't people know not to call before ten on a Saturday

morning? I snatched the phone, ready to yell at whoever it was. Until I heard Timothy's voice. I bolted up, suddenly wide-awake, and clutched the cordless to my ear.

"Are you still speaking to me?" Timothy asked. "I know I've been MIA for a while."

"I'm not mad at you, Timothy. I'd just like to see you. It's been three weeks."

*Squeak, squeak, squeak.* "Oh!! Oh yeah! Oh!!! Ohhhh!"

"I'm really sorry about that, Jane. I want to see you too, but things have been nuts here. I'm at the hospital right now."

"I understand, Timothy. I'm just dying to see that face of yours."

"That goes ditto for me. But they've got us working around the clock. This past week was so bad, I didn't even have a chance to go home once. That's why I haven't called. We've all been sleeping on cots. And it's gonna be bad for a while. But when it's over, I'm going to take you out for the most amazing dinner."

"Ohhhh! Oh yeah! Yeah, baby! Ohhh!!!"

"Sounds good," I said, pounding on the wall. "When do you think you might get some time?" Please say soon. Please, please, please.

"I can make a definite date for next Saturday night," he said. "I'm going to be working like crazy all week, but I'm off Saturday night until Sunday at two in afternoon. We'll have to do something low-key so I can get to sleep early. Is that okay?"

I jumped up and pumped my fist in the air like either a twelve-year-old or a tennis champ. I had my long-awaited fourth date! "That's absolutely fine. I can't wait to see you." I plopped back down on the futon, smiling so hard I thought my face would burst. He wasn't blowing me off! He *was* just being a doctor!

"I can't wait to see you either," he said. "I'll call to check in if I can. Otherwise, I'll see you next Saturday around seven-thirty or eight."

As we hung up, I realized my period was due next Saturday. Of course it was. Didn't Murphy's Law ordain that? Maybe Timothy wouldn't mind. After all—as everyone I knew kept reminding me—he *was* a doctor.

Friday, 3:14 p.m. I was tearing my cuticles to shreds. Today was the big day. Jeremy had promised to get back to me with his comments on the first three chapters and the outline of *The Stopped Starlet* by this afternoon, and I'd been a nervous wreck since noon. Any minute he'd call me into his office to discuss the partial. How I was getting through this day without ripping off the nicotine patch and bumming cigarettes from Eloise was beyond me. Thank God I could count on a Flirt Night Roundtable in four hours. I was in desperate need of a Cosmopolitan. Not only did I have raging PMS, but I was worrying myself into a frenzy. What if Jeremy ripped the chapters to shreds? What if they were off the mark? Too pornographic? Too self-help? Too not what he expected? What if the outline was a mess? Deep breath, deep breath, deep breath. Calm down. He'd loved the excerpt of Chapter One. He'd love the whole partial. Eyes on the little clock on my desk, I bit into another cuticle.

I'd placed the chapters and outline on Jeremy's desk at nine sharp this morning. I was proud of the partial, proud of Natasha for her hard work and excellent writing, proud of myself for spending the past two nights slaving over the manuscript with a pencil. I'd barely had to touch much of Chapter Two, and had only a bit of work to do midway through Chapter Three. The outline itself was in big, juicy, *New York Times* extended bestseller list shape. I'd done my job well, and I knew it. So why I had forgotten that since the clock struck twelve? *You did good,* I told myself. *You did damned good.* Jeremy *had* to like the partial.

Something suddenly occurred to me, something I hadn't given a thought to before now. If Jeremy approved the partial, that meant Natasha would go home, back to Santa Barbara and her proposing boyfriend. She wouldn't need weekly meetings or hand-holding to start the major work of writing the complete manuscript. Huh. No more Natasha to jangle her bracelets. No more tossing of the ringlets. No more phone calls at home or intense subway rides. No more *her.* I was just starting to get to know Natasha Nutley and, I had to admit, I was a bit curious to know her a little better. Not to sound like a self-help book, but in a way, the more I learned about Natasha, the more I learned about myself. Or at least that was how it seemed. I supposed I could even admit to *slightly* liking her. I knew she was staying in New York through a week or two of August; the boyfriend was flying in on the first, they'd go to Dana's wedding on the second, and they'd probably spend the following week walking up and down Madison Avenue, shopping for baby Prada clothes and furniture and accessories for the nursery. Then they'd fly back to the houseboat, and I'd hear from Natasha once a month or so, as she progressed with *The Stopped Starlet.* I'd planned to talk to her about the sequel Remke wanted once I had Jeremy's comments on *Stopped.* Overwhelming her with the idea of a second memoir before now would have been too much for her, and if Jeremy panned the partial, she might be less deflated if she knew he was behind her to the extent that Posh even wanted a sequel.

Tick-tock, tick-tock, tick-tock. Three-twenty.

The intercom buzzed, and I jumped. "Jaaane," whined Morgan. "Jeremy would like to see you in the conference room."

Ba-boom, ba-boom, ba-boom. I stood up and took a deep breath. The partial manuscript was good. There was no way Jeremy could say otherwise. Head held high, I smoothed my hair, picked a piece of lint off my Ann Taylor jacket, wiped my sweaty palms on my skirt and marched down the hall. I stopped by Eloise's office for a *you go, girl,* but she wasn't there.

The moment I entered the conference room, I saw the platter of cookies and the champagne and little plastic cups. Who was getting married now? Paulette? Daisy? Remke himself? I spotted Gwen behind Paulette; she was lifting Olivia into her arms from the baby carriage. If Gwen had turned up for this announcement, it had to be something big. Eloise was standing in the back, looking at the final cover mechanical for the *Skinny-Minny Wanna-Be* memoir. We caught eyes and I sent her a questioning look. She shrugged. The entire editorial and art departments were dotted around the room, plus Ian, the grumpy profit-and-loss number cruncher who I was forced to deal with way too often, and Irma, the temperamental contracts manager.

"Thanks for coming, everyone," Jeremy said, effectively stopping the chatter in the room. "Gwen has come in to make a special announcement."

What could she possibly have to announce? She was getting a divorce from Phoney-Baloney? The baby's poop was now green? Oh, God. Was she quitting?

"Hi everyone!" Gwen trilled as she handed Olivia to Morgan, who held the baby at an awkward distance from her body as though Olivia were contaminated. "I most certainly do have a special surprise announcement. I'd like everyone to get ready to clap their hands. Jane Gregg has been promoted to Editor!''

My mouth dropped open. Claps and cheers. Pats on the back. *Editor?* Had I heard right? Not *Associate* Editor? The champagne poured. I stared at Gwen, stared at Jeremy, stared at Remke, stared at Eloise. I finally clamped my mouth shut, but it fell open again. I'd gotten promoted!

"I'm so proud of you, Jane!" chirped Gwen. She took Olivia from Morgan and rocked her up and down in her arms, then came over to stand next to me. "Say hi-hi to Posh's newest editor, Livie-loo."

I played with Livie-loo's wispy blond curls. "I thought maybe I misheard, Gwen. I'm promoted to *full editor?*"

"You deserve it, Jane," Gwen said ostentatiously but welcomely gracious for once. "You were held at the editorial assistant level for a bit too long because you were so good and we didn't really need another editorial hand. And then you got stuck as an assistant editor for too long because of budget problems. You've proved you're editor level. Jeremy read Natasha's partial this morning, faxed me a copy, and we had a conference call with William. And *voilà.*"

"Yes, congratulations, Jane," Jeremy said, patting me on the back. "You've been very loyal to Posh, and we've all appreciated that and your hard work. The Nutley memoir really shows what you're capable of. It's dead-on."

Dead-on. Little currents of happiness started tingling at my toes and worked their way up to my fingers. Dead-on. I knew it! I couldn't wait to call Natasha and tell her.

"Good going, Gregg," Remke added. "And now that Natasha's working full speed ahead on the bulk of *The*

*Stopped Starlet,* you'll be taking on a couple of additional projects.''

"Your own projects," Jeremy added. "You won't be doing any more initial line-edits. You'll be doing your *own* edits."

I could feel myself beaming. I'd done it. I'd gotten my promotion. And not the perfectly fine promotion to associate editor. I'd leaped right over that to full editor! There were some accomplishments that no one could ever take away from you, and this was one of them.

"Okay, let's go, let's go, everyone," Remke snapped. "Drink up and let's get back to work."

Eloise squeezed me into a huge hug. "We are going to celebrate big time tonight!"

"Jane," Gwen said, settling Olivia in her baby carriage. "I'm so pleased about your promotion! When Jeremy called me to let me know he thought the memoir was proof of your readiness, I'd never been so proud! I mean, I taught you everything you know, so this really bodes well for my management skills. I've always said, I trained you well!"

I mentally rolled my eyes and smiled at her. "I appreciate everything you've done for me, Gwen. You've been really good to me." Good enough, actually.

She beamed and rocked the baby carriage back and forth. "You've blossomed, Jane. I've watched you grow from a twenty-two-year-old novice into a full editor. I'm just so proud. Ooh—guess who just made poopy face?" Gwen cooed to Olivia. "Jane, want to help me change her?"

"Um, I would, but I promised Eloise I'd go over the *Skinny-Minny* mechanicals with her, so…" A total lie. Changing a baby's dirty diaper wasn't exactly how I wanted to celebrate my promotion.

"Jaaane," Morgan said, two plastic cups of champagne in her hand. "Congratulaaations on your promotion. That's really greaaat. You definitely deserve it." She handed me one of the cups, then tapped mine with hers before heading to the table to snatch two chocolate-chip cookies.

Well, well. Would wonders never cease.

"Am I too late?"

I turned around at the sound of Natasha's voice and shocked myself by being glad to see her. We hadn't gotten together in three weeks, since the day of Dana's shower. She looked like herself again. She wore tight black leather pants, a tiny lavender microfiber tank top and high-heeled, lavender-black snakeskin slingbacks. Her perfect Nicole Kidman ringlets appeared sunlit, even indoors. She didn't look the least bit pregnant, but then again, she was barely three months along.

"Natasha, I got promoted to Editor!"

"I know." Her bracelets jangled as she tossed a few ringlets behind her shoulder. "Jeremy called and asked if I'd come over at three-thirty to celebrate. Congratulations! That must mean my chapters are coming along okay, huh?"

"He loved them!" I whispered. "So did Remke."

She flashed those super-white teeth in a dazzling smile. "Jeremy told me. I was so thrilled. You and I make a great team."

A team. Natasha and I. Huh. I hadn't thought of it that way before, but that was certainly what the editor-author relationship was.

"Champagne?" I kicked myself the moment the word was out of my mouth. Was I a total idiot or what? Hadn't I just read the fleshed-out outline of Natasha's life? The woman was a recovered alcoholic. Not to mention pregnant.

"No, thanks," Natasha said. "I don't drink. And neither does the baby." She patted her tummy.

Oh, God. I was an idiot. "I forgot for a second. I'm sorry."

"I'm glad you forgot." Natasha flipped a ringlet behind her back. "That must mean you're starting to see me as me, and not the mess in the book."

Huh. I most certainly was. Interesting. That was part of the realization I'd come to last week at the Flirt Night Roundtable. Unless you knew Natasha, really knew her, you wouldn't, *couldn't,* know her by reading her outline.

"So, it turns out I'm going to stay in New York for a while," Natasha added. "Sam doesn't think I should be flying around so early in the pregnancy. Isn't that crazy? He's such a silly worrier! So he's going to fly out on the first of August and spend a few weeks with me here. Wow, can you believe it's almost August? Dana's wedding will be here before we know it."

Yes, it would. In two measly weeks. And would Timothy be sitting next to me, making small talk with the Houseboat Dweller and twirling me around the mini-ballroom? I had no idea anymore. He hadn't called "to check in" this past week. Not once. All week I'd vacillated between He Likes Me, He Likes Me Not. I'd even plucked a flower from someone's first-floor window box and tried my luck; I'd ended on a He Likes Me Not. Why did this have to be so confusing? If he missed me, if he really liked me and wanted something to develop between us, wouldn't he have called? A three-second call on his way back from the bathroom or to lunch or to sleep. Wouldn't he want to talk to me? He'd found the time to call me last Saturday night, after all.

He was coming over tomorrow night. If he didn't give me the Can We Just Be Friends speech, the It's Not Me, It's You, I'd remind him of the wedding and make sure he knew how important it was to me that he be there. Surely for a special occasion he could get off duty. Couldn't he? Surely if it was really, really, really important to me. Right?

"Whoo-hoo!" Amanda yelled from our table in Evelyn's, a super-swanky Upper West Side bar. The Flirt Night Roundtable had the celebration of my promotion as its agenda. "Jane pays for everything now that she's a hotshot editor!"

I laughed. "Hey, my raise doesn't go into effect until the next pay period, and these drinks are nine bucks each!"

Eloise exhaled a stream of smoke. "You know what, Jane, my dear? You've got me raring to go. I'm gonna ask Daisy about a promotion on Monday. I'm due, too."

We all clinked our Cosmopolitans to that. "Okay, guys, I need to know what to do tomorrow night for Timothy's arrival. Do I doll up the place with scented candles and Marvin Gaye? Or is that too much?" I had absolutely no idea what was going to happen when Timothy showed up. Would we order in Chinese, watch HBO, make love and make plans for a next date? Or would I get one of the speeches? "Who am I kidding. He's coming to dump me." I slumped down on my chair.

"No way," Amanda insisted, "From what you described of his phone call, he's coming for a nice, low-key night with his honey, who he misses so much."

I brightened. "Do you really think so?"

"Guys don't come over to break up with you," Eloise

threw in. "They do it in public places so that you can't make a scene. You're totally safe."

I took a sip of my drink. "So what do you two think—candles and music and a little wine? Pizza and Coke? Nothing?"

Amanda and Eloise chewed their stirrers and mulled that one over. "I say doll up the place," Amanda said. "If you don't, that's like you expect something bad is going to happen."

"But what if something bad *does* happen?" I pointed out. "What if he *is* coming over to end it? Do I really want to be smelling vanilla and listening to Marvin Gaye when he dumps me? I'll never be able to listen to Marvin Gaye again."

"He is not going to dump you," Eloise declared with all the assurance of a best friend.

"I'll bet one hundred bucks he dumps me," I wagered.

Eloise exhaled a stream of smoke and smiled. "Jane, even though you're a hotshot editor at Posh, you still can't afford to lose a hundred bucks."

"Yeah," Amanda agreed.

"In fact," Eloise added, "I'll put up a hundred that Timothy tells you he's oh so sorry for his doctorly schedule, and he's gonna make it up to you by taking you to dinner at Gotham or Daniel."

"I'll put a hundred on Timothy, too," Amanda said. "I have faith."

"In him or me?" I asked.

Eloise swatted me with her stirrer. "You, you fool."

"*And* him," Amanda added.

"Fine," I said. "I wager my hundred that I get the 'Can we just be friends?' speech."

"Easy money," Eloise said, clinking glasses with Amanda.

This sucked. I was supposed to be celebrating my hard-won promotion with my buds tonight and my boyfriend tomorrow night, not chewing my cuticles to bits and taking bets on my love life. *Let my friends be right,* I prayed up in the direction of the crowded bar. *Let them win my hundred!* After all the *me too*s, after how compatible we seemed to be sexually, could Timothy just want to be friends? Things had been fine, so—

My heart stopped. Timothy Rommely was standing at the bar, waving a fifty at the bartender. I shifted my body so that I was blocked by Eloise, then peeked around her.

"What the hell are you doing?" she asked.

"Timothy! Straight ahead. He's at the bar!"

"Really?" Amanda asked. "I've never seen him in the flesh. Which one is he?"

"He's the one who looks like Greg from *Dharma and Greg,*" I reminded her. "He's the one who—"

Had just slung his arm over the shoulder of a woman who wasn't me.

Amanda sucked in a breath. "The one with the redhead?"

I couldn't speak. I couldn't even nod. Tears stung the backs of my eyes.

"He does look like Greg," Eloise said. "Too bad he's a two-timing asshole jerk—"

"Hey, wait a minute," Amanda insisted. "You don't know that. Maybe that chick's a co-worker and they just finished saving someone's life, or maybe she's his cousin or—"

We all watched as Timothy gave the redhead a flirtatious tug toward him and stuck his tongue in her mouth in a short but killer kiss. Now his back was to us. A bunch of people had come in and formed a second layer at the bar. At least they were blocking my view a bit.

"I'm so sorry, Jane," Amanda said, squeezing my hand.

"Are you okay?" Eloise asked. "Do you wanna get out of here?"

I still couldn't speak. I couldn't move. My heart had dropped to my feet. "I don't want him to see me," I managed. My mouth felt as though it were stuffed with cotton.

"Maybe you should go confront him," Amanda suggested. "Embarrass the son of a bitch."

Problem was, Timothy wouldn't be the embarrassed one. I'd take that honor. I was the spurned one. I'd be the one making the scene. Timothy would be the star of the show and get to go home with the redhead, besides.

I lunged for the pack of Marlboro Lights on the table. "I need a cigarette," I said, tapping one out.

"No!" Eloise whisper-yelled, grabbing the pack and stuffing them in her waistband. "You're not wrecking all that hard work for some asshole, Jane. He's not worth it."

Tears pooled in my eyes. I opened my mouth to speak, but nothing came out. I dared a peek. Timothy's back was still to our table. He and the redhead were sitting on stools at the bar, about seventy feet from where we sat. His arm was around her.

It was too much. The tears came and I couldn't stop them. My hands flew up to my eyes with a cocktail napkin. I felt Eloise rubbing my shoulder and Amanda squeezing my hand.

"We could sneak out without him seeing you," Eloise whispered into my ear. "C'mon, let's get out of here."

I stole another peek. Timothy and the redhead were now facing each other. Again he kissed her, and then they clinked glasses. He was probably saying, "Me too." I couldn't take my eyes off him, off the guy who was supposed to be mine. And because I was now staring at him, he turned in my direction.

Timothy Rommely and I were staring at each other, him with something akin to horror in his eyes. The redhead had swung her green-eyed gaze in my direction, too. I darted my gaze to my lap. "What do I do?" I whispered to Eloise and Amanda.

"You get the hell out of here," Eloise said. "C'mon, I've got your purse. Let's go."

And so we stood up and marched past Timothy and the redhead. I kept my eyes on the floor. I could feel him watch us leave. I ran up the steps leading to street level, tears falling down my cheeks.

"Jane, wait," he called out.

I turned around; Timothy was standing in the doorway, a beseeching look on his face.

Amanda and Eloise were on the top step. "We'll wait for you up here," Eloise said, a mixture of anger and concern in her expression.

And so I turned around and faced him, wondering what he could possibly want to tell me. It wasn't as though he could say, *Let's get a drink and talk about this;* his date was five feet away. "What's there to say, Timothy?"

"Jane, I know this looks bad."

What a classic. I didn't think anyone actually said that, even when it *did* look bad.

"It's just that things are really crazy at the hospital right now," Timothy said for the hundredth time since I'd met him, "and I guess it's easy to get involved with someone who's right there, going through what you're going through."

"So you've been seeing someone else?" I asked like an idiot. "That's why you haven't made plans with me?"

He nodded and had the decency to look deeply pained. "It's not serious or anything. And it's not like you and I had any conversations about exclusivity, Jane."

Did he not get it? Or was he just trying to save his butt?

He reached out to brush a strand of hair away from my face, and I stepped back. "I haven't seen you in so long that I forgot how pretty you are."

Was that a compliment? Was that supposed to make me melt and tell him everything was okay, he was right, we hadn't had that exclusivity conversation, and I couldn't wait till he came over tomorrow night to have sex with the moron who fell for his "Things are so crazy right now" crap?

"Tell me something, Timothy. What was all that *me too* bullshit?" I asked, hands on hips as though I were Aunt Ina. "Why'd you go so far to make me feel like we were headed somewhere, when you were never into it?"

He ran a hand through his hair. "I was into it, Jane. I really was. Our first few dates were great, but then I met..." He stared at his black shoes. "I'm sorry about the timing. I know it probably looked bad."

Fresh tears pooled in my eyes, and I tried to blink them back. So *that* was what he'd meant before by "knowing this looked bad." He wasn't trying to make excuses for himself. He was talking about the fact that he'd pulled his disappearing act right after we made love. He was talking about the timing. He'd met someone else and liked her better. I could see half of the redhead's hair at the bar. What was the point of talking to Timothy? He was only going to go back to the bar, win some sympathy from the redhead at "hurting some poor woman," and they'd both have a gin and tonic and forget all about me.

She'd probably comfort him later by giving him a blow job.

"So you were going to come over tomorrow night and what?" I asked. "Dump me? Or two-time the both of us?" I knew the answer to that. But I needed him to say it.

So, I wouldn't be Jane Greggely, after all. As if any editor worth her pencil didn't know that adverb-making "ly" was extraneous.

Timothy stared at his feet. "I'm really sorry, Jane. I didn't mean to hurt you."

I gnawed my lower lip, then turned around and ran up the steps. Eloise and Amanda were waiting with stricken expressions. I took one step toward them and burst into tears.

## Fifteen

I'd spent a picture-postcard summer Saturday afternoon (seventy-eight degrees and no humidity) under the blankets on my futon in the dark. Saturday night, Eloise had come up with Jiffy Pop to watch *Breakfast at Tiffany's* with me. When I was beyond depressed, only Audrey Hepburn singing "Moon River" could soothe me. But the moment Holly Golightly had set free her beloved Cat and then realized what she'd done, I'd sobbed so hard that Eloise had been afraid I'd ruptured something in my throat. She'd fast-forwarded to the part where Cat was sunning in someone's window, safe and sound, and I'd stopped crying.

Eloise had slept over. At around one or two in the morning, Opera Man had turned up the volume on *Götterdämmerung*—aka The Goddam Ring—and Eloise had pounded on the wall. All that had done was infuriate Opera Man and make him raise the volume. "You have to put up with this shit every night?'' Eloise asked. My tearstained nod must have looked really pathetic, because Eloise had flung off her half of the blanket, unlocked the door, stomped out into the hall and pounded on Opera Man's door. ''Shut that off!'' she'd screamed. ''It's two in the morning! Have some consideration for your neighbors!'' The volume had immediately lowered. Eloise marched back in, locked up and climbed into bed, muttering about the nerve of some people. I wasn't sure if she was aware that she'd managed to make me smile for the first time in twenty-four hours.

In the morning, Eloise had insisted on taking me for breakfast to celebrate my promotion since the whoo-hooing had been cut short Friday night. I wasn't exactly in the mood for celebrating, but Eloise refused to take moping for an answer. Amanda had called to check up on me as we were walking out the door. I'd assured her I was semi-okay, and then Eloise and I had gone to the diner on the corner of 79th and First Avenue, where I'd pushed scrambled eggs and home fries around on my plate. The three cups of awful coffee had helped, though.

And now, Eloise and I were making our way up the wide concrete steps to St. Monica's church. Eloise thought a midmonth candle-lighting for our mothers and my father and any other losses was in order. Mass was just ending as Eloise and I weaved our way through the throng of people exiting the church. The stained-glass windows alone were enough to make me feel better, no matter how down in the dumps I was.

Eloise lit a candle for her mother and for the end of her engagement to Serge, gave me a little smile and sat down in the last pew and hung her head. I lit a candle first for my father, and then my mother, and tried to picture them. I saw my father's face, so young, so handsome, so full of life and love and laughter. I saw him pointing out the Plaza Hotel and twirling me down Fifth Avenue the day before he died. I tried to picture my mother, but I couldn't. I tried again. And again, nothing. And suddenly, Max's face came to mind, and then Jeremy's, and then Timothy's. They floated past one another's. None of them had wanted me. I'd never been good enough to attract Jeremy, and both Max and Timothy had left me. Tears stung, and I blinked them back. Why hadn't they loved me? What was wrong with me? Why was I so unlovable? My knees started to wobble, and I dropped down beside Eloise and buried my face in my hands. She slid her arm around me. "It's okay, Jane."

"It's not," I croaked through a sob. "It's not okay."

"He didn't deserve you," Eloise whispered.

"More like I didn't deserve him. Or Max. Or Jeremy. No one ever wants me."

Eloise squeezed my shoulder. "Jane, that's not true."

"Oh yeah? So why'd I get dumped?" The tears fell fast down my cheeks. "Why do I always get dumped?" Eloise squeezed me closer, but all it did was make me cry harder. "Why did they leave me?" I whispered between sobs. "Why? Why?"

"Oh, Janey," Eloise murmured. "You'll meet someone else. Someone who'll love you forever."

My mother's face floated into my mind. She'd been forty-eight, and her hair had just started to gray. I could see her sparkling dark eyes and her slightly lopsided smile. My dad's face floated past hers. I remembered now. Remembered how I couldn't stop thinking about my parents' deaths those weeks and months after Max had dumped me. And now it was starting again. Their faces, almost like snapshots of times I recalled so vividly, flashed through my head. My mother. My father. Gone, gone, gone. My parents were dead.

"I lose everyone, Eloise," I whispered. "You were right. What's the point of caring about anything?"

"Jane, I'm going to throw your own words back at you. Your father and your mother wouldn't want to see you blaming them for leaving you. How do you think they'd feel? They'd want you to be happy. Living and having fun. Think how proud your mother would be about your promotion. Think how proud your dad would be that you gave your all to dating Timothy, a guy you really liked. They're up there rooting for you."

I stared up at the stained-glass portion of the ceiling and closed my eyes. "I lose everything and everyone. No one's ever gonna love me."

"*I* love you," Eloise told me, stroking my hair. "Amanda loves you. Your Aunt Ina loves you. God, Jane, I think even Natasha Nutley loves you."

"I miss my mom so much," I said, tears falling down my cheeks. "I want her back so bad. I just want my mother back."

"I know," Eloise said, leaning her head on my shoulder. "I know."

"Lay out the dress and the shoes and the jewelry," Aunt Ina said. I held the telephone at a safe distance from my ear. "Jane, are you listening to me? The wedding is next Sunday. If you don't have everything you need, you're going to be in trouble."

"I'm listening, I'm listening." I cradled the phone against my shoulder and tried to type title suggestions for the new memoir I'd been assigned. Remke and Jeremy hadn't been able to sign the Backstreet Boy, so they'd gone after a less well-known teenage singer who'd been a one-hit wonder in the year 2000. It was a told-to tell-all, which meant I'd be dealing with the hack writer and not the singer herself. I was grateful for all the work I'd been assigned. Concentrating on my job helped me not think about Dr. Did-Me-Wrong.

"Jane, are you typing, or are you listening?" Aunt Ina demanded.

"I'm listening," I snapped.

"Don't you take that tone with me, young lady," Aunt Ina said. "Just because you got a fancy promotion at work doesn't mean you have the right to act all superior with me. It's the twenty-second of July. The wedding is in eleven days. *Eleven days.* Do you hear me?"

"I have the dress and the shoes and the evening bag, okay? Can I go back to work now?" It was ten o'clock in the morning on Wednesday, and in ten minutes I had a meeting with my newest author, the told-to writer. I didn't have time to go over the outfit I'd spent way too much time and money on in the first place. And after the four days of pure heartbreak hell that I'd just been through, the last thing I wanted to think about was Dana Dreer's wedding.

Aunt Ina hung up on me. Great. Now I had to call her back to apologize. I punched in her number, but the line was busy. I tried again, but got the machine. "Aunt Ina, I'm sorry, okay? I'm just really busy at work and under a lot of pressure, okay?" Tears welled up in my eyes. I was becoming a regular crybaby.

My computer pinged to let me know I had e-mail. Amanda. *Hey, I have an idea. Remember Driscoll, the blind date you canceled? Why don't you call him and ask him out for the weekend? If it works out, you can invite him to the wedding! —P.S. No, I'm not crazy. Elo-*

*ise and I talked about it last night, and we think you should do it.*

Hello? Were they on drugs? Hadn't I been through enough? And what was I supposed to do, tell Driscoll that he had to pretend his name was Timothy at the wedding? I was over dating. For a long, long time. Clearly, I sucked at it. I'd rather become a workaholic. At least it gave something back, like a promotion and a raise.

The phone rang. Good. It was probably Aunt Ina calling me back. Like I needed the added stress of having my aunt mad at me?

"Jane, it's Natasha."

"Hey, how's everything going? How are you feeling?"

"Pretty good," she said. "I can't feel the baby kick yet, but my doctor says it's a bit early for that. The book's going well, too. I'm on Chapter Five."

"If you need me to look at pages, just send 'em. I'd be happy to read them for you."

"Thanks, Jane, but I think I'll be okay. I like the idea of writing out the entire manuscript and then going back over it to edit and polish before sending it to you. That okay?"

"Sure," I told her. "Are you still comfortable with the January fifteenth due date? If you need a few more weeks, that'll probably be okay."

"I think I'll be right on schedule, if not a little early, actually."

"Great. So, um, just curious, Natasha—have you spoken to your mom?"

"I tried," she said. I heard the jangle of her bracelets. "But she was her usual cold and clipped self. I'm ready to stop, I think. I'll send her pictures of the baby when he or she is born. Maybe that'll bring my parents around—or maybe not. I'm not going to let it kill me anymore, Jane. I can't.''

How did you do that? How did you decide not to feel something and then not feel it? Did it work that way? Or was Natasha kidding herself?

''The good news is that I called my aunt Daphne, my dad's sister, and though she was cold at first, she warmed up and told me she and my uncle Henry would love to see me! They live a few neighborhoods away in Kew Gardens. I'm going to spend the afternoon with them next weekend. Aunt Daphne said she'll work on my parents.''

I hoped her aunt would be successful! But at least she now had someone to turn to. I had no idea how worried I'd been for Natasha until now.

''Oh, by the way,'' she added. ''Dana called me yesterday and invited me to her bachelorette party, isn't that sweet? She said I'm as important a part of her past as anyone in her bridal party. I was so touched.''

Dana had invited Natasha to her bachelorette party? That was weird. Wasn't it? If Natasha had been so important to Dana, she'd *be* in the bridal party. And how big a part of Dana's life could Natasha have been? So she'd babysat her for a few years, so what? That gave her ''important'' status? I never understood my cousin and I never would.

''So I guess I'll see you next Friday night, then,'' I said. ''Oh, Natasha, my other line's ringing.'' That wasn't even a lie. It really was ringing.

''I'll let you go, then,'' Natasha said. ''See you next Friday! Wow, just think, two days after that and I'll finally get to meet this wonderful Timothy!''

I hung up and slumped over my desk. *No, actually, you will not get to meet him, Natasha, because he dumped me. First I made him up. Then I found him. Then I had him. And then, abracadabra, he was gone. Poof.* What the hell was I going to tell everyone about why Timothy wasn't at the wedding?

And why was I so bothered by the news that Natasha was coming to the bachelorette party? What did I care if she'd been invited to watch a bunch of Fabio types rip off their clothes and strut around? I pushed my second line. "Jane Gregg," I snapped into the receiver, my bad mood about to be taken out on whatever unfortunate person was on the line.

"Hi, Jane, this Driscoll Meyer. My friend Jeff gave me a buzz this morning and suggested I give you a call to see if you'd like to reschedule that blind date we never went on."

My mouth fell open. I was going to kill Amanda! Had she told Jeff to tell Driscoll to call me? "Um, hi, Driscoll. Can I put you on hold for a sec? Someone's buzzing me on the intercom."

Deep sigh. I put Driscoll on hold and opened my datebook and checked back to the Tuesday I was supposed to go out with him. June 9: *Driscoll Meyer. Five-eleven, 175, light brown wavy hair, blue eyes, senior accountant. A sweetie. 555-6536.*

A living, breathing, male person was on the other end of the phone, and, frankly, that was all I needed in a date for the wedding. I'd simply tell everyone that Timothy had emergency surgery, and that my dear friend Driscoll was attending the wedding with me instead. That way, I'd be doing them a favor. The $225 prime rib plate wouldn't go to waste. And Natasha and Dana would see cute, interesting Driscoll and marvel at how many good-looking, successful men I had in the hopper. They'd whisper among themselves at how successful *I* was, how I knew so many good-looking men, how lucky Timothy was to have me.

The tears threatened and I blinked them back. I felt like I'd been demoted in the boyfriend department. After all my hard work, I'd ended up with a big fat zero. And while I got nothing, Natasha—pregnant, boyfriend-proposing, bi-coastal, beautiful Natasha—had been invited to my cousin's bachelorette party at my family's wedding. *My family's.* She had her own family, dammit. Well, sort of. But the Dreers were *my* family. Mine. Couldn't I have anything of my own anymore?

*Ping: You've Got Mail.* Driscoll could wait three more seconds. This time the e-mail was from Eloise. *Jane, don't be pissed, but I told Amanda to call Jeff and tell him to tell Driscoll to give you a buzz. You never know. Plus, anyone named Driscoll is sure to have a tux in his closet! P.S. The Flirt Night Roundtable is being held at The Oyster Bar in Grand Central Station, same time. Are you mad? —E*

Deep sigh. I pressed the blinking extension. I was not showing up at Dana Dreer's wedding alone. I was not sitting at a table with Natasha Nutley, Mr. Proposing Houseboat Dweller and an empty seat. I wasn't. Driscoll Meyer was coming to the wedding with me, no matter how ugly, bad mannered, mean or rude he was.

Driscoll Meyer was adorable. He wore little round wire-rimmed glasses and laughed at everything. He was cute, smart, funny and warm. I sent the heavens a silent thank-you. It was Tuesday, exactly five days before the wedding, and sitting across from me at a charming little steakhouse was Mr. Potential.

"I'm so glad I called, Jane," Driscoll said, forkful of filet mignon poised midway to his mouth. "I was really disappointed when you canceled back in June. I had a feeling about you.''

''A feeling?'' I asked, sipping my red wine.

''The first girl I ever loved was named Jane,'' Driscoll explained, his blue eyes twinkling. ''Back in second grade. She crushed me, totally broke my heart.''

''I know a thing or two about that,'' I said. Suddenly I couldn't eat another bite of my twenty-one-dollar filet. I pushed peppercorns around on my plate.

''Heartbreaker, huh? I'd better be careful then.''

I smiled. ''Trust me, you've got nothing to worry about. I'm the one who's always getting crushed.'' Great. Now I sounded like a big loser. *Keep it up, Jane. He'll be dying to go with you to the wedding.*

''So I guess you need some cheering up,'' Driscoll said. ''Good thing I got us tickets to Dangerfield's.''

''You're kidding!'' I practically shouted. ''I love comedy clubs!''

''Tell me your best joke,'' Driscoll said.

''You asked. Just remember that.''

''Go ahead,'' he said, smiling. ''Give it your best shot.''

''A ham sandwich walks into a bar and asks the bartender for a beer, and the bartender says, 'Sorry, we don't serve food here.'''

Driscoll smiled. ''Good one. Did you hear that joke from a five-year-old?''

And suddenly I was laughing and trading jokes with a total stranger, a guy, someone who would make a very nice wedding date at this eleventh hour. *Oh, everyone, this is Driscoll,* I'd say. *Driscoll?* they'd whisper. *What happened to Timothy?* And I'd say, *Oh, we broke up, it was really bad, but I didn't want to worry anyone and take away from Dana's day, so I didn't mention it, and besides, now you get to meet my new boyfriend, Driscoll. Isn't that an interesting name?* And they'd whisper amongst themselves with worried expressions. *That Jane, such a trouper. So thoughtful. Didn't want to make us worry. She's so sweet. He's so cute and seems so nice.* I liked that scenario better than the one in which Driscoll was my dear friend.

A half hour later, Driscoll and I were smushed into seats at a tiny table at Dangerfield's, the comedy club owned by Rodney Dangerfield on the Upper East Side. Rodney was known to make impromptu visits. The place was packed with dates and large groups of friends. Driscoll and I ordered Cokes and a chocolate mud pie to split.

The first comic told a few scatological jokes to get the crowd roaring. "Ooh, lot of couples here tonight! You two, where you from?"

Oh, God. He was talking to me and Driscoll. "Um, here?" I said, a forkful of mud pie an inch away from my mouth.

"Are you asking me or telling me?" the comic asked. Was he related to William Remke? The audience found that very funny and roared. "No seriously, you're from New York?" We nodded. "So, you two engaged, married, what?"

"It's our first date," Driscoll called out.

"Oooh, first date," the comic sing-songed. The audience went wild. "You think you're gonna score? Huh? Think you'll get lucky?"

I felt my face turn bright red. I slid low in my seat, hoping he'd move on to some other couple.

"I think I'm lucky enough right now to have her just sitting next to me," Driscoll shouted back, to the delight of the audience. They *aahed* and cheered and clapped.

And I sat back up in my seat and beamed at Driscoll Meyer.

"So, let's see," Driscoll said, the warm breeze ruffling his light brown wavy hair as we walked up First Avenue. "We had dinner, then went to a comedy club and now I'd say it's definitely time for a drink so I can prolong this evening."

I grinned and looked at my watch. "Ooh—it's twelve-thirty, and I've got a killer day tomorrow. I'd better get my butt home."

"So, do I get to see you again?" he asked.

"I'd like that very much."

"Great," Driscoll said, beaming. "Only thing is, I'm leaving for a two-week vacation this Friday. I'm going to Belize."

Belize. Driscoll Meyer was going to Belize instead of to my cousin's wedding at the Plaza.

"Fine, whatever," I snapped, and turned to walk away. Half of me was mortified for being so childishly rude to Driscoll. But the other half had had it. And *that* half was about to burst into tears in the middle of First Avenue.

"Hey!" he called, following me. "What's your problem?"

"I just want to go home, okay?" I said, sticking my hand out for a taxi. My legs suddenly felt like rubber. "I just want to go home."

Since Dana's bachelorette party was Friday night, the Flirt Night Roundtable was being held on Wednesday night...on my fire escape. We had two bottles of wine, two loaves of French bread and two reduced-fat hunks of sharp cheddar cheese.

"You didn't!" Eloise said, exhaling a stream of smoke. "You said, *fine, whatever* and jumped into a cab?"

I nibbled a piece of cheese. "I said that I *hailed* a cab, not that I jumped into one. Driscoll insisted on knowing what he said that was so wrong, so I broke down and told him the whole sorry story on the curb."

"You're kidding! About the wedding and everything?" Amanda asked. At my nod, Amanda's and Eloise's mouths dropped open. "Then what happened?"

I cut off a piece of cheese. "He told me he was sick of being a pawn in women's head games. That he was glad he was leaving New York for a couple of weeks, that maybe he'd meet a woman down in Belize who wasn't a child and didn't have to resort to playing games."

"Geez, a little uptight," Amanda snapped. "Asshole."

"Yeah," Eloise agreed. "Who the hell does he think he is?"

"He wasn't totally wrong, guys," I said. "If the situation were reversed, I'd probably be pissed, too."

"So are you okay?" Eloise asked. "About showing up at the wedding alone?"

I shrugged. "I don't know. I did do a lot of thinking last night and today, though. There was something about Driscoll not being able to go to the wedding, after all that. Suddenly it all seemed so stupid. My whole self-worth tied up in having a *date?* That's what's pathetic. Not the ruse or the game."

"You do have a lot to be proud of, Jane," Eloise said. "So much." A car honking like crazy interrupted her. "And not just because of your promotion. That was simply the icing on the cake. I've done a lot of thinking too since our last visit to St. Monica's. All these years you've been on your own, working hard, falling in love, getting hurt, working hard, falling in love, getting hurt. That's what you should be proud of, Jane. *Both* of us should be proud."

"She's right, Jane," Amanda said, topping a cracker with a wedge of cheese. "It's the process that's important. And no matter what you guys have both been through, you've always picked yourselves up and kept going, never losing your spirit."

I thought of Natasha. That was what she was so good at. No matter what, she kept going. "So, I guess I'll just tell Natasha and Dana and my aunt and my grandmother that Timothy and I broke up. It's the truth, at least."

They nodded and nibbled cheese on crackers. "Yeah, that way at least you'll get their sympathy," Eloise pointed out. "They'll have to be extra nice to you. Hey, you know something? I noticed you stopped calling Natasha the Gnat."

Huh. I *had* stopped referring to her as the Gnat. When? I couldn't even pinpoint it.

"So we're both single again, Jane," Eloise went on. "So what? I'm thirty and I'm single, and I *am* proud of myself. Being thirty and single is something to celebrate. It means I didn't settle. I may not be married, but I also haven't fucked up by picking the wrong guy, either. God, Jane, I almost did that just to feel normal. *That's* what's sick. That's not what my mom would have wanted for me."

I squeezed her hand and grabbed Amanda's. "Let's toast to us." I held up my wineglass. "Let's toast to Eloise's bravery at giving Serge back his ring and Amanda's two-year anniversary and her skill at arranging blind dates in a jiffy. Let's toast my quitting smoking. And let's toast to the Flirt Night Roundtable. Six years running and still going strong as ever.''

"To the Flirt Night Roundtable," Eloise cheered.

"To the Flirt Night Roundtable," Amanda seconded.

"To friendship," I added, and we clinked.

## Sixteen

"Take it off!" shrieked the attendees of Dana Dreer's bachelorette party at the gyrating blond guy who looked like an escapee from a heavy metal rock band. The nine of us, seven bridesmaids, one maid of honor and one ex-babysitter, were seated at a long banquette table around the main stage of Hots, a Chippendales-type club in Forest Hills, where men danced around in G-strings for dollar bills. Tickets (thirty-five bucks each!) had been compliments of Aunt Ina, and both sets of grandmothers had given Karen an envelope of singles for each attendee to wave around and stuff in the G-strings.

*Embarrassing* was the only word to describe Hots. Naturally, Dreer party of nine seemed to be having fun, with the exception of the spoilsport sitting on the aisle (that would be me). Even Natasha, sitting across the table and dead center, of course (right next to the bride), was whooping and singing along with the music. Hots was packed with long table after table of screaming bachelorette parties, hordes of women waving bills around as though they'd never seen a three-quarters-naked man before.

Natasha had been so fawned over and fussed over by the group, you would have mistaken her for the bride—or a member of the wedding, for that matter. Dana was mostly responsible for all the attention Natasha had gotten. She'd said at least five times, "I can't believe a famous actress is at *my* bachelorette party and is coming to *my* wedding!" I'd been quiet since we'd all gathered about a half hour ago in the bar before sitting down to our table. Natasha and I hadn't arrived together; she'd wanted to spend the day sight-seeing again around Forest Hills. I'd arrived at Hots to find Natasha holding court with the bridesmaids. They'd complimented her nonstop. They loved her hair, and her slinky lavender sleeveless dress and strappy silver sandals and pounds of silver jewelry, and had anyone ever told her she looked so much like Nicole Kidman? They'd asked her question after question about her life, which she'd answered with almost talk-show-guest practiced ease. "You'll just have to buy the book!" I'd cut in at one point, and everyone had just looked at me. I'd thought it was quite clever.

"Welcome to Hots!" bellowed the Gyrater. He pumped his pelvis in and out in front of our table to a Bee Gees song. "Who's our lucky bride?"

The table shrieked and clapped and jumped up and pointed out Dana, who feigned humility and made a show of covering her happy blue eyes. Gyrater reached for Dana's hand and kissed it, then did erotic things with his body very close to her. He shook those hips and pumped that pelvis in and out à la Ricky Martin. Dana blushed and squealed. There was nothing sexy about the guy. First of all, he was missing a neck. Second of all, his hair—short on the sides and long in the back—was passé by 1985. Third of all, he was an erotic dancer. Gross! Finally he gyrated his way to the next banquette of shrieking bachelorettes.

"If only James could move like that," said one of the Julies. She sipped her frozen margarita. "James can't dance at all!"

"Omigod, your fiancé is a better dancer than mine," quipped skinny, short-haired Amy. "But whoever said how a guy dances is any indication of how he is in bed…"

Squeals and peals of laughter and shrieks.

"My fiancé is so amazing in bed," the other Julie said. "I don't know where he learned it or from who, and I don't care. I'll take him!"

More squeals and peals. This was how this group talked? Granted, the Flirt Night Roundtable got down and dirty about every last detail, but at least we discussed our sex lives with some degree of class.

"So how's Larry in bed?" I asked Dana before I could shut my big fat mouth. I was sorry the second it was out.

Silence. Eight faces peered at me.

"Jane!" Dana scolded. "I can't believe you! His sister is, like, right next to you."

I bit my lower lip and turned to my left to peer at Larry Fishkill's sister. "Sorry." The sister eyed me and sipped her frozen raspberry margarita.

"Let's toast to Dana's penultimate night as an unmarried woman!" Karen shouted. "Yay!" She sent me the fastest dirty look I'd ever seen, then resumed her big smile and began whoo-hooing the Gyrater.

Glasses raised and more peals and squeals followed. I shrank down on my seat and eyed Natasha, who was deep in conversation with the bridesmaid sitting next to her, a pretty blonde named Gayle. I could hear bits and pieces of Natasha telling Gayle about her boyfriend Sam and the houseboat.

I hadn't meant to ask Dana that inappropriate question. I most certainly did not want to know anything about Larry Fishkill's sexual ability. But being around these shrieking women in their bebe outfits and their Tiffany diamond rings was unbearable. And there, at the center of the table, was Natasha. The very Natasha who had the nerve to be invited, the nerve to be humanized, the nerve to be nice to me, the nerve to be a very good writer. I didn't even *like* these women—well, except for my cousin because I had to, and maybe Natasha because she was my author—and I *still* felt like the ugly duckling. The only one without a boyfriend. The only one without a proposing *someone*. The only one who went home to a futon and a Parsons table and nothing else, not even a pack of cigarettes. Talk about Plain Jane...

"So Jane, how's your boyfriend?" one of the Julies asked. "Didn't Dana say he was a doctor? Lucky you!"

My heart made a small twisting sensation in my chest. I managed a smile. "I am lucky," I said. "Hey, do any of you know where the bathroom is?" Karen, Miss Know-It-All, pointed me in the direction, and I fled.

Someone was smoking a cigarette in one of the stalls. I locked myself in a stall next door and inhaled deeply and squeezed my eyes shut. The familiar smell of smoke wafted around me. I wanted to climb on the toilet and reach over the stall and steal the cigarette out of the woman's hand. Deep breath, deep breath. The urge to smoke will pass whether you smoke a cigarette or not. Repeat until the craving passes.

It worked. Craving gone, I made my way back to the

table, where half the bridesmaids were waving dollar bills at a new Gyrater, another blonde with a shaved chest and the biggest biceps and triceps and deltoids I'd ever seen in my life. The other half of our table was in conversation, including Natasha. "I feel so bad for my older sister," one of the Julies said. "She's, like, twenty-eight and totally boyfriendless."

"I would die," Amy said. "You have to go out with the guy for a year to get engaged, then a year or two years until the wedding. Can you imagine being thirty and not married?"

"Well," Natasha said, "I'm twenty-eight and not married."

"Yeah, but you have that amazing-sounding boyfriend in California," Karen said. "And you're, like, *famous.*"

"I love your hair, Natasha," Amy said. "It's so gorgeous."

Dana ran out of singles to stuff in G-strings and joined the conversation. "What are we talking about?"

"How jealous we all are of Natasha's hair and how depressing it would be to be boyfriendless at our age," a Julie said, flashing her toothy smile. "This woman I work with, she's thirty and isn't even dating anyone. You know what they say—you have a better chance of getting killed by a terrorist than getting married after thirty."

I slid down lower on the leatherette bench, defeated. I grabbed my frozen margarita with both hands and slurped the straw and stared at the little wooden purple umbrella stuck in the lime wedged onto the side of the glass. I thought I was over this. I thought I was proud of myself. But these women, most of them strangers, had managed to make me feel like the insecure loser I'd felt like in junior high. Suddenly I felt like I'd intruded at the popular girls' lunch table. Why did I care so much what people said, what people thought? Why did my sense of self depend so much on the opinion of people I didn't even know? I hadn't known Natasha at all when I'd felt compelled to create a fake boyfriend. How could someone you didn't even know, hadn't even laid eyes on in ten years, have such power over you?

"Jane, you're so quiet!" quipped a Julie. "Aren't you having fun?"

I forced a smile. "I'm having a great time." And as if to punctuate the point, the Gyrater returned and thrust his pelvis so close to my face that I could maim him. But I should be grateful. According to one of the Julies, I had a better chance of getting shot by a terrorist than I did of ever getting this close to a penis in the flesh.

I woke up on Sunday morning to silence. Well, not silence exactly. I heard birds chirping on my fire escape. I heard cars driving up the block. But I did not hear the Oh Moaner. Perhaps Dana Dreer's wedding day was considered sacred even by Opera Man.

Compliments of Larry Fishkill's mother (but secretly, Aunt Ina suspected, Larry himself), the immediate female relatives were getting makeovers this morning at Zelda's, a la-di-da salon in my neighborhood that was being closed to the public for the morning. Makeup, hairstyling, manicures, pedicures, aka A Half Day of Beauty. I'd have to remember to bring earplugs to drown out the annoying conversation I was surely in for.

I'd tossed and turned Friday night and last night over what I was going to tell everyone about "my boyfriend." Because I hadn't mentioned the breakup at the bachelorette party when I'd been asked about him, it would seem weird to announce at the wedding that we'd broken up. My only option was to tell Dana and my aunt and Natasha that Timothy and I had broken up a couple of weeks ago, and that I hadn't wanted to mention it because I didn't want to take away from the excitement leading up to Dana's big day. That way, I'd still play the sympathy card and get a gold star. But after Friday night's festivities at Hots, all the "my fiancé this, my fiancé that" bullshit, how was I supposed to tell that group I'd been dumped? Like I needed Dana and the Julies to cast their pity-filled eyes at me? They'd probably throw riot gear at me and wish me luck against the terrorists.

I wasn't sure what I'd tell Natasha. I wouldn't know what would come out of my mouth until it actually did, at the reception. I just knew that I couldn't think about it anymore. Not right now, anyway. Because every time I did, Timothy's Thomas Gibson face floated before my eyes, dimples popping, and I heard him exclaim "Me too!" over and over. *Stop it, stop it, stop it,* I ordered myself. Get thee into a shower and wash that man right out of your hair.

The shower calmed me down, as hot water and green-apple shampoo and Dove pink soap always did. My Timothy-free hair towel-dried and in a ponytail, I fingered the peach bridesmaid dress hanging in my closet. Okay, it wasn't my color, but the dress *was* pretty. I hadn't tried it on once since picking it up. The seamstress at A Fancy Affair had tried to make me put it on there before I left, but I'd refused, claiming I was pressed for time.

It had been two years ago that I'd first heard Dana was planning to get married at the Plaza. Two years. Two boyfriendless, practically dateless years. Two years had seemed so far in the future that I never really expected the day to come. And now here it was, dawning bright and sunny and warm. A perfect summer day for a perfect summer wedding. According to Fox news, today was even a good hair day on the frizz-meter. Dana must be thrilled. Had it been raining, I wouldn't have been surprised if she'd postponed the wedding.

I slipped into the dress and the shoes and peered at myself in the full-length mirror. Interesting. The peach looked somehow softer and sweeter than it had in the bridal shop. The dress was floor length and straight, like a movie-star's gown for the Academy Awards. The high neckline was flattering, as was the empire waist, which was decorated by a delicate triple line of tiny peach-colored beads, which was repeated on the hem. I checked out the rear view in the mirror. I had to admit, I looked pretty good, even down to the peau-de-soie peach shoes. I should have taken Aunt Ina's advice and broken them in; they were a little stiff, and now I'd get blisters. I wanted to practice walking around in them, but walking around in shoes in an apartment in New York City was against the law, punishable by death if your best friend happened to live below you. Plus, it was eight in the morning on a Sunday.

I unlocked the door and walked up and down the sixth floor hallway. So far, so good. The shoes didn't hurt. If I could find some flesh-colored peds—

Opera Man's door opened. I was about to see Opera Man in the flesh for the first time! And I had no makeup on. Figured. Whenever you were about meet a Ricky Martin look-alike who had sex more often in a month than you had in a lifetime, you were bound to look like shit. Except that I was wearing a princess's dress. That counted.

Opera Man walked out of his apartment and started, obviously surprised by the vision in peach in the hallway. But he couldn't have been more surprised than I was. He didn't look like Ricky Martin at all. I was so shocked that

I couldn't take my eyes off him. "I'm uh, practicing walking in my shoes. They're new," I said. Lame, lame, lame, Jane.

Opera Man shot me a mean little smile, then resumed locking up his door.

"So we finally meet," I added. "I'm Jane Gregg. I live there." I pointed.

He narrowed his eyes at me. "I'm Archibald Marinelli."

Archibald?

"Look," he added. "I'm getting a little sick and tired of your passive-aggressive banging on the wall. It's really rude."

The jerk! "Well I'm getting a little sick and tired of listening to you blasting opera and your sex life."

"Then maybe you should get one of your own," Opera Man snapped before stomping down the hall and down the stairs.

By the time I thought of a good comeback, Opera Man was clomping out the building. I'd been right about the *A* standing for Asshole. But that the *A* really stood for Archibald gave me a small degree of revenge. Plus, after finally clapping eyes on Opera Man, I'd already gotten the only revenge I'd ever need. I'd never have to pound on the wall again. I'd never have to worry that everyone was having more sex than I was. Because worse than all that combined was the indisputable fact that A. Marinelli looked like a tall Elmer Fudd.


Through the windows of Zelda's Hair and Beauty Spa, I could see Aunt Ina and Grammy and Larry Fishkill's mother, his sister and two grandmothers. And there was Dana, the Princess, shoving clipped pages from bride magazines at Zelda herself.

"There she is," Aunt Ina announced, throwing up her hands and smacking her lips. "Fifteen minutes late, she waltzes in." She took the dress bag out of my hand and hung it up with everyone else's.

"The bus crawled and—"

"I don't need to hear your excuses," Aunt Ina said. "Sit down and roll up your jeans for your pedicure."

I said hello to the Fishkills and hugged Grammy and climbed onto the huge leatherette chair like a dutiful child. The second my feet hit the sudsy warm water I relaxed and closed my eyes. A Half Day of Beauty might be just what I needed.

"Hi, Jane," Dana said, climbing up to the chair next to mine. "What's that?" she asked, eyeing the bottle of red-black nail polish I'd set on the foot of the chair.

"It's fake Vamp. Isn't it great?"

Dana stared at me. "But we're all getting Precious Pink on our nails and toes."

"But you can't see our toes," I pointed out. "We're wearing *pumps*."

"I want us all to match," Dana said. "The bridal party should all have the same."

"I don't see the point if no one can see our toenails, Dana."

"Jane, if the bride wants you to get Precious Pink, you're getting Precious Pink," Aunt Ina snapped. "What's wrong with you?"

"That black color's disgusting," Grammy put in. "All the young girls wear it today. It's hideous."

"Fine, I'll get the Precious Pink that no one will see anyway," I announced.

"You're not doing anyone a big favor, Jane," Aunt Ina sing-songed. "You're doing what's expected. Do you believe her attitude?'' she said to Grammy, shaking her head.

I mentally shook my own head. It was nine in the morning, and already the day was off to an unbearable start. I took a deep breath, then closed my eyes and stuck my feet under the jet stream. My pedicurist grabbed a foot, set it on the footrest, said something in Korean to Dana's pedicurist and the two women laughed. I opened my eyes. Were they laughing at my feet?

"So, Jane, we're so psyched to meet Timothy," Dana said. "Mommy had been so worried about you, and now she's just thrilled."

I opened an eye and looked and Dana. She was flipping through *Modern Bride.* "Worried? Why?"

Dana stopped flipping and glanced at me, then resumed her flips. "Oh, nothing. I just meant she'd been worried about you being all alone."

"Alone? You mean without a boyfriend?"

Dana nodded. Flip, flip, flip.

"What is so terrible about me not having a boyfriend?" I snapped. "Maybe I'm concentrating on my career. Maybe I'm proud of myself for getting promoted, which, excuse me, no one seemed to think was such a big deal. Maybe I'm happy being *alone.*"

"Defensive, much?" Dana said, eyes on the magazine. "You're *not* happy, Jane. And you're not alone—you have a serious boyfriend. And you're still not happy. You haven't been happy for as long as I've known you. You probably never will be with *that* attitude of yours."

A burst of anger shot up from my stomach into my mouth. "Oh, like you know me so well?"

"Whose fault is that?" Dana asked, glancing at me.

"She's right, Jane," Aunt Ina said. "You never make an effort."

Why were they ganging up on me? What the hell did I do?"

"What is this nonsense?" Grammy hissed. "The Fish-kills will hear you." I eyed the Fishkills; the four were gabbing at the nail station and not paying us the least bit of attention. "Change the subject. This is Dana's wedding day, for God's sake."

"Fine, let's change the subject," Dana said. "So we're all looking forward to meeting Timothy."

Take knife, insert into gut. Then twist.

"He's coming to the ceremony, isn't he?" Aunt Ina asked. "Some people today, they just show up for the reception, the party. Do you believe that? It's disgusting."

*Deep breath, deep breath.* "Um, he might not be able to come at all," I said. "He's sort of on call."

"A little late to tell me," Dana snapped. "Does he know it's $225 a head?"

Bitch, bitch, bitch! I stared at Dana. "I'll pay it, okay?"

"That's not the point," Dana said. "It's called *consideration.*"

"You could have let us know," Aunt Ina added. She shook her head, slowly.

"I'm sorry, okay?" I yelled. "I'm sorry. God!"

The Fishkills all turned and stared at me. Grammy shook her head and flipped her magazine.

"You know what, Jane?" Dana closed *Modern Bride* and turned to face me. "I'm a little sick and tired of your attitude. I'm sick of the way you talk to my mother. I'm sick of how selfish and immature you are. And I'm sick of my mother worrying herself sick about you when you're too selfish to care."

My mouth dropped open.

"This is not the time or the place for this," Aunt Ina

said. "Let's just enjoy our morning, okay? We're in a beauty spa. Why don't I pour us all some of that nice complimentary tea—"

"I have to go the bathroom," I said. I lifted my soaking foot out of the water and startled the pedicurist. In the tiny bathroom I dropped down on the toilet bowl, shaking. How dare they! How dare they—

But suddenly I wasn't angry. I was…crying. Big, fat tears rolled down my cheeks into the creases of my mouth.

There was a knock on the bathroom door. "Janey?" Aunt Ina called. "Are you okay?"

I sat there, frozen, the tears falling faster and harder.

"Janey, open up, c'mon," Ina said. "I want to talk to you."

I got up and opened the door, my eyes on the floor. Aunt Ina took one look at me and squeezed inside the tiny room, shutting the door behind her. I sat back down on the toilet.

"Jane, look, Dana's just a little high-strung right now. It's her wedding day and—"

"Timothy dumped me," I said, burying my face in my hands. "Almost two weeks ago."

"Jane, why didn't you tell me?" Ina asked, kneeling down in front of me. She took my hands away from my face and clasped them in hers. "Huh? Why didn't you tell me?"

"I don't know," I said.

"I'm sorry, honey," Aunt Ina cooed. "What happened?"

I shrugged so pathetically that even I felt bad for myself. "I really liked him. I thought he liked me too, but he didn't. Or he just lost interest. Whatever. He dumped me. I always get dumped. Always." My hands flew back to my face. "And now Dana's getting married and you're getting all these new relatives—"

I hadn't realized just how threatened I felt by that until the words came out of my mouth. Aunt Ina's mouth had opened into an O and her hand touched her heart. "Jane, you're not losing us. Especially you're not losing *me*. Don't you know what you mean to me? You're my sister's only baby."

"I miss her," I whispered.

"I miss her too," Aunt Ina said. "She was my best friend, you know."

She hadn't been *my* best friend. I wouldn't let her be. And now I finally understood why. Because I'd been too afraid to be that close to her. Too afraid to love her to pieces and lose her the way I'd lost my father. And then I'd lost her anyway.

"I'm so sorry, Aunt Ina," I said, throwing my arms around her and falling into her. "I'm so sorry I've been such a brat."

Aunt Ina hugged me and squeezed me and stroked my hair. "I'll tell you what, Jane. You wash your face and then come out. I want to give you something."

I nodded and Aunt Ina grasped my chin and pulled me into another hug. And then she was gone. I took a deep breath but collapsed back down onto the toilet seat and buried my face in a mound of toilet paper. I got up and splashed cold water on my face, then pressed a scratchy brown paper towel against my eyes.

When I came out of the bathroom, Aunt Ina was waiting for me with a little box in her hand. Grammy and Dana were eyeing us. "I wanted you to wear this today," Aunt Ina said, handing me the box. "Go ahead, open it."

I pulled the top off and gasped. It was the delicate pearl

necklace my mother always wore for special occasions. I stroked the antique pearls, my eyes welling again.

"I gave that necklace to your mother on the day you were born," Aunt Ina said. "She was twenty-nine, and I was going to give you the necklace on your twenty-ninth birthday. But I think she would have liked you to wear this for Dana's wedding."

"Why?" I whispered, even though I hadn't meant to.

"You remember how we all thought your mom just had a nasty case of the flu the week before she passed on?" Aunt Ina asked. I nodded. "Well, Dana spent so much time with your mom those last few days. She was in high school and busy with boys and cheerleading, but she stopped by your mom's apartment a few times that week and just talked to her, gabbed in her ear about her boyfriends and classes and made her laugh."

I wish I'd made her laugh. I wish she'd had the flu. Instead, she'd had sneaky ovarian cancer. I hadn't known Dana had spent time with her. I hadn't known a lot. I especially hadn't known that the loss of my father and then the loss of my mother was so powerful a trigger that every time I lost something else, whether real like Max to another woman, or imagined like Aunt Ina to a son-in-law, I crumpled.

"Thank you, Aunt Ina," I said, and threw my arms around her.

"Go put the necklace in your handbag," Ina told me with a kiss on the cheek, "and then get back in that chair. You're missing your pedicure."

I smiled and climbed back into the chair next to Dana, the box in my hands. "Dana? Could you use something borrowed today?"

Dana looked at me and nodded. I knew that we had just become friends.

## Seventeen

The Plaza Hotel gleamed in the early afternoon sunlight. I stood in the exact spot on the east side of Fifth Avenue that I'd stood with my father the day before he died, the day he'd promised me the Plaza if I could find the guy. The memories seeped into me and filled me up instead of seeping out of me and making me cry. I hadn't found the guy, but I realized now that that wasn't my father's point. The point, I was just beginning to figure out, was finding happiness and peace and serenity and the very best for yourself, and that seemed to be a process, not something you could arrange by blinking your eyes and wishing on four blind dates in desperation. And the point was also not to be afraid of the process.

I'd come over with Aunt Ina, Dana and Grammy in a cab; the Fishkills had followed in another cab. Dana's photographer had shot the bridal party dressed naturally around the grounds of the hotel and in Central Park, and then everyone had gone inside to the dressing rooms near the mini-ballroom to change. I'd met the usher who was escorting me down the aisle; a frat-boy type named Glen who had a girlfriend. I'd told Aunt Ina I wanted to snap some photos of my own and that I'd join them all in five minutes. I pulled my disposable camera out of my little beaded peach purse (compliments of Dana for the brides-maids) and snapped one perfect photo of the Plaza Ho-tel—the Plaza Hotel my father had seen. And then I darted across the street and into the majestic hotel with my dress slung over my shoulder and my shoes in a tote bag.

Downstairs, the bridal party had their own dressing room. Karen and the Julies and the other bridesmaids had arrived and were slipping on their dresses. They all had Precious Pink on their toenails.

"Omigod, Jane, I still can't get over how amazing you look. I just love your hair like that!" a Julie exclaimed.

"And your makeup is so sophisticated," Karen added. "You really do look beautiful."

Huh. Did they suddenly have to be so nice just when I was feeling so humble? Or had they always been nice? I felt as though I had all this attention to pay now, to people and to things. I felt as though I was in for an annoying time of seeing things differently. Including my-self.

"Who's helping me get my dress on?" Dana called out as she and Aunt Ina whisked into the dressing room. "Karen, it's the maid of honor's job!"

The bridesmaids stood in a circle around Dana as Karen zipped and buttoned and fluffed. When Karen stepped away, everyone gasped. Dana truly looked like a princess. Her short, wispy blond hair had been coiffed to perfec-tion, and atop her head sat a delicate beaded headpiece with tiny rosebuds. Her makeup was practically translucent. Her cheeks glowed pink, her lips were slightly shimmery and her blue eyes had never been so clear and bright. And the dress. The simple, elegant gown was exquisite. The high-cut bodice was satin and fitted with a row of beading at the waist, and the skirt flared out like a ballerina's to the floor. Dana's eyes began to mist, and she twirled around to check out the rear view in the floor-to-ceiling mirror. When she turned back around, she was glowing.

"Something old," Dana announced, holding up her wrist, which was encircled by an heirloom diamond tennis bracelet that Larry Fishkill's mother had given her. "Something new." She gestured to the dress. "Something borrowed—" Dana reached into her tote bag and pulled out the box I'd given her. "Jane, will you help me put this on?" I smiled and draped my mother's pearls around her neck and clasped it. I stood back to admire it, to admire *her*. The murmurs from the bridesmaids said it all. "And something blue," Dana added, batting her eyelashes and opening her blue eyes wide.

Someone knocked at the door. "You've got a half hour before it's time for the photographer," Uncle Charlie called through it. "Then we'll do a mini-rehearsal of the lineup, and then it's showtime!"

"And now, ladies and gentlemen," the bandleader announced. "For the first time in public, give up a round of applause to…drum roll please…Mr. and Mrs. Fishkill!"

The two hundred and fifty guests clapped and cheered as Larry and Dana marched into the lavish reception hall, bursting with smiles. The newlyweds stood in the center of the dance floor, and the band began to play "The Wind

Beneath My Wings.'' I was so emotional on Dana's be-
half that I didn't even think a single snarky comment at
their choice of band. As Larry twirled his new bride
around the dance floor, I looked through the crowd of
guests for Natasha. I caught sight of her squeezed next to
a woman on her left and a man on her right, but I couldn't
tell if the man next to her was the Houseboat Dweller or
not. He looked a bit young for Natasha and to own a
houseboat. I'd spotted her once or twice at the wedding
itself, but I'd been so busy trying to think of what I was
going to say about the empty seat next to me at the party
that I hadn't paid attention to who she was with.

The wedding song over, the perky bandleader played
another boring slow song, which was my cue to find my
table. My cue to face the empty seat next to me at a table
for four. As I weaved my way over to table forty-two,
waving at Aunt Ina and Uncle Charlie, who'd weaved
their own way onto the dance floor, I noticed Natasha had
had the same idea as I had. She placed her little evening
bag on the table and sat down, eyeing the crowd. Before
I could even reach the table, someone had asked her to
dance and she accepted. The Houseboat Dweller, I assumed. Handsome. He appeared to be in his mid-thirties.
I dropped down at the table and gnawed on a roll from
the basket, the empty seat next to me taunting me, but
not to the point that I felt like crawling under the table.
I felt semi-okay. Mid-chew of the dinner roll I felt eyes
on me. I glanced in the direction of the stare and found
myself looking into the eyes of a cute guy. Very cute. He
looked something like Dr. Joel Fleishman from the television show *Northern Exposure*. He smiled, a little smile,
as though he wasn't sure I was *sans* date. Before I could
smile back, gobs of wedding guests got between us. The
song had ended.

Natasha appeared at the table alone. "Hi, Jane! You look so beautiful."

*Here goes nothing, as the cliché goes.* "Thanks, you too." And of course, she did. She wore a gorgeous pale pink dress of the thinnest material I'd ever seen. It slightly shimmered.

"Guess what?" she asked as she sat down across from me. "I had morning sickness today!"

I laughed. "And you're excited about that?"

"It was the first time," she said. "The first time I really felt something physical because of the baby." She put her hand on her tummy and smiled.

"So where's Sam?" I asked. "I'm dying to meet him."

Natasha glanced at the crowd. "He's not coming."

"Not coming?" I repeated. "Couldn't get a flight?"

"Couldn't care less is more like it," Natasha said, staring at her feet. "He broke up with me weeks ago. I kept meaning to tell you, but I just couldn't."

I stared at her, absolutely stunned. I closed my mouth, which, as usual, had fallen open practically onto the table. "Oh, Natasha," I said, understanding all too well. "I'm so sorry. When did this happen?"

The band was playing a Shania Twain song so loud that Natasha had to slide her chair around the table closer to mine so we could talk. "Remember that night I came over at midnight and had a breakdown in your apartment? He'd told me he met someone else, that it was over, that I was too needy and clingy."

"But what about the baby? I thought he was happy—"

Natasha took a deep breath. "I lied to you. He was the opposite of happy. He accused me of getting pregnant on purpose, then insisted he wasn't the father but he'd pay for an abortion anyway. Things had been pretty rocky for a while. It's why I was glad to escape to New York for a couple of months. But I thought we'd work it out. And when I found out I was pregnant, I'd hoped it would touch something in him. But I was wrong.'' Natasha's voice broke a bit and she closed her eyes for a second. "He crushed me pretty bad. Are you mad that I lied to you? I guess I was just too scared and humiliated to say it out loud, you know?"

I knew. Boy, did I. If her broken heart and my own weren't so painful, I'd probably be laughing my head off at the irony of it all. Plus, I felt as though I had some nerve (as Aunt Ina would say) whining about facing a wedding reception boyfriendless when she was facing motherhood husbandless, boyfriendless *and* parentless. But not friendless.

"So you must think I'm pretty pathetic, huh?" Natasha asked, her eyes on the empty plate in front of her.

I smiled at her. "Actually, I think you're pretty great. I think you're one of the strongest people I've ever known. I really admire you, Natasha.''

She looked up at me, biting her lip, and suddenly I knew what it was that Natasha Nutley had that made her so irresistible to everyone. The thing I'd wanted to know since I was twelve years old in Mrs. Greenman's sixth-grade class had finally come clear.

Natasha Nutley showed her vulnerability. Through the beauty, the strength and the supposed perfection of her existence, she exuded *vulnerability*. Not helplessness. Not fear. Vulnerability. And that was exactly what *I* had been so afraid to show my entire life. Terror at appearing vulnerable had kept me on the outside looking in, set me on the defensive and ready to attack to protect myself.

"I think you're pretty great, too," Natasha told me, a

smile on her shimmering pink lips. "So where's the good doctor?"

"Having sex with someone else," I admitted almost painlessly as the band began the theme song from *Dirty Dancing*. "He dumped me weeks ago, too."

"Oh, no!" Natasha said. "I'm so sorry."

My heart pinged a bit. "Aw, it's okay. You want to know a secret? When I met you in the Blue Water Grill for lunch back in June, I didn't even know him."

She tilted her head. "What do you mean?"

"I wanted to impress you, so I lied and said I had this fab boyfriend who owned a brownstone. And then I had to find some guy to bring to the wedding, so I went on a bunch of blind dates and one actually worked out: Timothy the doctor. Well, he worked out until two weeks ago. And then I scrambled to find a sub, just to feel okay enough to sit at this table with you. Talk about pathetic."

"Oh, Jane." She bit her lip "Is that how I make you feel?"

"Past tense," I said. "That's how I felt back in Forest Hills years ago. But I carried it with me, I guess, until I got to know you. And then I realized you were a person, just like me, just like everyone else." When had I realized that? Just now, perhaps. Or maybe that was what I'd hated about her all along. That with everything she had, she was just a girl, just a woman, just like me.

She smiled. "So you and Timothy clicked, and then what?"

"And then he dumped me for some redhead. I actually caught them together in a bar."

Natasha shook her head. "Men stink, huh?"

"They sure do."

"Too bad they're also so damned wonderful," Natasha

added. "And irresistible and cute and you just can't live without them."

"Yeah, I know." We both laughed.

Natasha sipped her ice water. There was a lemon floating in it. "In fact, that guy over there, a real cutie, has been staring at you for the past ten minutes."

Ha. Any guy staring in our direction was staring at Natasha, not me. I glanced over where Natasha's eyes were pointed. It was *Northern Exposure* Guy. Man, he was cute. And he did seem to be checking me out. His date was probably in the bathroom. No way was a guy that cute here solo. The band was now playing *Hit Me Baby One More Time* by Britney Spears. The dance floor was packed with guests, young and old.

I ripped off another piece of my dinner roll. "He is pretty cute," I agreed. "Maybe I'll get lucky and he'll ask me to dance."

"You could ask *him*," Natasha pointed out.

"Maybe later." Yeah, like never. I'd be ready to risk rejection sometime soon, but I'd been through enough for one wedding. "I'm sorry about Sam," I told Natasha. "Are you okay with everything?"

"Well, I'm taking it one day at a time and just thinking about the baby, doing what's good and right for her or him."

"That sounds like a good idea," I said.

"Actually, I'm lying again," Natasha confessed. "I'm scared to death. Really scared. But I think I'm gonna be good at it, after all. Motherhood, I mean. I love this baby so much already, Jane. I can't tell you how much."

I smiled and believed her. "I think you're going to be a great mother. Definitely."

She grinned and raised her water glass. I raised mine,

too. "Here's to keeping our chins up and to figuring it all out." We clinked.

"So are you staying in New York for good?" I asked.

She nodded. "Yeah. This is home. And I like the idea of being near my aunt Daphne and my parents, even if they hate me."

"I think your folks will come around, Natasha. I really do. Your aunt and uncle promised to work on them, right? And, since you're staying, maybe you'd like to come to the next Flirt Night Roundtable."

"What's that?" she asked.

"It's me and Eloise—you met her at Posh that day I got promoted, remember?" Natasha nodded. "And our friend Amanda. Every Friday night we go to some bar or restaurant and talk for hours. It's a tradition six years running."

I could tell Natasha was touched. "I'd love to come. Speaking of invitations," she said, "are you going to the Forest Hills High reunion in October?"

Ten-year high-school reunion. "I wasn't planning to. Are you going?"

"I'd like to, if you'll go. I'd be really happy to walk into that reunion with you as my friend, Jane."

Now it was my turn to be touched. "Deal."

I felt eyes on me again. It was *Northern Exposure* Guy. We locked eyes for a moment, then his attention was taken by the elderly man sitting next to him. There were so many people blocking my view of his table that I couldn't tell who was on his right. A date? Would he be checking me out if he was with a date?

"Ask him to dance," Natasha prodded. "Go ahead. Take a risk."

I gnawed my lower lip. "What if he says no?"

"What if he says yes?"

"Yeah, but what if he says *no?*"

Natasha laughed. "What if he says *yes.* Go."

I stood up before I lost the guts. But *Northern Exposure* Guy apparently had had the same idea, because he was standing right next to me!

"Would you like to dance?" he asked over the blast of a Madonna song. Six feet. Tux. Brown, wavy hair. Dark brown eyes. Perfect skin. Thirty, thirty-one, maybe? Did I mention he was beyond cute?

I smiled. That was answer enough for Fleishman's double. He took my hand and led me onto the crowded dance floor. I glanced back at Natasha and sent her a grin. She shot me a thumbs-up and was whisked onto the dance floor herself by a George Clooney look-alike.

It was too loud to talk or to even ask his name. We danced and smiled and flirted without saying a word. The band played the Backstreet Boys next, and I laughed and twirled around. And when the bandleader crooned the first note of a Frank Sinatra song, *Northern Exposure* Guy took my hand and put his other at my waist, and suddenly I was slow-dancing to Frank in a mini-ballroom at the Plaza Hotel. When Frank ended and Abba's "Dancing Queen" blasted, *Northern Exposure* Guy held up a hand and gestured to the bar. I smiled and nodded and followed him. Just as I was about to sit down next to him at one of the five stools around the bar, Aunt Ina and Uncle Charlie left the dance floor. Abba definitely wasn't their speed.

"Grammy's just tickled pink," Aunt Ina whispered in my ear. "She was going to introduce you to Ethan Miles, but you beat her to it."

Huh? Were they still trying to push Mr. Incinerator on me? I could find my own type myself, thank you very much. "I haven't met him." Thank God.

"Who do you think you just danced with to three songs in a row?" Aunt Ina asked.

My mouth dropped open. *Northern Exposure* Guy was Ethan Miles? Grammy's next-door neighbor? The very Ethan Miles who took out his trash in front of people and played chess with Uncle Charlie and carried Grammy's grocery bags from the elevator to her apartment? That Ethan Miles was my *Northern Exposure* Guy?

The man himself turned around at the bar and handed me a glass of red wine. "So, I don't even know your name," he said, a slight Texas drawl making his voice as sexy as he was.

"It's Jane," I told him, a smile tugging at my lips.

"I'm Ethan," he said in that drawl.

I couldn't hold back the laugh.

"Find that funny, do you?" he asked, his brown eyes twinkling.

"I'll tell you all about it later," I murmured. "After this dance?"

As Ethan Miles twirled me around the dance floor in the mini-ballroom of the Plaza Hotel, I closed my eyes and lifted my face to the tiny, twinkling lights adorning the ceiling and knew that my mother and father were both watching.

## Epilogue

February 14 found me at an engagement party in the arms of my beloved, wearing my Valentine's Day gift—small, sweet diamond stud earrings from Tiffany's. No, no, no. This wasn't *my* engagement party. It was Amanda and Jeff's. Jeff had popped the question on Christmas Eve and had given Amanda a rock. We're talking two carats. The party was being held in a West Village restaurant. Amanda's very tall, very blond, very Louisiana family had flown up for the occasion.

Ethan and I had very recently celebrated our sixth-month mark with a trip to Negril, Jamaica. Aunt Ina, Uncle Charlie, Dana, Larry and Grammy had been sure he'd propose there. I had a feeling Ethan and I were headed in that direction, but at six months, we were still getting to know each other, still getting to love each other. For the first time in my life, I felt as though I had all the time in the world.

Dana and Larry bought a huge house in Chappaqua, near the Clintons and the Welles; they made good use of all their France-inspired kitchen stuff by throwing barbecue after barbecue in their huge backyard. Ethan and I had attended their housewarming and two of the barbecues. Dana had joked that I'd be getting all of Great-Aunt Gertie's money now that I was with Ethan, who Grammy still couldn't stop raving about. I had to admit, I understood what all the fuss was about.

A very pregnant Natasha Nutley stood chatting with two other pregnant guests. Natasha had become close with Amanda. They'd bonded on that very first Flirt Night Roundtable Natasha had come to back in August. Eloise and Natasha had hit it off, too, and had become shopping friends. Natasha's parents still hadn't come around, but she was hopeful that when the baby was born, they might melt. I hoped so, too. Natasha's aunt Daphne promised to attend her baby shower, and I had a feeling her mom would show up with tears in her eyes. The baby was due in less than four weeks. Natasha had thought of a thousand names, but in the end she decided that she had to clap eyes on the little munchkin in order to name him or her. She'd finished the memoir a few days before Thanksgiving, and I'd edited it and turned it in to rave reviews from Jeremy, who, by the way, had married his *Vogue* executive in a small, family-only ceremony at the Plaza this past December. *The Stopped Starlet* was due out this coming December. I had made Remke very happy by signing Natasha to the sequel he wanted so badly. It was focused on self-esteem and recovery, not "sexy rehab." Natasha was hard at work on the outline.

Promotions had been aplenty at Posh these past six months. Right after Labor Day weekend, Eloise had finally gotten promoted from Assistant Art Associate to

Assistant Art Director, which pleased her to no end. She had decided to take a break from dating and was now passionately involved with kicking the nicotine habit. She'd gone back to SmokeNoMore for her free session and was two months nicotine free. Morgan Morgan had been promoted to Assistant Editor and was as on the lookout as ever. As for Remke, he'd stopped snapping so much ever since Gwen, who'd returned from maternity leave with a vengeance, managed to sign the Backstreet Boy.

Opera Man, aka Archibald Marinelli, moved last month, much to my joy. A very quiet young woman now resided in his apartment. I hadn't heard one *oh* since.

Ah, I almost forgot: Natasha and I had indeed attended our ten-year high-school reunion in October. Lisa and Lora Miner hadn't come, nor had Jimmy Alfonzo. But Robby Evers had been there. Nope, he wasn't bald or grossly overweight or a used-car salesman. He was better-looking than ever and the globe-trotting foreign correspondent he'd always wanted to be. And very happily married to a fellow globe-trotting foreign correspondent named Tatiana. I hadn't asked Ethan to attend the reunion with me because I already had a date. Natasha had been the hit of the reunion, naturally, and so had I, if I do say so myself. She'd played me up as Ms. Glamorous Important New York City Editor. I'd even been voted Most Changed in the class poll that had been announced at the close of the reunion; Natasha had been voted Least Changed.

We'd shared a good laugh at our wins. Natasha had never been what anyone thought she was. And I had only begun to change.

# One

## Tight lids and other theories of male behavior

It started with a message on my answering machine.

*"Guess who's getting married?"* came a voice I knew all too well.

It was Josh. My ex-boyfriend. Turned Someone Else's Fiancé. Not that I'd ever wanted to marry Josh, who suffered from an aversion to dental floss. "Did prehistoric man floss?" he would argue. "Is prehistoric man still around?" I argued back. We lasted only six months before I told him I couldn't see myself at sixty-five, making sure he took his teeth out at bedtime every night. "Okay, okay. I'll *floss*," he'd replied. But it was too late. The romance was gone.

Now he was getting married. To someone he'd met not

three months after we had broken up four years ago. And he wasn't the first ex-boyfriend to go this route. Randy, the boyfriend before Josh, was whistling the wedding march a mere six *weeks* after we had tearfully said our goodbyes. Then there was Vincent, my first love—he'd been married for nearly a *decade*. According to my mother—who lived within shouting distance of his mother in Marine Park, Brooklyn, and never failed to keep me updated—Vincent and his wife were already on their *third* kid.

One ex gets married, a girl can laugh it off. Two begins a nervous twitter. But three? *Three?*

A girl starts to take it personally. I mean, what was it about me that didn't incite men to plunk down large sums of money in the name of eternal love?

"It's the tight-lid dilemma," my friend Michelle said when I expressed my despair at sending another man to the altar without me.

"Tight lid?" I asked, awaiting some pearl of wisdom that might turn my world upright again. After all, in the time it had taken me to get a four-year degree in business administration that I no longer made use of, Michelle, who'd grown up three blocks away from me in Marine Park, had gotten a husband, a house and a diamond the size of New Jersey.

"You know the scenario," she continued. "You struggle for a good while trying to open a jar and the lid won't budge. But sure enough, next person you hand that jar pops the lid off, no problem. I mean, you don't really think Jennifer Aniston, cute haircut aside, would have landed Brad Pitt without the Gwyneth factor, do you?"

I couldn't deny the pattern, once Michelle had laid it out neatly before me. Clearly I had been instrumental in warming Josh, Randy and Vincent up for the next girl to come along and slap each one of them with a wedding vow. Gosh, I should have at least been maid of honor for my efforts.

Instead, I was nothing but the ex-girlfriend who might or might no get invited to the wedding, depending on how secure the bride felt about her future husband.

Suddenly I looked at Kirk, my current boyfriend, with new eyes. We had been together a year and eight months, by far the record for me since my three-year stint with Randy. We had become quite a cozy little couple, Kirk and I. I even got party invitations addressed to both of us—that's how serious everyone thought we were. The question was: Would Kirk be inviting me to his wedding someday or…?

"Kirk…sweetie," I said as we lay in bed together that night, a flickering blue screen before us and the prospect of sex lingering like an unasked question in the air.

"Uh-huh," he said, not removing his gaze from the cop show that apparently had him enraptured.

"Your last girlfriend…Susan?"

"Yeah?" he said, glancing at me with trepidation. Clearly he saw in the making one of those "relationship talks" men dread.

"You guys went out a long time, right? What was it, two years?"

"Three and a *half*," he said with a shudder that made me swallow with fear. Apparently I was heading for rough waters.

Still, I plunged on. "And you guys never talked, um, about…marriage?"

He laughed. "Are you kidding me? That's what broke us up. She gave me the old ultimatum—we get married or we're through." He snorted. "Needless to say, I chose door number two."

*Aha.* Relief filled me and I snuggled closer to Kirk, allowing him to sink back into his vegetative state as the cops on TV slapped cuffs on some unsuspecting first offender.

If Susan was the lid loosener, that could mean only one thing: I could pop this guy wide open. Hell, I could be married within the year!

The next day I met my best friend Grace for a celebratory lunch, which was always an event, as Grace, with her high-powered career and high-maintenance boyfriend, barely had time to get together at all anymore. As a concession to her hectic lifestyle, we met at a restaurant two blocks from her office on East Fifty-forth Street and Park Avenue. Of course, Grace didn't know I was celebrating until I clinked my water glass into hers and said, "Congratulate me. I'm getting married."

"What?" Grace said, her blue-gray eyes bulging with disbelief. Her gaze immediately fell to the ring finger of my left hand, which, naturally, was bare.

"Not *now*. But someday."

She rolled her eyes, sniffed and said with her usual irony, "Congratulations."

Leave it to Grace to laugh in the face of being thirty-three without a wedding band on her finger. She is the strongest, most independent person I know. Not only does she always manage to keep a killer boyfriend on hand, she has a killer job as a product manager for Roxanne Dubrow Cosmetics.

"Don't you ever worry, Grace? That you'll…wind up alone?" I asked, searching her face for some sign of vulnerability.

She shrugged. "A woman in this city can have everything she wants. If she plays her cards right."

Easy for Grace to say. Tall, voluptuous, with her chin-length, tousled blond hair and perfectly sculpted features, she was beautiful. While I...

I had always been little Angie Difranco—and still was—five foot four with a head of wavy black hair that defied all styling products, and thighs that threatened to turn into my mother's the minute I gave up my daily exercise regime. I sighed. It suddenly occurred to me that if I didn't marry Kirk, I didn't know what would become of me.

"What about you and Drew?" I asked now, wondering if Grace had been contemplating her current beau as a future husband. "Do you ever think about...you know?"

"Of course," Grace said. "Every girl thinks about it."

I felt relieved. At least I wasn't the only thirty-something unmarried hysteric. And Grace and Drew had been dating barely a year—at least eight months *less* than Kirk and me.

"But it's not everything," she said with a shrug.

Grace was right, I realized the next day as I headed for work. Marriage wasn't everything. I had so much going on right now, it was practically a nonissue. I was an actor, and at the moment a *working* actor, which was really something. Granted, my steady gig was *Rise and Shine,* a children's exercise program on cable access, but it was good experience in front of a camera, at least according to an agent I had spoken to, who refused to take me on until I had experience outside of the numerous off-off-Broadway shows I'd done.

But as I slid into the yellow leotard and baby-blue

tights that were my lot as the show's cohost, I wondered, for about the hundredth time, what exactly my résumé would say about me, now that I had spent six months leaping and stretching with a group of six-year-olds.

"Hey, Colin," I called out to my cohost once I entered the studio, cup of coffee firmly in grasp. One downside of this job was that it meant getting up at 5:00 a.m. to make the show's 6:00 a.m. taping time. Apparently it was the only time the station had allotted studio space for the program, which had a solid, albeit small, audience of upper-middle-class parents and the children they hope to mold, literally.

Colin looked up from the book he was reading, startled, before he broke out in his usual smile. Colin was the only person I knew who *could* smile at 6:00 a.m. It was his nature to be cheerful, which was why he was such a fabulous host for *Rise and Shine*. The kids loved him, and in the six months that I had gotten to know him, I loved him, too. He was warm, generous, loving, good with children. Not to mention gorgeous, with softly chiseled features, blue eyes surrounded by thick lashes, and short dark hair always cut in the most up-to-date style. Everything a woman would want in a prospective husband. In fact, I might have dated him until he married someone else—if he weren't gay, that is.

"You ready?" he said.

I sighed. "Ready as I'll ever be."

It still amazed me that I had even landed this gig at *Rise and Shine*—up until my audition, I hadn't exercised a day in my life. Yet there I was, every weekday morning, cheerfully urging a group of ten sleepy-eyed kids to stretch, jump, run and tone. Lucky for me, my baby-blue tights were thick enough to hide cellulite.

"Positions everyone," Rena Jones, our producer,

called out with a glare in Colin's and my direction. Well, mostly in my direction. She adored Colin. And tolerated me. Mostly because she was a stickler for timeliness, while I…wasn't.

Still, I took a certain satisfaction in the routine, assured that once the music—a strange mixture of circus rhythms and a singer who sounded like the love child of Barney the Dinosaur and Britney Spears—began, my feet would move into the steps of the opening warm-up dance right along with Colin's. That when we progressed into the series of stretches, squats and leg lifts, my body was not only limber enough to make all the maneuvers, but I could jog, jump and shimmer across the floor while I shouted out inspiring words to the ten little tumblers before us.

There was only the reassurance that when the clock against the back wall hit the thirty-minute mark, I would be able to heave a silent sigh of relief (which I disguised as a healthy exhale for the sake of my tiny followers) and bow down into the final stretch before leading the happy munchkins in the applause that ended the show.

"Hanging out with Kirk tonight?" Colin asked cheerfully as we headed to the small dressing area at the back of the studio.

"Of course," I replied with all the confidence a girlfriend should have at the stage Kirk and I were at in our relationship.

Later that very night, however, I realized that Kirk was at a different stage.

I was spending the evening at his place, where I spent most nights during the week. Not only because he lived on East Twenty-seventh and Third, which was somewhat closer to the studio on West Fifty-fourth than my East

Village apartment was, but because we liked to spend our every waking moment together—and every sleeping moment, which was often the case, as Kirk had a tendency to nod off early.

Besides, Kirk's doorman one-bedroom was a welcome respite from the cluttered two-bedroom walk-up I shared with Justin, my roommate and other best friend besides Grace. Kirk's place was an oasis of order, with his closet filled with rows of well-pressed button-downs and movie posters lining the walls with precision (yes, we both loved movies, though Kirk had an unsettling predilection for horror flicks, while I liked the classics and anything with Mel Gibson). Even his medicine cabinet was sight to behold, I thought, as I scrubbed my teeth before bed that night. The toothpaste was curled up neatly next to a shiny cup containing his brush; his shaving kit (a gift from the ex, which I once tried to replace with a packet of Gillettes, but to no avail) nestled sweetly next to a bottle of Chanel for men (from me, thank you very much, which he spritzed himself with only under serious duress). I even kept an antihistamine there—I had a tendency toward congestion at the slightest provocation: pollen, dust mites, mold. With a contented sigh I spit my mouthful of paste-and-water into the shiny white sink, carefully rinsing out the suds to return it to its porcelain perfection, before I returned to the bedroom, where Kirk sprawled on the bed, laptop in hand, studying the screen intently.

"Time to play," I said, bounding onto the bed in a pair of boxers (pirated from his bottom left drawer) and a T-shirt emblazoned with the logo of Lanix, the software company Kirk was working for when we first met.

"Just give me a minute, sweetie," he said, glancing up from the screen briefly to flash me a small smile of acknowledgment.

I settled in beside him, sparing a glance at the screen, which was covered in a series of incomprehensible codes, and picked up the book I kept on Kirk's bedside table, Antonin Artaud's *The Theatre and Its Double*. Turning to page five, the precise place I had been the past six times I had attempted to immerse myself, I started to read. Well, not exactly *read*—my gaze was too busy roaming over Kirk's profile.

He had the most beautiful brow line I had ever seen. Almost jet-black against creamy skin and normally smooth, though right now it was furrowed over his gray eyes as they studied the screen, almost without blinking. One of the things I had admired from the start about Kirk was his ability to concentrate against any odds.

I was hooked and hooked good from date one. Kirk was so different from all the men who had come before. For one thing, he made enough money to actually pay for dinner. And I couldn't help admire his ambition when he told me his dreams of running his own software company…or his well-toned physique, when things got to that level between us, honed from four times a week at the gym.

Now, as the warmth of that lean, muscled body seeped into my consciousness, I snuggled close, eyes intent on my book, until I felt his weight shift as he closed the computer and reached over to rest it on the night table.

Closing the book with a joyful snap, I thrilled to the feeling of triumph that winged through me, as it never failed to do, even almost two years into the relationship. Call me competitive, call me a nymphomaniac, I don't give a damn—there was nothing, to me, like the sight of Kirk smiling down at me, a predatory gleam in his eye.

"Come here, you," he said in a husky voice, as if *I* were the one who'd been resisting all this time.

Without hesitation I straddled him, reveling in the discovery that he had gone from software to hardware in seconds flat, even though you could barely tell I was female beneath the roomy T-shirt I was wearing. Still, his big hands unerringly worked their way under my shirt, found the somewhat meager mounds there and stroked.

I sighed, knowing what was coming. Because if there was one thing Kirk and I had down pat by now, it was sex. Like the scientist that he was, he had experimented endlessly on me to discover just what buttons to push to get me where I wanted to go. And it was never boring, despite this precision on his part, I thought, as he rolled me beneath him, did away with both of our boxers, then rested back on his heels momentarily to cover himself in latex procured from its ever-ready place in the nightstand.

I would have hated myself for being such putty in his hands if it hadn't been for the heat that inevitably overcame me as he slid inside me. My only complaint might have been that Kirk wasn't much of a kisser during sex. In fact, he rarely brought his mouth to mine once we were joined. But that was okay, I thought, gazing up at his flushed features, his dark lashes against his cheeks, his full mouth. The view was pretty damn good from here.

Rather than revel in the view, as I usually did, I closed my eyes. And just as I was settling into the rhythm, a sudden—and unexpected—image filled my mind, of Kirk peeling away my clothes, lifting me into his arms and depositing me on a canopied bed I had never seen before in my life. And when, in my mind's eye, I turned to look at the heap of cloth that had pooled at my feet as Kirk freed the last button on my—T-shirt?—I saw, to my horrified surprise, swaths and swaths of white silk. What looked to be, in my heated imagination—a wedding gown?

*Oh, God,* I thought as my body contracted—almost unwillingly, for it seemed *way* too soon—and I felt the biggest climax of my life shudder through me. My eyes flew open as the foreign sound of an earth-shattering moan left my mouth. I might even have thought it was Kirk who had cried out so freely (because, unlike me, he made no bones about noisily expressing his pleasure), if I hadn't found myself looking straight into his surprised gaze. Moments later, I felt and heard his own satisfied shudder—another shock, since Kirk usually prided himself on his smooth control during sex—as his body went lax on mine.

"Wow," he said when he lifted his head and met my gaze once more. "That was something," he continued, a smile lighting his features as he bent to graze my surprised mouth with a kiss.

"Yeah," I said breathlessly, studying his expression. It *was* something, I thought, hope beating in my breast. But did it *mean* something? I wondered, remembering the image of that dress in all its surprising detail. Well, clearly it did mean something, as sex between Kirk and me had always been a revelation. But this felt like a revelation of a very different kind. For me, I thought, gazing into his eyes and seeking out the foreign emotions that I felt racking my own heart and mind.

I did see something shining in Kirk's eyes, but what it was had yet to be determined. Until I heard his next words.

"I never felt you so…strongly. That must have been a big O, huh?" he said with a laugh, then leaned back with a look that told me exactly what *he* was feeling. Pride. The garden-variety male smugness over a sexual performance well done.

As if to punctuate my realization, he went into scientist

mode once more. "What do you think it was? I mean, it was the fucking missionary position, for chrissakes. Nothing special there." He pulled his hand away from my waist, where it had been gently massaging me, and thumped the bed. "Maybe it was this new mattress? God, had I known, I would have *tipped* that salesman at Sleepy's."

*Oh, brother.*

I might have been thoroughly disgusted at this point if Kirk hadn't rolled onto his back, bringing me with him, and pulled me into that solid body of his. Maybe it was the feel of his muscled chest beneath me. Of the tenderness in his hands as they slid over my back. Maybe I just wanted to believe that though Kirk was guy and thus given to fits of euphoria over the technicalities of sex, he did feel something more—something he couldn't possibly express—and that made me relent, pressing my body into his in an attempt to hold on to whatever that feeling was. At least until reality set in. and it soon did.

Glancing at the clock, Kirk sat up, suddenly disentangling himself from my limbs. "Oh, shit. Is it ten already? I gotta pack."

"Pack?" I asked, cool air crawling over me as he leaped from bed, pulled on a pair of boxers and headed for the closet.

"Damn, did I forget to tell you?" He turned to look at me, his expression baffled, as if he were mentally going over one of his meticulous to-do lists and realizing he'd forgotten one of the most important items on it: me.

Assuming he was going away to meet a client, I prepared to launch into a speech about how nice it would be to know these things in advance. Then I heard his next words.

"I'm going home this weekend."

That stopped me short. Kirk was going home to Newton, Massachusetts. To visit his parents. Parents, I might add, I had yet to lay eyes on myself.

"When did you decide this?" I asked, a vague panic beginning to invade my rattled senses.

"Mmmm…last week? Anyway, I just booked the ticket this morning. I was going to tell you…."

His voice faded away as my mind skittered over the facts: Kirk was going home for one of his semiannual trips, and he hadn't invited me. Again. The memory of Josh's taunting voice on my answering machine ran through my frazzled brain. While I was orgasming over wedding dresses, Kirk was planning a pilgrimage on the parental abode without me. Clearly I was *not* the woman who was about to pull the lid off this thing with Kirk. In fact, given that I was 0 for 3 when you tallied up the number of times Kirk had gone home in the past year and a half and not invited me, it might even seem as if his lid was still airtight.

Since I didn't know how to broach the subject of a meet-the-parents visit, I addressed the more immediate problem. "I wish you'd told me sooner…." *So I might have had a chance to rally for position of serious girlfriend,* I thought, but didn't say.

"I'm sorry, Noodles," he replied, contrite. "You know how busy I've been with this new client. Did I tell you that I'm designing a program for Norwood Investments? They have offices all over the country. If I land Norwood, I could have work lined up for the next few years…."

His words silence me for a moment. Maybe it was the injection of the nickname he had given me during the early days of our relationship, when I had ventured to cook him pasta, which, all-American boy that he is, he referred to as noodles and sauce. After I had teasingly told him that my Italian mother would toss him out on his ear if he ever referred to her pasta as "noodles," he had affectionately given me the name instead. But his warm little endearment wasn't the only thing that shut me up. There was also his subtle reminder that he was a software designer on the rise. That the program he had created six months earlier to automate office space was the only thing on his mind, now that prestigious financial companies like Norwood Investments had taken notice. In the face of all this ambition, I somehow felt powerless to express my desire to be considered parentworthy in Kirk's mind.

"Hey, Noodles?" Kirk said now, pulling a pair of jeans over his boxers and donning a T-shirt. "I'm gonna run down to Duane Reade and pick up a few things for my trip. Need anything?"

Yeah, I thought: my head examined. "Umm, no, I'm all right," I replied cautiously.

"Okay, I'll be back in fifteen, then." He gave me a perfunctory kiss on the forehead before making his way out the front door.

The minute I heard the door slam behind him, I picked up the phone. I needed another perspective. Specifically an ex-boyfriend's perspective. And since pride prevented me from calling back the newly engaged Josh just yet, I dialed up Randy, whose number I still had safely tucked in my memory banks. After all, not marrying the men in your life did have its advantages. I had managed to turn at least two of my ex-boyfriends into friends.

"I didn''t think you were into all that," Randy said after we'd exchanged greetings and I'd inquired about why the marriage issue had never come up for us.

"Into all *what?*" I asked.

"You know, marriage, kids. Hey, did I tell you Cheryl and I are working on our first?"

"That's wonderful," I said, in a daze. "What exactly do you mean I'm not into marriage, kids?"

Randy chuckled. "C'mon, Ange, you know as well as I do that your career came first. You always wanted to be a big movie star."

"Actor. I am an actor."

"Whatever."

When I hung up a short while later, I began to wonder if maybe I was projecting the wrong image. True, I had long been harboring the dream of making a career of the acting talent I had been lavishly praised for all through high school and college. And though I hadn't exactly landed my dream role in the four years since I had left my boring job in sales to pursue acting, *Rise and Shine* counted for something, didn't it?

Suddenly I had to start getting realistic if I hoped to ever get a grip on this particular lid. I was thirty-one years old. I wasn't getting any younger, as my mother lost no opportunity of reminding me. I needed to start looking like a wife.

# Out of the Blue

## Isabel Wolff

**This book is for every woman who has let a breeze of doubt turn into a full-blown hurricane!**

Faith Martin, AM-U.K.!'s face of the morning weather, is used to delivering the forecast, not being told the forecast—especially when it concerns her marriage.

When Faith's ultraglam best friend plants a seed of doubt about her husband's fidelity, she begins to question everything about her comfortable life.

"Wolff handles the breakdown of marriage with warmth and humor."
—*The Times*

out of the blue
isabel wolff

## RED DRESS INK™